Mysterious Cat Stories

Mysterious Cat Stories

Edited by John Richard Stephens
and Kim Smith

Galahad Books · New York

Published in 1994 by

Galahad Books
A division of Budget Book Service, Inc.
386 Park Avenue South
New York, NY 10016

Galahad Books is a registered trademark of Budget Book Service, Inc.

Published by arrangement with Carroll & Graf Publishers, Inc.

Library of Congress Catalog Card Number: 93-7981

ISBN: 0-88365-872-0

Printed in the United States of America.

This Book is Dedicated to

Marty Goeller

Marty and I have been best friends since we were both nine months old. We grew up together in San Diego.

—JRS

Contents

Acknowledgments

John Richard Stephens wishes to express his appreciation to Martha and Jim Goodwin, Scott Stephens, Mollie Seibert, Joyce Whiteaker, Danny Schutt, Bill and Norene Hilden, Doug and Shirley Strong, Frank and Marybeth DiVito, and my agent, Charlotte Cecil Raymond.

Kim Smith wishes to express her appreciation to Margaret Mannatt, Kristine Frey, Scott Cunningham, Robert Stoneman, Dale and Maxine Johnson, Mark Freundel, and lastly (though definitely not least) Matt Kramer.

Our thanks to the following, who have granted permission to reprint copyrighted material:

"Catnip" by Robert Bloch. Copyright © 1948 by Robert Bloch. Reprinted by permission of the author and the author's agents, Scott Meredith Literary Agency, Inc., 845 Third Avenue, New York, NY 10022.

"Weekend of the Big Puddle" by Lilian Jackson Braun. Reprinted by permission of The Berkley Publishing Group from *The Cat Who Had 14 Tales*, copyright © 1988 by Lilian Jackson Braun.

"The Man Who Turned Into a Cat" by J. Wentworth Day. Copyright © 1971 by J. Wentworth Day. From John Canning's *50 Great Horror Stories*. Used by permission of Souvenir Press, Ltd., 43 Great Russell Street, London WC1B 3PA, England.

"Balu" by August Derleth. Copyright © 1949 by August Derleth. Reprinted by permission of the author's estate and the author's agents, Scott Meredith Literary Agency, Inc., 845 Third Avenue, New York, NY 10022.

"The Tail" by M. J. Engh. Copyright © 1988 by M. J. Engh; first appeared in the *MosCon X Program Book;* reprinted by permission of the author and the author's agent, Virginia Kidd.

"Cat in Glass" by Nancy Etchemendy. Copyright © 1989 by Nancy Etchemendy. First published in *Fantasy and Science Fiction Magazine*, July 1989. Reprinted by permission of the author.

INTRODUCTION

Mysterious Cats

There are no ordinary cats.
—*Colette*

Cats are mysterious creatures. They have strong personalities which border on the eccentric; they are erratic and unpredictable; and they are strong individualists. You can make generalizations about cats, but you can always find at least one cat who refuses to act as you expect. This is one of the reasons why cats are such intriguing creatures.

The strange behavior of cats has resulted in many weird beliefs which have developed over the ages. These beliefs have, in turn, sparked the imaginations of many writers. As a result, there are many wonderful stories linking cats with the supernatural. We have collected together for the first time some of the best of these tales. The book you are holding is the result of a thorough search through literally hundreds of stories. As a result, the vast majority of these stories will be completely new to even the most avid collector of cat books.

The most famous mysterious cat tale is "The Black Cat" by Edgar Allan Poe. This is a gruesome tale where a severely mistreated cat takes his revenge on the murderer of his mistress. Many cat lovers find this often reprinted classic a bit hard to take. Instead of reprinting it once again, we have included two stories with interesting variations on this theme which we think cat lovers will find much more appealing. They are by two of the most famous horror writers, H. P. Lovecraft and Robert Bloch.

One of the strange powers often attributed to cats is an ability to see ghosts or spirits. Cats often seem to see or hear things we are oblivious to. This has caused some people to suggest that many cats are schizophrenic and live in a world of hallucinations. Whether you believe this or not, it can still be quite unsettling when your cat seems to be responding to the attentions of somebody else when you are the only person in the room.

My sister, Martha, once saw a cat reacting to something she couldn't see. She was staying at an old house in West Yorkshire when she walked by a room and heard a cat cry out. She went in and tried to coax the cat from under the bed but it ran out to a point a few feet away and started purring, jumping up on his hind legs, and arching his back with pleasure. She told me, "The cat was looking up at something and meowing just like it was being pet. And it was like— 'Ooh, I'm out of here! This cat is being pet by something and it's not me.' " This incident made such an impression on her that she never went into that room again. Other friends of mine have told me similar stories about that house. In another incident, reported in the *Occult Review* in 1924, a cat leapt into a spirit's lap and seemed amazed to find that she fell right through.

Marion Weinstein, a Wiccan author and radio show hostess, says, "Haunted houses are often frequented—or inhabited—by cats. And mediums often attest that they cannot keep their cats out of the room during a seance; in fact, even neighboring cats have been known to show up, eagerly, the moment that lights are dimmed and the table, or ouija board, is set up." Although many say cats like spirits, others say this is not always the case—it would seem to depend on the cat.

English ghost-hunter Elliott O'Donnell wrote in 1913, "From endless experiments made in haunted houses, I have proved to my own satisfaction, at least, that the cat acts as a thoroughly reliable psychic barometer. The dog is sometimes unaware of the proximity of the Unknown. When the ghost materializes or in some other way demonstrates its advent, the dog, occasionally, is wholly undisturbed —the cat never. I have never yet had a cat with me that has not shown the most obvious signs of terror and uneasiness both before and during a superphysical manifestation."

Several ghost stories are included in this book. Most of them are reported as factual accounts. We will leave it up to you to decide whether you feel they are frauds, hallucinations, or real ghosts. Of the two fictional ghost stories, one—by the famous mystery writer Lilian

Jackson Braun—highlights the cat's point of view, while the other—by Wilbur Daniel Steele—is a fascinating tale about a ghost ship which is found at sea with no one aboard but a cat.

The idea that people can turn into cats has been around for a long time. Throughout the Middle Ages, witches were said to turn themselves into cats more often than any other animal. One story from France tells of a cat who walked into a kitchen where a woman was cooking an omelet. The cat looked at the omelet and said, "It's done. Turn it over!" The woman was so insulted that a cat would presume to tell her how to cook that she threw the omelet at the cat, hitting it in the face. The woman said the next day she noticed burn marks on a neighbor's face.

In another story, which supposedly occurred in 1566, a group of French farmers wandering through a forest stumbled upon an assembly of cats engaged in mystic rites. The cats attacked them but the men were able to fight them off and escape. The next morning a dozen women in the village were said to have been found with wounds. They confessed, probably after being tortured.

German records tell of the burning of one witch, who—as the smoke rose up around her—suddenly let out a triumphant shriek and leapt from the flames in the form of a black cat, which disappeared into the crowd.

In one of the last witch trials, which took place in 1712, Anne Thorne claimed she was plagued by cats with the face and voice of Jane Wenham, the accused witch. This was corroborated by the testimony of two men. Wenham was convicted and sentenced to death by the jury. Fortunately the judge was quietly able to get her pardoned.

In some parts of Europe it was believed that all witches were actually cats transformed into human form. It was thought that cats turned into witches when they reached 7 to 12 years of age; then, when the witch turned 100 years old, she would become a cat once again.

In Egypt during the 19th century there was a belief, which may still survive today, that twins have the ability to turn themselves into cats. It's said that a traveler staying in Luxor, Egypt, once killed a cat who raided his storehouse. The next day the neighboring apothecary begged him not to kill any more cats explaining, "My daughter often visits you in the form of a cat to eat your dessert."

Of the several transformation stories we have included, "The Man

Who Turned into a Cat" is particularly interesting as it is set just
after the English Civil War when Oliver Cromwell was the dictator of
Britain.

Of course no book on cats would be complete without a story
about ancient Egypt—we have included four of them. Most people
are familiar with the Egyptian cat-headed goddesses, their cat temples, and cat cities. The ancient Egyptians saw their cats as intermedi-
aries between them and the gods—a role usually performed by priests
—and would often ask their cats to intercede with the gods on their
behalf. Because of this, cats were treated very well, and sometimes
were even treated as gods. The ancient Egyptians were the ultimate
cat-lovers.

The most notable of our Egyptian stories is the one by Bram
Stoker, the author of *Dracula*. To some cat lovers, he is also known
for "The Squaw." This short story is about a boorish American cow-
boy from Bleeding Gulch, Nebraska, who, as a tourist in Nuremberg,
accidently smashes a kitten with a rock and the kitten's irate mother
stalks him, seeking revenge. This grisly tale is spoiled by such outra-
geously unreal dialogue as: "Why, I'm as tender as a Maine cherry-
tree. Lor, bless ye, I wouldn't hurt the poor pooty little critter more'n
I'd scalp a baby. An' you may bet your veriegated socks on that!"
Although Stoker liked to write about America and Americans, his
knowledge on the subject was almost nil. "The Squaw" has often
been reprinted in cat books. That this is the main work by which
many cat lovers have come to know him is unfortunate because
Stoker was a particularly talented writer.

To help remedy this situation, we have included Stoker's much
neglected and virtually unknown cat story, *The Jewel of Seven Stars*.
This amazing tale of ancient Egypt easily rivals, and in some ways
surpasses, his masterpiece, *Dracula*.

The idea that cats can be extremely powerful and should never be
crossed is found in many parts of the world. Usually these cats are
thought to be evil. The Highlanders of Scotland tell of a gigantic
demon cat called Big Ears, who is master of all the subterranean
Black Cat spirits. This belief is echoed in Japan where there are tales
of a large demon cat heading a horde of phantom cats. The power of
this type of supernatural cat is brilliantly depicted in the excerpt from
James David Corrother's *The Black Cat Club*. This story also contains
much of the American folklore surrounding these creatures. We have

also included the rarely-printed legend of King Arthur's battle with a demon cat and Don Quixote's humorous run-in with what he thought were deadly demonic cats.

The ability to talk is a talent that is often attributed to cats. There is a wonderful tale from China which tells of a time when people were not much different from the rest of the animals and cats ruled the world. Back then, cats had the ability to speak and people couldn't. The cats governed the earth but they eventually grew tired of having to handle all of the planet's everyday affairs and decided they would much rather bask in the sun and take catnaps. So they looked at all the other animals for suitable candidates to take over for them and finally decided on the human race. In order for humankind to take over the job, the cats had to give people the ability to talk, which they in turn lost. Now people have the responsibility of the world on their shoulders while the cats get to spend all of their time doing what they enjoy most—and this is why they always seem to be smiling at us.

It is a common belief around the world that cats can understand human conversation and some say they can also speak when they want to. A few say cats can only speak after they are ten years old—presumably that is how long it takes them to learn our language. One Irish informant said, "There's something not right about cats . . . there's some have heard them together at night talking Irish."

Laurent Jean Baptiste Bérenger Féraud wrote that in 1875 there was a cat in Toulon, France, who actively took part in the evening discussions; that is, when the topic was interesting enough to keep him from falling asleep. His mistress often asked for and always followed the cat's advice. He would often wander off for days at a time and the family thought he took on human form during these absences.

Perhaps the ultimate story of cat communication is "Tobermory." This story by the famous Scottish author Saki is included in our book, along with a folktale of a talking cat as told by another popular Scotsman, Sir Walter Scott. Scott's version of the most widely told of all the cat folktales, "The King of the Cats," is relayed to us in an account of a visit with Sir Walter and his cats by Washington Irving, the author of "The Legend of Sleepy Hollow."

Actually, another of our stories about intelligent cats happens to contain the oldest known version of "The King of the Cats." It is included in the 16th century tale *Beware the Cat*. Although this wonderful story was the very first novel ever written in the English language, it is completely unknown outside of scholarly circles. This is the first time since it was written, over four centuries ago, that it is available to the general public in an easily understandable form. This story interprets cat behavior in light of the scientific knowledge of that time.

The strange behavior of cats has led to their being submerged in the mists of myths and folklore. These mysterious beasts are seen as symbols of freedom, independence, sensuality, and of the luminous ruler of the night—the moon. They are thought to be possessors of secret powers and abilities. They are associated with witches, invisible spirits, and other occult phenomena. They are sacred gods of the Pharaohs and wild hunters of the jungles and savannas. They are devoted, loving companions and possessors of a silent wisdom. This is how we see our cat—imbued with the aura of the unknown. It is this pervasive air of mystery which envelops cats that makes them such wonderfully fascinating beings to be around.

Beware the Cat

(1553)

Based on the original by

William Baldwin (ca. 1518–1563?)

Beware the Cat is considered by scholars to be the first English novel, though some may question whether it actually qualifies as a novel since it is about the length of what we would today consider to be a short story. Unlike many of its contemporary works, it is amusing, fast-paced, and conversationally intimate in tone. The actual setting for this tale is based in fact. Baldwin really did attend court in 1550 to produce a play for the young king, Edward VI, and many of the characters and locations mentioned were real. This story contains the earliest known version of the popular folktale "The King of the Cats." Interestingly enough, we find the popular version that has come down to us today is actually only half of the story. *Beware the Cat* sheds a completely new light on this folktale. It also contains what may be the first use of the name Grimalkin, which was later popularized by Shakespeare as the name for a witch's familiar (*Macbeth*, 1606). The manner in which Baldwin originally wrote *Beware the Cat* makes it extremely difficult to read; therefore John Richard Stephens has completely rewritten and enhanced the story, making it accessible to the general public for the first time since it was written over four centuries ago. The result is highly enjoyable.

Rewritten by

John Richard Stephens (born 1958)

Stephens is the author of *The Enchanted Cat* and *The Dog Lover's Literary Companion*. He has spent many years studying people's beliefs and is one of America's most knowledgeable experts on British fairy folklore. His dream is to live in the Highlands of Scotland and spend his time writing, wandering the moors, and drinking ale.

The Argument

During the Christmas season of 1550, it happened that I was at the King's Court in London with Master Ferrers, who was master of the winter festivities for His Majesty the King. During the days we were actively planning and organizing the King's recreation and entertainment; while at night we would often discuss the work we had carried out. Four of us were sleeping in a single large chamber upon pallets of straw. Besides Master Ferrers and myself, there was Master Willot, his astronomer, and Master Streamer, his divine.

One night—I think it was the twenty-eighth of December—a controversy arose between Master Streamer and myself over whether or not animals possess the ability to reason. It had come to my attention that the King's players were rehearsing a play by Aesop in which all the characters were birds. I objected to this, saying that it was totally ridiculous to apply human attributes, such as the ability to think and speak, to brute beasts. Master Streamer responded that animals not only have the ability to reason, some are even more intelligent and perceptive than ourselves. At this point, Master Ferrers and his astronomer awoke to our discussion and, though they listened intently, both refused to take one side or the other of our argument.

As proof of his assertion, Master Streamer cited cases of elephants who walk on tightropes; hedgehogs who can predict the weather; foxes and dogs who return home from a night of killing geese and sheep and slip their necks back into their collars so as to give the perception of innocence of their crimes; parrots who mourn their keeper's death; swallows who open their babies' eyes by using a type of plant which is well known for its effect on vision; and hundreds of other examples.

I denied that this was proof of any reasoning abilities. I put forward that these could just be instances of instinct and learning—and as proof I cited the authority of our greatest scientists and philosophers.

"Well, I know animals can reason," said Master Streamer, "and not from the secondhand information of some supposedly great people that I've never met. I have proved it for myself."

"And what was it that convinced you of all this?" I asked.

Calmly he replied, with all seriousness, "I have heard them speak as clearly as I hear you, and they made just as much sense as you do."

Master Ferrers burst out laughing, but I could tell Master Streamer really believed what he was saying. I could not dismiss him lightly because I knew he was an intelligent man with more experience than myself in such matters. I have heard unusual and mysterious things before and I don't claim to know everything, so I tried to keep an open mind. I asked where and when this happened to him and what kind of animals they were.

He thought for awhile and then said, "If you will allow me to talk without interruption. I will tell you something which will amaze you and will erase all your doubts; but if anyone interrupts me, whether out of humor or serious curiosity, I will immediately stop and you will hear no more."

We consented to his stipulation and put more wood upon the fire. He adjusted himself on his bed so we could hear him better and he told us what follows.

The First Part of
Master Streamer's Oration

I was staying at a friend's house which stands at the end of Saint Martin's Lane, so close to the town wall that part of the house actually sits on top of the wall. I lodged in a chamber which had a bay window opening onto a garden where the earth is piled almost as high as the top of the nearby Saint Anne's Church. On the other side of this garden there is a door and a staircase which leads up to the lead-covered roof of Aldersgate, where sometimes the bodies of executed criminals—or rather the parts thereof—dangle from poles.

For as you know, the penalty for certain crimes—treason being chief—is to be hanged. The unfortunate criminals are then cut down before life escapes them and they are disemboweled and quartered. The head is placed on a pike on London Bridge and the quarters are distributed to the various gates of the city—such as Aldersgate—where they are hung from the poles.

Though I don't know why we continue this loathsome and atrocious practice, I sometimes wonder if it might not be from the influence of evil spirits—spirits who loved the taste of blood. Perhaps these had sacrifices made to them in the past. Perhaps they subconsciously influenced tyrants to commit hideous acts of butchery upon their innocent populations. And now, missing these sacrifices, they influence us to display the remains of our criminals in this manner. Thus, they still have their sacrifices and they still get their blood.

I have often seen ravens—which may be manifestations of these spirits—feeding on these mangled corpses . . . and at night, many cats gather below and make such a noise as to prevent the possibility of one ever obtaining any sleep.

One evening after supper I was sitting by the fire conversing with certain members of this household and I began talking about the tremendous caterwauling which lasted from ten o'clock until one on the previous night, rendering it impossible for me to either sleep or study. This led us to a discussion on whether or not cats possess communication and comprehension. Some insisted they did, but I was skeptical and argued against it—as you do now.

To prove their point, one of the men who worked at the printing house next door said, "Back when I dwelled in Staffordshire, I knew of a man who raised a cat from when it was but a kitling. This man would often relax after a day's work by playing games with his cat.

"One night he was called away on business and was riding through Kank Woods, when suddenly something that looked very much like a cat leapt out of a bush in front of his horse and called him by name.

"The poor man was so startled he could not speak. The cat called out his name a couple more times, but receiving no response she finally said, 'Commend me unto Pfeffa-Rah and to thy cat, and tell her Grimalkin is dead.' With that she vanished into the forest, leaving the very dazed and confused man to continue on about his business.

"Later in the evening, after he had returned home, he was sitting in front of the fire with his family and he began to relate his curious adventure. When he told them the strange cat's message, his cat suddenly looked up at him and said, 'So, Grimalkin is dead now.' The cat shook her head sadly and slowly rose and walked over to the door. Not surprisingly the man did not hesitate to open it for her. She slipped out into the night and was never seen again."

As the printer finished his story, Thomas, a friend of my host, asked him when this all happened. He replied that he could not be certain, but that it must be within the past forty years because his mother was friends with the man in this story and his family.

Thomas said, "Aye, that may well be . . . for about that time I heard of how Grimalkin was slain. I was traveling in Ireland when I was told this story, but I gave it little credit until now.

"At that time, Mac Murrough and the other wild lords were the enemies of the King; the Fitzharrises waged war against the Priory and Convent of the Abbey of Tintern, who remained loyal to the King; and Cahir Mac Art made daily raids into County Wexford, looting and burning towns until the entire county—from Clonmines to Ross—lay waste. Even now it has yet to recover and much of the land has been taken over by wilderness.

"One night I was at a feast with one of Fitzharris's churls—which is what they call all farmers and husbandmen. Our conversation eventually turned to the strange and mysterious . . . and to cats. It was then that he told me this tale:

"Less than seven years past, he said, there was a peasant soldier who was stationed at the estate of John Butler in the wilderness of Bantry. He was one of a number of soldiers who were to guard this Englishman's estate from the rebel Irish. This soldier, named Patrick Apore, decided to make a raid into the country of Cahir Mac Art, who was his master's enemy.

"He put on his armor, which consisted of a corset of chain mail and a helmet of gilt leather crested with otter fur. After summoning his boy—which is what they call their horse keepers no matter what their age—the two of them rode off into the morning sun. By nightfall they found a town consisting of two houses. They then broke in and slaughtered all within. When they finished this, they looked around for their reward. The only cattle they could find as plunder were a cow and a sheep, so they took them and headed for home.

"The curs belonging to their victims soon raised such a tempest of noise that they began to fear they would be pursued and overtaken, so they rode as quickly as they could with such plunder. Soon they came upon a church and took refuge inside, confident that no one would think of looking for them there. They also knew that all the wild Irishmen held churches with such reverence that they would never harm a man on holy ground, even if he had murdered their own fathers.

"So Patrick and his boy settled down to wait until midnight had passed and then they would continue on their way. It wasn't long before they realized they were famished, as they had eaten little that day. The soldier sent his boy out to gather up some sticks while he butchered the sheep. Using his flint to start the fire, they soon had it blazing away inside the church. Then they tossed the sheep on top of the fire in order to roast it in the usual Irish manner.

"Just as their meal was ready and Patrick was about to take a bite, a cat wandered into the church and sat down near them. 'Sin feoil,' she said, which is Gaelic for 'give me meat.' Patrick was so amazed—having never heard a cat talk before—that he handed over the quarter he held in his hand. The cat immediately swallowed it whole and asked for more. They acquiesced and soon the cat had eaten the entire sheep . . . but it still wanted for more.

"Realizing there was something strange going on here and—not knowing whether this was some evil spirit in disguise or something equally as dangerous—Patrick thought it prudent to do his best to please this strange cat, so he butchered the cow and placed its carcass on the fire to roast.

"While it was cooking, they busied themselves with making leather coverings for their shoes from pieces of the cow's flayed hide. These coverings would protect their feet and, when they got hungry and were unable to find anything else to eat, they could cook them for food, as soldiers often do when they can't find anything to hunt or plunder. All while they were doing this, they kept one eye on the cat, who calmly went about washing herself.

"When the cow was done, they began giving quarters of it to the cat. After three quarters had been devoured and the cat still asked for more, Patrick began to fear that after the last quarter was gone the cat would start on them next. So while the cat was working on the last of their plunder, they quickly fled the church. Grabbing their horses, they frantically rode off across the countryside into the blackness of the night.

"After they had covered a couple of miles, the moon slowly began to break through the clouds. It was then that the boy spotted the cat sitting on Patrick's horse right behind his master's back. He immediately brought this fact to the soldier's attention. Patrick quickly grabbed his dirk and swung around, running the cat clean through. She let out a bloodcurdling screech as she died.

"No sooner had the cat done this, than they found themselves surrounded by such a throng of the most furious cats they had ever seen in their lives. They were sorely set upon and a tremendous battle ensued. They fought their best, but to no avail. The boy was soon ripped apart and devoured, leaving nothing but a few of his glistening bones scattered about the bloody battle site. The soldier continued to fight with renewed effort and was barely able to escape with his life. The remaining cats fled into the forest screeching what were probably terrible curses upon him and succeeding generations.

"When he finally arrived home, his wife set about feeding him and tending to his wounds. As she worked, he proceeded to tell her of the misfortunes that had befallen him after his successful raid. When he reached the part of his adventure where he stabbed the cat, his wife's kitling—who was not yet half a year old—jumped up and cried, 'Thou hast murdered Grimalkin!' The kitling suddenly plunged onto his face, clawing it to ribbons. Before his shocked wife had a chance to react, the kitling flew out the door and disappeared, leaving Patrick with more skull than face remaining. He survived a few miserable hours before finally giving up his ghost.

"It was thirty-three years ago that I heard this story," concluded Thomas, "and at that time less than seven years had passed since this incident had occurred; therefore, I am led to believe this is the same Grimalkin you told of in your story."

Another of our party, who also argued against the animals having the ability to reason and communicate, immediately piped up.

"This is too fantastic for serious belief. How could a cat in Staffordshire know about the death of another cat over in Ireland?"

"Why, the same way we do," replied Thomas. "News from Ireland

—yea, from all over the world—is carried to us by ships . . . and there are very few ships that do not have at least one cat on board."

"But how could a cat possibly eat so much meat and why should other cats care that Grimalkin was killed?"

"I am afeared that this is beyond my ken," said Thomas, "but we can make conjectures. Perhaps Grimalkin was like one of our religious leaders, in whose name the faithful will not only scratch and bite, but will gladly kill, torture, and burn. How often we have seen Christianity's representatives destroy the innocent only because they did not believe the same things that the clergy proclaimed to be truth. At least the cats had good reason to exact their revenge."

At this point I spoke up saying, "Still, I find it difficult to believe that an actual cat could possibly swallow an entire sheep and cow. It is physically impossible."

"I have repeated the tale exactly as I heard it," said Thomas. "I too found it fantastic at first, but, after hearing the first story, I am now inclined to believe it is based in fact, though I am sure some distortion or exaggeration of the story has taken place.

"Perhaps Grimalkin did not actually eat all the meat. She may have in some way used deception—or perhaps even wizardry—to convey the plunder to her cohorts. A congregation of cats would have no trouble disposing of such a feast."

Another of the printers added, "Aye, it is true that cats have a fellowship and are concerned for one another's welfare. I know this by experience for my cousin was once hired for twenty shillings to roast a live cat, as is often done at festivals. He fastened the beast to a spit and set about his task. I know not whether it was the smell of the singed fur or else her cry, but there appeared such a company of cats. It was only by the quick actions of myself and the other hardy men present in releasing the beast that prevented my cousin from being hard pressed by the company."

"Indeed," said Throckmorton, who was a scholarly man, "there appears to be a certain amount of communication among animals . . . but as for this Grimalkin, I am inclined to think of her more as a witch than as a cat. It is common knowledge that witches often assume the likeness of cats; in fact, this is the origin of the proverb that a cat has nine lives—which is to say, a witch may take on a cat's body nine times."

"This is strange," I said. "I have heard of spirits appearing in the likeness of the dead and of succubi, dryads, fairies, nymphs, and the like taking on other forms at will, but I have never heard of anything with a body as large as that of a person straining themselves down into a form as small as that of a cat. I do not perceive how such a thing can be."

"Well, Master Streamer," replied Throckmorton, "I know you are not as ignorant as you present yourself. I realize it is your manner to make men believe you are not as learned as you are in truth. As you understand many tongues, such as Arabic and Latin, I am sure you possess greater knowledge in these matters. So to say you cannot comprehend how a person can assume the form of a cat is ridiculous, for you are well aware that the Church teaches that the body of Christ himself is brought down out of heaven to replace the bread and wine, leaving only the appearance of bread and wine remaining. And did not Christ transform five loaves and two fish into enough to feed five thousand men, plus women and children?

"Although witches may take the form of cats, it is likely they do not reduce their bodies in size and shape; they either transfer their soul into a cat's body or they delude the seer through some form of enchantment.

"When I make a candle out of horse brains and brimstone, the candle's light causes everyone's head to appear as horseheads. The heads are not actually transformed, it is the false light which creates the illusion within the seer's eye."

As a side note, you may be interested to know that Throckmorton was later arrested for suspicion of magic because he had tried to get a condemned man to promise his soul to him after he was hanged. He eventually died from disease while he was imprisoned at Newgate jail waiting for his trial. But to continue his narrative:

"I am not certain how witches make their transformations; I only know that I have heard many tales of this both here and in Ireland—aye, and in Scotland and Wales, too.

"Witches are feared far and wide for their conjurations. In Ireland no man will buy a red swine. This is because witches used to send many red swine to market. These swine would continue in this form until the unfortunate buyer led them to water, whereupon they were transformed back into piles of hay, old rotten boards, or some such worthless rubbish. Then the buyer would have nothing to show for the money or cattle he exchanged for the swine. How the water removed the illusion, I know not, but I do believe it was the spirits we call demons who animated those bodies until the enchantment was revealed.

"Also in Ireland there are men and women who, after a space of seven years, are turned into wolves. They abide in the woods in this shape until a further seven years have past, whereupon they are once again returned to their former shape. If they survived the seven years and are returned to their former selves, then another man or woman is condemned to take their place.

"This was told to me by a man who was one of these wolves. His wife was slain during her final year. He told me of the men whose cattle he had killed and showed me the scars he had received from these men. His story was documented and attested to by the Bishop, who had sent it on to the Pope.

"St. Augustine, in his book *De Civitate Dei*,* wrote of similar transformations taking place in Italy. He tells of one old hermit woman who would give cheese to a traveler in order to transform him into an ass so she could ride him to the market.

"Perhaps witches have devised some sort of ointment which makes men appear as wolves for seven years or themselves as hares or cats. No matter how these sorceries are carried out, one thing is certain— witches are exceedingly malicious . . . and if one method is closed to them, I am certain they will find another.

"You can think what you like," Throckmorton concluded. "As for myself, I have only told you what I myself have seen along with a few obvious conjectures which any man may make."

"You have spoken well," said the printer, "for once when I was at Oxford on business, a credible clerk of the University told me of a woman who was tried as a witch. Her accusers said she had entered their homes as a cat in order to steal or to poison them in their sleep. One accuser said he threw a firebrand at the cat, singeing it. The complaint was proved true when a search of the witch's body revealed the spot where her skin was burned. Therefore I must agree with your conjecture that Grimalkin was a witch in the likeness of a cat. Also, because of her wit and craft, it is likely natural cats—who are not as wise as her—would hold her and her kind with reverence, thinking her to be merely a natural cat as themselves; just as some

---

* *The City of God* (5th century A.D.).

men who claim to be holy—and who are reverenced by many—are, in fact, devils in disguise."

"If you believe these speaking cats are actually witches in disguise," I asked, "how then is it that you think natural cats can also reason and communicate among themselves?"

"Because all animals have such understanding among their kind. It was this that caused Pythagoras—as I'm sure you know—to believe the souls of the dead could enter into the body of beasts. Because of this, his followers held a cat up to his dying lips so his soul could enter the body of the cat. Although this belief has since been proved false, the evidence which brought him to this conclusion stands true; which is that some beasts are intelligent and can perform amazing and wondrous acts, while some men are dull and brutish in their ignorance.

"As for communication among beasts, witness the story of the Bishop of Alexandria, who either purged his brain with the use of fumes and drinks, or enhanced his brain by natural medicines so that he could understand all manner of animal speech.

"It is recorded that he was seated at a meal with his friends when a sparrow came chirping about the house. The bishop harkened to the chirping and smiled. When one of his companions inquired about the reasons for his mirth, he replied that the bird was telling of how a sack of grain had fallen from a horse and burst open about a quarter mile away. The sparrow, he said, was inviting all his friends to the feast.

"The bishop's friends decided to test his claim by seeing if there was indeed a broken sack of grain on the highway, and it was so."

It was at this point in our conversation that the clock struck nine and our party disbanded. I returned to my chamber to study but found myself unable to concentrate for the remembrance of these tales I had heard, so I carefully considered what each man had spoken.

The Second Part of
Master Streamer's Oration

I had not been lost in thought long when the cats—who had so disturbed me the night before—had once again assembled upon the roof of the gate. Soon they were creating such an infernal noise that it could have easily been the choir of hell led by Old Horny himself. There were no chords or melody to this music, just utter pandemonium. Some cats shrieked out high notes while others bellowed out low notes. Try as I might, I could make no sense of any of it.

Thinking that I might be able to better understand their meaning and the cause of their assembly if I could but see their gestures, I quietly moved to the chamber containing the window that opened onto the roof of the town wall near the gate.

Standing in the dark, I peered through the trellis as best I could to observe them without being noticed. My curiosity was rewarded. Their behavior was completely orderly and they greeted one another with gestures of respect. In particular, there was one large gray cat with large sparkling eyes who sat in the midst of the crowd. On either side of her sat her lieutenants. Before her stood three other cats, one of which mewed continuously—pausing only when the gray cat had something to say—and whenever this cat began to mew again, she would first bow her head in a sign of respect and obedience. Often, at certain points in this cat's monologue, the crowd would suddenly cry out as if they were laughing at what the cat had said and then they would fall silent again in rapt attention to the speaker.

I watched them from 10 o'clock until midnight, when suddenly a loud noise emanated from the kitchen below causing the cats to jump up upon the house to investigate. Fearing they might discover my presence and perhaps think I had thrown something at them, I silently retreated to the safety of my own chamber where my lamp was still burning. I sat down and ruminated on the phenomenon I had just witnessed. Eventually I came to the conclusion that the gray cat was some sort of leader who was treated with dignity and respect, while the cat who spoke to her was relating an account of some matter.

I was unable to sleep the rest of the night as my mind was racing, trying to determine some way in which I might be able to understand them. At one point, I recalled a passage in a book titled *Liber Secretorum** by the great German scholar and wizard, Albertus Magnus. Quietly I stole down to my host's library and located the volume I was looking for. After jotting down a few notes on how to make a philter for this purpose, I returned to my bed and continued to ruminate until the golden rays of the morning sun crept in through my window and slowly crawled across my chamber floor.

By late afternoon I had gathered up all the required ingredients and I immediately set about preparing them according to Magnus's recipe. "If thou wilt understand the voices of the beasts," the book had said, "find one of their number which has died of natural causes and remove its tongue." This was the most difficult of the ingredients to find; fortunately, I was successful in locating a fresh feline donor. I placed the tongue in a mortar with some nightshade, garlic, pepper; added an equivalent portion of fresh cat's dung; and pulverized the lot. I then put in enough wine to turn the mixture into a paste, from which I formed several one ounce lozenges. "Place this lozenge under thy tongue to dissolve," the recipe concluded, "and thou shalt have thy purpose; and whosoever thou kissest shall understand them as well as thyself." After taking one, I placed the remaining lozenges in a fancy box and happily went down to join my host for our evening meal.

On my way I passed through the kitchen where a shrewd young boy—one of the servants—noticed my box and asked me what it contained. Because of his sauciness, I told him it held "presciencial pills" which could make one understand wonders and tell prophecies. Upon hearing this the boy sorely entreated me to permit him one. Finally I acquiesced and gave it to him. He greedily popped it in his mouth and chewed it up. Suddenly a look of disgust came over his face and he began coughing and spitting pieces all over the kitchen floor.

"God's holy trousers," he cried. "That's a cat's turd!"

All those present began laughing and I exclaimed, "It works! Already he is a prophet!"

This caused several of the staff to fall to the floor with laughter. When our mirth finally subsided a bit, I showed him the lozenge

---

* *The Book of Secrets* (13th century). Though primarily remembered as a sorcerer, Albertus Magnus is also a Catholic saint.

under my tongue to prove that it was not evil and so he would not hold it against me. Replacing my lozenge I proceeded to join my host for our meal.

As we finished eating, I heard someone call out, "What Isegrim, what Isegrim." Whereupon, I asked, "Who is this Isegrim I hear being called?"

My companions said they had never heard the name and could hear no one calling. All they heard, they said, was a cat mewing on the roof of the gate. Suddenly realizing the truth of what they said, I was the happiest man alive. Excusing myself, I quickly ran up to the window from which I had secretly watched the cats on the previous night.

The cat was still calling for Isegrim when I made myself comfortable. I placed another lozenge under my tongue and two in my nostrils so as to obtain a full effect. Then I waited to see what would happen.

The Third Part of
Master Streamer's Oration

The cats began to assemble as they had on the previous night. Soon the large gray cat arrived and assumed her place of honor. The cat who had been calling sat down beside her and said, "Grisard, we were becoming concerned. I am glad to see no ill has befallen you." Another cat sat to her other side, while the others approached her one at a time and touched their noses to hers as a sign of greeting and respect.

"My dear friends and fellows," she began, "I apologize for my delayed arrival. Earlier this evening I crept into the magistrate's kitchen a few blocks from here in order to steal some meat for my supper. Before I knew what was happening, a wench came in and placed a lid on the pot, not realizing I was inside. I'm afraid it took me a while to regain my freedom. Then, as I rushed across the housetops in order to get here, I ran head first into a pair of thieves who were attempting to pry open a window at the old sea captain's place. Fortunately I startled them as much as they startled me. Finally, that new hound of the vicar's gave me a run for my life again—the malicious creature! At any rate, I have arrived . . . a little late, but none the worse for wear.

"I see by the position of the Great Star of Bast that the fifth hour of night rapidly approaches. As you know, this is my last night here, for tomorrow I must return to Her Majesty Cammoloch."

At the mention of this name, all of the other cats raised their left paws near their left ears and cried, "Pheffa-Rah save and protect her!"

In response, Grisard raised and lowered her left paw. Continuing, she said, "As our time is limited . . . Mouse-slayer, pray continue where you left off last night."

The cat sitting before Grisard bowed her head. "Thank you m' lady," she began. "We are saddened that this is to be your last night with us and are very grateful that you took time out from your busy schedule to grant us this visit. We also extend our appreciation to your two confidants, Isegrim and Pol-noir."

Mouse-slayer nodded her head to each of the two cats sitting on either side of the gray cat. "Grisard, as chief counselor to Her Majesty Cammoloch—who became queen of the empire through election and inheritance after the treacherous murder of her mother, Grimolochin, by the infamous Patrick Apore— . . ."

"Curses upon the infidel's evil soul!" shouted the cats.

". . . you must judge this complaint," continued Mouse-slayer, "that has been lodged against me by that snake-tongued furball, Catch-rat. For the past two nights I have declared before you and this assembly my life's story—from the blind days of my kitlinghood through my fourth year—in order to prove my honesty and innocence. I trust that when I have concluded, you will understand that it is my accuser who is being deceitful to this august body and who beareth me malice because I refused his lecherously offered delights.

"I shall now continue, m' lady, from where I left my narrative yesternight. As you will recall, my master and mistress had left the city to dwell in the country, and I was taken with them.

"My mistress was old and in ill-health. After a period of time she lost her eyesight and became bedridden, whereupon the parish priest was summoned.

"As he prepared to say the Mass, all were removed from the chamber. I closely observed him from where I lay near the fire. After a rather dull monologue, he poured some wine and held up a wafer saying, 'Wipe your eyes, woman, and behold thy Maker.' She did so and her health and eyesight were restored to her. As a result of this miracle, a few of our number have told me that they have seen their masters and mistresses secretly saying Masses in their chambers."

"If I may . . . ," interrupted Pol-noir. "Could it be that the priest first used some magical art to blind your mistress and then used the same sorcery to cure her? Or perhaps it was something in the Mass itself? If it is the latter, it may be possible that our kitlings could be delivered from their blindness sooner if such a Mass were said over them."

"I have already tried this," replied Mouse-slayer. "I have since kittened in the chamber of another mistress where a Mass was said everyday and their eyesight was none the better for it—yea, it was worse; therefore, I conclude that it wasn't the Mass which brought about the cure. Sorcery remains a possibility. Bird-hunt, who dwells with the priest, is watching him closely but has yet to catch him at it. Still, the priest is a sly one and I wouldn't put it past him."

Pol-noir nodded his head in approval.

"To continue," Mouse-slayer said, "I then moved on to another mistress. This woman kept a boarding house for young men. Secretly she also kept a bevy of fair wenches in order to satisfy their desires. She was a crafty woman who would soak the young gentlemen for all they had and then cast them out into the streets. Many of these men, in order to be allowed to stay, would go out in the night and return the next morning with money, jewels, or even apparel for my mistress. She would take the jewelry—the rings, chains, and such—melt them down and sell them to the goldsmith. Sometimes the young gentlemen would return in the morning cursing their ill fortune, with nothing to show for their adventures except cuts and bruises.

"Notwithstanding these practices, my mistress was a very devoutly religious woman. Every night when she and I were alone in her chamber, she would kneel before the crucifix on the wall above her bed and pray . . . sometimes for an entire hour. Usually she prayed that the Lord should protect her and her guests from danger and shame, promising to continue to serve the Lord during the remainder of her lifetime.

"While she was at this, I would often play on the rug near the hearth. Sometimes I would take her necklace and jump at it as if it were a golden snake. Then I would put it over my head and run with it about my neck. Often I would hear her say, 'I know thou hearest my prayer, Lord, because I can see your image smiling at the gambols of my cat.'

"Never did this mistress do me any wrong, save once. One of her boarders came to her and told her that he had become enamored with the beautiful young wife of a merchant, but, even though he used all his wiles, he was unable to persuade her to satisfy his lust. He had offered her great banquets, rich apparel, and many precious jewels—but to no avail. The young lady was too concerned with her honesty and what others would think of her. Thus, he pleaded with my mistress for help, promising her anything she would require, for he was about to go mad with desire.

"My mistress—who was considered a decent and godly woman throughout the parish—contrived some excuse to have the young lady over for dinner the next day. She then fed me a piece of pudding full of mustard. Soon as I had eaten this, my eyes began to water and continued to do so all the next day. Shortly before the dinner, she blew pepper in my nose which made me sneeze.

"After she had shown the young wife around her house, the two of them sat down to dinner together. They were busy gossiping—for women love to gossip almost as much as we do—when I wandered in and sat down, as I was want to do at meal times. On noticing me cough and weep continuously, the young lady inquired of my mistress what ailed me. At this my mistress fell herself to weeping and replied, 'In faith, my friend, I must be the most unfortunate woman alive, for God hath poured forth all his plagues at my feet. My husband (an honest and devoted man if ever there was one) and my heir and only son (as handsome and hardworking as any that ever graced this land) have both been taken from me by His angel of death. And though this were not enough, He has turned my daughter (who was a fair woman and well-married) into this likeness you see before you. For the past two months she has continuously wept, lamenting her miserable fate. I must admit, I am at a loss whether I should comfort my daughter and reproach our God; or to blame her and pardon Him.'

"The young lady was astonished at this and asked my mistress what had brought all this about.

" 'It is a sad story,' my mistress replied. 'As I said, my daughter was well-married and devoted to her husband. No thought of infidelity ever crossed her mind. She was very beautiful, and it was this beauty that caught the eye of a young gentleman. This man proclaimed his love for her and offered her all manner of tokens and gifts, but she spurned his attentions, saying she must remain loyal to her husband. The young man was deeply besotted with my daughter and persisted in his attentions.

" 'Finally my daughter came to me for advice. On hearing all this, I told her that she was doing the proper thing and should on no account give in to this gentleman. She was encouraged by my advice and tried to shake him off with shrewd words and threatening answers.

" 'Seeing his case to be hopeless, the young man went home and fell ill. He languished on his bed for three days, refusing to eat or drink. Perceiving that the hand of death was upon his shoulder, he sent a letter to my daughter, which I have here.

" 'Although I am unable to read or write, my daughter could. If you are able, you may read what it says.' My mistress handed her the letter which read:

The Nameless Lover to the Nameless Beloved, without whose love he may not live.

Cursed be the time when love for another first entered this miserable carcass. Cursed be the hour which first you entered my life. Yea, cursed be that unhappy hour when I first saw those piercing eyes which so inflamed my heart with unquenchable desire. Lo, for those innocent days when I yet had the desires and dreams of other men—the dreams of success and conquest. In one fatal moment all my former concerns were ripped from my life, to be replaced by a new concern alien to my former existence. One that is devastatingly beyond my grasp. A beautiful lure and a constant reminder of what I shall never be able to have.

It is a sad thing to have but one desire in life—that of spending every waking hour in devotion and fulfilling the pleasures of another. As this desire is beyond all hope of fulfillment, there is no longer any motivation for me to continue in this life.

I do not blame you my sweet unloving love for pouring showers of cruel words upon me and extinguishing the few remaining burning embers of hope in my soul. I do respect your fidelity to wedlock and, though I wish to God it were not, I have to admit your faithfulness is worthy of praise.

The hour is late and my destiny draws near. All I ask is that you find it in your heart to grant me but one request: Please pay a last visit to one whose mind has not been quiet these past three months, who has not slept this past fortnight, who has taken no food nor drink these past three days, and who is dead while yet alive. Let those lovely white hands of yours close up the windows to my soul, through which your beauty first entered into my heart. If you cannot do this, then at least see me honestly buried.

If you refuse to do this, then I beseech God (to whom I shall go shortly) that He either soften your merciless heart or change your tremendous beauty, so that none other may be entrapped in a similar fate.

Yours always, G.S.

"After reading this letter, the young lady, on the verge of tears, said, 'I am very sorry for your unhappiness and much more for this gentleman's but, most of all, I am sorry for your daughter. What did she do upon receiving this letter?'

" 'As with her previous responses, she sent him a rough reply, but he died before he received it. Within two days, my daughter's husband died after being thrown from his horse. Two days later, while lamenting her husband's death, we heard a voice cry out, "Hard-hearted woman, repent thy cruelty!" and my daughter was transformed into the likeness you see her in now. All this because she valued honesty and fidelity more than preventing cruelty.

" 'I hold myself responsible, as it was I who advised my daughter to take the course which has brought us to this miserable state.'

"All this weighed heavily on the young lady's mind and, taking leave of my mistress, she sent word to her young suitor that she would meet him the next day.

"In the meantime, I had decided to take revenge on my mistress for the mustard and pepper which made me so miserable. My mistress abhorred mice with a passion, so I caught one and released it underneath her frock. To her intense horror, it ran straight up her leg. How she cried out and how pale she became. Pretending I was coming to her rescue, I leapt at the mouse with claws extended and went to work on her thighs. I dare say it took her two months to recover from those wounds.

"Shortly after this, the young lady begged my mistress to allow her to take care of me and, thus, I went to dwell with my new mistress, with whom I until recently resided.

"As all of the cats who know me will attest, I have always abided within the law and have been a loyal subject to our empire. I have never refused the advances of any male, with only one exception. Yea, I admit that I refused Catch-rat and bit and scratched him, as the law forbiddeth. I shall now explain why.

"Earlier this year, when I was great with kitlings and food was scarce, I came upon Catch-rat in the gutter eating a bat he had caught. As I am sure you know, m' lady, when we are in this way, we often develop a desire for certain things—for me, I had developed a wild craving for churchmouse. Added to this was my starved state and my fear that I would lose my kitlings if I could not find something to eat.

"I humbly asked Catch-rat if I could have a piece of the leathery wing to chew on, but the ravenous churl refused with bitter words and quickly devoured it all. He told me that I had only wanted it out of wantonness and not from actual need. This grieved me, especially as I was ill for the next two days for the lack of nourishment. If it wasn't for Bird-hunt, who brought me a piece of mouse—leading me to believe it was bat—I am sure I would have kittened ten days before my time.

"After recovering from my illness, I again met Catch-rat. This time he made his advances, not caring that I had not yet had my kitlings. I did my best to dissuade him, but to no avail. (Truly, I believe he had been eating catnip.) When he made it clear he intended to ravish me by force, I cried out as loud as I could and, to defend myself until help arrived, I bit and scratched as hard as I could. Had it not been for the rapid arrival of Bird-hunt and her son, Lightfoot, I am sure he would have marred me for life. They are both here and can attest to the truth of what I say.

"The law forbiddeth us females from refusing any males not exceeding the number of ten in a night. I have abided by this law except for this solitary instance. Now you, m' lady, must judge whether I was justified or not."

Mouse-slayer, having completed her narrative, bowed her head as the other cats watching the proceedings began talking among themselves. Then all became silent as Grisard began to speak.

"In the third year of the reign of Glascalon, at the court held in Catwood, as appeareth in the records, they issued the decree which forbiddeth any male from forcing his desires on any female against her will; therefore, you are free from guilt. In truth, we were satisfied of this during the first night of your life's account, but we found it so interesting that we could not cause ourselves to bring an end to it. As briefly as you can—for I see that Felis is low on the horizon indicating that the goblins' hour approacheth—please tell us how your life was with your new mistress."

Mouse-slayer bowed her head again and continued.

"My new mistress made much of me, thinking I was my old mistress's daughter. She often told this story to her friends. My new master also made much of me because I used to eat my meat by holding it in my paw.

"Also in this house there was my mistress's father, who loved to play tricks. One day he took four walnut shells and filled them with soft pitch. Placing them on my feet, he put them in cold water so that the pitch hardened and then let me go.

"How strange it was for me to go around in shoes. They vexed me terrible. Not only did it make walking difficult, it made climbing impossible. Try as I might, I could not get the horrible things off. Finally, out of disgust, I hid myself in my mistress's and master's chamber and spent the remainder of the day there. That night, after all were asleep, I spied a mouse playing on the floor. I immediately tried to catch it, but my shoes made such a racket that I ended up chasing it all around the room.

"My master, who is very fearful of spirits, shot up in bed and cried out. The servants also heard the noise, as it sounded like a herd of horses tramping across the wooden floor. I had a hard time keeping from being stepped on by my master and mistress as they headed for the door. Soon the whole house was in an uproar.

"Finally, the father—the same one who had shoed me and one of the bravest men in the parish—crept back to see what was causing the noise. As he slowly climbed the stairs, I came out to meet him. When he saw my gleaming eyes in the darkness, he screamed and fell over backwards down the stairs. The entire household—with the father leading the way—ran naked into the street screaming that the specters of the Wild Hunt were riding through the house.

"They were soon joined by all the neighbors. In the mean time I returned to hunting for the mouse. Eventually the priest was roused from his slumber and put in charge of the affair. He entered the house, armed with a crucifix and a candle in one hand and holy water in the other. He was followed by the rest of the people.

"I heard him coming up the stairs, saying prayers, and thought we would have a Mass as I had often seen before. Once again I ran to greet them but this had the same effect as it had on the father. As the priest toppled over backwards, he took the others down with him. I ran down among them where they lay in heaps and sought out my mistress. Finding me rubbing against her and mewing, she called out, "It is only my cat," at which the others began to laugh.

"Although they suspected and cursed the one who had shoed me, they were never able to prove it and he refused to admit it. In any case, hot water was soon brought and the shoes were removed, much to my joy. After agreeing that no one else—outside of those present—should ever hear what had happened on this night, they all crept off to bed very embarrassed by the night's proceedings."

After all of the cats, and I too, had laughed over this for a bit, Mouse-slayer continued. "My mistress began seeing increasingly the young gentleman she had formerly resisted until my bout with the mustard and pepper. Eventually I began to pity my master because those two were secretly spending his money faster than he could make it. Even though his business was prospering, I was sure he was close to ruin.

"My mistress's paramour often visited her when my master was away. On one of these occasions, my master suddenly arrived home unexpectedly while they were both in bed. The young man grabbed up his clothes and hid behind a tapestry. He stood there as still as a corpse, and just as pale. My mistress was just able to throw on her frock before he entered the room.

"She threw her arms around her husband and kissed him as she usually did when he arrived home. She then did her best to get him to leave the room, but to no avail. He was so tired, he just rolled onto the bed and asked her to bring his dinner up to him. Seeing no means to budge him, she went to the kitchen and brought him some potato stew and a piece of stale bread; whereas earlier, she and her lover had dined on capons, hot venison, and other delicacies.

"On seeing this, I decided to give my master some reality orientation. I strolled behind the tapestry and proceeded to use the young man's bare legs as a scratching post. Realizing where the greater danger lie, he did not move nor make a sound. I was not about to give up. Claws extended, I leapt into the air and took a swipe at his genitals. Letting out a tremendous scream, he grabbed me by the neck and was in the process of strangling me when my master tore back the curtain. The young man released his grip and I took a flying leap out of the window. I have not been back since, and durst not for fear of my life.

"Thus I have laid my life's story before you. To my knowledge, I have never violated any laws and I trust you will so certify before my liege Cammoloch."

Mouse-slayer once again bowed her head. Grisard, Isegrim, and Pol-noir praised her and then said that Cammoloch would hold her next court on St. Catherine's day at Caithness. With that, the cats departed. I wandered off to bed, thankful for what I had heard and sorry for what I had not understood on the two previous nights.

The next morning I was sitting in the garden, when I overheard two cats talking nearby. One cat asked what had happened during the proceedings. The other answered that Mouse-slayer had cleared herself of a crime that was laid to her by Catch-rat, and that she had declared the entire six years of her life. During the first night she had told of the private deceits of five masters: a baker, a lawyer, a broker, a butcher, and a priest. On the second night she had exposed the cruelty, cunning, waste, and oppression of six masters: a bishop, a knight, a lord, a goldsmith, an apothecary, and an alchemist. On the final night she had told of Catch-rat and three mistresses, but that this was nothing compared to the two previous nights.

After breakfast, I discovered my power to understand cats had gone and, though I could see their gestures, I could not comprehend their words.

So now I have told you of this wonderful matter. Some other time I will tell you of other mysteries and experiences I have had which even surpass this, but now it is late and time for us to sleep.

With that, Master Streamer concluded his narrative and we all drifted off to the land of Nod.

An Exhortation

I know it seems marvelous that cats should be able to communicate, have rulers, and be obedient to laws. I would not believe it myself were it not for the approved authority of my sources. Since I know the persons and places described herein, I am less doubtful. Seeing that cats are able to understand us, watch our secret doings, and describe them to other cats (and to any persons who have taken the proper medications), I would therefore counsel everyone to be careful what they do in secret, lest it become known to the world. I would also caution them not to put away their cat, as this would be a sure sign that they have something to hide.

Therefore let us live openly so that, even though our cat has access to all our secrets, she will not have anything to declare against us, save what is good and just. And wherever thou goest, be mindful of this proverb: *Beware the Cat.*

The Empty Sleeve

(1911)

Algernon Blackwood (1869–1951)

Blackwood was an English novelist and short story writer who began writing as a journalist for newspapers in New York City. Called by H. P. Lovecraft "the one absolute and unquestioned master of weird atmosphere," Blackwood was one of the most prolific writers of ghostly tales. His stories are characteristically set against macabre and pagan backgrounds, reflecting his lifelong dedication to occult studies. Outside the dedicated cult of horror fans, Blackwood is little known—one of those authors unaccountably neglected by the literary community as a whole. This story originally appeared in the January 1911 issue of *The London Magazine*.

I

The Gilmer brothers were a couple of fussy and pernickety old bachelors of a rather retiring, not to say timid, disposition. There was gray in the pointed beard of John, the elder, and if any hair had remained to William it would also certainly have been of the same shade. They had private means. Their main interest in life was the collection of violins, for which they had the instinctive *flair* of true connoisseurs. Neither John nor William, however, could play a single note. They could only pluck the open strings. The production of tone, so necessary before the purchase was done vicariously for them by another.

The only objection they had to the big building in which they occupied the roomy top floor was that Morgan, liftman and caretaker, insisted on wearing a billycock with his uniform after six o'clock in the evening, with a result disastrous to the beauty of the universe. For "Mr. Morgan," as they called him between themselves, had a round and pasty face on the top of a round and conical body. In view, however, of the man's other rare qualities—including his devotion to themselves—this objection was not serious.

He had another peculiarity that amused them. On being found fault with, he explained nothing, but merely repeated the words of the complaint.

"Water in the bath wasn't really hot this morning, Morgan!"

"Water in the bath reely 'ot, wasn't it, sir?"

Or, from William, who was something of a faddist:

"My jar of sour milk came up late yesterday, Morgan."

"Your jar sour milk come up late, sir, yesterday?"

Since, however, the statement of a complaint invariably resulted in its remedy, the brothers had learned to look for no further explanation. Next morning the bath *was* hot, the sour milk *was* "brortup" punctually. The uniform and billycock hat, though, remained an eyesore and source of oppression.

On this particular night John Gilmer, the elder, returning from a Masonic rehearsal, stepped into the lift and found Mr. Morgan with his hand ready on the iron rope.

"Fog's very thick outside," said Mr. John pleasantly; and the lift was a third of the way up before Morgan had completed his customary repetition: "Fog very thick outside, yes, sir." And Gilmer then asked casually if his brother were alone, and received the reply that Mr. Hyman had called and had not yet gone away.

Now this Mr. Hyman was a Hebrew, and, like themselves, a connoisseur in violins, but, unlike themselves, who only kept their specimens to look at, he was a skillful and exquisite player. He was the only person they ever permitted to handle their pedigree instruments, to take them from the glass cases where they reposed in silent splendor, and to draw the sound out of their wondrous painted hearts of golden varnish. The brothers loathed to see his fingers touch them, yet loved to hear their singing voices in the room, for the latter confirmed their sound judgment as collectors, and made them certain their money had been well spent. Hyman, however, made no attempt to conceal his contempt and hatred for the mere collectors. The atmosphere of the room fairly pulsed with these opposing forces of silent emotion when Hyman played and the Gilmers, alternately writhing and admiring, listened. The occasions, however, were not frequent. The Hebrew only came by invitation, and both brothers made a point of being in. It was a very formal proceeding—something of a sacred rite almost.

John Gilmer, therefore, was considerably surprised by the information Morgan had supplied. For one thing, Hyman, he had understood, was away on the Continent.

"Still in there, you say?" he repeated, after a moment's reflection.

"Still in there, Mr. John, sir." Then, concealing his surprise from the liftman, he fell back upon his usual mild habit of complaining about the billycock hat and the uniform.

"You really should try and remember, Morgan," he said, though kindly. "That hat does not go well with that uniform!"

Morgan's pasty countenance betrayed no vestige of expression.

"At don't go well with the yewniform, sir," he repeated, hanging up the disreputable bowler and replacing it with a gold-braided cap from the peg. "No, sir, it don't, do it?" he added cryptically, smiling at the transformation thus effected.

And the lift then halted with an abrupt jerk at the top floor. By somebody's carelessness the landing was in darkness, and, to make things worse, Morgan, clumsily pulling the iron rope, happened to knock the billycock from its peg so that his sleeve, as he stooped to catch it, struck the switch and plunged the scene in a moment's complete obscurity.

And it was then, in the act of stepping out before the light was turned on again, that John Gilmer stumbled against something that shot along the landing past the open door. First he thought it must be a child, then a man, then—an animal. Its movement was rapid yet stealthy. Starting backwards instinctively to allow it room to pass, Gilmer collided in the darkness with Morgan, and Morgan incontinently screamed. There was a moment of stupid confusion. The heavy framework of the lift shook a little, as though something had stepped into it and then as quickly jumped out again. A rushing sound followed that resembled footsteps, yet at the same time was more like gliding—someone in soft slippers or stockinged feet, greatly hurrying Then came silence again. Morgan sprang to the landing and turned up the electric light. Mr. Gilmer, at the same moment, did likewise to the switch in the lift. Light flooded the scene. Nothing was visible.

"Dog or cat, or something, I suppose, wasn't it?" exclaimed Gilmer, following the man out and looking round with bewildered amazement upon a deserted landing. He knew quite well, even while he spoke, that the words were foolish.

"Dog or cat, yes, sir, or—something," echoed Morgan, his eyes narrowed to pin-points, then growing large, but his face stolid.

"The light should have been on," Mr. Gilmer spoke with a touch of severity. The little occurrence had curiously disturbed his equanimity. He felt annoyed, upset, uneasy.

For a perceptible pause the liftman made no reply, and his employer, looking up, saw that, besides being flustered, he was white about the jaws. His voice, when he spoke, was without its normal assurance. This time he did not merely repeat. He explained.

"The light *was* on, sir, when last *I* come up!" he said, with emphasis, obviously speaking the truth. "Only a moment ago," he added.

Mr. Gilmer, for some reason, felt disinclined to press for explanations. He decided to ignore the matter.

Then the lift plunged down again into the depths like a diving-bell into water; and John Gilmer, pausing a moment first to reflect, let himself in softly with his latchkey, and, after hanging up hat and coat in the hall, entered the big sitting room he and his brother shared in common.

The December fog that covered London like a dirty blanket had penetrated, he saw, into the room. The objects in it were half shrouded in the familiar yellowish haze.

II

In his dressing-gown and slippers, William Gilmer, almost invisible in his armchair by the gas-stove across the room, spoke at once. Through the thick atmosphere his face gleamed, showing an extinguished pipe hanging from his lips. His tone of voice conveyed emotion, an emotion he sought to suppress, of a quality, however, not easy to define.

"Hyman's been here," he announced abruptly. "You must have met him. He's this very instant gone out."

It was quite easy to see that something had happened, for "scenes" leave disturbance behind them in the atmosphere. But John made no immediate reference to this. He replied that he had seen no one—which was strictly true—and his brother thereupon, sitting bolt upright in the chair, turned quickly and faced him. His skin, in the foggy air, seemed paler than before.

"That's odd," he said nervously.

"What's odd?" asked John.

"That you didn't see—anything. You ought to have run into one another on the doorstep." His eyes went peering about the room. He was distinctly ill at ease. "You're positive you saw no one? Did Morgan take him down before you came? Did Morgan see him?" He asked several questions at once.

"On the contrary, Morgan told me he was still here with you. Hyman probably walked down, and didn't take the lift at all," he replied. "That accounts for neither of us seeing him." He decided to say nothing about the occurrence in the lift, for his brother's nerves, he saw plainly, were on edge.

William then stood up out of his chair, and the skin of his face changed its hue, for whereas a moment ago it was merely pale, it had now altered to a tint that lay somewhere between white and a livid gray. The man was fighting internal terror. For a moment these two brothers of middle age looked each other straight in the eye. Then John spoke:

"What's wrong, Billy?" he asked quietly. "Something's upset you. What brought Hyman in this way—unexpectedly? I thought he was still in Germany."

The brothers, affectionate and sympathetic, understood one another perfectly. They had no secrets. Yet for several minutes the younger one made no reply. It seemed difficult to choose his words apparently.

"Hyman played, I suppose—on the fiddles?" John helped him, wondering uneasily what was coming. He did not care much for the individual in question, though his talent was of such great use to them.

The other nodded in the affirmative, then plunged into rapid speech, talking under his breath as though he feared someone might overhear. Glancing over his shoulder down the foggy room, he drew his brother close.

"Hyman came," he began, "unexpectedly. He hadn't written, and I hadn't asked him. You hadn't either, I suppose?"

John shook his head.

"When I came in from the dining-room I found him in the passage. The servant was taking away the dishes, and he had let himself in while the front door was ajar. Pretty cool, wasn't it?"

"He's an original," said John, shrugging his shoulders. "And you welcomed him?" he asked.

"I asked him in, of course. He explained he had something glorious for me to hear. Silenski had played it in the afternoon, and he had bought the music since. But Silenski's 'Strad' hadn't the power—it's thin on the upper strings, you remember, unequal, patchy—and he said no instrument in the world could do it justice but our 'Joseph'— the small Guarnerius, you know, which he swears is the most perfect in the world."

"And what was it? Did he play it?" asked John, growing more uneasy as he grew more interested. With relief he glanced round and saw the matchless little instrument lying there safe and sound in its glass case near the door.

"He played it—divinely: a Zigeuner Lullaby, a fine, passionate, rushing bit of inspiration, oddly-misnamed 'lullaby.' And, fancy the fellow had memorized it already! He walked about the room on tiptoe while he played it, complaining of the light—"

"Complaining of the light?"

"Said the thing was crepuscular, and needed dusk for its full effect. I turned the lights out one by one, till finally there was only the glow of the gas logs. He insisted. You know that way he has with him? And then he got over me in another matter: insisted on using some special strings he had brought with him, and put them on, too, himself— thicker than the A and E *we* use."

For though neither Gilmer could produce a note, it was their pride that they kept their precious instruments in perfect condition for playing, choosing the exact thickness and quality of strings that suited the temperament of each violin; and the little Guarnerius in question always "sang" best, they held, with thin strings.

"Infernal insolence," exclaimed the listening brother, wondering what was coming next. "Played it well, though, didn't he, this Lullaby thing?" he added, seeing that William hesitated. As he spoke he went nearer, sitting down close beside him in a leather chair.

"Magnificent! Pure fire of genius!" was the reply with enthusiasm, the voice at the same time dropping lower. "Staccato like a silver hammer; harmonics like flutes, clear, soft, ringing; and the tone— well, the G string was a baritone, and the upper registers creamy and mellow as a boy's voice. John," he added, "that Guarnerius is the very pick of the period and"—again he hesitated—"Hyman loves it. He'd give his soul to have it."

The more John heard, the more uncomfortable it made him. He had always disliked this gifted Hebrew, for in his secret heart he knew that he had always feared and distrusted him. Sometimes he had felt half afraid of him; the man's very forcible personality was too insistent to be pleasant. His type was of the dark and sinister kind, and he possessed a violent will that rarely failed of accomplishing its desire.

"Wish I'd heard the fellow play," he said at length, ignoring his brother's last remark, and going on to speak of the most matter-of-fact details he could think of. "Did he use the Dodd bow, or the Tourte? That Dodd I picked up last month, you know, is the most perfectly balanced I have ever—"

He stopped abruptly, for William had suddenly got upon his feet and was standing there, searching the room with his eyes. A chill ran down John's spine as he watched him.

"What is it, Billy?" he asked sharply. "Hear anything?"

William continued to peer about him through the thick air.

"Oh, nothing, probably," he said, an odd catch in his voice; "only —I keep feeling as if there was somebody listening. Do you think, perhaps"—he glanced over his shoulder—"there is someone at the door? I wish—I wish you'd have a look, John."

John obeyed, though without great eagerness. Crossing the room slowly, he opened the door, then switched on the light. The passage leading past the bathroom towards the bedrooms beyond was empty. The coats hung motionless from their pegs.

"No one, of course," he said, as he closed the door and came back to the stove. He left the light burning in the passage. It was curious the way both brothers had this impression that they were not alone, though only one of them spoke of it.

"Used the Dodd or the Tourte, Billy—which?" continued John in the most natural voice he could assume.

But at that very same instant the water started to his eyes. His brother, he saw, was close upon the thing he really had to tell. But he had stuck fast.

III

By a great effort John Gilmer composed himself and remained in his chair. With detailed elaboration he lit a cigarette, staring hard at his brother over the flaring match while he did so. There he sat in his dressing-gown and slippers by the fireplace, eyes downcast, fingers playing idly with the red tassel. The electric light cast heavy shadows across the face. In a flash then, since emotion may sometimes express itself in attitude even better than in speech, the elder brother understood that Billy was about to tell him an unutterable thing.

By instinct he moved over to his side so that the same view of the room confronted him.

"Out with it, old man," he said, with an effort to be natural. "Tell me what you saw."

Billy shuffled slowly round and the two sat side by side, facing the fog-draped chamber.

"It was like this," he began softly, "only I was standing instead of sitting, looking over to that door as you and I do now. Hyman moved to and fro in the faint glow of the gas logs against the far wall, playing that 'crepuscular' thing in his most inspired sort of way, so that the music seemed to issue from himself rather than from the shining bit of wood under his chin, when—I noticed something coming over me that was"—he hesitated, searching for words—"that wasn't *all* due to the music," he finished abruptly.

"His personality put a bit of hypnotism on you, eh?"

William shrugged his shoulders.

"The air was thickish with fog and the light was dim, cast upwards upon him from the stove," he continued. "I admit all that. But there wasn't light enough to throw shadows, you see, and—"

"Hyman looked queer?" the other helped him quickly.

Billy nodded his head without turning.

"Changed there before my very eyes"—he whispered it—"turned animal—"

"Animal?" John felt his hair rising.

"That's the only way I can put it. His face and hands and body turned otherwise than usual. I lost the sound of his feet. When the bow-hand or the fingers on the strings passed into the light, they were"—he uttered a soft, shuddering little laugh—"furry, oddly divided, the fingers massed together. And he paced stealthily. I thought every instant the fiddle would drop with a crash and he would spring at me across the room."

"My dear chap—"

"He moved with those big, lithe, striding steps one sees"—John held his breath in the little pause, listening keenly—"one sees those big brutes make in the cages when their desire is aflame for food or escape, or—or fierce passionate desire for anything they want with their whole nature—"

"The big felines!" John whistled softly.

"And every minute getting nearer and nearer to the door, as though he meant to make a sudden rush for it and get out."

"With the violin! Of course you stopped him?"

"In the end. But for a long time, I swear to you, I found it difficult to know what to do, even to move. I couldn't get my voice for words of any kind; it was like a spell."

"It *was* a spell," suggested John firmly.

"Then, as he moved, still playing," continued the other, "he seemed to grow smaller; to shrink down below the line of the gas. I thought I should lose sight of him altogether. I turned the light up suddenly. There he was over by the door—crouching."

"Playing on his knees, you mean?"

William closed his eyes in an effort to visualize it again.

"Crouching," he repeated, at length, "close to the floor. At least, I think so. It all happened so quickly, and I felt so bewildered, it was hard to see straight. But at first I could have sworn he was half his natural size. I called to him, I think I swore at him—I forget exactly, but I know he straightened up at once and stood before me down there in the light"—he pointed across the room to the door—"eyes gleaming, face white as chalk, perspiring like midsummer, and gradually filling out, straightening up, whatever you like to call it, to his natural size and appearance again. It was the most horrid thing I've ever seen."

"As an—animal, you saw him still?"

"No; human again. Only much smaller."

"What did he say?"

Billy reflected a moment.

"Nothing that I can remember," he replied. "You see, it was all over in a few seconds. In the full light, I felt so foolish, and nonplused at first. To see him normal again baffled me. And, before I could collect myself, he had let himself out into the passage, and I heard the front door slam. A minute later—the same second almost, it seemed —you came in. I only remember grabbing the violin and getting it back safely under the glass case. The strings were still vibrating."

The account was over. John asked no further questions. Nor did he say a single word about the lift, Morgan, or the extinguished light on the landing. There fell a longish silence between the two men; and then, while they helped themselves to a generous supply of whisky-and-soda before going to bed, John looked up and spoke:

"If you agree, Billy," he said quietly, "I think I might write and suggest to Hyman that we shall no longer have need for his services."

And Billy, acquiescing, added a sentence that expressed something of the singular dread lying but half-concealed in the atmosphere of the room, if not in their minds as well:

"Putting it, however, in a way that need not offend him."

"Of course. There's no need to be rude, is there?"

Accordingly, next morning the letter was written; and John, saying nothing to his brother, took it round himself by hand to the Hebrew's rooms near Euston. The answer he dreaded was forthcoming:

"Mr. Hyman's still away abroad," he was told. "But we're forwarding letters; yes. Or I can give you his address if you'll prefer it." The letter went, therefore, to the number in Konigstrasse, Munich, thus obtained.

Then, on his way back from the insurance company where he went to increase the sum that protected the small Guarnerius from loss by fire, accident, or theft, John Gilmer called at the offices of certain musical agents and ascertained that Silenski, the violinist, was performing at the time in Munich. It was only some days later, though, by diligent inquiry, he made certain that at a concert on a certain date the famous virtuoso had played a Zigeuner Lullaby of his own composition—the very date, it turned out, on which he himself had been to the Masonic rehearsal at Mark Masons' Hall.

John, however, said nothing of these discoveries to his brother William.

IV

It was about a week later when a reply to the letter came from Munich—a letter couched in somewhat offensive terms, though it contained neither words nor phrases that could actually be found fault with. Isidore Hyman was hurt and angry. On his return to London a month or so later, he proposed to call and talk the matter over. The offensive part of the letter, lay, perhaps, in his definite assumption that he could persuade the brothers to resume the old relations. John, however, wrote a brief reply to the effect that they had decided to buy no new fiddles; their collection being complete, there would be no occasion for them to invite his services as a performer. This was final. No answer came, and the matter seemed to drop. Never for one moment, though, did it leave the consciousness of John Gilmer. Hyman had said that he would come, and come assuredly he would. He secretly gave Morgan instructions that he and his brother for the future were always "out" when the Hebrew presented himself.

"He must have gone back to Germany, you see, almost at once after his visit here that night," observed William—John, however, making no reply.

One night towards the middle of January the two brothers came home together from a concert in Queen's Hall, and sat up later than usual in their sitting-room discussing over their whisky and tobacco the merits of the pieces and performers. It must have been past one o'clock when they turned out the lights in the passage and retired to bed. The air was still and frosty; moonlight over the roofs—one of those sharp and dry winter nights that now seem to visit London rarely.

"Like the old-fashioned days when we were boys," remarked William, pausing a moment by the passage window and looking out across the miles of silvery, sparkling roofs.

"Yes," added John; "the ponds freezing hard in the fields, rime on the nursery windows, and the sound of a horse's hoofs coming down the road in the distance, eh?" They smiled at the memory, then said good night, and separated. Their rooms were at opposite ends of the corridor; in between were the bathroom, dining-room, and sitting-room. It was a long, straggling flat. Half an hour later both brothers were sound asleep, the flat silent, only a dull murmur rising from the great city outside, and the moon sinking slowly to the level of the chimneys.

Perhaps two hours passed, perhaps three, when John Gilmer, sitting up in bed with a start, wide-awake and frightened, knew that someone was moving about in one of the three rooms that lay between him and his brother. He had absolutely no idea why he should have been frightened, for there was no dream or nightmare-memory that he brought over from unconsciousness. and yet he realized plainly that the fear he felt was by no means a foolish and unreasoning fear. It had a cause and a reason. Also—which made it worse—it was fully warranted. Something in his sleep, forgotten in the instant of waking, had happened that set every nerve in his body on the watch. He was positive only of two things—first, that it was the entrance of this person, moving so quietly there in the flat, that sent the chills down his spine; and, secondly, that this person was *not* his brother William.

John Gilmer was a timid man. The sight of a burglar, his eyes black-masked, suddenly confronting him in the passage, would most likely have deprived him of all power of decision—until the burglar had either shot him or escaped. But on this occasion some instinct told him that it was no burglar, and that the acute distress he experienced was not due to any message of ordinary physical fear. The thing that had gained access to his flat while he slept had first come— he felt sure of it—into his room, and had passed very close to his own bed, before going on. It had then doubtless gone to his brother's room, visiting them both stealthily to make sure they slept. And its mere passage through his room had been enough to wake him and set these drops of cold perspiration upon his skin. For it was—he felt it in every fiber of his body—something hostile.

The thought that it might at that very moment be in the room of his brother, however, brought him to his feet on the cold floor, and set him moving with all the determination he could summon towards the door. He looked cautiously down an utterly dark passage; then crept on tiptoe along it. On the wall were old-fashioned weapons that had belonged to his father; and feeling a curved, sheathless sword that had come from some Turkish campaign of years gone by, his fingers closed tightly round it, and lifted it silently from the three hooks whereon it lay. He passed the doors of the bathroom and dining-room, making instinctively for the big sitting-room where the violins were kept in their glass cases. The cold nipped him. His eyes smarted with the effort to see in the darkness. Outside the closed door he hesitated.

Putting his ear to the crack, he listened. From within came a faint sound of someone moving. The same instant there rose the sharp, delicate "ping" of a violin-string being plucked; and John Gilmer, with nerves that shook like the vibrations of that very string, opened the door wide with a fling and turned on the light at the same moment. The plucked string still echoed faintly in the air.

The sensation that met him on the threshold was the well-known one that things had been going on in the room which his unexpected arrival had that instant put a stop to. A second earlier and he would have discovered it all in the act. The atmosphere still held the feeling of rushing, silent movement with which the things had raced back to their normal, motionless positions. The immobility of the furniture was a mere attitude hurriedly assumed, and the moment his back was turned the whole business, whatever it might be, would begin again. With this presentment of the room—however—a purely imaginative one, came another, swiftly on its heels.

For one of the objects, less swift than the rest, had not quite regained its "attitude" of repose. It still moved. Below the window curtains on the right, not far from the shelf that bore the violins in their glass cases, he made it out, slowly gliding along the floor. Then, even as his eye caught it, it came to rest.

And, while the cold perspiration broke out all over him afresh, he knew that this still moving item was the cause both of his waking and of his terror. This was the disturbance whose presence he had divined in the flat without actual hearing, and whose passage through his room, while he yet slept, had touched every nerve in his body as with ice. Clutching his Turkish sword tightly, he drew back with the ut-most caution against the wall and watched, for the singular impres-sion came to him that the movement was not that of a human being crouching, but rather of something that pertained to the animal world. He remembered, flash-like, the movements of reptiles, the stealth of the larger felines, the undulating glide of great snakes. For the moment, however, it did not move, and they faced one another.

The other side of the room was but dimly lighted, and the noise he made clicking up another electric lamp brought the thing flying forward again—towards himself. At such a moment it seemed absurd to think of so small a detail, but he remembered his bare feet, and, genuinely frightened, he leaped upon a chair and swished with his sword though the air about him. From this better point of view, with the increased light to aid him, he then saw two things—first, that the glass case usually covering the Guarnerius violin had been shifted; and, secondly, that the moving object was slowly elongating itself into an upright position. Semi-erect, yet most oddly, too, like a creature on its hind legs, it was coming swiftly towards him. It was making for the door—and escape.

The confusion of ghostly fear was somehow upon him so that he was too bewildered to see clearly, but he had sufficient control, it seemed, to recover a certain power of action; for the moment the advancing figure was near enough for him to strike, that curved scimitar flashed and whirred about him, with such misdirected violence, however, that he not only failed to strike it even once, but at the same time lost his balance and fell forward from the chair whereon he perched—straight into it.

And then came the most curious thing of all, for as he dropped, the figure also dropped, stooped low down, crouched, dwindled amazingly in size, and rushed past him close to the ground like an animal on all fours. John Gilmer screamed, for he could no longer contain himself. Stumbling over the chair as he turned to follow, cutting and slashing wildly with his sword, he saw half-way down the darkened corridor beyond the scuttling outline of, apparently, an enormous—cat!

The door into the outer landing was somehow ajar, and the next second the beast was out, but not before the steel had fallen with a crashing blow upon the front disappearing leg, almost severing it from the body.

It was dreadful. Turning up the lights as he went, he ran after in to the outer landing. But the thing he followed was already well away, and he heard, on the floor below him, the same oddly gliding, slithering, stealthy sound, yet hurrying, that he heard weeks before when something had passed him in the lift, and Morgan, in his terror, had likewise cried aloud.

For a time he stood there on that dark landing, listening, thinking, trembling; then turned into the flat and shut the door. In the sitting-room he carefully replaced the glass case over the treasured violin, puzzled to the point of foolishness, and strangely routed in his mind. For the violin itself, he saw, had been dragged several inches from its cushioned bed of plush.

Next morning, however, he made no allusion to the occurrence of the night. His brother apparently had not been disturbed.

V

The only thing that called for explanation—an explanation not fully forthcoming—was the curious aspect of Mr. Morgan's countenance. The fact that this individual gave notice to the owners of the building, and at the end of the month left for a new post, was, of course, known to both brothers; whereas the story he told in explanation of his face was known only to the one who questioned him about it—John. And John, for reasons best known to himself, did not pass it on to the other. Also, for reasons best known to himself, he did not cross-question the liftman about those singular marks, or report the matter to the police.

Mr. Morgan's pasty visage was badly scratched, and there were red lines running from the cheek into the neck that had the appearance of having been produced by sharp points viciously applied—claws. He had been disturbed by a noise in the hall, he said, about three in the morning. A scuffle had ensued in the darkness, but the intruder had got clear away. . . .

"A cat, or something of the kind, no doubt," suggested John Gilmer at the end of the brief recital. And Morgan replied in his usual way: "A cat, or something of the kind, Mr. John, no doubt."

All the same, he had not cared to risk a second encounter, but had departed to wear his billycock and uniform in a building less haunted.

Hyman, meanwhile, made no attempt to call and talk over his dismissal. The reason for this was only apparent, however, several months later when, quite by chance, coming along Piccadilly in an omnibus, the brothers found themselves seated opposite to a man with a thick black beard and blue glasses. William Gilmer hastily rang the bell and got out, saying something half intelligible about feeling faint. John followed him.

"Did you see who it was?" he whispered to his brother the moment they were safely on the pavement.

John nodded.

"Hyman, in spectacles. He's grown a beard, too."

"Yes, but didn't you also notice—"

"What?"

"He had an empty sleeve."

"An empty sleeve?"

"Yes," said William; "he's lost an arm."

There was a long pause before John spoke. At the door of their club the elder brother added:

"Poor devil! He'll never again play on"—then, suddenly changing the preposition—"*with* a pedigree violin!" And that night in the flat, after William had gone to bed, he looked up a curious old volume he had once picked up on a secondhand bookstall, and read therein quaint descriptions of how the "desire-body of a violent man" may assume animal shape, operate on concrete matter even at a distance; and, further, how a wound inflicted thereon can reproduce itself upon its physical counterpart by means of the mysterious so-called phenomenon of "re-percussion."

King Arthur Versus the Great Cat

(13th century)

As told by

Lady Jane Francesca Wilde (1826–1896)

Lady Wilde's infamous son, the prolific and colorful writer Oscar Wilde, has served to obscure his mother's literary contributions. Lady Wilde published many works of both prose and poetry under the pen name of "Speranza." Some of her works were for the "Young Ireland" party and were quite inflammatory. One of her special areas of study was Irish legends and folklore. Originally from Dublin, Lady Wilde moved to England after the death of her husband, a famous surgeon, in 1876. Despite persistent financial problems, she ran a literary salon for many years which was considered to be the finest in London. She died the year after Oscar was sent to prison. This legend is from the thirteenth-century prose romance *Lestoire de Merlin*, which is also known as *Merlin* and *The Vulgate Merlin*. This book was written in ancient French and, after an extensive search, this is the only English translation of this story that we have found. We have heard of a version of this story where the cat kills King Arthur, but we have been unable to find any trace of it.

Merlin told the King that the people beyond the Lake of Lausanne greatly desired his help, "for there repaireth a devil that destroyeth the country. It is a cat so great and ugly that it is horrible to look on."

57

For one time a fisher came to the lake with his nets, and he promised to give Our Lord the first fish he took. It was a fish worth thirty shillings; and when he saw it so fair and great, he said to himself softly, "God shall not have this; but I will surely give him the next." Now the next was still better, and he said, "Our Lord may wait yet awhile; but the third shall be His without doubt." So he cast his net, but drew out only a little kitten, as black as any coal.

And when the fisher saw it he said he had need of it at home for rats and mice; and he nourished it and kept it in his house, till it strangled him and his wife and children. Then the cat fled to a high mountain, and destroyed and slew all that came in his way, and was great and terrible to behold.

When the King heard this he made ready and rode to the Lake of Lausanne, and found the country desolate and void of people, for neither man nor woman would inhabit the place for fear of the cat.

And the King was lodged a mile from the mountain, with Sir Gawain and Merlin and others. And they clomb the mountain, Merlin leading the way. And when they were come up, Merlin said to the king, "Sir, in that rock liveth the cat"; and he showed him a great cave, large and deep, in the mountain.

"And how shall the cat come out?" said the King.

"That shall ye see hastily," quoth Merlin; "but look you be ready to defend, for anon he will assail you."

"Then draw ye all back," said the King, "for I will prove his power."

And when they withdrew, Merlin whistled loud, and the cat leaped out of the cave thinking it was some wild beast, for he was hungry and fasting; and he ran boldly to the King, who was ready with his spear, and thought to smite him through the body. But the fiend seized the spear in his mouth and broke it in twain.

Then the King drew his sword, holding his shield also before him. And as the cat leaped at his throat, he struck him so fiercely that the creature fell to the ground; but soon was up again, and ran at the King so hard that his claws gripped through the hauberk to the flesh, and the red blood followed the claws.

Now the King was nigh falling to earth; but when he saw the red blood he was wonder-wrath, and with his sword in his right hand and his shield at his breast, he ran at the cat vigorously, who sat licking his claws, all wet with blood. But when he saw the King coming towards him, he leapt up to seize him by the throat, as before, and stuck his fore-feet so firmly in the shield that they stayed there; and the King smote him on the legs, so that he cut them off to the knees, and the cat fell to the ground.

Then the King ran at him with his sword, but the cat stood on his hind-legs and grinned with his teeth, and coveted the throat of the King, and the King tried to smite him on the head; but the cat strained his hinder feet and leaped at the King's breast, and fixed his teeth in the flesh, so that the blood streamed down from breast and shoulder.

Then the King struck him fiercely on the body, and the cat fell head downwards, but the feet stayed fixed in the hauberk. And the King smote them asunder, on which the cat fell to the ground, where she howled and brayed so loudly that it was heard through all the host, and she began to creep towards the cave; but the King stood between her and the cave, and when she tried to catch him with her teeth, he struck her dead.

Then Merlin and the others ran to him and asked how it was with him.

"Well, blessed be our Lord!" said the King, "for I have slain this devil, but, verily, I never had such doubt of myself, not even when I slew the giant on the mountain; therefore I thank the Lord."

"Sir," said the barons, "ye have great cause for thankfulness."

Then they looked at the feet which were in the hauberk, and said, "Such feet were never seen before!" And they took the shield and showed it to the host with great joy.

So the King let the shield be with the cat's feet; but the other feet he laid in a coffin to be kept. And the mountain was called from that day "the Mountain of the Cat," and the name will never be changed while the world endureth.

Don Quixote and the Cat Demons

(1605)

Miguel de Cervantes Saavedra
(1547–1616)

Cervantes is considered to be "Spain's greatest literary genius and among the most esteemed figures in world literature." Before taking up writing, Cervantes was a soldier. He was captured by pirates and held as a slave for five years. After four unsuccessful escape attempts, his family finally paid a ransom and he was released. He returned to Spain to find his family in poverty. After an affair with an actor's wife, which produced his only child, he married a woman half his age. The marriage was a complete failure and he spent twenty years as a nomad before becoming a purchasing agent for Philip II's Spanish Armada. This position resulted in many problems and accusations which brought him to trial several times, landed him in prison at least twice, and caused his excommunication from the Church. It was while he was in prison that he began his masterpiece and most famous work, *El ingenioso hidalgo Don Quijote de la Mancha (The Ingenious Gentleman Don Quixote of La Mancha)*. This book was published in two parts. The first portion, consisting of 52 chapters, initially saw print in 1605. This same year a nobleman was killed outside his house and he was charged with complicity in the murder, but he was later cleared. Although he was a prolific writer, almost a decade passed and the second portion of *Don Quixote* still had not appeared, so plagiarists and forgers began producing their own sequels to Cervantes' work.

This finally roused him to finish the book and the four final chapters appeared in 1615. Even though his books were extremely popular, he spent his final years in distress over the immoral conduct of his daughter and fighting off poverty.

We left the great Don Quixote profoundly buried in the thoughts into which the love-sick Altisidora's serenade had plunged him. He threw himself into his bed; but the cares and anxieties which plagued him, like so many fleas, would not allow him to sleep, and the misfortune of his torn stocking added to his affliction.

But as time is swift and nothing can bar its course, he glided through the hours and the dawn finally arrived. At the return of light, Don Quixote, more early than the sun, forsook his downy bed and put on his chamois apparel. Drawing on his riding boots, he concealed in one of them the disaster of his stocking. He threw his scarlet cloak over his shoulders and clapped on his valiant head his cap of green velvet edged with silver lace. Over his right shoulder he hung his belt, the sustainer of his trusty executing sword. About his wrist he wore the rosary, which he always carried about him. And thus accoutered, he strutted with a great deal of pomp and majesty towards the antechamber, where the duke and duchess were ready dressed, and, in a manner, expecting his coming.

As he passed through the gallery, he encountered Altisidora and her damsel friend, who had purposely placed themselves in his way. The moment Altisidora caught sight of him, she pretended to fall into a swoon and dropped into the arms of her companion, who in haste began to unclasp her bosom.

When Don Quixote saw this, he approached them and said to the damsel, "I know well the meaning of all this, and from whence these faintings proceed."

"You know more than I do," replied her friend, "for this I am sure of, there is no damsel in all this family who is in better health than Altisidora. I've never heard so much as a sigh from her in all the time I've known her. A curse upon all the knights-errant in the world, say I, if they are all so ungrateful! Pray, my lord Don Quixote, for pity's sake leave this place, for this poor young creature will not come to herself while you are near."

"Madam," answered the knight, "I beg that a lute to be left in my chamber to-night so that I may comfort this poor damsel as far as I am able; for love in its early stages is most easily cured by prompt undeceiving."

He then retreated, to avoid observation.

Altisidora, immediately recovering from her swoon, said to her companion, "By all means we must let him have the lute; for, without a doubt, the knight intends to give us some music, and we shall have some sport."

Then they went and acquainted the duchess with this incident and Don Quixote's desire for a lute. Whereupon, being overjoyed at the occasion, she plotted with the duke and one of her maids to play a trick on the Don.

With great glee, therefore, they waited for night, which stole upon them as quickly as had done the day. The duke and duchess passed the meantime in agreeable conversation with Don Quixote. At last, at eleven o'clock at night, Don Quixote retired to his chamber. Finding a lute there, he tuned it, opened the window, and perceiving there was somebody walking in the garden, he ran over the strings of the instrument. Having tuned it again as nicely as he could, he coughed and cleared his throat. Then with a voice somewhat hoarse, but not unmusical, he sang the following song, which he had composed himself that very day:

> "Love, with idleness its friend,
> O'er a maiden gains its end;
> But let business and employment
> Fill up every careful moment;
> These an antidote will prove
> 'Gainst the poisonous arts of love.
> Maidens that aspire to marry,
> In their looks reserve should carry;
> Chastity their price should raise
> And be the herald of their praise.
> Knights, whom toils of arms employ,
> With the wanton laugh and toy;
> But the modest only choose
> When they tie the nuptial noose.
> Love that rises with the sun,
> With his setting beams is gone:
> Love that guest-like visits hearts

When the banquet's o'er departs,
And the love that comes today,
And tomorrow wings its way
Leaves no traces on the soul
Its affections to control.
Where a sovereign beauty reigns,
Fruitless are a rival's pains—
O'er a finished picture who
E'er a second picture drew?
Fair Dulcinea, queen of beauty,
Rules my heart and claims its duty;
Nothing there can take her place,
Nor her image can erase.
Whether fortune smile or frown,
Constancy's the lover's crown;
And, its force divine to prove,
Miracles performs in love."

No sooner had Don Quixote made an end of his song—which was heard by the duke and duchess, Altisidora, and almost all the people of the castle—when suddenly, from an open gallery directly over Don Quixote's window, a rope was let down to his window, to which over a hundred tinkling bells were fastened. This was immediately followed by a huge sackful of cats, each furnished with smaller bells tied to their tails.

The jangling of the bells, and the squalling of the cats made such a dismal noise, that the very contrivers of the jest themselves were alarmed. Don Quixote himself was panic-struck.

At the same time, as ill-luck would have it, two or three frightened cats leaped in through the bars of his chamber-window, and began running up and down the room like so many evil spirits that one would have thought a whole legion of demons were flying about the chamber. They put out the candles which lighted the chamber in their frantic efforts to escape. Meanwhile the rope, with the bigger bells upon it, was pulled up and down, adding to the discord, so that those who knew nothing of the secret plot were greatly scared.

Don Quixote jumped up and, seizing his sword, he made wild thrusts at the air and towards the window, crying out, "Avaunt, ye

wicked enchanters! Avaunt, ye infernal scoundrels! for I am Don Quixote de la Mancha, your wicked arts cannot prevail against me."

And then, running after the cats that darted about the room, he
began to swing at them furiously, while they made desperate attempts
to get out. At last they all made good their escape through the window, except for one, who finding himself hard pressed by the knight,
flew in his face; grabbing onto his nose with claws and teeth and
causing him such pain that the Don began to roar as loud as he could
as he dashed about the chamber.

The duke and duchess immediately guessed the cause of his outcry
and ran to his assistance. After opening the door of his chamber with
a master-key, they found the poor knight struggling hard to disentan-
gle the cat from his face.

By the light of candles they brought with them, the duke saw the
unequal combat and attempted to come to Don Quixote's assistance;
but the Don refused his aid.

"Let nobody take him off," he cried; "Leave me on my own to
battle hand to hand with this devil, this sorcerer, this necromancer!
I'll teach him what it is to deal with Don Quixote de la Mancha!"

The cat, however, paid no heed to these bloodcurdling threats. It
just growled and hung on like grim death; until at length the duke
finally got its claws unhooked from the knight's flesh, and put the
beast out at the window.

Don Quixote's face was hideously scratched, and his nose was in
even worse condition. Yet nothing vexed him so much as that he had
been rescued out of the hands of that villainous demon before he'd
had a chance to properly chastise it.

Immediately some ointment was sent for, and Altisidora herself,
with her own lily-white hands, bound up his wounds. While dressing
him, she whispered in his ear, "Cruel hard-hearted knight, all these
disasters have befallen thee as a just punishment for thy willful stub-
bornness and disdain. May thy squire, Sancho, forget to whip himself,
that thy darling Dulcinea may never be released from her enchantment, nor thou ever be blessed with her embraces in the bridal bed—
at least so long as I, thy neglected adorer, lives."

To all this Don Quixote answered only with a profound sigh, and
then stretched himself at full length upon his bed, thanking the duke
and duchess—not for their assistance against that rascally, bell-ring-

ing crew of caterwauling enchanters, which he despised—but for their good intent in coming to his aid.

His noble friends then left him to rest, not a little grieved at the depressing result of their joke; for they never dreamed it would prove so fatal to the knight, as to cost him five days' confinement to his chamber. During this period, another adventure befell him which was much more pleasant than the last, but which cannot be here recorded.

Balu

(1949)

August Derleth (1909–1971)

Among horror fans, Derleth is best known as the preserver of H. P. Lovecraft's body of works and as one of the creators of Arkham House, an unparalleled publishing venture. While dedicating over 30 years to these pursuits, he still found time to publish a number of works in his own style, which differs markedly from that of his mentor, Lovecraft. The tale offered here is reminiscent of the atmospheric stories produced by M. R. James. It originally appeared in the January 1949 issue of *Weird Tales*.

Within the week after his father's funeral, Walter moved in with his widowed Aunt Thea. He was now an orphan, but he did not feel any different. True, he had a sense of loss, he missed his father, but not quite everything had been taken from him. He still had Balu, though his aunt and his cousin Harold, who, at eleven, was one year his senior, eyed the great black cat with its intense green eyes with disgust and manifest misgivings, and he was aware, with the instinct peculiar to childhood, that Balu would be the object of their attempts to rid the house of him.

Stout-hearted, he took possession of the room given him, and made a place for Balu, despite his aunt's mild suggestion that perhaps "the cat" could sleep in the basement or the attic, where there were mice.

"This is a special cat," he informed her. "This is Balu. Daddy brought me Balu from Egypt. Balu is like a person, but he's very old. Balu is older than I am; he's older than this house. Daddy said Balu is older than America."

Aunt Thea showed her disapproval, but said nothing.

His trunks followed him—one filled with clothing, the other with books and mementoes of life with his father, his mother having died almost beyond the limits of his memory. He was fair, with curly hair, sturdily built, in contrast to his thin, gangling cousin Harold. He was self-contained, for he had lived a long time in his father's apartment, while his father had been away on his trips of exploration.

"I hope you will like it here, Walter," said Aunt Thea when he came down to dinner the first night. "We'll try to help you forget your loss."

"Thank you, Aunt Thea," he said gravely.

But he was not deceived. Harold resented him. He did not know how much Aunt Thea was getting for taking care of him, but he suspected she was being well paid. It would be difficult with Harold not liking him, and it would be difficult about Balu. But he meant to survive.

Before he had been in his new home two days, Harold was at him about "that cat." Harold was particularly annoying because of his superior air, as if mere birthdays gave him an intangible edge over Walter.

"My mother says there's nothing different about your cat," he said, perched on Walter's bed.

"There is so," retorted Walter.

"There is not."

"My Daddy got him in Egypt. He ought to know. He got him from some kind of priest. A priest of Thoth, he said. Balu is a very special person."

"A cat can't be a person."

"Balu is."

Balu, curled on top of Walter's bureau, took no notice of the conversation. He made a great, black cushion there, reflected in the mirror. His ears were tufts of black that stood straight up. His whiskers were long and handsome. His eyes were as green as jade. He half sat, half lay, looking coldly into distance far beyond the room's confining walls.

"Besides," continued Harold, sneering, "my mother says Uncle William was weird."

"He was not!"

"He was, too!"

"My Daddy was a great explorer. What was your daddy?"

Harold could not answer that. He was routed.

Balu raised up, humped his back, stretched himself with infinite grace. He descended, leaped lightly over to Walter, and rubbed against him, muttering a throaty purr. Very plainly, he approved of Walter. He walked carefully, haughtily, around Harold.

"Balu doesn't like you," said Walter soberly.

"I don't like Balu, either."

Harold's second attack came within the week. He came complaining that the servants were frightened of Balu. There were but two. It was true that the servants were frightened of Balu; they had always been. Walter remembered very well an old laborer who had worked a while for his father. He had shunned the cat; more than that, he had walked carefully all around it. In this house, it was worse because the servants were women. Women always carried on so. He had heard them. He had heard them say, "Lord, that cat is a witch-cat!" He had heard them say, "Balu has got a spirit in him. He's old. He's old as the world."

"Balu scares old Lou," said Harold. "And Melissa, too."

"Some people are scared of Balu," said Walter scornfully. "You know why?"

"No. Why?"

"Because they know. They know about Balu. Daddy said some people could feel things we can't feel. They feel how old Balu is. They feel Balu is special."

"You're talking foolish."

"No, I'm not."

"You are so. You're talking lies, that's what they are."

Walter was outraged. "I never lie. I don't have to. Balu is . . ."

"Balu is an ugly black cat," interrupted Harold, "who ought to be poisoned or something."

"You get out of here—saying things like that!" Walter clenched his fists.

"Who's going to make me?"

"I am."

Balu broke in with a curious sound of anger. His tail was thick, thick as an upraised club.

"If that cat scratches me—I'll kick it," said Harold.

"Balu doesn't scratch."

"Is he any good besides just sitting there?"

"Balu catches mice and rats."

"You feed him plenty from our table," said Harold accusingly.

"I guess that's paid for."

"Anyway, if you don't get rid of that cat, we might lose Lou and Melissa. And if we do, my mother is going to be plenty mad."

"Balu goes where I go," said Walter firmly. "I stay where Balu is."

A muted purr came from Balu, though the cat did not lift its head.

Aunt Thea had noticed the vindictiveness of Harold, and the rift between the boys. She regretted it and fluttered, but she hoped that it would soon be over and done. There would be a period of adjustment; that could not be helped. But, being foolish, she could not help unwittingly abetting Harold by talking carelessly of William Bayle— how fruitless his explorations had been, how queer a man he was, how little attention he had paid to Walter, and so on.

Harold remembered.

It was difficult for Walter. It made him realize how much he missed his father. It brought home to him for the first time that he did not have his father's protection, nor did he have that wonderful freedom to do as he liked, when only the governess had kept a beneficent eye on him, seldom interfering, only guiding gently and keeping him from harm. How he wished sometimes that his father were still alive, and everything were once again as it had been!

One day he caught Harold in his room tormenting Balu. Balu was in a corner, and Harold was throwing books at him—Walter's books. Walter leaped on Harold, beating him with his fists. Harold, trying to escape, fell to the bed.

"You dirty beast!" cried Walter. "If I ever catch you doing that again, I'll—I'll kill you."

Harold recovered his feet, and backed against the wall. "I didn't hurt him," he said sullenly.

Walter went over to Balu, stroking the cat, petting him, talking to him. Over his shoulder he said, "Get out of my room."

"This is *our* house—not yours," said Harold defiantly.

Walter turned on his haunches and glared at him. "Get out!"

Harold sidled toward the door and vanished.

Walter looked to his cat once more. "Did he hurt you, Balu?"

Balu seemed to understand. Balu came to him, rubbing against him, purring.

He felt Balu all over. The cat flinched at no touch; so he was not hurt. He began to pick up the books Harold had thrown. "I'll kill him," he muttered balefully.

Balu's tail switched from side to side. He nuzzled one of Walter's fingers. He licked the back of Walter's hand.

Thereafter, he would not confine Balu to his room. Balu went with him everywhere. He disdained to notice the cowering blacks, though it was extraordinary the way they flattened to the wall when Balu passed, the way they muttered strange gibberish under their breath. In a confiding moment, Harold told him that the black delivery boys from down-town stores no longer stopped to talk, but left their baskets and were off; they had heard about Balu. They believed Balu had strange powers.

Aunt Thea was upset and angry, but there was William's money to consider. While she was not indigent, it meant a good deal to her. Somehow, for all his extravagance and carelessness, William Bayle had managed to gather a lot of money, and she meant to have all she could before Walter reached his majority.

Harold found ways to trouble Walter.

If they played tennis in the court behind the house, and Balu was there, Harold managed at least once each time to bat the ball at the cat. Walter knew he did it on purpose, but he could not prove it; invariably, he stopped playing immediately, went sulking to the house, morose with anger he could not vent upon his cousin.

If they sat inside playing cards or any other household game, Balu beside them, Harold never missed an opportunity to step on Balu's tail. Curiously, the cat never screamed, but only drew away and licked its tail, and Walter's cries of rage were ended by his aunt's defense of Harold. "Anyone could see it was just an accident, Walter," she said, time after time. But Walter knew it was no accident.

When he ignored Harold, his cousin came to his room. Always at him about Balu . . .

"That cat scared Melissa so today she busted a dozen eggs . . .

"That cat hasn't caught a mouse since she was here. Two whole months, almost three . . .

"That cat's been sharpening her claws on our good furniture . . .

"Mother says your dad wasn't quite all there . . ."

But in the end, Harold returned to methods more direct.

Thinking Walter at the dentist's one afternoon, he invaded Walter's room with an ingenious weapon—a toasting fork extended and tied to a broom-handle. Carefully securing doors and windows, so that the cat could not escape to the hall or the adjoining storeroom, where it might find shelter among old boxes and trunks, Harold got after Balu.

He had inflicted two gashing wounds when Walter came.

When Walter had finished with Harold, Harold had several long scratches and gashes from his own improvised weapon, and in his vindictiveness, Harold blamed the wounds upon Balu, so that Aunt Thea talked to Walter and insisted that Balu must be "done away with." Walter stood his ground, but told no word of Harold's perfidy.

In the night he was awakened by Balu's insistence.

The cat lay on his belly on the bed, his green eyes shining in the dark.

"What is it, Balu?"

The cat purred commandingly. One paw pulled at the covering sheet, his tail switching impatiently back and forth. "Come and see," he seemed to say.

Walter stirred.

Balu leaped to the floor and stood waiting, turned to see whether Walter was coming.

Walter put on the light and watched the cat jump up to the bookcase. On the second shelf a book jutted forth. Balu clawed downward, and the book fell to the floor. Balu came after, walking back and forth across the opened book.

Walter came down to his knees and gazed at it. It was his father's Egyptian book with his pencilled notes. *Book of the Dead.* He gazed at Balu, walking impatiently back and forth. Clearly Balu expected something of him. He began to page through the book, and at once Balu came to sit opposite him, intent upon his paging.

Abruptly, Balu thrust forth a paw, laid it upon a page, and looked at him. The cat's green eyes seemed to swim before him, to enlarge.

They were pools, ponds, oceans, and within them moved a strange procession of all manner of beings—ancient men in Egyptian garb, wearing masking head-dresses, the priests of Bast, winged creatures and four-footed ones, cats, and men, men and cats through ages past. The illusion passed.

Walter bent to read his father's notes.

What he read was stranger still. He read it carefully, over and over, memorizing it. He tried to understand. What it said was something about transforming one person into another. The words were there, the directions were given.

Balu watched him intently.

Walter put the book back in its place and pondered. He went to bed and dreamed—dreamed of great gulfs of time and space, of towering pyramids and ancient men, of things beyond his knowledge, things lost in far time.

Three days later he invited Harold to his room to play a game. "What kind of game is it?" asked Harold.

"It's a new game," said Walter. "It's a transforming game."

"I never played it before."

"No, I guess you never did."

Harold trooped along to the room and looked at the changes Walter had made. "Gee, you moved things around a little."

"I had to."

"What're those circles for?"

"They're part of the game."

"You'll catch it—chalking up the floor."

"Now you stand here, Harold, in the middle of this circle, and Balu has to sit in the middle of the other one—like this."

"Does that cat know how to play this game?"

"Yes, he does. Balu's very smart, Harold. Balu's smarter than I am or you are. He's smarter than anybody is."

"Oh, cut that out. That's not part of this game."

"I guess in a way it is."

"Well, what next?"

"Now I have to kneel in front of you and say some words, and then something happens."

"Aw, stuff!"

"Really it does. Harold, please, just stay and play it once."

"Well, all right."

Walter hoped that he had understood his father's notes. Balu sat attentively in one of the chalked circles, and Harold stood in the other. Harold looked curiously at all the little signs and hieroglyphs Walter had copied.

"What're those things?"

"They're part of the game."

"What are they?"

"I don't know, really, Harold. It's just part of the game. You're supposed to do it that way."

"I'm going to be twelve next week. I'm getting too old to play kids' games."

"Now, listen."

He read. He intoned words.

For a moment nothing happened. Then abruptly the cat leaped into the air, tail thick, every hair taut and extended. He began to spit and claw the air; his tongue stuck from between his teeth, and the sounds that rose from his throat were like bestial, half articulate human words. But no words came.

Shaken, Walter looked at Harold.

But Harold was somehow different. There was a light in his eyes that had never been there before. His eyes were—like Balu's eyes. As Walter looked, Harold sank to his knees, then to his belly. Stretched out flat, he leaned forward and licked Walter's hand.

When, after a long period of silence, while Walter was confining the cat that had once been Balu, and accustoming himself to Harold in his transformation, Aunt Thea could no longer ignore the absence of the boys and called to find out where they were, Walter answered, somewhat tremulously.

"Up here, Aunt Thea."

"Up where, Walter?"

"In my room."

"Is Harold there, too?"

"Yes, Aunt Thea."

"What on earth is he doing?"

Walter swallowed and said that Harold was reading. He could not very well tell Aunt Thea what Harold was doing. At the moment Harold was in the storeroom catching mice. Walter hoped earnestly that the early hangovers from the previous incarnation would soon be lost, or else Aunt Thea might ask him questions he could not answer. Yet he felt that he could count on Balu.

When Aunt Thea wrote her next monthly letter to the executor of William Bayle's estate, an estimable Southern gentleman who saw to it that she was paid for Walter's keep, she could not resist a paragraph about the changed circumstances of the household.

"You will be delighted to learn that the boys, who were once so quarrelsome, get along beautifully together now. It is so inspiring to witness such a transformation. Harold, who had not been kind to Walter, I must admit, now seems actually to fawn upon him—not disgustingly, of course; but certainly he is extremely fond of his cousin. And Walter, now that we have had to dispose of his cat (which apparently went into fits one day in his room and could not be brought out of them), has the somewhat quaint habit of calling Harold *Balu*, after his cat. Oddly enough, the servants, who once adored Harold, now seem to be unable to tolerate his presence. But, I suppose, one must expect the servants to be a little strange . . ."

The Cat Ghost of Seedley

(1913)

Robert Dane

As told to

Elliott O'Donnell (1872–1965)

O'Donnell was a famous British ghost hunter. Originally he was a stage and film actor before he took up writing. He was the author of about 60 books, almost all of which were supernatural nonfiction. Although he did believe in ghosts, he was careful to point out that he was not a spiritualist. This account appears in his book, *Animal Ghosts: or Animal Hauntings and the Hereafter* (1913).

 WARNING: This story may upset the more sensitive cat lover. Such persons should bypass this tale.

Here is another case in the veracity of which I have every confidence. . . .

It was related to me by Mr. Robert Dane, who was at one time a tenant of No. ** Lower Seedley Road, Seedley [a suburb of Manchester, England]. I quote it as nearly as possible in his words, thus:—

"When we—my wife and I—took No. ** Lower Seedley Road, no possibility of the place being haunted crossed our minds. Indeed ghosts were the very last things we reckoned on, as neither of us had the slightest belief in them. Like the generality of solicitors, I am stodgy and unimaginative, whilst my wife is the most practical and matter-of-fact little woman you would meet in a day's march. Nor was there anything about the house that in any way suggested the superphysical. It was airy and light—no dark corners nor sinister staircases—and equipped throughout with all modern conveniences. We began our lease in June—the hottest June I remember—and nothing occurred to disturb us till October.

"It happened then in this wise. I will quote from my diary:

"*Monday, October 11th.*—Dick—that is my brother-in-law—and I, at 11 p.m., were sitting smoking and chatting together in the study. All the rest of the household had gone to bed. We had no light in the room—as Dick had a headache—save the fire, and that had burned so low that its feeble glimmering scarcely enabled us to see each other's face. After a space of sudden and thoughtful silence, Dick took the stump of a cigar from his lips and threw it in the grate, where for a few moments it lay glowing in the gloom.

" 'Jack,' he said, 'you will think me mad, but there is something deuced queer about this room to-night—something in the atmosphere I cannot define, but which I have never felt here—or indeed anywhere—before. Look at that cigar-end—look!'

"I did so, and received a shock. What I saw was certainly not the stump Dick had had in his mouth, but an eye—a large, red and lurid eye—that looked up at us with an expression of the utmost hate.

"Dick raised the shovel and struck at it, but without effect—it still glared at us. A great horror then seized us, and unable to remove our gaze from the hellish thing, we sat glued to our chairs staring at it. This state of affairs lasted till the clock in the hall outside struck twelve, when the eye suddenly vanished, and we both felt as if some intensely evil influence had been suddenly removed.

"Dick did not like the idea of sleeping alone, and asked if he might keep the electric light on in his room all night. Tremendous extravagance, but under the circumstances excusable. I confess I devoutly wished it was morning.

"*Tuesday, October 12th.*—I was awakened at 11:30 p.m. by Delia saying to me, 'Oh, Edward, there have been such dreadful noises on the landing, just as if a cat were being worried to death by dogs. Hark! there it is again.' And as she spoke, from apparently just outside the door, came a series of loud screeches, accompanied by savage growls and snarls.

"Not knowing what to make of it, as we had no animals of our own in the house, but concluding that a door or window having been left open, a dog and cat had got in from outside,-I lit a candle, and opened the bedroom door. Instantly the sounds ceased and there was dead silence, and although I searched everywhere, not a vestige of any animal was to be seen. Moreover all the doors leading into the garden were shut and locked, and the windows closed. Not wishing to frighten Delia, I laughingly assured her the cat—a black Tom—was all right, that it was sitting on the roof of the summerhouse, looking none the worse for its treatment, and that I had sent the dog—a terrier—flying out of the gate with a well-deserved kick. I explained it was my fault about the front door being left open—my brain had been a bit overstrained through excessive work—and asked her on no account to blame the servants. I grow alarmed at times when I realize how easy lawyering makes lying.

"*Friday, October 21st.*—On my way to bed last night I encountered a rush of icy cold air at the first bend of the staircase. The candle flared up, a bright blue flame, and went out. Something—an animal of sorts—came tearing down the stairs past me, and on peering over the banisters, I saw, looking up at me from the well of darkness beneath, two big red eyes, the counterparts of the one Dick and I had seen on October 11th. I threw a matchbox at them, but without effect. It was only when I switched on the electric light that they disappeared. I searched the house most carefully, but there were no signs of any animal. Joined Delia, feeling nervous and henpecky.

"*Monday, November 7th.*—Tom and Mable came running into Delia's room in a great state of excitement after tea to-day. 'Mother!' they cried, 'Mother! Do come! Some horrid dog has got a cat in the spare room and is tearing it to pieces.' Delia, who was mending my socks at the time, flung them anywhere, and springing to her feet, flew to the spare room. The door was shut, but proceeding from within was the most appalling pandemonium of screeches and snarls, just as if some dog had got hold of a cat by the neck and was shaking it to death. Delia swung open the door and rushed in. The room was empty—not a trace of a cat or dog anywhere—and the sounds ceased! On my return home Delia met me in the garden. 'Jack!' she said, 'I have probed the mystery at last. The house is haunted! We must leave.'

"*Saturday, November 12th.*—Sublet house to James Barstow, retired oil merchant, to-day. He comes in on the 30th. Hope he'll like it!

"*Tuesday, November 15th.*—Cook left to-day. 'I've no fault to find with you, mum,' she condescendingly explained to Delia. 'It's not you, nor the children, nor the food. It's the noises at night—screeches outside my door, which sound like a cat, but which I know can't be a cat, as there is no cat in the house. This morning, mum, shortly after the clock struck two, things came to a climax. Hearing something in the corner and wondering if it was a mouse—I ain't a bit afraid of mice, mum—I sat up in bed and was getting ready to strike a light— the matchbox was in my hand—when something heavy sprang right on the top of me and gave a loud growl in my ear. That finished me, mum—I fainted. When I came to myself, I was too frightened to stir, but lay with my head under the blankets till it was time to get up. I then searched everywhere, but there was no sign of any dog, and as the door was locked there was no possibility of any dog having got in during the night. Mum, I wouldn't go through what I suffered again for fifty pounds; I've got palpitations even now; and I would rather go without my month's wages than sleep in that room another night.' Delia paid her up to date, and she went directly after tea.

"*Friday, November 18th.*—As I was coming out of the bathroom at 11 p.m. something fell into the bath with a loud splash. I turned to see what it was—there was nothing there. I ran up the stairs to bed, three steps at a time!

"*Sunday, November 20th.*—Went to church in the morning and heard the usual Oxford drawl. On the way back I was pondering over the sermon and wishing I could contort the Law as successfully as parsons contort the Scriptures, when Dot—she is six to-day—came running up to me with a very scared expression in her eyes. 'Father,' she cried, plucking me by the sleeve, 'do hurry up. Mother is very ill.' Full of dreadful anticipations, I tore home, and on arriving found Delia lying on the sofa in a violent fit of hysterics. It was fully an hour before she recovered sufficiently to tell me what had happened. Her account runs thus:—

" 'After you went to church,' she began, 'I made the custard pudding, jelly and blancmange for dinner, heard the children their collects, and had just sat down with the intention of writing a letter to mother, when I heard a very pathetic mew coming, so I thought, from under the sofa. Thinking it was some stray cat that had got in through one of the windows, I tried to entice it out, by calling "Puss, puss," and making the usual silly noise people do on such occasions. No cat coming out and the mewing still continuing, I knelt down and peered under the sofa. There was no cat there. Had it been night I should have been very much afraid, but I could scarcely reconcile myself to the idea of ghosts with the room filled with sunshine. Resuming my seat I went on with my writing, but not for long. The mewing grew nearer. I distinctly heard something crawl out from under the sofa; there was then a pause, during which you could have heard the proverbial pin fall, and then something sprang upon me and dug its claws in my knees. I looked down, and to my horror and distress, perceived, standing on its hind-legs, pawing my clothes, a large, tabby cat, without a head—the neck terminating in a mangled stump. The sight so appalled me that I don't know what happened, but nurse and the children came in and found me lying on the floor in hysterics. Can't we leave the house at once?

"*Wednesday, November 30th.*—Left No. ** Lower Seedley Road at 2 p.m. Had an awful scurry to get things packed in time, and dread opening certain of the packing-cases lest we shall find all the crockery smashed. Just as we were starting Delia cried out that she had left her reticule behind, and I was dispatched in search of it. I searched everywhere—till I was worn out, for I know what Delia is—and was leaving the premises in full anticipation of being sent back again, when there was a loud commotion in the hall, just as if a dog had suddenly pounced on a cat, and the next moment a large tabby, with the head hewn away as Delia had described, rushed up to me and tried to spring on to my shoulders. At this juncture one of the servants cautiously opened the hall door from without, and informed me I was wanted. The cat instantly vanished, and, on my reaching the carriage in a state of breathless haste and trepidation, Delia told me she had found her reticule—she had been sitting on it all the time!"

In a subsequent note in his diary a year or so later Mr. Dane says: "After innumerable enquiries *re* the history of No. ** Lower Seedley Road prior to our inhabiting it, I have at length elicited the fact that twelve years ago a Mr. and Mrs. Barlowe lived there. They had one son, Arthur, whom they spoilt in the most outrageous fashion, even to the extent of encouraging him in acts of cruelty. To afford him amusement they used to buy rats for his dog—a fox-terrier—to worry, and on one occasion procured a stray cat, which the servants afterwards declared was mangled in the most shocking manner before being finally destroyed by Arthur. Here, then, in my opinion, is a very feasible explanation for the hauntings—the phenomenon seen was the phantasm of the poor, tortured cat. For if human tragedies are re-enacted by ghosts, why not animal tragedies too? It is absurd to suppose man has the monopoly of soul or spirit."

The Black Cat Club

(1902)

James D. Corrothers (1869–1917)

James David Corrothers was a well-known Chicago journalist but, as an African American born shortly after slavery was abolished, his rise to this position was very difficult. His mother died while giving birth to him and he was the only black child in his hometown in Michigan. He often related with relish his numerous battles to preserve his skin. His pugilistic skills proved sufficiently potent to ensure him a peaceful life. He worked a variety of low paying jobs—such as bootblack in a barbershop—and was ordained as a Baptist preacher in 1894. His friends finally urged him to become a writer. *The Black Cat Club*, from which these excerpts were taken, was his primary work. Although he was very proud of his accurate rendition of the "colored dialect," we have had to tone it down considerably so as not to offend the modern reader. Still, this selection contains an incredible amount of American catlore which is presented in a hilariously cartoonish fashion, making this piece quite entertaining.

Promptly at nine o'clock on Friday night, the nine members of the "Black Cat Club" met in Billy Spooks' rear room.

The club was seated in a semicircle or crescent, with Sandy and his cat in the middle, and every member had a rabbit's foot and a silver spoon in his pocket; likewise a silver quarter in the toe of his shoe, and a newly sharpened razor near at hand. . . .

Before any other business was attended to, good-natured Spooks was unanimously elected an "onry" member of the society, and he was asked to choose between treating the club to an oyster supper and having his luck crossed by the black cat. He treated.

Then a prayer was offered to Mesmerizer by the Rev. Dark Loudmouth, after which Sandy arose, with as much dignity as a full stomach and a starchy new suit of tailor-made clothing would allow, and made the following remarks on the subject of cats—cats in general and black cats in particular:

"Gentlemen," he said, "we bear an honored name. The cat—in pertickler the Black Cat—has been a powerful and respectable gentleman since Time first began to wheel his eternal flight of circumlocution through endless ages of nitric acid, quintessence of floating protoplasm, and parliamentary usage!"

(The whole club fell to the floor, face downward, fanned itself, and passed the bottle around, while Saskatchewan Jones stretched out in a dead faint. It required the entire contents of Sandy's bottle to bring him to.)

"Long before the earth was made or the archangel Gabriel had cut his milk-teeth, the Black Cat had graduated from a singing school in Mars, and had created the planet of Juan Fernandez and the island of Mesopotamia!

"The cat is a practical person. He is no spring chicken. He is generally calculated to have nine lives, but this the conjuring man around the corner assures me is a sad mistake. He has nine hundred and ninety-nine lives, lives as long as he wants to every time, and, like the good Christian, is 'born again' almost any ole time. That's why the Theosophists sing their sacred solo, 'The Cat Come Back.'

"When the earth was made without form or void, the Black Cat was there, watching the whole business, and a-laying his wires for to send Grover Cleveland to the United States senate and Dick Crokah to the happy land of Canaan! First thing he did was to cross our foreparents' luck in the beautiful Garden of Eden, and sent poor Adam out to play football with the rattlesnakes and In'juns in the lonely Province of West Virginny. The Black Cat is prone to evil, as sparks fly upwards. He is a lover of the back fence, the telegraph pole, and the midnight serenade. Bootjacks, pistols, policemen's clubs, and missiles cannot stop his rapturous ditty to the pale-face moon. He is a gentleman! He is the marvel of the nations!

"You might ask me what the Black Cat have done for suffering humanity. I answer: He is the inventor of the watermelon, corn pone, sweet potatoes, liquor, and opossum; and was the first one to teach us of the advisability of eating pork chops when you're flush and liver when you're hard up." *(Great applause by the club.)* "Oh, the Lord will provide! That's why he gave us ole Mesmerizer here to bring us good luck wherever we go in the United States of America, while some of our good ole mothers is a-bending over the wash-tub, 'way down yonder in Dixie-land, shedding briny tears and a-sighing—'Where's my wandering boy to-night?'

"And while she's working and fretting, her traveling son's down on the corner, sunning himself and shooting dice, and a-singing:

> " 'Bells are a-ringin' in Memphis—
>   Bells are a-ringin' in Cairo—
> The sun has sunk, and the alligator's
>   Dreaming in the deep bayou;
> The ole folks have gone to church,
>   The little folks have gone to sleep—
> 'Way down on the ole homestead.
>   I expect they're gripeing about me;
> But they've got to do without me,
>   Tho' I was the sweetest blossom
> In the ole homestead—

Huh! seven-eleven!' "

"That's him!"

(Cries of: "That's right, Sandy!"—"Ain't it so?" and "Had a good ole mother myself.")

"Gentlemen," Sandy continued, "the Black Cat has always been somebody. Look, what a pull he had with ole Isis, one of the richest men in Egypt, thousands of years ago: Cat came along one day, he did, and crossed Mr. Isis's luck, and that fellow didn't do a thing but beg the cat's pardon, and built a sacred temple to him. That's all he did to *him!* And don't you think he can take care of *us?*—his needy and faithful children? All we've got to do is to work our rabbit's foot, and say nothing, and things'll come our way.

"Gentlemen, as I close, a vision of the future comes before me: I see the Black Cat seated on a throne so high that he can touch Jupiter with his tail and use the moon for a cuspidor! I see him get between the earth and the sun and there won't be no daylight till he moves! And the same way with the rain; he licks that up as it falls. And every time he arch his back, there's a hundred billion earthquakes and tornadoes on the earth! And there ain't nobody got no influence with the cat but the members of this club; and people is a-falling at your feet, throwing us their money and jewels and rabbit's feet, and such, and a-totin' us all the good eatin's in the known world. And every member of this club'll have a brass band to escort him around; and a golden crown on his head, and a club in his hand to kill critics with!—children to scatter flowers in front of him and behind him, and on both sides of him, and forty college graduates to carry his trailing robes!"

Sandy sat down, out of breath, but well satisfied with his address, and the club, as soon as it could regain its proper functions, tendered him a rising vote of thanks.

"Great day!" yelled Saskatchewan Jones, "am I here or yonder? What was it struck me, and where did all them stars come from?"

Then Sa..ly, who had recovered his breath, read his latest poem—

"THE BLACK CAT CROSSED HIS LUCK"
I
"O, the Black Cat caught ole Sammy Lee,
  As he came home from a jamboree
The cat sat up in a juniper tree,
  Shaking of his sides with glee.
The moon was sailing overhead—
  Sam's heart felt like a lump of lead.
Black Cat grinned and winked one eye,
  Licked his paws and gave a sigh,
And then he cried: 'Me-ow, me-ow—
  Upon my soul I've got you now!
Fall down and pray, poor simple man,
  For the ole Black Cat has called your hand.'

II
"Sam lost his job the very next day;
  And when he went to get his pay,
Got bit by a poor man's dog—
  Policeman beat him with his log—

Got arrested, put in jail—
Had to hustle hard for bail—
Lost his lawsuit, sprained his jaw
Wrangling with his mother-in-law—
Lost his best of lady loves—
Got knocked out with the boxing gloves—
Got held up and lost his roll—
Robber almost took his soul!
Sam went to the hospital—
Three weeks passed before he got well.
Played the races—got broke flat;
And all because of that Black Cat!

III

"Then to the conjurin'-man Sam sped,
And this is what the conjurin'-man said:
'Black Cat is a powerful man;
Ruinin' mortals is his plan.
Ole Satan and the Original Sin
Is the daddy and mammy of him.
He's got nine hundred and ninety-nine lives—
Nineteen thousand and ninety-nine wives—
He's kin to cholera and allied
To smallpox on his mammy's side.
And all the evils on the earth
Started at the Black Cat's birth!—
Just stop and die right where you're at,
If your luck's been crossed by the ole Black Cat!'

IV

"And then Sam read in history
That a cat crossed Pharaoh by the sea,
And buried him, as sure's you're born,
Too deep to hear ole Gabriel's horn!
And that the cat crossed Jonah once,
And made him act a regular dunce.
Crossed Bonaparte at Waterloo,

And got James Blaine* defeated, too.
'Oh, Lord a-mercy now on me!'
Cried Sam, 'and on this history!'
And then Sam went and killed the cat—
Swore he'd make an end of that;—
Buried him in the light of the moon,
With a rabbit's foot and a silver spoon.
But the Black Cat rose, and swallowed him whole—
Burnt his house and took his soul!"

"Doc," said one of his hearers, "that cat was a warm chicken and a moving chile!'

"Yes," remarked another, "black cats are dead bad luck. They've hoodooed me more than once."

Then the club adjourned, amid stories of experiences with black cats. . . .

The telling of ghost stories, and the relating of hard-luck experiences occasioned by a black cat's having crossed the storyteller's luck or that of some friend, were in order at the next meeting of the club. The meeting was held at its old headquarters in its president's apartments, and every member of the society was present.

"Gentlemen," said Sandy, "suppose to-night we have a few stories on ghosts and black cats and such."

Bad Bob Sampson took the floor.

"Gentlemen," he began, "before I joined the Black Cat Club, all the ghosts and black cats in the city had me for a good thing. One night I'd been down-town, drinkin' a little bit. That was about six years ago, when I was kind of half-way respectable. Well, jest as I started home, the durndest, biggest ole black cat in the United States crossed my path. I was about half 'shot'; but I knew that cat was fatal to me! I kept on though, and just as I passed the Twelfth-street viaduct, I look back over my left shoulder, and I see something that makes my wool stand up! Good Lord, it scares me now!

"I saw a man about twelve feet high, and I always will believe 'twas the devil. His eyes shone like two new moons. His nose puffed smoke like a tar-kiln. His lips looked like two chunks of roast beef without

---

* James Blaine (1830–1893) was a U.S. senator who ran for president in 1884, but he was narrowly defeated by Grover Cleveland.

the gravy. His ears hung down like a tobacco leaf. He had horns and tail, and one of his feet was a black cat and the other was a snake! O my Lord! And then he speaks, saying: 'Sampson, I'm a-going to slap the taste out of your mouth!' Great Day! I felt for my razor, and it was gone! And the way I tore up sidewalk with my corn plantations and burnt the air with my coat-tails was a caution! I expect they heard me a mile away, and thought it was a storm a-coming! Why, I tore up all the railroad tracks I crossed! And when I got home, I didn't have on no more shoes than a rabbit! Couldn't go no where until my partner caught policy, and bought me some new shoes. And I was trustee in the Methodist church, too!—and was kind of setting to the preacher's daughter. And she was pretty as a peach! Make your mouth water to look at her!

"Well, before God, I was so badly hoodooed that I had a falling out with my girl; got turned out of church—and mighty nigh went to the dogs. Lord knows I was glad when ole Sandy organized this club!"

"That reminds me," said the Rev. Dark Loudmouth, "of when I was pastor of a little Methodist church in Indianapolis: A black cat crossed me one day on Locerkby Street, right in front of Brother James Whitcomb Riley's. I turned around three times and spit on the ground, over my left shoulder, and walked backwards until I passed the spot where the black cat crossed me. Then I rubbed my rabbit's foot, and went over to the other side of town, and took supper and drank a little egg-nog with one of the sisters of my church. But I couldn't help feeling a little dubious about that cat!

"That evenin', about eleven, I was goin' home, and just as I was a-ambulatin' by the big store, I saw a stylish gentleman a-standin' there, and, thinkin' he was one of the owners of the place, I took my hat off to him, and was just fixin' up my mouth to ask him to help my church, when—name of God!—the man reaches up and pulls his head off and hands it to me, with the mouth a-workin', and the blood a-drippin' on the sidewalk!

"Says I: 'Saints in heavenly rest!—Mister, I don't want none of your money, nor nothin' you've *got!*' And away I took—down the street—like a runaway horse! But the first thing I knew, I had done collided with the biggest Irish policeman in Indianapolis, and we were a-cussin' one another and tryin' to gouge each other's eyes out.

"Says he: 'What in the devil's the matter with you?'

"Says I: 'What in the devil's the matter with *you?*'

"Says he: 'You don't know who I *am*, do you?'

"Says I: 'Yes, and you don't know who *I* am, neither!'

"Says he: 'Are you crazy?'

"Says I: 'Mr. Officer, I has just seen the worst ghost that ever scared a grown *man!*' And then I told him the whole story.

" 'You can go home,' says he; 'that's the same thing that made my partner, Officer Muggins, drop his club and run last night, after he had been lushin'. Git home with you! But mind you don't mix your drinks like *that*, no more. That privilege is only for the boys of the force.'

"I took the streetcar, and went home. But, before God, I was turned out of conference that year, and I ain't had no luck since." And Loudmouth sat down.

"Before I came to Chicago," said Saskatchewan Jones, arising, "I had an experience that I never will forget as long as I live. I was living in my native home in Tennessee, at the time, and had been to see a lady I was setting to, and was coming home, late one Sunday night. Had about four miles to go; but the moon was shining kind of dismal like, and I had my razor, and didn't feel afraid—though there was a strip of woods and a old-fashioned country graveyard with a deserted church in it between me and home. There were *haunts* in that grave-yard, too! But I couldn't stop for that, if I wasn't but fifteen years old; because me and my gal had the wedding day all set. And I had to get home, so I wouldn't lose my job.

"Just as I was telling my lady-love goodnight, her mammy's ole black cat ran betwixt me and her, and my heart leaped into my mouth. But I started out, and got through the woods all right—except that a screech-owl scared me some—and was just getting abreast of the church, when I see the same identical black cat, with a candle burning in her belly, come walking straight to me on her hind legs, playing the fiddle, and singing:

> " 'Great big house, and nobody living in it—
>   Nobody living in it, nobody living in it—
>   Great big house, and nobody living in it—
>   Down in Tennessee.'

"Every step that cat took, she got bigger and bigger! By the time she got front of me, she was big as a cow! Then she wheels around, facing me, and blows a stream of fire out of both sides of her nose, and says:

" 'In the name of Father, Son, and Holy Ghost, I forbid you going to see Miss Lucy Ann any more. I love you myself. You are to be my partner at the Witches' Dance to-night. Let me take your arm.'

"And she reaches for me. Good Lord! I whips out my razor, and I slashes at her—cutting her plum' in two! But she gathers herself up, and grows bigger than an elephant in ten seconds, and stands with her arms spread clean across the road, right in front of me. And smoke a-rolling out of her nose, like a volcano! Great Day! It was do or die! I shut my eyes, and plunges to one side. The cat grabs at me as I pass, but Lord!—these feet of mine had wings!—seemed like I just got up and flew—winging with the angels, and my coat-tails ahgafying with the wind!

"The cat must have got discouraged, just looking at me tread air! How I got home is a mystery to me to-day; for I never knew nothing till I fell in the front door. My shins were barked, my nose was bleeding, my back was all scratched up and muddy—my shoe soles were gone, and both big toe-nails was off! Got discharged, lost my gal, and the story got out that I'd been drunk, and I had to come to Chicago to hide my disgrace." And Jones sat down, laughing with the rest.

"My father used to tell a tale," said K. C. Brighteyes, "that used to scare us children most to death. I've been actually too scared when he was tellin' it to get up and get myself a drink of water. And the water bucket stood on the table, right in the room where we was settin'. Still, somehow or another, I liked that story, and when us children used to be a-settin' around the fireplace of a evenin', eatin' goober-peas, and listenin' to the wind sighin' out of doors, and a-whistlin' in through the chinks in the cabin wall, us little ones would coax Pap to tell it, and sit mouth-open, holdin' our breath, till he said the last word. And he always told it alike—never knew him to change. Got so, by'm-by, I could tell it myself. I expect some of you has heard the story. It ran like this:

" 'One evenin' in potato-diggin' time, when the woods was turnin' yellow, and the nights were growin' long, me and some of my friends down in ole Virginny, where I was bred and born, started out a rac-coon huntin'.

" 'There was me, first and foremost, the spryest one in the lot,—and "Big Eagle," a six-foot man with ham fists, measurin' seven foot from tip to tip, with his wings spread. He could knock a mule down with his natural hand! Then there was Bill Thompson, the conjurin' man; Tom Johnson, the fiddler; Jones Lee, Rubin Calloway, June Tatro, Pompey Colefax, Bud Mason and Buck Jackson, who could out-butt any ram in the place. Then there was ole Uncle Ephram, the best coon hunter in Rockbridge county. The ole man had the rheumatism so bad he hadn't walked in twelve years; but we carried him along for the pointers he could give us on catchin' coon—totin' him, first one then another, on our shoulders. We took along the hounds, guns and axes, a jimmyjohn of good liquor and a lot of right greasy cracklin' bread, and was the happiest set of hunters in the world.

" 'Never will forget that night the longest day I live! Moon shinin' *bright!*—sky was clear, and there was scarcely a breath of wind stirrin' —just the time for coon huntin'! We hunted till along about mid-night, when we run the biggest coon I ever saw up a big gum tree, about four miles from home. Hounds appeared so crazy to get at that coon, it seem like they'd tear the tree down. And ole Uncle Ephram, about a rod away, was fairly sweatin' and foamin' with anxiety. I blazes away at the coon, and misses; loads and fires again, and hits him in the same place. And by this time every fellow in the party was shootin' away like mad—but missin' every crack. "Aim for his eyes!—aim for his eyes!" cried Uncle Ephram, "and all of you shoot at once!"

" 'Bi-oo! went the guns. But the coon only grins, much as to say, "Never touched me!" "Wait till I get hold of you, ole fellow," says Big Eagle, "*I'll* take some of the sass out of you!"

" 'By this time our ammunition was gone, and we began to throw clubs. But the coon never budged.

" ' "Chop down the tree! Chop down the tree, you nummies!" yells Uncle Ephram, rollin' and groanin' with his rheumatism, "and be sure you throw it away from *me!* Keep your eye on the coon, and, as the tree falls, set the dogs on him."

" 'We cut down the tree, and as it fell, the coon simply jumped to the next tree. Chop that down, and he jumped again.

" 'Says Uncle Ephram: "Somethin' mighty curious about that

coon! I hope he ain't the Black Cat Haunt I've heard my father tell about. If 'tis, God help these poor ole bones of mine! Ask him who he is in the name of Father, Son, and Holy Ghost."

" 'I went up to the tree and said: "In the name of Father, Son, and Holy Ghost, who are you that we've gone an' treed?"

" 'The thing turns immediately to a big black cat, blows a forked red flame out of his mouth—and all the leaves on the tree wither to a crisp! "Who?—who?—who?" he says, jumpin' from limb to limb. And the hounds commence to a-whinin' like whipped curs.

" ' "God-a-mercy! God-a-*mercy!*" moans Uncle Ephram, buryin' his face in the leaves, "Lord God-a-mercy on my poor, ole weakened soul! Spare me, Lord, spare me! and give me the use of these weary, achin' limbs for just a little while, and I'll give you a dollar note and praise you evermore! Great God of Shadrach, Meshach, and Abed-nego, spare thy servant now!"

" 'By this time, the thing's eyes was as big as saucers, and as red as fire. It took to jumpin' from limb to limb again an' sayin':

> "Sunday night—Monday night—
> Tuesday night—Wednesday night—
> Thursday night—Friday night—
> Saturday night, and Sunday night again
> And poor coon gets no rest!"

" 'And down he comes—ka-plumpup! right in our very midst! Away went the dogs, and away went Uncle Ephram after them, screamin'— Do the best you can for yourselves, children, the ole man's treadin' air!"

" 'Every one of us tore out in a different direction—Big Eagle in the lead—scratchin' our faces against the brush, barkin' our shins, fordin' creeks, and swimmin' fish-ponds and rivers, and splashin' mud-holes dry, and ruinin' crops and breakin' down fences—every-where we went! And it was noon the next day before all of us got home! Uncle Ephram outran the dogs, and beat them home. And from that day till he died, he was never pestered with no more rheu-matism! and coon meat he despised. *I* never cared much about it, no way. Big Eagle almost butt his brains out against the Natural Bridge—never saw it till he hit his head against it. Bill Thompson, the conjurin' man, and Buck Jackson like to run their fool selves to death!

Each of them thought the other was the haunt, and they ran till they gave out, and fell over the top of one another. They were the last ones home.'

"That was father's tale," concluded Brighteyes.

"Now, here's something *I* done," said Roustabout Thompson. "I don't have to go back, like you young fellers, and rake up something my father did. I'm man enough to speak for my own individual self!

"One day last summer I was walking along the street, when a feller in a leather suit, big boots, and sombrero, pulls his gun on me and says:

"I'm Wile Pete from the wild West and I'm looking for something tough! Where's the toughest place on the levee?'

"Says I: 'It's pretty middling tough right along here. Is you hunting trouble, honey?'

" 'Yes,' says he, and just then a black cat runs between me and him, and I knew I was duty bound to carve that man.

"Says I: 'Peel your linen, and look out for me!' And with that I carved him—furious, wide and deep. 'Any message you wants to send to your friends?' I asked, bending over him, as he was breathing his last.

" 'Yes,' he whispers, 'tell 'em the hundred-armed grizzly bear was too many for me, but that I died game!'

"I sent the telegram to his mother, and paid his funeral expenses; but, sir, that very night I saw his ghost! I got a silver quarter, and wore it in the toe of my shoe; but that feller pestakates me sometimes, still."

Whittington's Cat

(1934)

Lady Eleanor Smith (1902–1945)

Lady Eleanor Smith's great-grandmother was a gypsy, and it was her father's stirring recollections of her life that launched Eleanor on her successful literary career. Her novels include *Flamenco* (1925), *Ballerina* (1928), *Tzigane* (1935), and *The Man in Grey* (1941), which was made into a movie in 1943. This tale is from the American edition of *Satan's Circus* (1934). It was not included in the earlier British edition. The story refers to the well-known fairytale *Dick Whittington and His Cat*. Sir Richard Whittington (c. 1358–1423) was the Lord Mayor of London three times. The fairytale that became attached to his name tells how he came to London in poverty and sold his cat for a fortune in a mouse-plagued country that had never seen a cat before. It is the great Horatio Alger story of Britain. A monument to Whittington's cat still stands in London today and at least one pantomime theater still exists in London.

Martin was the name of the young man who went alone nearly every evening to the local pantomime. Usually, he sat in the dress circle, but sometimes he patronized the stalls, and he had even been seen on more than one occasion seated—still quite alone—in a stage box. The programme girls knew him by sight, and discussed him very frequently, for the regularity of his attendance made him appear something of an oddity in their eyes. Always, however, they decided that he must be in love either with the Principal Boy or with the Principal Girl. Very often, when they had nothing better to do, they had bets with one another as to which of the two had caught his eye. Unless, of course, this eye had fallen upon someone else—upon Columbine, for instance, or upon the Fairy Queen. . . .

Martin himself was quite unconscious of their interest. Nor was he in love with anyone, with the possible exception of Marlene Dietrich. His reasons for visiting the Burford Hippodrome so constantly were, in fact, purely aesthetic—he was engaged in compiling a book that was to be entitled *Pantomime throughout the Ages.*

Why such a subject ever in the first place appealed to him is impossible to understand; he knew nothing of pantomime, nor was he acquainted with anyone likely to be of assistance to him in this direction; all he knew was that he felt the urge to write, and to write, what is more, upon this particular subject. Hence these nightly visits to the Burford Hippodrome.

Early that autumn, visiting a local curiosity shop, he had stumbled by chance upon a series of spangled prints representing characters from popular pantomimes; fascinated by the glitter and gaiety of these little pictures, he had bought the lot, and hung them in his bedroom; he was determined to reproduce them as illustrations to the book, and it is conceivable that his fondness for the collection may have influenced his choice of subject.

There was no particular reason why Martin should have bothered to write a book at all. He was rich, and had no need to work. In Burford and its neighborhood he was considered a *parti*, and the eyes of those mothers whose daughters were marriageable rested very fondly and very frequently upon him.

His own mother had died when he was very young, and his father, a retired mill-owner, had left him pleasantly endowed upon departing this life about a year before the pantomime mania became manifest.

Life, then, for Martin, was comfortable if dull. He continued to inhabit the ancestral home, a large pleasant villa in a fashionable suburb of Burford, and his every want was ministered to by Mr. and Mrs. Renshaw, who were respectively manservant and cook, and who had attended to his father many years before. His life was perhaps inclined to be lonely. He was only twenty-five. Provincial society sometimes seemed tedious to him, and then he would toy with the idea of living in London, or cruising round the world, or spending a winter in Monte Carlo. But in the end he was always too timid, too conservative, to embark upon adventures so tremendous. Burford had, after all, been good enough for his father before him and for his grandfather before that, and he had a curious idea that he might, in London, find himself more lonely than was already the case. In Burford he knew everyone, everyone of Burford consequence, that is, and he dined out regularly, and was respected by the tradesmen, and made an impressive appearance each Sunday in his parish church.

He supposed that one day he would have to marry, and beget children, and carry on his family name, but whenever this idea occurred to him he felt slightly uncomfortable, for he had never, with the sole exception of the doctor's niece, met anyone who in the least attracted him, and his own natural shyness made it difficult for him to appear at his ease in the society of women. He invariably decided, after such reflections, to live a life of great austerity, a life devoted uniquely to the pursuit of literature. Then he discovered the pantomime prints, and from that moment his destiny seemed assured.

Unfortunately, the famous book was by no means swift in materializing. He had always supposed that it would keep him occupied for at least five years, but whenever he came to ponder upon the magnitude of his task and his own ignorance of his subject, he decided that ten years might be an optimistic time-limit to put upon his labors.

And now every night he sat at the Burford Hippodrome to watch *Dick Whittington*, and it was really discouraging to realize how very little nearer he was even to beginning his book. So many trivial matters seemed to occupy his mind whenever he tried to concentrate upon the technique of pantomime. He could not help speculating, for instance, upon the adenoids of the Principal Girl, and wondering why she had never had them removed in childhood; it irritated him when the Principal Boy sang flat, which he very often did; and sometimes he suspected the Dame of being ever so slightly intoxicated.

That it would have been possible to scrape up an acquaintance with any of these people never once occurred to him; he would have been too timid, in any case, to take the first step, and actually he was interested in them not as people, nor as actors, but merely as the traditional characters of Christmas pantomime.

One frosty day, early in January, he informed Mrs. Renshaw that he would once again be dining at six o'clock.

"Yes, sir," she answered politely, but she seemed to hover in the

doorway, and he was conscious that she had not yet finished with
him. He was correct in this surmise; she coughed for a moment, and
then asked, casually:

"The pantomime again, Mr. Martin?"

He was conscious that the Renshaws must think his behavior absurd, and he therefore answered curtly, "Yes," hoping that that would
be an end of the matter.

And it seemed to be, for Mrs. Renshaw changed the subject. She
said: "I hope that cat didn't keep you awake last night, Mr. Martin?"

"What cat? I didn't hear anything. . . ."

"There was one howling all night on the roof. Renshaw threw a
shoe at it, and then it stopped for a bit."

"No, I didn't hear anything," Martin repeated.

He was bored with the subject, for he disliked cats at the best of
times. He added, hoping to get rid of Mrs. Renshaw: "Six o'clock,
then."

And this time she went.

That night, Martin sat in the front row of the dress circle to watch
the tribulations of Dick, Alice Fitzwarren and the Emperor of Bagh-
dad. During the performance something happened that he had always
known would happen if he continued to haunt the Burford Hippodrome. His natural shyness made him long to avoid such an embarrassing encounter, yet to many men, less courageous perhaps than
himself, what he dreaded would not have seemed so very terrible.

During a certain scene, Dick Whittington's Cat left the stage to
climb up to one of the stage boxes, thence to swing itself along the
circle, where it was wont to engage one or other of the spectators in
badinage, much to the delight of the entire audience.

Now it was Martin's turn to be picked out, and the odd thing is
that he had known this all night. He turned scarlet, gripping the rail
with both hands, while the Cat scrambled straight towards him, and
small boys nearly split their sides with laughter. Just opposite to him
the Cat paused, balancing itself astride the circle; it thrust its mask
close to him, and as he flinched away, the audience roared its delight
at the embarrassment of this young ninny.

The Cat wore a suit of shaggy black hair. It seemed enormous,
almost like a giant, as it peered towards him, and he could discover no
human lineaments beneath the fiercely whiskered mask. Even as he

recoiled he tried to force a ghastly smile, and then the Cat, approaching nearer still, whispered to him:

"Poor Tom's a-cold . . ."

Then it vanished, swinging away faster than it had come.

Martin felt self-conscious for the remainder of the evening. He decided that he would never again patronize the circle—he was too well known locally to endure such ridicule. He went home, made a few notes, and poured himself out a glass of beer. As he was finishing his drink, his eye fell upon the open notebook at his side. He read:

Origin of the Catskin

This hairy, faun-like garb, the introduction into pantomime of the feline grotesque, is believed to date from the days of Daemonology, or Devil-Worship. The Cat . . .

He read the paragraph once more, shaking his head. It was, after all, entirely surmise. He shut the book and went to bed.

That night his sleep was inclined to be fitful, and once when he woke just before dawn, he could hear distinctly the miowling of that stray cat which had already disturbed the Renshaws. Too sleepy, too comfortable to care very much one way or the other, he buried his head in his pillows and soon dozed off once more. Then he dreamed, a vague, perplexing dream, during the course of which he sat once more in the Hippodrome circle, and the Pantomime Cat, thrusting its mask close to his face, muttered in his ear: "Poor Tom's a-cold."

When he woke in the morning he found that he himself was cold, the bedclothes having tumbled upon the floor during the course of his restless night. It was a clear frosty day, and there were ice-flowers trailing across his windowpane. He ate his breakfast with enjoyment and remembered that he was lunching with his oldest friend, the doctor who had brought him into the world.

Dr. Browning was a sharp-witted little man in appearance rather like a dried-up russet apple. He was something of a gourmet; he had a pretty niece named Gwen, and Martin always enjoyed lunching with him very much indeed.

Today they were alone; Gwen was spending Christmas with an aunt in London.

"Still haunting the pantomime, Martin?" the doctor asked quizzically.

"Yes. I go nearly every night."

"Do tell me what it is that fascinates you so much about that very shoddy show? Is she blonde, brunette, or auburn-haired?"

"I've told you, sir, about fifty times, that—"

"Oh, I know all about that famous book. And a very excellent excuse, if I may say so. I only wish I'd practiced authorship instead of surgery."

While the doctor was engaged in his favorite pursuit of teasing Martin, something uncomfortable happened. The household cat, a large sluggish tabby, suddenly saw fit to spring from beneath the table where she was concealed, on to the guest's knee; with an exclamation of horror, Martin flung out his hand and threw poor Tabitha most violently from his lap, whereupon she gave a screech of anger and bolted from the room.

"I'm so sorry," Martin cried. He had jumped to his feet all prepared to brandish his napkin, to which he clung as though it were a sword.

"There's no need to be so rough!" rebuked the doctor, who was exceedingly fond of Tabitha, and who much disliked seeing her upset. "Nerves a bit jumpy, aren't they?"

"I'm so sorry," Martin said again.

He sat down, feeling incredibly foolish.

The doctor repeated his question.

"No," said Martin, in reply to this, "my nerves aren't in the least jumpy, really they're not. It's only—you know cats always give me the creeps. I know it sounds idiotic, but honestly it's the truth."

"Pantomimes—cats—what on earth next?" was the doctor's retort to these excuses. "God bless my soul, Martin, you're growing into an old maid before my very eyes! Why don't you get away from Burford for a bit—travel—see the world—meet other young people? Cats, indeed!"

And he snorted most violently, with the result that his guest felt sulky and resentful, and the lunch immediately turned into something of a failure.

None the less Martin went off to the pantomime once more that same evening.

He was sitting all alone in a box, musing as to the probable origin of Pantaloon, when the Frightful Thing occurred. And it was really very frightful indeed. On the stage, a transformation scene was in progress. Tinsel roses were melting into a gilded bower, peopled with dancing elves, when suddenly he felt a touch upon his neck. This touch was indescribably horrible—it was so soft, so furtive, so obviously the contact, not of a hand, but of a padded, cushiony paw. He turned, to see the Cat bending over him. In the darkness of the box the Cat's eyes gleamed emerald. In one second Martin realized the appalling truth—the Cat was no longer an actor in a shaggy suit, but a real Cat, a giant Cat, a Cat nearly six feet tall.

Martin sprang to his feet. He felt faint, but had no desire to cry out. The Cat said again, suggestively: "Poor Tom's a-cold." It put its paw upon his shoulder, patting him, obviously conciliatory, and with that sickening and velvety caress his will-power suddenly failed him. He had no longer any will of his own; it was all in one moment surrendered.

Swiftly it had passed, this will of his, like a dark wave, right away from him into the personality of the Cat.

He watched his companion dumbly, waiting to see what was wanted of him.

And it pointed, with one paw, at his overcoat that hung upon a peg in the box, together with his hat and muffler. Vaguely he grasped what this gesture signified; it was desirous of escape, and it could only succeed in this project were it disguised in the outward lineaments of a human being.

He picked up his overcoat and held it out towards his companion. Slowly, snake-like, the Cat slid itself into the coat. It twined the muffler dexterously about its chin, so that the black mask was at least partly concealed; the felt hat it jammed forward upon its ears so that still more was hidden; then having regarded itself critically in the mirror at the back of the box, it motioned to Martin.

"Home," it commanded briefly.

And Martin, that was now no longer Martin so much as an animated puppet, a Robot taught only to obey, found himself opening the door of the box that his companion might precede him. The Cat strolled through this door with an air almost nonchalant; had it not been for a plume of black tail protruding beneath the overcoat, it might well have passed for some sober Burford citizen.

Outside it was snowing.

The air was thick with a cloud of drifting snowflakes, and the pavement was already powdered as though with icing sugar.

The Cat moved quietly by Martin's side.

Martin wondered whether this was some ghastly nightmare from which he would presently awake. Glancing behind him, fearful of curiosity, he observed with a curious detachment the footprints of the Cat, walking beside his own in the snow, round, padded, clear-cut, the prints not of a man but of the gigantic beast that it was. He shivered. They walked on in silence. Soon they had arrived at Martin's house, and he was obediently fumbling for his latchkey even while he prayed most desperately for escape.

How could he possibly introduce this fiend, this specter, into the pleasant, humdrum security of his own home? For one second, then, his apathy changed into the fierce frightened rebellion of a wild thing, and then he turned to face the Cat, although his tongue clove to the roof of his mouth and his knees were shaking.

"You can't—"

But two eyes, like fixed and glaring emeralds, bore like searchlights into his own, and in one moment his defiance had withered away, so that he was once more the slave of this thing that his own imagination had created from an actor's motley. The Cat stepped over the threshold before him, and that he knew was a significant moment in the history of this strange adventure. From that instant he realized that the Cat was to be master of his home.

He shut the door behind him.

Very deliberately the Cat divested itself of overcoat, hat and muffler. It stretched itself, then, so that a ripple of movement slid through all its body, and he was reminded of the many dozing tabbies that he had seen stretch thus on the hearthrugs of his friends.

It said: "Supper?"

He could not in any way define its voice. He would have been unable to describe it. Was it husky, miowling, high-pitched, or gruff? Was it perhaps not so much a voice as the sinister reflection, perfectly comprehended by him, of the Cat's own immediate desires? The interpretative shadow of its dark mind? He did not know; all he knew was he himself moved, spoke, and thought in some hideous trance; he was passive obedience to the will of the Cat; he felt sick, and would have cut his own throat had he been so commanded.

"What sort of supper?"

And his own voice for the matter of that, sounded totally unfamiliar to him. A rusty creak that seemed to come from a long way away. If he pinched himself, perhaps he would awake from all that this night-mare meant . . . he pinched, but nothing happened. The nightmare was still there.

The Cat appeared to ponder.

"Some fish, some milk," it said, at length.

He tried to tell himself: "That's all right. Fish and milk—why, of course. It's just an ordinary cat. Nothing at all to worry about."

Aloud, he said: "Will you come into the dining-room?"

The Cat at once followed him into the respectability of this apart-ment, where Martin's father had so often stayed alone to drink his port. It sat down at the head of the table. Its bushy tail stuck out from behind the chair. It said, and again he sensed a menacing inflection:

"Don't be long. Tom's hungry."

He found himself in the larder without knowing how he got there. He discovered some tinned sardines, half a lobster and a jug of milk. He hastened back into the dining-room.

The Cat ate—like other cats. Exactly like other cats. That, too, should have been reassuring, but it wasn't. When it had finished eat-ing, it washed its face meticulously, licking its great paws first, again like other cats.

It looked at Martin

"Where is poor Tom's room?"

He was not astonished by this question. He had known from the first moment his companion entered the front door that it was there to stay. He knew, too, that sleep for him would not be possible with such a presence in his home.

"I'll show you," he said, "the three spare rooms."

In silence they made a tour of the bedroom floor. On the threshold of each room the Cat hesitated, peered and shook its head. One room was too cold, another faced the wrong way, and the third looked damp.

"Show your room."

So that was it! He longed, at that moment, for some last remaining feeble flicker of defiance, or courage, or self-respect; he longed in vain; his will was still the will of the Cat. When it ordered, he must obey, since he could not cast off this hateful thrall.

"This is my room."

The Cat glanced at the great glowing fire, the soft comfortable bed, the warm curtains, all the luxury and security of this pleasant apartment.

It seemed to grin.

"This will do."

And in one moment, the detestable black furry form had glided into Martin's own bed, had insinuated itself beneath his silk eiderdown, had cushioned its whiskered head upon his own pillows. He was dispossessed; the Cat was most certainly master now.

He returned to the farthest spare room, where he made himself up a bed. The night passed slowly; he was too terrified to sleep, and, even had he wished to do so, the persistent yowling of cats on the roof outside would probably have interfered with his slumbers.

Mrs. Renshaw, the next morning, was disturbed by Martin at an unusually early hour. He looked ghastly, and demanded a cup of tea. He then said to her in hesitating accents:

"Mrs. Renshaw, I don't want either you or Renshaw to go near my room today."

Mrs. Renshaw seemed astonished.

He continued:

"I—the fact of the matter is that I met an old friend of mine last night. He—he's ill; he's got a bad chill, and what's more, he's in quarantine for—for scarlet fever. I'm going to nurse him myself, and I don't want anyone else to go near him."

Mrs. Renshaw continued to look astonished. She said, at length:

"But I've had the scarlet fever, Mr. Martin, and if there's any trouble—"

He interrupted her harshly.

"I shall look after my friend myself. I don't wish germs to be carried all over the house. And now, will you get some haddock for breakfast? Some haddock, and a glass of warm milk. . . ."

"Whatever's happened to Martin?" Gwen Browning asked her uncle, about a week later.

The doctor glanced vaguely up from his crossword.

"I didn't know anything had happened to him. I haven't seen him for about a fortnight."

"That's just what I mean," said the girl. "He's never even been to see me since I got back from London. Shall I ring him up and ask him to supper?"

"Of course, my dear. Ask him by all means."

The doctor thought, not for the first time, how pleased he would be if Martin married his niece, and then at once forgot them both in the mysteries of his crossword.

"I don't think Mr. Martin can come to the telephone," Renshaw told Gwen shortly afterwards, in a cautious tone of voice.

"Why not? He's in, isn't he? I'll hold on."

"He's upstairs. He's engaged. Could you leave a message, miss?"

Gwen gave her message, not without a slight feeling of rebuff. That afternoon, Renshaw rang her up to say that Martin was sorry he would be unable to come to supper—he was confined to the house with a bad cold.

"We'll ask him again in a day or two," commented the doctor. He added that Martin's cold did not surprise him—the weather was as treacherous as he ever remembered.

That same evening, just before dusk, as the doctor was returning home after his rounds, he heard from the curb opposite to where he was walking the well-known wail of the cats'-meat man. He crossed the road immediately; he was always ready to give Tabitha a treat. He was, however, just too late. As he approached he heard the man say to another customer:

"That's the lot, sir. You've cleared me out for the day."

The customer turned, saw the doctor, and looked thoroughly dismayed. It was Martin, his pockets stuffed full of cats' meat.

"Thought you had a cold?" the doctor said, with brisk humor.

Martin hesitated. At length, he stammered: "I—I have."

The doctor suddenly noticed that even by twilight the boy looked drawn and ill.

"You ought to be indoors, you know."

"I'm just going home."

"Whatever possessed you to come out, with an east wind like this? Surely not just to buy cats' meat?"

And the doctor roared with laughter at his own joke.

"I'm going now," Martin muttered.

"Well, I'll walk with you to the corner."

They set off in silence.

"Come in and have supper, when you're feeling better. Gwen hasn't seen you since she went away."

"Is she well?" Martin asked listlessly.

"She's all right. But you've lost weight since I saw you last, Martin. Sure you wouldn't like me to look you up professionally?"

"Oh, no, indeed not," Martin protested, with such violence that the doctor was almost inclined to take offense. He was, however, good-natured; he felt sorry for the boy, and at length he tried another topic of conversation.

"You probably caught a chill at your beloved pantomime."

"I haven't been there for a week."

"By the way, talking of the pantomime, did you read about that odd theft down at the theater, the other day?"

"No. What was it?"

"You remember Dick Whittington's Cat? But of course you do, as you went every night. Well, someone apparently stole the Cat costume from a dressing-room just before the show, and so the poor fellow who acts the Cat had to go on and play the part in his ordinary clothes. They got another costume down from London the next day, but the funny part is, they've never found the other one. Fancy you not seeing that!"

Here, to his great astonishment, the doctor found that he was addressing the air. Martin had vanished round the corner with a quite extraordinary celerity and with no word of farewell whatsoever.

"That boy's mad," the doctor told Gwen later, "stark, staring mad. Mooning about, looking like death, buying enough cats' meat to stock a Cats' Home, and treating me, me, who brought him into the world, with the most infernal puppy-dog impudence! Running away from me, I tell you! He's as mad as a hatter!"

Gwen said: "But Martin hates cats."

"He's mad, I tell you," the doctor repeated.

"But I tell you he hates them. He dreads them. He can't even be in the room with Tabitha."

"I don't wish to discuss the young cub any further."

But the doctor had by no means finished with Martin, although at the moment he really imagined that he had.

The next morning Renshaw arrived, while Gwen and her uncle were at breakfast, requesting the favor of an immediate interview.

"Show him in," said the doctor, "and give me another cup of tea, Gwen."

Gwen obeyed.

"Do you want to see the doctor alone?" she asked Renshaw, who appeared perturbed.

"No, miss, not particularly. That is, what I have to say is private, but I'd be glad all the same, and so I'm sure would Mrs. Renshaw, if you'd listen to what I have to say, as well as Dr. Browning."

"Influenza, I suppose?" queried the doctor, eating toast and marmalade.

"Nobody's ill, sir, not at home. Not as far as we know, that is. But Mrs. Renshaw will be soon, if it isn't stopped."

The doctor began to show signs of interest.

"Suppose you sit down, Renshaw, and tell us quite slowly what's worrying you. Take your time—I'm in no particular hurry at the moment. It's Mr. Martin, I suppose?"

"In a way," Renshaw admitted cautiously.

He sat down as he was told, and began:

"More than a week ago Mr. Martin told us he had this friend sick in his own bedroom, and that we weren't to go inside the room or disturb him in any way. He said the gentleman was an old friend of his, and eccentric—didn't like servants, and would only eat food brought to him by Mr. Martin."

"Did you see this mysterious friend when he arrived?"

"No, sir. He came back with Mr. Martin late one night. We didn't know he was in the house until the next morning. We thought it queer, but we did just as Mr. Martin said. Mrs. Renshaw cooked for him, and Mr. Martin always took it up, and meanwhile Mr. Martin was sleeping in the spare room. At last I asked whether one of us mightn't go up to the gentleman, just to sweep, and make his bed."

He paused.

"Well?"

"Well, sir, Mr. Martin flew into the most dreadful passion. He turned pale, and shouted at me, and swore, and asked me if I didn't understand plain English. He said that if he ever found either of us messing about near that bedroom, he'd have to make different arrangements. I asked him, then, how long the gentleman was going to stay, and he flew up again. Said it was none of my business, and told me to get out of the room and not interfere."

"And then?" the doctor wanted to know.

"For the last few days Mr. Martin has looked as white as a sheet, and seems a regular bundle of nerves—quite unlike his usual self. He keeps on complaining, too, to Mrs. Renshaw, about the gentleman's food—says it isn't fit to eat, and the gentleman *must* be humored. He's never complained about Mrs. Renshaw's cooking before, sir, nor has anyone else."

"What sort of food, by the way, is being sent up to the gentleman?" Dr. Browning asked.

"Fish, sir, mostly. Sometimes a little chicken, and any amount of milk. The odd thing is, sir, that—well, he must eat all the bones, for none ever come down on the tray. We can't quite make it out."

There was a pause. For the first time a vague sensation of apprehension obtruded itself into the pleasant room.

Then the doctor asked: "Anything else, Renshaw?"

The man glanced across at him, and then dropped his eyes. "Yes, sir, since you mention it. Something a bit queer. I don't scarcely expect you to believe it, although Mrs. Renshaw will bear me out."

"I think we'd better hear it," the doctor decided, in a kind tone of voice, "if I am to be of any help to you. What was this queer thing, eh?"

Renshaw licked his lips, smiled nervously, and began:

"Well, it was like this. The cats have been very bad round the house, lately, screeching all night. It hasn't been easy to sleep, with so much row. Last night I'd just dropped off when Mrs. Renshaw woke me up. She said she heard someone moving about downstairs. It was nearly two o'clock, so it worried us both. I listened and heard footsteps. I thought it was perhaps Mr. Martin, in a restless fit, but all the same, we couldn't very well leave it at that. We got out of bed and went downstairs, as quiet as we could. I had my electric torch."

He paused.

"Go on," encouraged the doctor. "What happened then?"

"There was nothing, sir, although we'd both heard footsteps. But all the same, there was something funny in the drawing-room—you know the great goldfish bowl that belonged to Mr. Martin's mother? Well, there it was, standing in the middle of the floor, with a lot of water slopped out of it, and all the fish gone—every one."

"An odd thing to steal, goldfish!"

"That's not all, sir. As we tiptoed upstairs we determined to go past Mr. Martin's bedroom, to see if the strange gentleman was awake."

"Yes!" Gwen's voice was eager now.

"We did so, miss. There was a thread of light under the door. We stopped a minute to listen."

He paused once more, averting his eyes.

"Well?"

"Dr. Browning, there's something in that room that's not human. I swear there is: I'm not easily scared."

"Go on, Renshaw."

"We stopped to listen, as I told you. We both heard it moving about. It wasn't walking—it was *padding*, like a great beast. And we heard it snarling, as though it was growling away to itself, and I tell you that noise made your blood run cold."

"Anything else?"

"No, sir. Only, while it was still growling, the cats outside started again, and then the Thing in the room became quiet. We went back to bed, and this morning, after we'd talked it over, we both decided I should come to you."

"A queer story," commented the doctor; "tell me, Mr. Martin has been nervous and irritable since the arrival of this mysterious guest, I think you said. Has he shown any other signs of being unlike himself?"

Renshaw said simply: "He seems afraid, sir." He added: "And he looks very bad."

The doctor jumped up.

"I'll come over with you now, Renshaw. Wait while I get my hat."

"Can I come, too?" Gwen wanted to know.

Her uncle looked doubtful.

"Oh, do let me! Perhaps—if he's ill—perhaps Martin might want me."

"All right, you can come. But hurry up."

They were silent, all three of them, as they walked across the busy streets of Burford towards Martin's home.

When they arrived at the house they were admitted by Mrs. Renshaw, who looked pale and anxious.

"Where's Mr. Martin?" asked the doctor.

"I don't know, sir. I haven't seen him since he took the gentleman's breakfast upstairs."

"How long ago was that?"

"It must be about an hour, sir."

"We'll go and see for ourselves," the doctor said to Renshaw. "Don't worry—I'll take all responsibility. Gwen, you go into the drawing-room and wait."

"But, Uncle—"

"Do as I tell you, there's a good girl. For all we know, there may be a lunatic at large upstairs. Come on, Renshaw, and bring a stout walking-stick from the umbrella stand there. I've got mine."

The house seemed very still as they walked upstairs. Only the guttural ticking of a grandfather clock disturbed the silence of the hall. They paused outside the bedroom, but all was quiet there, as well.

"If it's locked," whispered the doctor, "we must break it open. Are you ready?"

But the door was not locked. When the doctor turned the handle, it opened immediately, and they walked in without any difficulty whatsoever.

The room was in a strange condition. Sheets and blankets had been stripped off the bed and flung haphazard about the floor, which was still further cluttered up with piles of feathers, as though someone had been plucking chickens, gnawed bones, dirty plates, dishes, and empty glasses that had at one time probably contained milk. The windows were closed, and the room smelled of stale food. There was another odor, too, one more difficult to define—the strong, harsh stink of an animal's body.

At first sight, the room was empty.

Then the two men caught sight of something dark lying on the floor, at the foot of the bed.

"That's it," the doctor muttered.

Gingerly they approached the heap of black fur that lay coiled so still. A second afterwards the doctor burst out laughing. His laughter was rather forced.

"Fooled again," he said.

For the black object upon the floor was nothing more nor less than a shaggy suit, with mask attached, of the kind worn by actors impersonating animals in Christmas plays. For a moment all horror was removed; the hairy skin, the papier-mache mask, brought back immediately reassuring memories of *Peter Pan*, of other pleasant, childish, homely amusements. The doctor picked up the suit and held it, dangling limply from his hand, nothing more nor less than an empty, grotesque, tousled cat's skin.

Then Renshaw, moving across to the other side of the bed, gave a sudden cry of fear and horror. The doctor dropped the cat's suit more abruptly than he had picked it up.

"Look, sir!"

On the floor near the fireplace Martin's body lay sprawled. It was concealed by the bed; that was why they had not seen it before.

The doctor knelt down and gently lifted the boy's head. It was then, as he afterwards said, that he himself, with all his fund of grim experience, felt physically sick. Martin's throat was bleeding profusely. It was lacerated, torn—a mass of fiendish, slashing, brutal wounds. The mark of the Beast; for such fury of destruction by tooth and claw no human being could ever have been responsible.

"Good God!" whispered Renshaw. "Is he dead?"

The doctor answered brusquely: "Get me a basin of water. Quickly, do you hear? *Quickly!*"

It was many, many weeks afterwards that Martin, still looking ghastly pale and with his neck swathed in bandages, lay back on his sofa and asked Dr. Browning if he might speak to him for a few minutes.

"It's about all this," he said. "I've never felt like mentioning it before, either to you or to Gwen, but I've got to face it one day, and I believe I'm feeling up to it at last. Won't you please sit down?"

The doctor obeyed. He looked worried; he had been dreading this moment.

"Well, Martin?"

"Well, doctor? Won't you tell me the truth? Did I go off my head for a time? Did I live like an animal and in the end try to commit suicide? Or did a real lunatic dress himself in that skin and take possession of my house?"

"What do you yourself really think?" the doctor asked him gravely.

"What do I think? My opinion has never changed—I think as I did then. I am still convinced, absolutely and completely convinced, that some frightening thing, materializing as a gigantic cat, took entire possession, not only of my house, but of my mind and of my soul. Hypnotism—it was more than that, far far more. I was the will of this creature, whatever it may have been. I existed only to do its bidding.

Then, one day, I suppose it grew angry with me for some reason or other, or perhaps grew tired of being here, and it attacked me, before it disappeared. That sounds like a madman's explanation, doesn't it? But frankly, I have no other. Now tell me what you think."

The doctor lighted his pipe.

"I think you're very lucky to be alive."

"What else?"

"I'll tell you, Martin, since you want to know. What I've got to say is unethical and the world would probably laugh me out of the medical profession if it heard me talking to you, but I'll chance that." He took a pull at his pipe. "Look here, Martin, it's not good for any young man to live so much alone as you've been doing. This lonely house, these books—it's not a healthy existence. You're inclined to be imaginative, you're a bit neurotic into the bargain, and all that combined is tempting Providence."

"Well?"

"Merely this: let us suppose for a moment that there do dwell, on the borders of this world and some other world, unclean spirits, evil elementals, forever in search, so to speak, of pliable human minds on which to impose their own will—suppose, I say, just suppose, such creatures exist, you yourself would undoubtedly have been an ideal victim for their experiments. Do you see?"

There was a pause.

"I see," Martin said, slowly, "that at least you understand my story and don't think me mad."

"I don't think you mad. . . . Go abroad for six months, and when you come back to Burford try to interest yourself in something less solitary than study. Buy a car, but learn to repair it yourself. Keep a horse, but groom it. And don't go mooning about by yourself at pantomimes any more. Take some children with you next time."

"There won't be any next time," said Martin.

It was only when he was alone once again that Martin noticed something curious.

He was looking—for the first time for many weeks—at the pantomime prints of which he was so fond. How pretty they were, how gay, how bright were their spangles—there were Pantaloon and Harlequin, and the Demon King, and there was Columbine, and there the Cat—but no, that was the funny thing—the form of the Cat had disappeared entirely from its frame, and although the spangled background of the print remained the same, the space once occupied by the little figure was now blank and empty.

The Cat had vanished; could it, he hoped, be for ever?

The Last Temptation of Tony the C.

(1992)

Christopher Fahy

Christopher Fahy is the author of the horror novel *Dream House* and the suspense novels *Lyssa Syndrome* and *Eternal Bliss*. *Eternal Bliss* was written as an update to John Fowles' *The Collector*. Oddly enough, it turned out that Stephen King had the same idea. As *Eternal Bliss* was being published, King came out with his update to Fowles' novel which he titled *Misery*. Fans of *Misery* really should check out Chris's novel. Stephen King himself called Chris "a wonderful writer." He is also the author of a book of poetry, *The End Beginning*, a home repair book, *Home Remedies*, and a collection of short stories, *One Day in the Short Happy Life of Anna Banana and Other Maine Stories*, which won the Maine Arts Commission's fiction competition. His stories have appeared in many magazines, including *The Twilight Zone Magazine*, *Gallery*, and *The Fiction Review*. New stories are scheduled to appear in the anthologies *Santa Clues* and *Dead Elvis*. Recently he completed a mainstream novel, *Fever 42*, which is scheduled to be made into a motion picture. The following example of his work is a tour de force in a hard-bitten, raw style—a refreshing contrast to the somber, antique style of so many supernatural stories. Chris lives with his wife on the coast of Maine.

He couldn't believe she liked this halfassed town any better than he did—she simply refused to admit it, the stubborn bitch. Why the hell had he stuck with her all this time? Why hadn't he ditched her ages ago, before they left Paris?

Because she'd had money and even a shot at a job back then, that's why. And he had been lonely, she'd wanted some company on her travels—so here they were.

The job was supposed to be at the Peggy Guggenheim, but when they got down to Venice they learned it was gone. The bastards had hired some other artist, another American, right off the street instead. They figured that Tara had changed her mind, they said. Just because she was two weeks late. The bastards. The news didn't faze her, though: She had money. And jobs opened up at the Peggy G. all the time, she said, and if they could hang around for a little while, she'd score for sure.

So they hung around for a month, and nothing came up, and prices were high—not as high as they'd been in Paris, but high—and drugs weren't easy to get, so they split for Florence. They stayed in a little hotel in the center of town, saw Dante's tomb, Giotto's tower, the paintings at the Uffizi and lots more stuff—and he'd actually had a desire to pick up a brush. Nothing strong, not as strong as the urge for some good cocaine, but a definite twinge. They found some grass and some decent speed, one balanced the other out pretty good, and they ate good and slept good too.

In Vienna it wasn't so good, it rained a lot, and Tara had stomach cramps—from something she ate in Florence, no doubt. She was crabby and wouldn't sleep with him, and stayed at the pensione while he roamed the museums and walked the gray Danube's banks in the dreary rain.

In Berlin they had one whale of a fight. She had talked about going back to New York, as she missed her cat (her mother who lived in Queens was keeping it), and he'd told her she liked her goddamn cat better than him. "Well, Tony, I've known Sugar longer than you," she said in her lazy, sleepy way, with that curl of her upper lip he had grown to hate. "And she's nicer than you, and she doesn't blow all my money on drugs the way you do."

Her money. Sure. Like her CEO daddy had nothing to do with it, right? And she'd known from the very beginning he wasn't a saint. Well that was the last straw, that wiseass remark, and he'd stormed out into the street and hit the bars. Got away from lil' ol' Tara a while. Tara, Jesus, what kind of a name was that? The name of that mansion in *Gone With the Wind*? Her real name was probably Mary or Sue. That Southern accent—give me a break. When she'd grown up in Queens?

In one of the bars, quite late in the day, he'd found a dude who sold him something, and after a night that was lost forever he'd woken up in a tattered room with a headache the size of a house. He'd found Tara (Linda? Jane?) back at the hotel, drinking hot chocolate and reading the *Trib*, just as cool as could be. And the look in her eyes said quite clearly: You goddamn fool.

Then Amsterdam. Warm sunny days, bike rides, cheap tasty Indonesian food, cheap drugs—who could ask for anything more? Except maybe the turn, the change he had come to Europe for, the change that would break through the blockage that numbed his desire to paint. Every so often he got just a flicker, like back there in Florence, but nothing that said: This is it!—Like it used to in Omaha and his first days on Riverton Street. That change hadn't come.

And it sure wasn't going to come in Amsterdam's opposite, *this* friggin' place, zero city, he thought as he rounded another bleak corner. The weight of these buildings, their dark brown baroque facades, crushed the juices right out of his soul. How could anyone ever paint in a burg like this? The Avenue Louise was sleepytime, the Grand Place medieval glitz, the cops wouldn't even let you stick your sore feet in the public pond. Everything was *verboten* here. Bunch of tight-assed bourgeoisie. Whatever happened to Bruegel's peasants, dancing around with their dicks sticking up, swilling beer, eating platters of pig? They were rednecks, yeah, but at least they had *life*. *These* schmucks. . . . And as for drugs—a billionaire couldn't buy a joint in this goddamn hole.

Why had he ever left Amsterdam? Now *there* was a city, a place where folks knew how to *live*. The kids smoked cigar-sized joints in the public parks while they waded around in the ponds, and nobody said boo. Cocaine, acid, smack, you could get it all. And the town even gave you clean needles! To go from that freedom to this was too much, too much. But when Tara had "done" the Van Gogh Museum, the Rijksmuseum and cruised the canals, it was time to move on, she said. To this. Verbotenville.

And now it was starting to drizzle again. Same thing as Berlin and Vienna. His hair was already wet, Jesus, where *was* this place?

When he looked up again, he saw it: *Musée Royaux Des Beaux-Arts.*
Not bad-looking. Huh.

He stopped for a moment and reached in his pocket and took out a
foil square. Looked around—no cops—then opened the foil and
popped the two pills in his mouth.

He'd gotten the pills in Amsterdam, and this was the end, sad to
say. He'd done one yesterday and it wasn't bad: brought a bright
clean edge and a mellow cool. A little too mellow, actually, and
that's why he'd taken a double this time. Try to sharpen things up
a bit.

As he walked through the entrance door, his depression deepened.
Ahead he saw ornate gold frames and stern portraits of soldiers and
kings.

Am I really ready for this? he asked himself.—Then shrugged,
bought a ticket and went inside.

A portrait by Jan van Eyck, 1434. Lotta water under the bridge
since those days, man. Porcelain people: they looked like they'd shat-
ter to bits if you knocked them down. Hands and fingers so white, so
thin. Big nose on the dude, and the cuffs on the chick's robe two feet
long. Good technician, van Eyck. The grain in the wood floors,
amazing.

Stuff by Aertsen and van der Goes, and some others that left Tony
cold. Good old Rembrandt, of course. Soldiers. Yeah, it was good—
but *soldiers?*

On to a Bruegel—a famous one—*Landscape with the Fall of Icarus.*
Old Ick is head down in the water, drowning, and who gives a damn?
Life goes on. Hey, you fly too close to the sun, you fry your
tailfeathers, right? And here was one of those peasant paintings, the
dancing, the drinking—and what was that stuff going on in the corner? Somebody getting roughed up, getting robbed. Even back then,
man, the world was royally screwed.

Then Rubens. He'd had a good deal: sketch out the compositions
and paint the heads, get your lackeys to do the rest. Rake in the
dough and keep most for yourself. Tony scowled at the canvas. Were
all broads big mamas back then? Or was that all that guys liked to see
in the buff?

Another room. Franz Hals. His smiling peasants had never made
Tony joyous, not in the least. It was something about their teeth. He

squinted. Ugly teeth, mean ratlike teeth. He thought: The pills are kicking in.

After Hals he had just about had enough. He was crossing another gloom-packed room when a triptych on a table caught his eye. He stopped.

A Bosch? No kidding. He hadn't expected that. Even though Bosch was Belgian, the Prado had most of his stuff, though God knew why. Tony had seen it his first trip to Spain.

He looked at the brass plate attached to the painting's frame. "Attributed to Hieronymous (Jeroen) Bosch, c. 1508."

Attributed to. Well it looked like the real thing, all right. Good old Hieronymous, Jerry the B., as they used to call him in art school. Now *there* was a painter, there was a guy who *knew*.

The triptych was smaller than most—each panel was only about two feet high and a foot across—and was darker than other Bosches that Tony had seen. Or was that the effect of the drugs? Couldn't tell. He squinted, leaned close.

The first of the panels, the one on the left, was brighter than the other two, with a lovely lush garden and naked slim people (no Rubens heavyweights here). Way off in the distance, however, some bad shit was coming down: an ugly knot of insectile limbs was rolling across the green hill.

In the next scene—again, pure Bosch—things were radically falling apart. Some poor naked dude pulled a huge wooden wagon that overflowed with green corpses; an arrow was buried between his shoulder blades. Another nude guy slumped against a stone wall while a huge fish with legs stuck long pins through his neck. There was one of those giant pathetic tree-men, fishing boats stuck to his severed limbs, and his broken-egg body was chock full of fat priests and nuns doing something obscene. Fishlike birds with thin murderous bills and the legs of humans sailed through the dark blue sky, as crowds of milk-pale people below were nibbled by monster rabbits. Above it all, Jesus sat on a cloud, shrugging and raising his arms as if saying: Hey man, I mean what can you do with these fools?

The third panel depicted all hell breaking loose—quite literally. The sky was a flaming red cauldron of sparks, and people were being devoured by cow-sized rats. A fat yellow pig had one sad skinny dude

by his ankles, and dipped him head-first into lava. Another doomed
sucker puked bilious green bubbles, out of which black roachlike in-
sects came crawling to feast upon babies' eyes. Not a fun time at all.

Tony wished he had waited till later to do those pills, whatever the
hell they were. He wasn't feeling the same way he'd felt when he'd
done them before; and now that he thought of it, these had been
different, a different color, red, not blue, like yesterday's. Old Bosch
was plenty without added zip, these golden haloes, these buzzing
sounds, these shimmering wavy lights, and he thought: Maybe Jerry
the B. used to take something too, like mushrooms or something,
whatever they had in those days. Whatever, he'd gone all the way.
You bet. It was almost as if he had actually been there, had actually
visited hell and come back with the news. Or maybe to him the
everyday world looked like this, like the underworld. Maybe that was
it.

Despair sank its talons in Tony's heart. That vision, that singular
way of seeing—what did it take to achieve it? He was starting to think
—no, he'd thought for a while now—that he'd never be able to break
through like that, make it over the edge.

He stared at the painting, that hellish third panel, and thought:
Fantastic! I'd give *anything* to be able to see like that, take *anything*. . . .

Shaking his head in awe, he turned away—and suddenly realized
something.

He was all alone in this room. There was nobody else in sight, not
even a guard.

He looked back at the painting, then up at the sign on the wall.
C'est interdit à toucher les peintures. Well, that was the same everywhere, no museums would let you touch paintings, that went without
saying. But how delicious to touch one right here in Forbidden City!

He looked around quickly—left, then right—then caught his
breath and did it: reached out and touched the right panel, the blazing inferno—specifically, a snarling cat—with the tip of his right index finger.

Ow! Gasping, he jerked his hand back.

An electric shock! The bastards had wired the paintings! Real
sweethearts in charge of this place, oh yeah, the least they could do
was tell you the damn things were juiced! He looked at his stinging,
tingling hand, and his fingers were yellow and green.

He'd done some stuff in Santa Fe that had made his hand look like that, some peyote—or maybe mescaline. Made him puke like a dog all night and half the next day. Not *that* again, he said to himself. Man—

A guard was in the doorway now. He'd come out of nowhere, poof, like a friggin' ghost, and stood there scowling. Had he seen? Had the painting set off an alarm? Couldn't be—or the guy would be on him for sure.

He was one weird dude, that guard, one *mean*-lookin' dude. His hair stuck up in silver spikes and his yellow-green teeth looked like fangs. His hands were black, with blue-black nails, like a friggin' gorilla's hands. I am *outta* this place, Tony said to himself.

As he started to walk, the floor seemed to ripple. The paintings, especially their golden frames, seemed to shine with an inner light. Not bad, he thought. Looks like I'll get something out of this stuff after all.

On the street, though, the light hurt his eyes, and his pupils contracted with sudden sharp pain. The rain had stopped, but the sky was still brooding and gray. Good thing the sun's *not* out, Tony thought, I'd be damn near blind.

The street was deserted—except for a guy at the end of the block, on the corner, waiting for the light to change. The light was huge, a blood-red sun, even this far away. Tony squinted against its glare.

It shifted to splintery emerald green and the guy crossed the street. He was hunched down, bent, was wearing gray, and looked for all the world like a giant bird. His nose was as sharp as a sandpiper's beak, and his arms in his floppy gray cape looked like wings. And—what? Did he actually lift off the ground and fly a few feet?

This stuff was *bad*, even worse than that Santa Fe crap or that junk he had done in Chicago with . . . yeah, Drusilla. A chick with a name like that, he shoulda known better. Drusilla, Tara—how come he always got stuck with these weirdo women?

When he reached the corner, his feet felt soft on the curb, soft and light. His whole body felt light, like he might float away if he didn't watch out, or like if he jumped—

He tried it; jumped. And got up. He got *up*—into slam-dunk range. Impossible, he thought. There isn't a drug in the world that could—

Someone was staring. She (*was* it a she?) stood in one of those dark baroque doorways, her thick eyebrows furrowed, skin doughy and pale, her huge eyes like lumps of black coal. Okay, so I jumped, Tony thought. So what is it, a crime? Is jumping forbidden too? As he finished this thought, those black eyes blinked, and a serpent's red tongue darted out from the woman's blue lips, sprouting spirals of flame.

Whoa!

He walked in the other direction. Bad stuff, and how long was it going to last? The Santa Fe garbage had taken three days to metabolize—and this shit seemed stronger than that.

It dawned on him then that he wasn't walking—not walking, but *capering* down the street. I don't want to do this! an inner voice said, I am making a fool of myself! But he couldn't stop.

They stared. The whole lot of them stared. They were naked or wrapped in rags, their eyes burning, beaks clacking, their vicious horns slicing the air. He snarled at them as he capered by and they shrank back or slashed with their claws.

Whoa!

Shaking their fists, they spat as he passed. "I don't speak your friggin' language!" he tried to say, but it came out all garbled, a jumble of noise.

His shoes were suddenly killing him. He tore them off quickly and dropped to all fours. That felt better, much better, yes.

Which way was home? Down here, this street? Yeah, down—

When he turned the corner, the world was fire. Flames poured from the roofs and windows of towering flat wooden buildings. The heat was unbearable. Christ! Where the hell were the fire trucks?

In the flickering darkness between two tenements, crowds of naked people screamed as coals rained down on their flesh. Lizard men with slick skin and long snouts lashed another nude throng with black whips. Further along the cobblestone street giant weasels chewed people's thighs. Much worse than Santa Fe, Tony thought. *Much worse.*

Then it hit him: It wasn't the pills.

He had touched the painting—had touched the forbidden painting and caused all this. The painting had been the gate, and he, Anthony Catalano, a sinner—

No! Tony said in his mind, his skin flooded with sweat, it's just the pills!

—And a bird rushed at him, huge and blue. It brandished a thick black stick in its claws and the funnel-like hat on its head spouted purple-green smoke. Its beak went wide, snapped shut again, went wide, and the clamor that issued forth from that scarlet gash made Tony's blood run cold. He tried to scream, Stop! but the sound that came out was a hiss. The bird was on him, stretched its neck—

And Tony charged it, biting its leg. It screeched, flapped its sandpaper feathers at Tony's hot head. He ran—and ran, past grinning goats and toads with red coats and black tongues.

His stomach suddenly cramped with a horrid pain. He moaned and squatted, pushed—and out of his heat came steaming eggs which cracked and spewed forth monster crabs that clicked their claws and pursued. He ran. Had to get back to Tara, the room, lock the door, call a doctor—

He craned his head and the street was full of them, after him, all of them, lizards and fish-men, men with diaphanous wings and bright scissors where fingers should be. Foxes with beaks and long ears that hung down to the ground, giant snakes with the faces of men. The sky was roiling with sulfurous clouds and his breathing was filled with brimstone, he couldn't go on—

And suddenly here it was! This was it, this was it, his building! He yanked on the heavy entrance door, ran inside, slammed it shut.

And if she was a demon too? he thought as he crouched in the shadows, fighting for breath. If this hell was the way things really were—and touching that painting had merely allowed him to see it? No, he told himself, that can't be it, she'll help, she will, she *has* to help.

He raced up the high dark stairs, turned right, and there was the door to the room. He pounded on it. Tara! Tara! he tried to shout, but the noise he made, it sounded like—

"Did you have to shoot him?" she asked, looking down at the hallway floor. "Did you have to *kill* him?"

"Ah yes," the policeman said in his heavy accent. "He was dangerous. Quite dangerous, he bit one of us in the leg. He was wild, wild."

"It seems such a shame," Tara said.

The policeman shrugged. "He maybe had some kind of sickness? We'll have him examined."

"What kind of a cat is he, anyway?" Tara asked.

"I don't know," the policeman said. "I don't know cats."

"Such an ugly thing. Those teeth, those claws . . ."

With a look of disgust the policeman said, "I don't want to touch him, I'll send a man out right away." He nodded. "Sorry for all the trouble, madame. Goodbye."

"Goodbye," Tara said.

Brushing her stringy hair away from her eyes, she went back inside. The thought of that cat made her naked toes curl. So ugly-looking, so mean. They had plenty of weird things back in Queens, but they didn't have cats like that.

She went to the window and looked at the street. Still gray, still raining. Depressing.

Yeah, Tony was right, this city could get you, could bring you down bad. It was time to move on again.

She'd tell him that as soon as he came home.

The Man Who Turned into a Cat

J. Wentworth Day (1899–1983)

James Wentworth Day was a journalist, writer, and editor in London. He was the author of over 40 books, primarily on sports. Oliver Cromwell was the Puritan who lead the rebels in the English Civil War. He abolished Parliament and the monarchy—beheading King Charles I—and established the Commonwealth, with himself as lord protector. He ruled England, Scotland, and Ireland for 11 years. After his death in 1658, the protectorate fell apart and the royalists restored both Parliament and the monarchy, by returning Charles II —the son of Charles I—to the throne.

Cambridge creeps with ghosts. Since it is a city near as old as written English history, that is as one should expect it to be. This place of chiming bells, of soaring towers and rose-red battlements, of alley-ways of legend and courts of splendor, is haunted not only by memories of great men and by the shades of donnish eccentrics who have vanished like gray moths into the dusk of time, but it has also here and there an inheritance of macabre horror.

Consider Jesus College. It began as the nunnery of St. Radegund in the twelfth century. It sits behind a long sun-warmed, very old wall of red brick which marches along one side of Jesus Lane full of color and warmth and old stories, full of reflected memories of men who passed this way, talking and laughing, and then died and perhaps linger on as amiable spirits. It is the sort of old wall which, like the faded gilt and smooth leather of an old book, promises flowers within. Scent of thyme and lavender and lilies, tall in the sun, and of roses, whose far wild roots sprang from the fields of Navarre.

All these sights and sounds and memories and people this old wall seems to promise. You feel it is the guardian of them all. And so indeed it is.

It is a sure and certain thing that Cromwell's Roundheads came here. They clattered down this stone path, stamped and rattled under that great doorway and kept their guard in what is now the Porter's Lodge. They slept in the rooms of the Gate Tower. And it is in that tower that we shall find our first ghost of Jesus College.

The tale starts in 1643. Strafford had been beheaded two years earlier. Charles I, having lost his one strong man, was waging the Civil War with all the indecision of a weak and kindly man. Cromwell had occupied Cambridge with his Bible-banging, psalm-singing soldiers of the Eastern Counties Association.

Like all self-proclaimed "soldiers of the Lord," they were the biggest humbugs unhung. Vandalism and sacrilege were everyday affairs. Their violent behavior and willful damage were appalling. They gloried in destruction. With the zest of the ignorant, the fury of the envious, they smashed works of art, broke windows of old beauty and hammered lovely stone tracery to rubble.

Contemporary records in colleges tell the damning tale. They were men of mean souls, enemies of loveliness, haters of tradition, downcasters of beauty and sanctity.

Before that sad summer of 1643 had run its course of fear and trembling, fourteen of the sixteen Fellows of the College had been expelled. Two only remained in residence. With them were about half a score of scholars. The rest of the College was full of Cromwell's ranting, canting troops.

The two Fellows who remained were John Boyleston and Thomas Allen.

Allen committed suicide. That bald statement hides a lot. First, we must bear in mind that six months before Allen died, that ignorant fanatic, William Dowsing, the scourge of churches and chapels, descended on Cambridge like a plague. He was armed with Parliamentary powers to "reform" churches and, for that matter, college chapels. This ignorant oaf wrought monstrous damage in Cambridge. It is on record that on 28 December, 1642, in the presence of John Boyleston, he "digg'd up the steps" (i.e. the College chapel altar) "and brake down Superstitions and Angels, 120 at the least."

A certain Doctor John Sherman, a Fellow of Jesus, took careful note of these barbaric proceedings. He incorporated the whole disgraceful tale in his Latin History of the College, which was later published when Charles II ascended the throne and English air was once more fit to breathe. Sherman records that Boyleston was not the only witness of the desecration of the altar. Thomas Allen was there also. Dr. Sherman remarks: "The one (i.e., Boyleston) stood behind a curtain to witness the evil work; the other, afflicted to behold the exequies of his Alma Mater, made his life a filial offering at her grave, and, to escape the hands of wicked rebels, laid violent hands on himself."

So far, so good. It was for long taken for granted, by those who did not know the darker side of the picture, that Allen had committed suicide. Sherman did not know—or perhaps did not remember a certain Adoniram Byfield. This man, Byfield, was a Roundhead chaplain, attached to Cromwell's troops in Cambridge. You can get some idea of the mean, cribbed character of the man, full of fanaticism and dark superstition, if you burrow about in the library of Jesus until you come on a pudgy leather-bound collection of old sermons of the Commonwealth times. Among the sermons is one dated 1643 and described as:

"A FAITHFUL ADMONICION of the Baalite sin of 'Enchanters & Stargazers', preacht to the Colonel Cromwell's Souldiers in Saint Pulcher's (i.e., Saint Sepulchre's) church, in Cambridge, by the fruitfull Minister Adoniram Byfield, late departed unto God, in the yeare 1643, touching that of Acts the seventh, verse 43, Ye took up the Tabernacle of Moloch, the Star of your god Rempham figures which ye made to worship them; & I will carrie you away beyond Babylon."

The title of this sermon, if it can be dignified as such, lays bare the mind and soul of Byfield. He stands revealed as one of those fanatical Bible-thumpers, who played remorselessly on the ignorance of the Roundhead troops and inflamed their superstitious prejudices against the "carnal learning" of the University scholars. Byfield was almost as ignorant as the men. He was quite as superstitious. He was one of those raving preachers whose like is still found in the eastern counties today, where the country people dismiss them, in one telling word, as "ranters."

This weasel of a man, with his dark mind, was given rooms on the first floor of the entrance tower of Jesus, immediately above the Great Gate. Below his bedchamber was the Porter's Lodge. The troops quartered in the College used it as their armory. There they kept their swords, pistols and muskets. Above Byfield's rooms, on the third and last floor of the Gate Tower, "kept" Thomas Allen.

He was a man of mystery. Byfield saw him only half a dozen times in the first three months of his sojourn in the Gate Tower. The truth is that Allen probably kept to his rooms as much as possible, at any rate by daylight, because the moment he appeared in the College he was hooted, whistled at and insulted by the soldiers. For when the Long Vacation of 1643 began, Allen was the only member of the College still in residence. Apart from his natural reluctance to expose himself to insults and possible showers of mud and stones, Allen was a mystic. His mind and enthusiasm were deep in the sciences of mathematics and astronomy. Both were regarded in those days as little less than black magic. Mathematicians were branded as necromancers. Thomas Hobbes says that, in his own days at Oxford, mathematics was held to be "smutched with the black art." Many a country squire and noble lord refused to send his son to Oxford University for fear that the youth's mind and soul should become poisoned by the "black art" of mathematics.

It is scarcely to be wondered at, therefore, that the small black pit of ignorance which represented the mind of Adoniram Byfield should be seething with prejudice and hatred against such "stargazers" and "enchanters" as Allen. Hence his sermon. There was a reason for his delivery of that sermon. First of all, a Cromwellian cornet, full of holy faith and little sense, fell down one of the steep, dark staircases of the College one night and broke his neck, just after he had left a prayer-meeting in an upper chamber. Then two or three soldiers were stricken down with dysentery. These occurrences started a great deal of gossip. The soldiers were convinced that the last scholar in the College, the mysterious Allen, was cursing them with his "black art," bewitching them with his spells. All this sank into the little mind of Byfield. There it gathered force until he was convinced that Allen was a magician.

We cannot altogether blame Byfield, for, night after night, he heard the voice of his mysterious neighbor in the room above, mumbling on in a ceaseless rise and fall of conversation. It went on hour after hour. No other voice gave answer. None of the words made any intelligible sense to the listening ears of Byfield.

More than once he caught sight of Allen standing before a blackboard, mounted on an easel. It was chalked with white figures and symbols, probably the most elementary mathematical calculations. To Byfield's mind they were the visible signs of "black magic," the alphabet of the Devil.

On more than one night of stars Byfield stood in the courtyard below and watched Allen's lighted window. More than once he saw Allen come to the window, put his spy-glass to his eye and turn it towards the stars. What else could this be but a ghastly telegraphy with the black spirits of the night?

Once, he swore, he heard the ceaseless mumble and muttering above him change to a sudden, shrill, high cry. He heard three words, charged with evil and terror:

"Avaunt, Sathanas; Avaunt!"

What else could that be but the magician, the necromancer, the dabbler in devilries, shrinking in terror from his dark master, Satan himself, who had just paid him a visit in the oak-paneled chamber above Byfield's head?

A few nights later something happened which gave the Roundhead parson fresh grounds for fear. He heard Allen's door open cautiously above him. He heard Allen creep quietly down the steep, unlit, oaken staircase, past his own door, a flickering candle in his hand.

Byfield saw the thin line of pale yellow light under his own door.

Cautiously he lifted the latch of his door, opened it, crept down the stairs and saw Allen pass into the armory beneath, the room which is the Porter's Lodge today. Byfield slipped down the stairs and into the court below. Through the lighted window, Byfield saw Allen walk up to a rack of pistols hanging on the wall. He took one down, cocked it, raised it to his eye as though taking aim, then lowered it, tried the weight of it in his hand and finally put it back again. Then he crept quietly out of the armory and trod silently up the staircase, by the light of his flickering candle, to his own mysterious room high in the top of the tower. Next day one of the sick soldiers died. Byfield put two and two together. They added up to all that he had ever suspected, and worse.

Then began a new source of terror. Night after night, as Byfield lay quaking in his bed, muttering psalms to keep his spirits up and the evil spirits at bay, he heard Allen's door open. Immediately afterwards soft quick footsteps pattered down the narrow oaken staircase. They fled past his door to the bottom of the stairs and vanished, noiseless, into the night.

Two or three hours later, the same quick, soft steps returned, pattering at unnatural speed up the oaken stairs—pitch-dark, be it remembered—and into the room above. Then he heard Allen's door close.

Each night Cromwell's parson lay cold with fear in his bed, listening, praying, clutching his Bible, calling on his God to save him, racking his brains to know what those ghastly steps might mean.

He decided that they were the footsteps of the Evil One himself But in what form did Satan visit his slave and servant in that room of mystery and cabalistic symbols overhead?

Finally, Byfield screwed up his courage.

He waited, candle in hand, prayers on his lips, until one night the soft swift feet fled by his door. Then he opened the door, holding the candle high aloft, and peered down the dark stairs. He saw nothing.

The following night, pale with fright and grim with resolve, he flung the door open again as the feet fled downstairs. Luckily, a lantern in the armory threw a pale, yellow shaft of light across the foot of the stairs. By its light Byfield saw a cat, huge and black, whisk down the stairs and vanish into the dark night. He knew that two hours later it would return.

Faintly, up the stairs, above his head, Byfield heard papers rustling in the wind in Allen's room. The door stood half-open. A flickering candle shed yellow quavering light down the stairs. Not a sound came from the room. The muttering undertones of the necromancer's voice were stilled. Only the wind and the night silences possessed the room of magic.

Quietly Byfield crept upstairs. He peered through the half-open door of the top-floor room. The room was empty. He entered softly. There was the blackboard with its magic figures and numerals. There were the open books writ in Latin—that ungodly tongue. And papers and quill pens and endless pages of close writing—the visible signs of the Devil's work that went on night after night. There, on a small table by the window, stood the spyglass, the prisms and other Devil's instruments, at whose foul use he could only guess. There was no Thomas Allen. Yet no human footsteps had descended the staircase since dusk had gloomed into darkness.

What, then, was the cat, huge, black, swift and foul, that had whisked down the stairs on feet soft and quick as the wind? Was it the Devil in the form of his own favorite animal? Or was it Thomas Allen, translated by his own magic into the body of a great cat and now launched into the starlit night on another errand of death? Who would be the next victim among the soldiery by dawn? What Christian spirit was even now being caught up in the foul web of the muttering enchanter? Adoniram Byfield asked himself these questions. There could be only one answer. He pursed his thin lips and crept quietly down to the armory.

The horn lantern still hung from a chain in the ceiling. Its fat, tall candle shed yellow light out of the open door into the entrance arch, flooding the bottom steps of the stairs. Whatever returned to Allen's chamber—man, cat or Devil, or all three in one form—must pass through that broad belt of yellow light.

Adoniram turned his eyes to the rack of six horse-pistols hanging on the wall. There were only five! He took one down, primed it carefully from a tiny flask of fine priming powder. Then he took up a larger powder horn, full of pistol powder of a coarser grain, tipped a full charge down the barrel, rammed down a bullet as thick as his little finger, cocked the pistol, taking note that the lock clicked sweetly, and made sure that the priming powder lay well and truly in the pan beneath the flint. Then he shrank into the shadows of the wall, his eyes fixed on the lighted space without the door.

An hour passed. He heard the bells of Cambridge ring out to the wheeling stars their carillon of midnight. They boomed and chimed.

So midnight came and went. Well Adoniram knew that from now till two or three of the clock was the time when ghosts rose whitely from the graves, tombs opened, spectral choirs sang in softly-lit chapels of abomination, and dark spirits were abroad on creaking wings.

Still he stood there, stiff against the wall, pale and grim, too intent to feel the cold, too fanatic to allow his ghostly fears to let his trigger-finger tremble.

Any minute now, within the next hour, the Thing—cat or man or Devil—would return. What if it flashed past him before he could fire? What if it fled up the stairs ahead of him, entered his own room and cast its black spell therein?

Suddenly he became aware of a presence. Unseen, unheard, it was out there in the darkness. Yet he felt it.

Then, without sound or movement, It was there—in the patch of light—not six feet away. A cat, black, malign, green-eyed with fury, fur on end.

Adoniram leveled the great horse-pistol. He cried, triumphant, hoarse:

"God shall shoot at them, suddenly shall they be wounded"—and fired.

The heavy report thundered and echoed in the stone archway, up the narrow oaken stairs and re-echoed with a crash of sound from the far walls of the inner grass-grown court.

A ghastly cry, not animal, not human, stabbed the night. It was the scream of a soul in torment. The cat, if it were a cat, whisked into the darkness with the speed of the Devil.

Adoniram put the smoking horse-pistol—it had jumped in his hand, with the heavy recoil, like a bucking horse—back into the rack. He felt exultant. A great glow warmed his heart and soul. The deed was done. The Evil Spirit had fled. He clambered the stairs to his chamber, not bothering to creep quietly, slammed his door and felt at peace. He slept soundly that night.

No pattering footsteps fled swiftly by his door. No streak of candlelight or shuffling foot of man told of the return of Thomas Allen to his room above. The door of his room stood open all night. The questing wind ruffled his papers, sent them fluttering like sprites down the stairs. His candle burnt low, guttered and died. Thomas Allen did not come home that night.

Next morning, when the troopers went with leathern buckets over to the King's Ditch to draw water for their horses, they found the body of Thomas Allen lying dead in the grove of trees which border that ditch to this day. A great horse-pistol bullet had torn a jagged hole through his chest. His mouth was open. His tongue would mutter its midnight spells no more. His eyes were wide—and full of horror. They had seen something in the stars at last to quiet their evil questing for ever.

There was a trail of blood, thick gouts of it, from the foot of the staircase by the Porter's Lodge, through the college and across the grass to the grove where the body lay. A pistol was missing from the rack in the armory. One or two soldiers had heard the shot in the small hours. It was clear enough—the necromancer, haunted by his own evil, had shot himself outside the armory door, and, by a super-human effort, walked or dragged himself here to the grove, to die under the stars with whom he had communed for too long. Suicide. That was the general verdict. Byfield said nothing.

In his fanatic mind, he was convinced that he had shot Allen in the form of the cat. Already he saw himself facing his God on the dread Judgment Day, the curse of Cain heavy on his soul, Heaven denied him, Hell his remorseless end, because he had committed the un-forgivable sin of murder. In his mind's eye he saw the Book opened, the Accuser confronting and the Judgment pronounced:

"Now art thou cursed from the earth."

That night, he heard men with slow and lumbering steps and mut-tered words bring the dead body up the narrow stairway to the room above. They laid the dead man on his own bed, there in the empty room, with his books of magic, his prisms and evil instruments, his magic scribblings on the blackboard. They closed the door and went away.

The silence was paralyzing. It dropped like a pall on the Gate Tower. There was no man in the armory below and a dead man in the room above.

Adoniram was utterly alone. The silent horror of the night gripped him. He fell on his knees and prayed in agony of mind that the dead might come alive again, that his sin might pass from him, that the curse of Cain be lifted from his soul, and all be as it was before he fired that pistol shot.

As he finished praying, he heard the door above open. Soft patter-ing steps crept down the stairs. They passed his door. They were gone before he could open it—had he dared. For a moment he felt a wave of relief. His prayer had been answered. He was not alone. The dead had come to life. No longer did the curse of murder lie on his soul.

Then fresh horror seized him. Allen was dead enough. He had seen that for himself. What then was this soft, pattering Thing which had gone out into the night?

He opened his door and listened. Not a sound. Allen's door above was open. So was his window. Adoniram Byfield heard again the soft rustle of the wind in the dead man's papers, felt the soft night breeze pass on his cheek. Somehow he must close that door, before the pattering, furry-footed Thing returned. He must shut off the mutilated body of Allen, with its staring eyes, pathetically open mouth, from his foul Spirit, which would assuredly return to possess it. Perhaps if he could do that, he, Adoniram Byfield, might earn pardon on the Judgment Day.

He steeled himself to creep up the stairs. At any moment the Thing might return. He reached Allen's door. It stood open. A new and guttering candle lit the room. The bed was empty. No dead man, shot-mangled, with staring eyes lay there. The coverlet was white and smooth.

A sharp breath of wind through the open window caught the candle flame. It wavered sideways, like a little yellow pennon. It flickered— went out.

Byfield stood there in the pregnant, listening dark. Then he heard it. Soft, furry footsteps were coming up the open stairs. Stealthily. Menacingly. There was no quick, cat-like scamper. They were stalking him.

Byfield shrank back, and yet back, into the darkened room—towards the bed. The furry feet were on the last stairs. They came softly over the threshold of the door.

Then, in the pitch-blackness, he saw it. In a lambent radiance he saw the cat—mangled, menacing, its chest and neck sagging in a bloody apron of tattered flesh. It crept towards him. Its eyes smoked with evil. It crouched to spring. Adoniram Byfield backed towards the bed. The cat followed, low as a tiger to the floor. The bed touched the back of his knees. He dropped down upon it, sitting. The crouching cat, bloody and torn, sprang through the air. . . .

"Oh, my God, make haste for my help!" babbled Adoniram Byfield in a last surge of words. He fell upon the bed, his hands scrabbling at the coverlet. They closed on the dead, stiff hands of the body of Thomas Allen.

When dawn came a few minutes later, greening in the east and palely lighting the chamber, there was no cat. The stiff body of

Thomas Allen asked only for burial. Adoniram Byfield was on his knees gabbling for forgiveness.

And, as you will remember from the preface to his sermon, now in the College library, he died that same year.

How Diana Made the Stars and the Rain

(1880)

As recorded by

Charles G. Leland (1824–1903)

Leland was a folklorist who lived with native American tribes and spent many years studying gypsies and tinkers. While gathering material in Italy, he came in contact with a woman named Maddalena, who claimed to descend from an old Witch family. She gave Leland a manuscript of the "Old Religion," which he published as *Aradia; or the Gospel of the Witches* (1880). It contains an interesting mix of the ancient Roman religion, Christianity, and fairy folklore. There is a great deal of controversy surrounding the authenticity of this work. It has been suggested that the entire piece is a fabrication, while on the other hand, many hail it as definitive proof of the existence through the ages of a true cult of witches—or Wiccans, as most modern witches prefer to be called. Regardless of this controversy, there is no doubt that among modern occultists, *Aradia* has had an unparalleled influence and, together with Margaret Murray's works (*God of the Witches* and *Witch Cults in Central Europe*), can be said to be the direct inspiration for the formation of the modern Neo-Pagan movement. "How Diana Made the Stars and the Rain" is an excerpt from *Aradia*, and is a delightful nature tale, told in a simple and whimsical style.

Diana was the first created before all creation; in her were all things; out of herself, the first darkness, she divided herself; into darkness and light she was divided. Lucifer, her brother and son, herself and her other half was the light.

And when Diana saw that the light was so beautiful, the light which was her other half, her brother Lucifer, she yearned for it with exceeding great desire. Wishing to receive the light again into her darkness, to swallow it up in rapture, in delight, she trembled with desire. This desire was the Dawn.

But Lucifer, the light, fled from her, and would not yield to her wishes; he was the light which flies into the most distant parts of heaven, the mouse which flies before the cat.

Then Diana went to the fathers of the Beginning, to the mothers, the spirits who were before the first spirit, and lamented unto them that she could not prevail with Lucifer. And they praised her for her courage; they told her that to rise she must fall; to become the chief of goddesses she must become a mortal.

And in the ages, in the course of time, when the world was made, Diana went on earth, as did Lucifer, who had fallen, and Diana taught magic and sorcery, whence came witches and fairies and goblins—all that is like man, yet not mortal.

And it came thus that Diana took the form of a cat. Her brother had a cat whom he loved beyond all creatures, and it slept every night on his bed, a cat beautiful beyond all other creatures, a fairy: he did not know it.

Diana prevailed with the cat to change forms with her; so she lay with her brother, and in the darkness assumed her own form, and so by Lucifer became the mother of Aradia. But when in the morning he found that he lay by his sister, and that light had been conquered by darkness, Lucifer was extremely angry; but Diana sang to him a spell, a song of power, and he was silent, the song of the night which soothes to sleep; he could say nothing. So Diana with her wiles of witchcraft so charmed him that he yielded to her love. This was the first fascination; she hummed the song, it was as the buzzing of bees (or a top spinning round), a spinning-wheel spinning life. She spun the lives of all men; all things were spun from the wheel of Diana. Lucifer turned the wheel.

Diana was not known to the witches and spirits, the fairies and elves who dwell in desert place, the goblins, as their mother; she hid herself in humility and was a mortal, but by her will she rose again above all. She had such passion for witchcraft, and became so powerful therein, that her greatness could not be hidden.

And thus it came to pass one night, at the meeting of all the sorceresses and fairies, she declared that she would darken the heavens and turn all the stars into mice.

All those who were present said—

"If thou canst do such a strange thing, having risen to such power, thou shalt be our queen."

Diana went into the street; she took the bladder of an ox and a piece of witch-money, which has an edge like a knife—with such money witches cut the earth from men's foot-tracks—and she cut the earth, and with it and many mice she filled the bladder, and blew into the bladder till it burst.

And there came a great marvel, for the earth which was in the bladder became the round heaven above, and for three days there was a great rain; the mice became stars or rain. And having made the heaven and the stars and the rain, Diana became Queen of the Witches; she was the cat who ruled the star-mice, the heaven and the rain.

The Great God Mau

(1983)

Stella Whitelaw

Stella Whitelaw is a journalist and the author of many romance novels. She works in the Parliamentary Press Gallery at the House of Commons, Westminster. She is also the author of over 150 published short stories, many of which are about her favorite subject—cats. Her books include *Collected Cat Stories, Cat Tales: A Treasury, True Cat Stories*, and *More Cat Stories*. Her book *New Cat Stories* (1990) was recently published in America as *The Cat Who Wasn't There*. This story comes from a book she co-authored, called *Grimalkin's Tales* (1983). She resides in Surrey, England, with her husband and three cats.

In the calendar-less days before man, violent changes within active volcanoes threw rock into new mountain ranges and created immense ravines flooded with water. At the same time a new species of animal appeared. It was a small, short legged animal with a sleek body and a long tail. It was called Miacis. It was destined to found a family of mammals—the dog, the weasel, the raccoon, civet, hyenas and the cat.

When Man emerged, he hunted for food but he did not eat cats. He found them too useful merely to eat. He discovered that they could protect his precious stores of grain by keeping down the rats and mice. So the cat became the protector of granaries and in Ancient Egypt was as sacred as the Gods themselves.

The cat goddess was called Bast, or Bastet. She was also known as Pasht. She was portrayed as a tall, slim woman with a cat's head, holding a musical instrument, a shield and a basket of kittens. Her temple was built at Bubastis, east of the Nile delta and was more beautiful than any other temple.

The cat of Ancient Egypt was an elegant, strikingly marked spotted tabby, long of neck and shoulder, reddish brown in colour and altogether a handsome creature with great poise and presence. Cats were also kept to guard the family from poisonous snakes, and there were strict laws to protect them. To kill a cat meant the death penalty.

Mau was one such valued cat of Ancient Egypt. He was regularly taken to the vast temple of the cat goddess at Bubastis. The long journey was made in a gold boat from Thebes to the temple and Mau was accompanied by his own servants. The Pharaoh travelled in another boat and so did his Queen. They arrived with pomp and ceremony for feasts held in honour of Bastet.

Mau was always a little in awe of the splendour of the temple, but he did not show it. Towering red granite blocks dominated the great square, with canals on either side one hundred feet wide and in the centre was the shrine to the goddess surrounded by tall date palms. The walls of the temple were richly decorated in every colour with scenes of kings presenting gifts to the goddess. She was as important as the great god Ra.

Almost the same reverence was bestowed upon Mau. He was allowed to roam the deck of his boat, returning to his silken pillow to sleep. He wore a gold ear-ring in his large, pointed ear and he had a jewelled collar studded with emeralds to match his fathomless eyes. On special days he also wore a bronze chain and sacred pendant hung about his neck, and an amulet of the sacred eye which represented the solar eye of the god Horus. Mau tolerated the jewels, though he was always glad when they were removed and put away in a golden chest.

There was also a cat cemetery at Bubastis and many Egyptian families would bring the embalmed bodies of their pet cats for ritual burial. The small bodies were wrapped in linen or in simple cases made of straw. Some came in a casket or cat-shaped box.

Mau knew nothing of these burials. He was venerated by the Pharaoh and his Queen, and lived a life of luxury in return for the remarkable power which the great God Bastet could evoke against sickness and evil. But Mau was not worshipped as Bastet was worshipped, although to the Pharaoh, the cat was sacred and no one cared to dispute the fact.

Mau's sacred role began in this way. One day the Pharaoh and his Queen were hunting in the Nile marshes when suddenly the cat appeared among the reeds with three waterfowl. He had one bird gripped in his jaws and the two others held tightly in his claws.

The royal party were overcome by the sudden presence of Mau. It seemed to them that the cat was a reincarnation of the cat depicted on the tomb painting of Pharaoh Thutmoses II and his Queen Hatshepsut, who had been gathering lotus blossoms in their light papyrus boat when a similarly remarkable cat had appeared to them.

It was taken as a special sign and Mau returned with them to the Pharaoh's palace and was proclaimed sacred. Not being born to such nobility, Mau insisted on a certain degree of freedom. The palace covered a large area and Mau spent his days inspecting the great halls and vast granaries. He knew every inch of the spacious courtyards, gardens and rooms, as if he had been the architect himself.

Each morning he went to the pool with its shady trees, where he could sharpen his claws and frighten the silly ducks. He watched the servants drawing water from the wells, then skirted the cattle yards and dog kennels. He did not care for the smells from these places.

His favourite part of the palace were the stewards' rooms next to the kitchens and food stores, for although Mau was fed with chicken and fish from a golden bowl at the Pharaoh's table, a little snack never came amiss. Here the servants gave him delicious nibbles and goats' milk.

The Pharaoh never knew of these early morning visits and would often remark: "How fastidious Mau is with his food. See how he picks only the best from the fish. How little he eats. A true god is fed from the spirit within."

In fact the true god was rarely hungry for he also visited the Queen's suite and her women's rooms where they teased him with sweetmeats and brushed his fur with silver brushes. They painted his nails with a shining coloured enamel, and Mau thought this peculiar and rather pointless.

At mid-day Mau strolled through the great audience hall to the Window of Appearances where the Pharaoh held his daily public court and gave gifts and rewards. Mau always appeared with him. He sat in the portico, long and elegant, quietly unmoved by the cheering crowds. The people thought it an excellent sign that he should be there. It meant that Bastet was regarding them with favour.

A servant was sweeping the floor between the two rows of columns in preparation for a great feast that was to be held. Mau liked the servant; his name was Thut. He was a simple but strong young man and he was kind to Mau, sometimes forgetting that he was a god and treating him as an ordinary cat. Mau appreciated this and he also liked Merya, the girl that Thut was always talking to in the kitchens. She had beautiful hair that rippled like silk.

Mau watched the broom of rushes sweeping rhythmically across the floor. He crouched down, his long black-tipped tail whipping from side to side. He would dearly love to pounce on that broom and send it skidding across the marble tiles. Thut realized that Mau was watching and gave the broom a few quick jerks to tease the cat.

Mau's whiskers twitched. He would not be able to resist it much longer. A small growl grew in his throat. The Pharaoh heard the sound and felt that Bastet must be displeased. He immediately doubled the gold he was about to give to an old steward who was leaving after many years in his service. The old man fell on his arthritic knees and mumbled his astonished thanks.

At night Mau was put to sleep on a gold silk pillow in a special shrine in the chapel. The pillow was slippery and uncomfortable, so he often toured the granaries at night, roaming the vast storehouses and inspecting the corn bins. Then towards dawn he would go to the servants' quarters. He knew the room that Merya shared with the other women and he would curl up at her feet, careful not to wake her.

"Oh Mau," she whispered one night in a terrified voice. "Something terrible will happen to me if I am caught sleeping with a god."

When there were ceremonies in the Sanctuary, Mau awoke to the sound of the priest chanting hymns. He allowed them to bath him in perfume and put a wide collar of linked gold round his neck. Then Mau was carried in his boat shrine by a procession of priests to the outer court of the Great Temple. Granite statues of the Pharaoh towered above him, each toe the size of a table, and the great columns rose to the roof and into sunburst paintings of reeds and the papyrus flower and lotus buds. It was very spectacular and the endless singing was enough to send him to sleep. If he began to doze, the priests whispered among themselves, so Mau kept himself awake with day dreams of catching the painted birds that decorated the columns.

"We will go down the Nile to the Valley of Kings," said the Pharaoh. "I want to see how my work is progressing."

Mau was quite happy to go anywhere. They disembarked at one of the landing stages and were led along a causeway to the foot of the cliffs. A large number of ramps were in place, and stones were being dragged on sledges up the slopes by lines of workers roped together. There were thousands of workers drawn from the peasants who could not work in the fields when the Nile was flooded. Long convoys of barges had brought the stones from distant quarries and oxen had dragged them from the banks. The skilled masons were shaping and preparing the rocks and the noise was deafening.

Mau thought it all very dusty and noisy. He sneezed twice. So many people milling about . . . he was glad that Thut was among the servants carrying his gold food bowls. He watched the water being poured in front of the sledges to help them slide up the ramps, and tried to close his ears to the man beating time with clappers so that the strength of the workmen could be united. The men groaned and gasped under the hot Egyptian sun as they strained to drag the huge blocks of stone up the ramps into position.

Mau could not see the point of all this frantic activity when they could fish in the Nile or merely sit in the sun and doze. He made a pretense of lordly supervision for about ten minutes, but then boredom took over and he retreated to the shade of his boat shrine and went to sleep.

"See, the great god Mau is content," said the Pharaoh with satisfaction. "He is pleased with the work. He is meditating with the gods and leaves this great work in my hands."

The workers cheered, believing him, though the Pharaoh had not touched one trowelful of soil. And the work went on.

One night some time later, Mau was prowling among the granaries when he became aware of people hurrying. The fur on his back stood up—the atmosphere had changed. It was charged with something he did not understand. For a moment, he was alarmed, every sense alert.

"But where is the great god Mau?" they whispered among themselves. "Where is Mau? We must find Mau."

"Here he is," said Merya, with tears in her voice.

A procession of boats left Thebes and went down the Nile. Mau lost count of the number of boats. He had never seen such a procession, each boat laden with rare carvings and statues, jars of wine and oil, pitchers of milk, chests of gold and jewels, papyrus scrolls and valuable ornaments. There were platters of fruit and bread, even live birds caught by the legs with twine. Perhaps they were going to have a special feast, thought Mau, as they reached the landing stage. It certainly looked like it. He watched with interest as the birds fluttered helplessly. He was not hungry, but he always enjoyed a quick pounce.

A long line of priests and servants formed by the landing stage. They began dragging a boat-shaped sledge covered with lotus flowers. The Queen followed, wailing and weeping, throwing dust on her head.

The procession went first to the Mortuary Temple where rituals were carried out and jars filled with organs. Mau could not understand why no one would look at him, not even Thut. The priests then carried out the ceremony of Opening of the Mouth in front of the chapel and the sacred tablets were put on the eyes and mouth of the dead Pharaoh by his eldest son. Mau felt a cold shiver along his spine even though the sun was hot as the mummy was lowered down the shaft.

Mau found himself being carried through a narrow entrance into the rock and then along a dark passage. He did not like it, but could see from the flickering torches that the walls were carved with inscriptions and scenes from the Pharaoh's life—hunting and fishing and feasting. They passed storehouses filled with furnature and household goods. The procession went deeper and deeper into the heart of the rock and Mau could smell the dampness even though wells had been dug to drain away flood water.

They came at last to a small chamber where the mummy was placed in a great stone sarcophagus. The walls were covered with paintings and the scent of musk and spices was strong.

"I think it's cruel," muttered Thut. "The practice of burying the king's household was abandoned years ago, thank goodness," he added, thinking of his own skin and Merya's.

"The great god Mau will ensure the safe passage of our dead king through the underworld," said a priest. "He will help him answer the questions of the forty-two animal and human-headed gods. Then the god Osiris will see that Mau is returned to us. You will see."

Thut hoped he was right. He was very fond of Mau, god or no god. The cat had given him comfort and, in a strange way, a hope for the future.

Mau was sitting alert on his golden cushion, his pointed ears pricked for any new sound that would solve the mystery of the day's events. He was wearing the heaviest of his ceremonial collars and that was a bad sign. The collar rubbed on his shoulder bones and he hoped Thut would take it off soon.

They all heard a low rumble and then the chamber resounded with thuds as the work began of filling in the shaft with rocks and earth. The priests hurried through their last ceremonies although they were in no danger.

Thut put his hand briefly on Mau's head and touched the short reddish fur. "Farewell, old friend," he whispered.

The movement caught the attention of a priest "You dare to touch the great god Mau," he hissed. "You will be punished."

"Only for luck, for luck," the young Thut pleaded, bowing his head. "I am humble before the god. I am his servant."

"Out of the way," the priests swept past and retraced their steps through the passageways and staircases to the main entrance of the tomb. They gave the command for the entrance to be sealed and hidden.

Mau did not pay much attention to his surroundings at first. He thought it a pretty odd game and waited for someone to come and fetch him. He knew where a mouse was biding in the granaries and was keen to chase him out.

He sneezed as the dust settled around him, and the noise stopped echoing in the chamber. He had the feeling he was alone. He stretched his legs and jumped off the cushion. It was then he discovered that his collar was fastened with a length of chain to the ornamental carved stool on which lay his cushion. He growled at the chain and shook it angrily. He tugged and leaped this way and that but he was jerked back by the linked gold plates hard against his neck.

He crouched at the full length of the chain, his tail flicking with fury. But he was feeling his first tremors of fear. He had never been chained before. Again he attacked the chain, the stool, the cushion. He lay exhausted and slept.

When he awoke he thought he was back at the palace, near the gardens and shady tree-lined pool. Then he remembered from the darkness, the smell and the heavy collar that he was still a prisoner. He twisted and turned in the collar, flattening his ears and trying to drag it over his skull. He began to scratch at the carved stool but it was a hard wood, and it seemed hours before his claws made even a small groove.

He cried out, a loud strident call that echoed down the passageways. The candles fluttered in deep pools of wax and the incense drifted away to the ceiling of the tomb. It was getting very cold.

As time passed Mau was racked with hunger and thirst. He knew he was getting weaker. He knew he must find food before he lost the strength to move. With a tremendous effort he dragged the stool across the rock floor, the collar biting into his neck and almost choking him. Many times he had to stop and rest. Then he knocked into one of the pitchers and it fell over, water flowing onto the floor and gathering in little pools. Mau drank eagerly, his parched tongue lapping in weak gulps like a kitten.

He found wide necked earthenware jars of corn and dates. His primeval ancestor, the Miacis, had eaten fruit. Mau chewed, not caring what he ate. Perhaps if he was very quick, he would catch a lizard. His neck was a mass of open sores from dragging the stool around. He grew thinner and the collar began to get loose, but still he could not pull his head free. The craftsman who had made the heavy gold ornament had measured him carefully.

Days and weeks went by. Mau was living in hell. He was constantly in pain from the festering sores. The corn and dates had long since gone and now he ate the candle wax from the dark pools. He had almost forgotten the outside world, but he clung to life. His dreams were confused, and his thin limbs twitched with memories.

He hardly heard the soft footsteps of the robbers as they crept stealthily and warily down the passageway. Their burning torches cast long shadows on the walls and it was this light that Mau first noticed through half-closed eyes. He kept quite still as the figures crept into the burial chamber. Mau trusted no one.

The men were dark-faced and in ragged robes. They were whispering and trembling with nerves. They touched the stone sarcophagus with awe at first, but they had levers in their hands and were soon seeking a crack. Mau lay in the shadows, watching them, his fluttering heart beating weakly against his ribs.

A flame spluttered and threw a brief streak of light onto Mau's collar. One of the robbers saw the gleam of gold. His eyes glinted.

"Gold," he whispered excitedly. "Look at this! It's solid gold." He peered at the corpse of a dead cat lying in the gloom. His gnarled fingers fumbled at the heavy clasp of the collar and found the way to unfasten it. It snapped open. Mau gathered his remaining strength to emit a piercing howl.

"M . . . A . . . U . . ." He yeowelled with ear-splitting clarity.

The robbers shrieked with fear, dropped their levers and fell over each other in their haste to leave the chamber. They ran, moaning with fear, their hands over their ears as Mau's cries rang through the passageways.

"Mau . . . the great god Mau," they whimpered as they stumbled through the darkness. Mau flew after them, brushing through their legs in the dark, and the touch of his fur sent them into further paroxisms of terror. "Ah . . . the god . . . the god. Save us, be merciful and save us," they cried.

They clambered and slithered over the rocks that they had dug through at the entrance, their hands slippery with sweat. Mau smelled the fresh air and leaped in front of them, sensing freedom at last. He streaked towards the glimmer of light, unseen in the grey shadows, a great surge of willpower giving him strength.

He tumbled out of the narrow hole into the desert night. He paused momentarily, amazed at the brightness of the desert stars in the velvet black sky and the heady oxygen of the cool night air. Then he fled like the wind, not caring in which direction he ran, rejoicing in the feel of the balmy air that stirred through the wisps of fur on his sore skin and the sheer joy of being free. . . .

The new Pharaoh had brought his own servants and all the former servants were sent to do other work. Thut had become a brickmaker and he worked hard making bricks from the mud of the fields after the annual floods. Merya spun cloth and brewed beer for the workers and they lived together in a small terraced house that had only a matting of reeds for a roof.

Thut was laying bricks in the sun to dry when Mau approached him. The cat had been walking for many days and his fur was matted with dust. At first Thut was frightened, like the robbers, but when Mau twisted himself round Thut's bare ankles, demanding attention,

Thut realized that this was no spirit but Mau alive. He wrapped the cat in a piece of linen and took him to Merya.

"Look at his poor sores," she said, tears in her eyes. "And he's so thin. Bastet has sent him to us to be cared for."

She fed him goats' milk and fish that Thut had caught in the river, and put a soothing ointment on the sores. Mau did not move as she administered the herbal balm. The matted hut was no palace but it seemed he still had his servants.

That night he curled up at Merya's feet, a deep purr of contentment throbbing and swelling in his throat. He would sleep now, with complete trust in the two humans.

"But if they know that we have the great god Mau, we will be punished," Thut whispered to his wife, too distracted to sleep.

"Ssh . . ." said Merya, stroking his thick dark hair as if he were a child. "Who will know? One cat is very much like another. And who would expect to see Mau here? Of all places?"

She got up very early the next morning before it was light and took a file from her small box of precious possessions. Mau again sat quite still as she patiently filed away at his claws. It was ticklish and occasionally he twitched at the light sensation, longing to lick between his toes and be done with the pedicure.

Carefully Merya gathered every fragment of gold off his claws and put it away in a small pouch. Then she gently eased the heavy gold ear-ring out of his ear and put that with the gold dust

"Now no one will recognize you," she said. "And we will spend the gold wisely when there is a time of need."

Mau stretched and yawned then licked at her hand with his rough pink tongue. He shook his head delightedly. He had always hated that ear-ring.

Outside the sun was burning on the marshes, and Mau sniffed at the odorous air. There were wild fowl to chase and scare, birds to catch, fish to eat, mice to stalk and tease. He leaped out to begin a new dynasty.

The Tail

(1988)

M. J. Engh

Mary Jane Engh is the author of *Arslan*, which was originally published in paperback. It was "rediscovered" a decade later and published in hardcover. It has also been published as *A Wind from Bukhara*. She is also the author of the science fiction novels, *Wheel of the Winds* and *Rainbow Man*, and the fantasy children's book, *The House in the Snow*. She is currently hard at work on a historical trilogy set in the Late Roman Empire. Her short stories have appeared in a number of anthologies. This tale is from the *MosCon X Program Book*, which was the program book for Moscow, Idaho's 10th annual science fiction convention. "The Tail" is a delightful short piece reminiscent of Edgar Allan Poe in its use of the first-person singular and the protagonist's obsessive musings. Though not apparent from the story itself, it is set in Chicago. After living in the Midwest and Asia, she has finally settled in Washington state—"the part without rain," she says.

I blame the birds. I enjoy watching birds as a rule—the stimulation is very pleasant—but at times they are intolerable. It was one of those dry winter days that set the fur a-tingle, and the birds were maddening. They were hopping about on the bare branches just outside the window, bobbing their little heads and flirting their little tails at me, and all the while cheeping insultingly. I felt the fur rising along my spine, my tail twitching, and when one of the little beasts actually made a pass at the window, banking off at the last moment with that titillating motion of theirs, I sprang from the sill in a fury and raced up and down the apartment until I felt calmer. Sitting down again, I lashed my tail once or twice to get rid of the last tingles of rage.

Then, with a sudden spasm, it lashed itself.

I do not think you can understand. Perhaps if your right hand suddenly struck you in the face you would feel something of what I felt. But a hand cannot compare with a tail. At all times, a tail has its own character. It is not a *part*, like a hand or paw; it is a whole.

Now it lay curled on the floor beside me, and I stared at it. Could my own tail have (to put it so) seceded from me? Perhaps, after all, what had seemed like independent action had been only a violent twitch, certainly the birds had never been so infuriating. Tentatively, gently, I switched it.

Like a mouse in panic it leaped away, flinging itself out at full length. And, panicked too, I raced crazily through the rooms, as if I could escape by flight the second half of my backbone. I took refuge at last under the table where my humans sat at one of their interminable meals. There I lay flat, and beside me the tail lay twitching. It looked just as it always had—or did it? How often I had cleaned and sported with it, my familiar tabby tail; how often snuggled it neatly around my paws, and yet never (I saw now) truly observed it. Its tip was black. I knew that, of course, but exactly how many black rings should it have? I looked along the length of it, turning slowly to see if it was indeed attached to me. Attached yes, but no longer mine; or mine, let us say, but not me. Faceless and footless it lay, like a blind furred serpent and nervously twitched. And I realized that I had no sensation in that tail.

With caution, if not with prudence, I laid a paw upon it. At the first touch it grew perfectly still, then violently it tried to jerk away. Instinctively I clutched it.

It was stronger than I had known. It plunged, it twisted, in frantic struggle we rolled and tumbled, knocking against the feet of the humans, and so burst out into the open again. It had escaped my grasp. We lay prone and watchful, as before.

I became aware that they were laughing at me. One does not expect much understanding from humans, but one all too easily grows fond of them. Hurt, mortified, I collected myself as best I could and stalked away to fight my strange battle in privacy. Behind me, the thing hung and followed stiffly. I shuddered as I walked.

In the hall, with the laughter of the humans still pursuing me, it struck. I felt an actual yank at the base of my spine, as if some rude child had tugged my tail sideways, and then another. It was lashing violently from side to side, thumping hard against my flanks. Like a spanked kitten, I scampered down the hall and bounded into the next room.

But I had had enough humiliation. I turned, at bay, and slashed at it. It was quick—as quick as I—and hard to hold. Round and round we plunged, one way and then another, in mutual flight and attack, a hideous parody of kittenhood tail-chases. And now, with fury it flung itself at me, whipping and pounding about my legs. With a lucky snatch I pinned it down and buried my teeth in its thick fur. But it tore convulsively away, lashed to the other side, fell lightly back, and lay twitching at full length.

Cautiously, I looked over my shoulder at it. A prickling shiver rose along my spine, and I began to feel my tail again. I turned slowly and patted it with my paw, and in paw and tail alike, I felt the touch. With some trepidation I flexed it. My tail—yes, it was mine, my own. Very thoughtfully I began to wash it.

And now I wait. And if sometimes I bite at it with a kind of tentative anger, if more often I lick it with a reluctant gentleness, if long I sit gazing or lie brooding upon it, I have my reasons, yes. You do not understand.

The Ghostly Visitations to a Georgia Farmhouse

(1891)

From the

San Francisco *Examiner*
(November 29, 1891)

The little hamlet of Oakville, lying seven or eight miles east of this city, on the Savannah river, is much agitated at present over a ghostly sensation which appears to be more substantial than is usual with such excitements, to use a paradoxical expression. About three weeks ago the family of a small farmer named Walsingham began to be annoyed by certain disturbances in their household matters, which at first they attributed to the malice or mischievous propensity of some outsider. Those disturbances generally took the form of noises in the house after the family had retired and the light extinguished, continual banging of the doors, things overturned, the door bell rang and the annoying of the house dog, a large and intelligent mastiff. It was the conduct of this animal, says a Statesborough, Ga., correspondent of the Chicago *Press*, that first caused the Walsinghams to believe there was something more in those occurrences than appeared on the surface, though they were reluctant to attach any supernatural significance to them; being a family of educated, practical persons and avowed skeptics on the subject of spooks, etc.

Don Caesar, the mastiff, would be seen to start suddenly from a
nap and run at full tilt as if from some one, or to start suddenly back
while walking leisurely down a path as if he again met that some one.
But he soon lost his temper and varied these pacific proceedings by
snarling at every door that was opened, as if he expected an enemy to
enter, and often drawing back with threatening bark and displayed
fangs to warn his unseen annoyer from him. One day he was found in
the hallway barking furiously and bristling with rage, while his eyes
seemed directed to the wall just before him. At last he made a spring
forward with a hoarse yelp of ungovernable fury, only to fall back as if
flung down by some powerful and cruel hand. Upon examination it
was found that his neck had been broken.

The House Cat Enjoyed It.

The house cat, on the contrary, seemed rather to enjoy the favor of
the ghost, and would often enter a door as if escorting some visitor in,
whose hand was stroking her back. She would also climb about a
chair, rubbing herself and purring as if well pleased at the presence of
some one in the seat. She and Don Caesar invariably manifested this
eccentric conduct at the same time, as though the mysterious being
was visible to both of them. This kept up until no doubt could be
entertained that the animals saw something of a supernatural character, which was also making itself very disagreeable to the Walsinghams.

It did not long content itself with petty annoyances, but finally took
to rousing the family at all hours of the night by making such a row as
to render any rest impossible.

This noise, which consisted of shouts, groans, hideous laughter
and a peculiar, most distressing wail, would sometimes proceed, apparently, from under the house, sometimes from the ceiling, and at
other times in the very room in which the family was seated. One
night Miss Amelia Walsingham, the young lady daughter, was engaged at her toilet, when she felt a hand laid softly on her shoulder. Thinking it her mother or sister, she glanced in the glass before her, only to be thunderstruck at seeing the mirror reflect no

form but her own, though she could plainly see a man's broad hand lying on her arm.

She brought the family to her by her screams, but when they reached her all sign of the mysterious hand was gone. On another occasion the girl was startled by beholding the knob of her door turn softly, the door open and then close as if some one entered and shut it behind them. She strained her eyes trying to make out some form or the cause of the phenomenon, but nothing appeared. She vacated the room, however, feeling sure something was in it with her. Mr. Walsingham himself saw footsteps form beside his own while walking through the garden after a light rain.

The marks were those of a man's naked feet, and fell beside his own as if the person walked at his side. After some minutes the steps left him and led toward the house, where Don Caesar was lying on the front piazzi. The dog sprang up, barking furiously, but retreating as the steps approached him.

Blood Dripped from the Ceiling.

Matters grew so serious that the Walsinghams became frightened and talked of leaving the house when an event took place that confirmed them in this determination. The family was seated at the supper-table with several guests who were spending the evening, when a loud groan was heard in the room overhead.

This was, however, nothing unusual, and very little notice was taken of it until one of the visitors pointed out a stain of what looked like blood on the white tablecloth, and it was seen that some liquid was slowly dripping on the table from the ceiling overhead. This liquid was so much like freshly-shed blood as to horrify those who watched its slow dropping. Mr. Walsingham, with several of his guests, ran hastily up stairs and into the room directly over the one into which the blood was dripping.

A carpet covered the floor and nothing appeared to explain the source of the ghastly rain; but, anxious to satisfy themselves thoroughly, the carpet was immediately ripped up and the boarding found to be perfectly dry and even covered with a thin layer of dust, and all

the while the floor was being examined the persons below could swear
the blood never ceased to drip. A stain the size of a dinner plate was
formed before the drops ceased to fall. This stain was examined next
day under the microscope and was pronounced by competent chem-
ists to be human blood.

The Walsinghams left the house the next day, and since then the
place has been apparently given over to spooks and evil spirits, which
make the night hideous with the noise of revel, shouts and furious
yells. Hundreds from all over this county and adjacent ones have
visited the place, but few have the courage to pass the night in the
haunted house. One daring spirit, one Horace Gunn, of Savannah,
however, accepted a wager that he could not spend twenty-four hours
in it, and did so, though he declares that there is not enough money
in the county to make him pass another night there. He was found
the morning after by his friends with whom he made the wager in an
insensible condition, and was with difficulty brought out of the
swoon. He has never recovered from the shock of his horrible experience, and is still confined to his bed suffering from nervous prostra-
tion.

His story is that shortly after nightfall he endeavored to kindle a
fire in one of the rooms and to light the lamp with which he had
provided himself, but to his surprise and consternation, found it impossible to do either. An icy breath, which seemed to proceed from
some invisible person at his side, extinguished each match as he
lighted it. At this peculiarly terrifying turn of affairs Mr. Gunn would
have left the house and forfeited the amount of his wager, a considerable one, but he was restrained by the fear of ridicule of his story not
being believed in. He seated himself in the dark with what calmness
he could, and waited developments.

For some time nothing occurred, and the young man was half dozing when, after an hour or two, he was brought to his feet by a sudden
yell of pain or rage that seemed to come from under the house. This
appeared to be the signal for an outbreak of hideous noises all over
the house. The sound of running feet could be heard scurrying up
and down the stairs, hastening from one room to another, as if one
person fled from the pursuit of a second. This kept up for nearly an
hour, but at last ceased altogether, and for some time Mr. Gunn sat in
darkness and quiet, and had about concluded that the performance

was over for the night. At last his attention was attracted by a white spot that gradually appeared on the opposite wall from him.

This spot continued to brighten, until it seemed a disk of white fire, when the horrified spectator saw that the light emanated from and surrounded a human head, which, without a body or any visible means of support, was moving slowly along the wall about the height of a man from the floor. This ghastly head appeared to be that of an aged person, though whether male or female it was difficult to determine. The hair was long and gray and matted together with dark clots of blood, which also issued from a deep jagged wound in one temple. The cheeks were fallen in and the whole face indicated suffering and unspeakable misery. The eyes were wide open and gleamed with an unearthly fire, while the glassy balls seemed to follow the terror-stricken Mr. Gunn, who was too thoroughly paralyzed by what he saw to move or cry out. Finally the head disappeared and the room was once more left in darkness, but the young man could hear what seemed to be half a dozen persons moving about him, while the whole house shook as if rocked by some violent earthquake.

Seized by the Ankle.

The groaning and wailing that broke forth from every direction was something terrific, and an unearthly rattle and banging as of china and tin-pans being flung to the ground floor from the upper story added to the deafening noise. Gunn at last roused himself sufficiently to attempt to leave the haunted house. Feeling his way along the wall in order to avoid the beings, whatever they were that filled the room, the young man had nearly succeeded in reaching the door when he found himself seized by the ankle and was violently thrown to the floor. He was grasped by icy hands, which sought to grip him about the throat. He struggled with his unseen foe, but was soon overpowered and choked into insensibility. When found by his friends his throat was black with the marks of long, thin fingers, armed with cruel, curved nails.

The only explanation that can be found for these mysterious manifestations is that about three months ago a number of bones were discovered on the Walsingham place which some declared even then to be those of a human. Mr. Walsingham pronounced them, however, to be an animal's, and they were hastily thrown into an adjacent limekiln. It is supposed to be the outraged spirit of a person to whom they belonged in life that is now creating such consternation.

Weekend of the Big Puddle

(1988)

Lilian Jackson Braun

Lilian Jackson Braun's *The Cat Who . . .* mysteries—featuring Jim Qwilleran and his pair of siamese cats, Koko and Yum Yum—are among the most popular mysteries being written today. This series—which began with *The Cat Who Could Read Backwards* (1966)—now consists of no less than fifteen books. Less familiar to her mystery fans may be her numerous short stories, also featuring cats. The scope and quality of these short pieces is such that the greatest difficulty the editors of this book encountered was in choosing only one to be included! "Weekend of the Big Puddle" won out because it combines elements of mystery, supernatural phenomena, humor, and because we both thought the story's hero was a great character. It originally appeared in her short story anthology, *The Cat Who had 14 Tales* (1988). Braun lives in Michigan and North Carolina.

Ghosts were no novelty to Percy. In England, his birthplace, they had them all the time. But British ghosts had always shown their good breeding; the uncouth pair that turned up at Percy's summer residence in Michigan left him outraged and chagrined.

Percy was a comfortable middle-aged bachelor with quiet tastes and fastidious habits, who distributed his contempt equally among small children, yipping dogs, and noisy adults. His own manners were impeccable, his reputation blameless. In fact, Percy would have been considered somewhat stuffy, had he been a man. Being a cat, he was admired for his good behavior.

He was a portly silver tabby with a gray-and-black coat patterned as precisely as a butterfly's wing. Something about his strong, fierce face gave an impression of integrity, rather like a benevolent man-eating tiger.

Percy spent summer weekends at a rustic chalet in the north woods —on the shore of the exclusive Big Pine Lake. Here he dozed away the hours in the company of Cornelius and Margaret or stared unblinking at the placid lake.

Cornelius was a comfortable middle-aged attorney with equally quiet tastes. He too was portly and had Percy's look of integrity. On weekends Cornelius worked jigsaw puzzles, took untaxing strolls with his wife, or went through the motions of fishing. Margaret knitted sweaters or puttered lovingly in the push-button kitchen. When they entertained, their guests were calm, temperate, and middle-aged, with no great desire to exert themselves. Everything was quite civilized and dull—the way Percy liked it—until the weekend of the big puddle.

Bill Diddleton and his wife had been invited to spend Saturday and Sunday at the chalet. The bar was stocked with the expensive brands that Cornelius took pride in serving, and the refrigerator contained Margaret's specialties: shrimp bisque, veal in aspic, and blueberry buckle. Her chief delight was the feeding of guests; for Cornelius the greatest pleasure came when he tied on a chef's apron and broiled the steaks that he ordered from Texas.

"I wonder what Bill's new wife will be like," Margaret murmured over her knitting as they awaited the arrival of the Diddletons. "I hope she appreciates good food."

"A piece of this puzzle is missing," said Cornelius, frowning at a jigsaw version of the Mona Lisa.

"It's under your left foot, dear. Do you think Percy will object to Bill? He's rather a boisterous character."

At the sound of his name Percy raised his head. He noticed the ball of yarn unwinding, but it failed to tempt him. He never disturbed Margaret's knitting or Cornelius's jigsaw puzzles.

The man beamed a brotherly smile at the silver tabby. "Percy, the gentleman you are about to meet is an excellent client of mine, and we shall all endeavor to tolerate his bombast for thirty-six hours."

Percy squeezed his eyes in casual consent, but when the Diddletons arrived, shouting and squealing and creating a general uproar, he retired to the balcony where he could observe from a discreet distance.

The woman, small and nervous, spoke in a shrill voice, and Percy put her in the classification with small yipping dogs. Nevertheless, he stared in fascination at her jewelry, which flashed in the shafts of sunlight slanting into the chalet. The man was muscular, arrogant, and active, like some of the boxer dogs Percy had encountered. The silver tabby had strong opinions about that particular breed.

Upon entering the chalet Bill Diddleton caught sight of a horizontal beam spanning the living room, and he jumped up and hand-walked the length of it. The irregularity of this conduct made Percy squirm uncomfortably.

"Well, well!" said Cornelius in his best genial tone. "After that exhibition of athletic prowess I daresay you are ready for a drink, my boy. And what is Mrs. Diddleton's pleasure, may I ask?"

"Call me Deedee," she said.

"Indeed! So I shall. Now, might I offer you a fine eighteen-year-old Scotch?"

"I've got a better idea," said Bill. "Just show me the bar and I'll mix you a drink you'll never forget. Got any tomato juice?"

"Bill's famous for this cute drink," said his wife. "It's tomato juice, ginger ale, Scotch, and . . ." Rolling her eyes upward to recollect the fourth ingredient, she shrieked. A disembodied head with staring eyes was wedged between the balusters of the balcony railing.

"That's only our Percy," Margaret explained. "He's not as menacing as he looks."

"A cat! I can't stand cats!"

Percy sensed that the weekend was beginning poorly, and he was right. For lunch Margaret had planned a lobster soufflé, to be followed by her special salad that she prepared at the table, basking in the flattering comments of guests. On this occasion Bill Diddleton insisted, however, on presiding at the salad bowl.

"You sit down and take it easy, Meg honey," he said, "and I'll show you how the experts toss greens."

"Isn't it wonderful the way Bill takes over?" Deedee said. "He's a wonderful cook. He made one of his wonderful cakes for this weekend."

"I call it a Lucky Seven torte," Bill said. "Seven layers, with seven different kinds of booze. It has to ripen twenty-four hours before we can eat it. . . . What's the matter, Meg? Afraid of a few calories?"

"Not at all," said Margaret lightly. "It's just that I had planned—"

"Now let's get this straight, honey. I don't want you folks going to a lot of trouble. It was great of you to invite us up here, and we want to do some of the work."

"Bill is so good-hearted," Deedee whispered to Margaret.

"And that's not all, folks. I've brought four fantastic steaks, and tonight I'll show you how to grill good beef."

"Indeed! Well, well!" said Cornelius, abashed and searching for a change of subject. "By the way, do you people like old cemeteries? There's an abandoned graveyard back in the woods that's rich in history. The tombstones," he explained, picking up speed, "bear the names of old lumberjacks. At one time this was the finest lumbering country in the Midwest. There were fifty sawmills in the vicinity, and fifty saloons."

Cornelius was launching his favorite subject, on which he had done considerable research. He told how—when the log drive came down the river in the spring—thousands of loggers, wearing beards and red sashes, stormed the sawdust towns, howling and squirting tobacco juice and drinking everything in sight. The steel calks on their boots, sharp as ice picks, splintered the wooden sidewalks. They punctured stomachs, too, when a fight started. Loggers killed in saloon brawls were either dumped in the lake or—if they had any wages left—given burial in the cemetery. Twelve dollars bought a tombstone, inscription included.

"After the lumbering industry moved west," Cornelius went on, "the sawdust towns were destroyed by fire, but the tombstones can still be seen, with epitaphs referring to smallpox and moosebirds. When a lumberjack was killed—or sluiced, as they used to say—he was said to be reincarnated as a moosebird. Smallpox was a term used to describe a man's body when it had been punctured by steel calks."

Margaret said: "We have two favorite stones—with misspelled inscriptions. Morgan Black was 'sloosed' in 1861 and Pigtail Beebe 'died with his corks on' in that same year."

"Let's go!" Bill shouted. "I've got to see that boneyard. I feel like an old moosebird myself."

"Is there any poison ivy?" Deedee asked, shrinking into her chair.

"Absolutely none," Margaret reassured her. "We visit the cemetery every weekend."

Percy was glad to see the party leave for their stroll. They returned all too soon, and it was apparent that the adventure had captured the imagination of Bill Diddleton.

"It's a filthy shame to let that cemetery go to pot," he said. "It would be fun to clear out the weeds, straighten the tombstones, and build a rail fence around it. I'd like to spend a week up here and fix it up." A significant silence ensued, but he was not discouraged. "Hey, do any of those boys ever walk? What I mean, do you ever see any ghosts around here?"

His wife protested. "Bill! Don't even suggest it!"

"I'll bet I could go into a trance and get a couple of spirits to pay us a visit tonight." He winked at Cornelius. "How about if I have a try at Morgan Black and Pigtail Beebe?"

They were sitting around the fireplace after dinner. Bill threw his head back, stiffened his body, rolled his eyes and started to mumble. An unearthly silence descended on the chalet, except for the snapping of logs in the fireplace.

Margaret shivered, and in a moment Deedee screeched: "Stop it! It's too spooky! It makes me nervous."

Bill jumped up and stirred the fire. "Okay, how about a nightcap? We better hit the sack if we're going fishing at five in the morning. Hey, Meg honey, I'm leaving the Lucky Seven on the bar to ripen overnight. The cat won't get into it, will he?"

"Of course not," Margaret said, and Percy—who had been watching the proceedings with disdain—turned his head away with a shudder.

After the others had retired he prowled around the chalet in the dark, stretching with a sense of relief. The fire had burned down to a dull glow. It was a peaceful moonless night with nothing beyond the chalet windows but black sky, black lake, and black pine trees.

Percy settled down on the hearth rug and was moistly licking his fur in the warmth of the waning fire when a sound in the top of the pines made him pause with his tongue extended. It was like the moaning of the upper branches that gave warning of a storm, yet his whiskers told him this had nothing to do with weather. As he peered at the black windows a presence came through the glass. It came gently and soundlessly. A gust of chilled air reached Percy's damp fur.

The presence that had entered the chalet began to utter a low, painful lament, swirling all the while in a formless mass. Then, as Percy watched with interest, it took shape—a beefy human shape.

Apparitions were nothing new to Percy. As a young cat in England he had once tried to rub his back against some ghostly ankles and had found nothing there. This one was larger and rougher than the silver tabby had ever seen. As it became more clearly defined he observed a figure with a beard and a fuzzy cap, a burly jacket, and breeches stuffed into heavy boots. *Click-click-click* went the boots on the polished wood floor.

"Holy Mackinaw!" said a hollow, reverberating voice. "What kind of a shanty would this be?" The apparition looked in wonder at the luxurious hearth rug, the brass ornaments on the fieldstone chimney breast, the glass-topped coffee table with half-finished jigsaw puzzle.

Percy settled down comfortably to watch, tucking his legs under his body for warmth. A musty dampness pervaded the room. *Click-click-click* again. He turned his head to see another figure materializing behind him. Though dressed in the same rough clothing, it was smaller than the first and beardless, and it had a rope of hair hanging down its back.

"Pigtail Beebe!" roared the first apparition in a harsh voice without substance. It was a sound that only a cat could hear.

"I'm haywire if it ain't Morgan Black!" exclaimed the other in the same kind of thundering whisper. The two loggers stood staring at each other with legs braced wide apart and arms hanging loose. "I got a thirst fit to drain a swamp," Pigtail complained.

"Me, I got a head as big as an ox," said Morgan, groaning and touching his temples.

"Likely we was both oiled up when we got sluiced. How'd you get yours, you orie-eyed ol' coot?"

"A jumped-up brawl in the Red Keg Saloon." Morgan sat down wearily on the pine woodbox, removing his head and resting it on his lap, the better to massage his temples.

Pigtail said with a ghostly chuckle: "They got me on the Sawdust Flats. I'd had me a few drinks of Eagle Sweat and was on the way to Sadie Lou's to get m'teeth fixed, as the sayin' goes, when along came this bandy-legged Blue Noser, and I give him a squirt o' B&L Black right in the eye. 'Fore I knowed it, seven o' them Blue Nosers come at me. When they got through puttin' their boots to m'hide, I had the best case o' smallpox you ever did see. . . . Never *did* get to Sadie Lou's."

"That was in '61," said Morgan's head noiselessly. "Good drive on the river that spring."

"An' I was a catty man on the logs. I could ride a soap bubble to shore, I could."

"Still braggin'."

Pigtail sat down cautiously in Cornelius's deep-cushioned leather chair. "Holy Mackinaw! This shanty is sure-thing candyside!" The logger began to sing, in an eerie whine. "Oh, our logs was piled up mountain high, and our cots was on the snow . . . in that godforsaken countree-e-e of Michigan-eye-o!"

"Pipe down," said Morgan. "My head's aimin' to go off like dynamite."

"You think you're bad off? I got a thirst that'd dry up the Tittabawassee River. I could chaw an ear off the tin-plated fool what called us back! Why couldn't they leave us be?"

Morgan carefully fitted his head back on his shoulders. "It's nigh to daylight. We'll be goin' soon."

"No sense goin' without leavin' a sign," said Pigtail. "I'm feelin' stakey. Yahow!" he yelled in a ghostly facsimile of a logger's howl as he upended the coffee table and pulled the needles out of Margaret's knitting. Percy cringed in horror.

Then the logger began to swagger around the room. *Click-click-click* went his calks, although they left no mark on the polished wood floor. "What's this jigamaree?" he said, as he pushed the seven-layer torte off the bar. It landed on the floorboards with a sickening splash. "Yahow-w-w!" There was a distant echo as a rooster at one of the inland farms announced the break of day.

"Pipe down, you furriner!" Morgan warned, getting up from the woodbox with clenched fists. "You aimin' to split m'head open? If I could get holt o' you, I'd—"

"Hit the gut-hammer!" Pigtail sang out. "It's daylight in the swamp!"

Morgan Black lunged at him, and the two figures blended in a hazy blur.

"Da-a-aylight in the swamp!" was the last fading cry Percy heard as the cock crowed again. The blur was melting around the edges. It wilted and shrank until nothing was left but a puddle on the polished wood floor. Then all was quiet except for the swish of waves on the shore and the first waking peeps of the sandpipers.

Thankful that the raucous visitors had gone, Percy curled on the hearth rug with one foreleg thrown over his ears and slept. He was waked by a voice bellowing in consternation.

"It's a rotten shame!" Bill Diddleton roared, pacing back and forth in his fishing clothes. "It's a filthy rotten shame!"

"I fail to understand it," Cornelius kept repeating. "He has never been guilty of any mischief of this sort."

"It took me three hours to make that cake—with eighteen eggs and seven kinds of booze!"

The disturbance brought the two women sleepily to the balcony railing.

"Look at my torte!" Bill shouted up at them. "That blasted cat knocked it on the floor."

Margaret groped her way downstairs. "I can't believe Percy would do such a thing. Where is he?" Percy—aghast at Bill's accusation—sensed it might be wise to disappear.

"There he goes!" Bill shouted. "Sneaky devil just ran under the couch."

Then Margaret cried out in shocked surprise. "Look at my knitting! He pulled the needles out! Percy, you are a *bad cat!*"

Percy laid his ears back in hopeless indignation, alone in the dark under the sofa.

"It is quite unlike him," said Cornelius. "I fail to understand what could have prompted such . . . Margaret! My jigsaw puzzle has been swept off the table! That cat must have gone berserk!"

Now Deedee was coming slowly downstairs. "Do you know the floor's all wet? There's a big puddle right in the middle of the room."

"I can guess what that is!" said Bill, looking cynical and vindictive.

"Percy!" shouted Margaret and Cornelius in unison. "What-have-you-done?"

Recoiling at the unjust accusation, Percy shrank into his smallest size. He was a fastidious cat who observed the formalities of the litterbox with never a lapse.

Margaret circled the puddle. "Somehow I can't believe that Percy would do such a thing."

"Who else would leave a puddle on the floor?" said Bill with a cutting edge to his voice. "A ghost?"

"Ghosts!" cried Deedee. "I knew it! It was that crazy stunt of yours, Bill!" She peered into an oversize brandy snifter on the bar. "Where's-my-diamond-ring? I put it in this big glass thing when I helped Margaret in the kitchen last night. Oh, Bill, something horrible happened here. I feel all cold and clammy, and I can smell something weird and musty. Let's go home. Please!"

Bill stood there scratching his right ankle with his left foot. "We'd better get back to the city, folks, before she cracks up."

"Let me prepare breakfast," Margaret said. "Then we'll all feel better."

"I don't want breakfast," Deedee wailed in misery. "I just want to go home. I've got some kind of rash on my ankles, and it's driving me nuts!" She displayed some streaks of white blisters.

"That's ivy poisoning, kiddo," Bill said. "I think I've got the same thing."

"It couldn't be," Margaret protested. "We've never seen any poison ivy at the cemetery!"

The Diddletons packed hastily and drove away from Big Pine Lake before the sun had risen above the treetops.

Percy, his pride wounded, refused to leave his refuge under the sofa, even to eat breakfast, and for some time following the weekend of the big puddle he remained cool toward Cornelius and Margaret. Although they quickly forgave him for all the untoward happenings, he found scant comfort in forgiveness for sins he had not committed. The incident was related to a new houseful of guests each weekend, and the blow to Percy's reputation caused him deep suffering.

At the end of the season Deedee's diamond ring was found behind the pine woodbox. The Diddletons paid no more visits to the chalet, however. Nor did Cornelius and Margaret return to the loggers' graves; almost over-night the entire cemetery became choked with poisonous vines.

"Very strange," said Margaret. "We've never before seen any poison ivy there!"

"I fail to understand it," said Cornelius.

The Cats of Ulthar

(1920)

H. P. Lovecraft (1890–1937)

The works of Howard Philips Lovecraft originally appeared in pulp magazines or amateur presses. He remained virtually unknown until well after his death. It was through the persistent efforts of his friends and admirers that he finally received a wider and ever-growing audience. Two fellow-writers—one of whom was August Derleth—tried to convince publishers to reprint posthumous collections of Lovecraft's work. Their efforts were unsuccessful, so they formed Arkham House Publishers and released the books themselves. He is now one of the best-known authors of horror and supernatural fiction. He was the creator of the "Cthulhu Mythos," a collection of stories which are widely imitated and supplemented. His most famous stories are "The Call of Cthulhu" and "The Dunwich Horror." Many of his stories have been made into movies. His works are now continually in print and have been anthologized numerous times. This story was originally accepted for publication in *Weird Tales* in 1923.

It is said that in Ulthar, which lies beyond the river Skai, no man may kill a cat; and this I can verily believe as I gaze upon him who sitteth purring before the fire. For the cat is cryptic, and close to strange things which men cannot see. He is the soul of antique Aegyptus, and bearer of tales from forgotten cities in Meroe and Ophir.

He is the kin of the jungle's lords, and heir to the secrets of hoary and sinister Africa. The Sphinx is his cousin, and he speaks her language; but he is more ancient than the Sphinx, and remembers that which she hath forgotten.

In Ulthar, before ever the burgesses forbade the killing of cats, there dwelt an old cotter and his wife who delighted to trap and slay the cats of their neighbours. Why they did this I know not; save that many hate the voice of the cat in the night, and take it ill that cats should run stealthily about yards and gardens at twilight. But whatever the reason, this old man and woman took pleasure in trapping and slaying every cat which came near to their hovel; and from some of the sounds heard after dark, many villagers fancied that the manner of slaying was exceedingly peculiar. But the villagers did not discuss such things with the old man and his wife; because of the habitual expression on the withered faces of the two, and because their cottage was so small and so darkly hidden under spreading oaks at the back of a neglected yard. In truth, much as the owners of cats hated these odd folk, they feared them more; and instead of berating them as brutal assassins, merely took care that no cherished pet or mouser should stray toward the remote hovel under the dark trees. When through some unavoidable oversight a cat was missed, and sounds heard after dark, the loser would lament impotently; or console himself by thanking Fate that it was not one of his children who had thus vanished. For the people of Ulthar were simple, and knew not whence it is all cats first came.

One day a caravan of strange wanderers from the South entered the narrow cobbled streets of Ulthar. Dark wanderers they were, and unlike the other roving folk who passed through the village twice every year. In the market-place they told fortunes for silver, and bought gay beads from the merchants. What was the land of these wanderers none could tell; but it was seen that they were given to strange prayers, and that they had painted on the sides of their wagons strange figures with human bodies and the heads of cats, hawks, rams, and lions. And the leader of the caravan wore a head-dress with two horns and a curious disc betwixt the horns.

There was in this singular caravan a little boy with no father or mother, but only a tiny black kitten to cherish. The plague had not been kind to him, yet had left him this small furry thing to mitigate his sorrow; and when one is very young, one can find great relief in the lively antics of a black kitten. So the boy whom the dark people called Menes smiled more often than he wept as he sat playing with his graceful kitten on the steps of an oddly painted wagon.

On the third morning of the wanderers' stay in Ulthar, Menes could not find his kitten; and as he sobbed aloud in the market-place certain villagers told him of the old man and his wife, and of sounds heard in the night. And when he heard these things his sobbing gave place to meditation, and finally to prayer. He stretched out his arms toward the sun and prayed in a tongue no villager could understand; though indeed the villagers did not try very hard to understand, since their attention was mostly taken up by the sky and the odd shapes the clouds were assuming. It was very peculiar, but as the little boy uttered his petition there seemed to form overhead the shadowy, nebulous figures of exotic things; of hybrid creatures crowned with horn-flanked discs. Nature is full of such illusions to impress the imaginative.

That night the wanderers left Ulthar, and were never seen again. And the householders were troubled when they noticed that in all the village there was not a cat to be found. From each hearth the familiar cat had vanished; cats large and small, black, grey, striped, yellow, and white. Old Kranon, the burgomaster, swore that the dark folk had taken the cats away in revenge for the killing of Menes' kitten; and cursed the caravan and the little boy. But Nith, the lean notary, declared that the old cotter and his wife were more likely persons to suspect; for their hatred of cats was notorious and increasingly bold. Still, no one durst complain to the sinister couple; even when little Atal, the innkeeper's son, vowed that he had at twilight seen all the cats of Ulthar in that accursed yard under the trees, pacing very slowly and solemnly in a circle around the cottage, two abreast, as if in performance of some unheard-of rite of beasts. The villagers did not know how much to believe from so small a boy; and though they feared that the evil pair had charmed the cats to their death, they preferred not to chide the old cotter till they met him outside his dark and repellent yard.

So Ulthar went to sleep in vain anger; and when the people awaked at dawn-behold! every cat was back at his accustomed hearth! Large and small, black, grey, striped, yellow, and white, none was missing. Very sleek and fat did the cats appear, and sonorous with purring content. The citizens talked with one another of the affair, and marvelled not a little. Old Kranon again insisted that it was the dark folk who had taken them, since cats did not return alive from the cottage of the ancient man and his wife. But all agreed on one thing: that the refusal of all the cats to eat their portions of meat or drink their saucers of milk was exceedingly curious. And for two whole days the sleek, lazy cats of Ulthar would touch no food, but only doze by the fire or in the sun.

It was fully a week before the villagers noticed that no lights were appearing at dusk in the windows of the cottage under the trees. Then the lean Nith remarked that no one had seen the old man or his wife since the night the cats were away. In another week the burgomaster decided to overcome his fears and call at the strangely silent dwelling as a matter of duty, though in so doing he was careful to take with him Shang the blacksmith and Thul the cutter of stone as witnesses. And when they had broken down the frail door they found only this: two cleanly picked human skeletons on the earthen floor, and a number of singular beetles crawling in the shadowy corners.

There was subsequently much talk among the burgesses of Ulthar. Zath, the coroner, disputed at length with Nith, the lean notary; and Kranon and Shang and Thul were overwhelmed with questions. Even little Atal, the innkeeper's son, was closely questioned and given a sweetmeat as reward. They talked of the old cotter and his wife, of the caravan of dark wanderers, of small Menes and his black kitten, of the prayer of Menes and of the sky during that prayer, of the doings of the cats on the night the caravan left, and of what was later found in the cottage under the dark trees in the repellent yard.

And in the end the burgesses passed that remarkable law which is told of by traders in Hatheg and discussed by travellers in Nir; namely, that in Ulthar no man may kill a cat.

A Case of Possession by a Cat

(1881)

From the

Shanghai *North-China Herald*
(November 1, 1881)

The *North-China Herald and Supreme Court & Consular Gazette* was Shanghai's English-language newspaper. The *Shên-pao* was a Chinese-language newspaper.

The *Shên-pao* contains a characteristic witch-story, curiously illustrative of a certain form of superstition, apparently of Buddhist origin, which enters widely into the popular folk-lore of the country. It is very generally believed that if any person kills an animal, from wantonness or cruelty, its soul will return and take possession of the murderer's body until his guilt is expiated. An instance of this is said to have occurred recently at Yangchow. There were a man and his wife, who had a pet cat, the mother of three kittens. Like most other domestic animals, however, the feline family had somewhat thievish propensities, and were constantly stealing sundry tid-bits and delicacies that the servant-girl had put by for her own private eating. At last she got so exasperated that, after a course of systematically ill-using the cats, she killed them, one after another, in different ways. But in a short time she was taken violently ill, mewing and scratching like a cat, and displaying all the symptoms of rabies. Her mistress, suspecting the true cause of the girl's attack, thereupon apostrophized the dead cat, demanding for what reason it had come to haunt her body. The cat, speaking through the girl's mouth, then recounted the ill-treatment it had received from her during its life, and told her how its little ones had been killed before its eyes. One had been drowned, another worried by a dog, and a third burnt. Last of all the cat herself had been killed, and its spirit had now come to inflict its fearful visitation upon the murderess. All this, be it understood, was said by the girl herself, in the character of the cat, between her paroxysms. At last, however, justice was satisfied, and the girl died in convulsions at the feet of her mistress.—It is scarcely necessary to add that stories of this description are firmly believed in by the Chinese, who are after all no more superstitious than Europeans themselves were at a comparatively recent date. Indeed many similar survivals might without much difficulty be found at the present day among the peasantry of several countries in the West.

Catnip

(1948)

Robert Bloch (born 1917)

Robert Bloch is one of America's pre-eminent masters of the horror and fantasy tale. His association with these fields is a long and very prolific one, which began when he was the teenage protégé of H. P. Lovecraft. One of his most famous contributions to the genre, *Psycho*, has surely influenced more than one generation of film goers and which of us, having viewed Hitchcock's masterly treatment of the novel, hasn't at least once recalled the film uncomfortably while showering in a presumably empty house? Since 1934 he has written hundreds, if not thousands, of books, stories, and screenplays. His works include *Out of the Mouths of Graves*, *Mysteries of the Worm*, *The House that Dripped Blood*, *Asylum*, *Psycho II*, *American Gothic*, and *Twilight Zone—The Movie*. His early works were heavily Lovecraftian in tone and style, though in later years he developed a deft handling of the basic absurdity in human nature which is clearly illustrated in the story "Catnip." This story originally appeared in the March 1948 issue of *Weird Tales*. Bloch currently lives in California.

Ronnie Shires stood before the mirror and slicked back his hair. He straightened his new sweater and stuck out his chest. Sharp! Had to watch the way he looked, with graduation only a few weeks away and that election for class president coming up. If he could get to be president then, next year in high school he'd be a real wheel. Go out for second team or something. But he had to watch the angles—

"Ronnie! Better hurry or you'll be late." Ma came out of the kitchen, carrying his lunch. Ronnie wiped the grin off his face. She walked up behind him and put her arms around his waist.

"Hon, I only wish your father were here to see you—"

Ronnie wriggled free. "Yeah, sure. Say, Ma."

"Yes?"

"How's about some loot, huh? I got to get some things today."

"Well, I suppose. But try to make it last, son. This graduation costs a lot of money, seems to me."

"I'll pay you back some day." He watched her as she fumbled in her apron pocket and produced a wadded-up dollar bill.

"Thanks. See you." He picked up his lunch and ran outside. He walked along, smiling and whistling, knowing Ma was watching him from the window. She was always watching him, and it was a real drag.

Then he turned the corner, halted under a tree, and fished out a cigarette. He lit it and sauntered slowly across the street, puffing deeply. Out of the corner of his eye he watched the Ogden house just ahead.

Sure enough, the front screen door banged and Marvin Ogden came down the steps. Marvin was fifteen, one year older than Ronnie, but smaller and skinnier. He wore glasses and stuttered when he got excited, but he was valedictorian of the graduating class.

Ronnie came up behind him, walking fast.

"Hello, Snot-face!"

Marvin wheeled. He avoided Ronnie's glare, but smiled weakly at the pavement.

"I said hello, Snot-face! What's the matter, don't you know your own name, jerk?"

"Hello—Ronnie."

"How's old Snot-face today?"

"Aw, gee, Ronnie. Why do you have to talk like that? I never did anything to you, did I?"

Ronnie spit in the direction of Marvin's shoes. "I'd like to see you just try doing something to me, you four-eyed little—"

Marvin began to walk away, but Ronnie kept pace.

"Slow down, jag. I wanna talk to you."

"Wh-what is it, Ronnie? I don't want to be late."

"Shut your yap."

"But—"

"Listen, you. What was the big idea in History exam yesterday when you pulled your paper away?"

"You know, Ronnie. You aren't supposed to copy somebody else's answers."

"You trying to tell me what to do, square?"

"N-no. I mean, I only want to keep you out of trouble. What if Miss Sanders found out, and you want to be elected class president? Why, if anybody knew—"

Ronnie put his hand on Marvin's shoulder. He smiled. "You wouldn't ever tell her about it, would you, Snot-face?" he murmured.

"Of course not! Cross my heart!"

Ronnie continued to smile. He dug his fingers into Marvin's shoulder. With his other hand he swept Marvin's books to the ground. As Marvin bent forward to pick them up, he kicked Marvin as hard as he could, bringing his knee up fast. Marvin sprawled on the sidewalk. He began to cry. Ronnie watched him as he attempted to rise.

"This is just a sample of what you got coming if you squeal," he said. He stepped on the fingers of Marvin's left hand. "Creep!"

Marvin's sniveling faded from his ears as he turned the corner at the end of the block. Mary June was waiting for him under the trees. He came up behind her and slapped her, hard.

"Hello, you!" he said.

Mary June jumped about a foot, her curls bouncing on her shoulders. Then she turned and saw who it was.

"Oh, Ronnie! You oughtn't to—"

"Shut up. I'm in a hurry. Can't be late the day before election. You lining up the chicks?"

"Sure, Ronnie. You know, I promised. I had Ellen and Vicky over at the house last night and they said they'd vote for you for sure. All the girls are gonna vote for you."

"Well, they better." Ronnie threw his cigarette butt against a rose-bush in the Elsners' yard.

"Ronnie—you be careful—want to start a fire?"

"Quit bossing me." He scowled.

"I'm not trying to boss you, Ronnie. Only—"

"Aw, you make me sick!" He quickened his pace, and the girl bit her lip as she endeavored to keep step with him. "Ronnie, wait for me!"

"Wait for me!" he mocked her. "What's the matter, you afraid you'll get lost or something?"

"No. *You* know. I don't like to pass that old Mrs. Mingle's place. She always stares at me and makes faces."

"She's nuts!"

"I'm scared of her, Ronnie. Aren't you?"

"Me scared of that old bat? She can go take a flying leap!"

"Don't talk so loud, she'll hear you."

"Who cares?"

Ronnie marched boldly past the tree-shadowed cottage behind the rusted iron fence. He stared insolently at the girl, who made herself small against his shoulder, eyes averted from the ramshackle edifice. He deliberately slackened his pace as they passed the cottage, with its boarded-up windows, screened-in porch and general air of withdrawal from the world.

Mrs. Mingle herself was not in evidence today. Usually she could be seen in the weed-infested garden at the side of the cottage; a tiny, dried-up old woman, bending over her vines and plants, mumbling incessantly to herself or to the raddled black tomcat which served as her constant companion.

"Old prune-face ain't around!" Ronnie observed, loudly. "Must be off someplace on her broomstick."

"Ronnie—please!"

"Who cares?" Ronnie pulled Mary June's curls. "You dames are scared of everything, ain't you?"

"*Aren't*, Ronnie."

"Don't tell *me* how to talk!" Ronnie's gaze shifted to the silent house, huddled in the shadows. A segment of shadow at the side of the cottage seemed to be moving. A black blur detached itself from the end of the porch. Ronnie recognized Mrs. Mingle's cat. It minced down the path towards the gate.

Quickly, Ronnie stooped and found a rock. He grasped it, rose, aimed, and hurled the missile in one continuous movement.

The cat hissed, then squawled in pain as the rock grazed its ribs.

"Oh, Ronnie!"

"Come on, let's run before she sees us!"

They flew down the street. The school bell drowned out the cat-yowl.

"Here we go," said Ronnie. "You do my homework for me? Good. Give it here at once."

He snatched the papers from Mary June's hand and sprinted ahead. The girl stood watching him, smiling her admiration. From behind the fence the cat watched, too, and licked its jaws.

It happened that afternoon, after school. Ronnie and Joe Gordan and Seymour Higgins were futzing around with a baseball and he was talking about the outfit Ma promised to buy him this summer if the dressmaking business picked up. Only he made it sound as if he was getting the outfit for sure, and that they could all use the mask and mitt. It didn't hurt to build it up a little, with election tomorrow. He had to stand in good with the whole gang.

He knew if he hung around the school yard much longer, Mary June would come out and want him to walk her home. He was sick of her. Oh, she was all right for homework and such stuff, but these guys would just laugh at him if he went off with a dame.

So he said how about going down the street to in front of the pool hall and maybe hang around to see if somebody would shoot a game? He'd pay. Besides, they could smoke.

Ronnie knew that these guys didn't smoke, but it sounded cool and that's what he wanted. They all followed him down the street, pounding their cleats on the sidewalk. It made a lot of noise, because everything was so quiet.

All Ronnie could hear was the cat. They were passing Mrs. Mingle's and there was this cat, rolling around in the garden on its back and on its stomach, playing with some kind of ball. It purred and meeowed and whined.

"Look!" yelled Joe Gordan. "Dizzy cat's havin' a fit 'r something, huh?"

"Lice," said Ronnie. "Damned mangy old thing's fulla lice and fleas and stuff. I socked it a good one this morning!"

"Ya did?"

"Sure. With a rock. This big, too." He made a watermelon with his hands.

"Weren't you afraid of old lady Mingle?"

"Afraid? Why, that dried-up old—"

"Catnip," said Seymour Higgins. "That's what he's got. Ball of catnip. Old Mingle buys it for him. My old man says she buys everything for that cat; special food and sardines. Treats it like a baby. Ever see them walk down the street together?"

"Catnip, huh?" Joe peered through the fence. "Wonder why they like it so much. Gets 'em wild, doesn't it? Cat's'll do anything for catnip."

The cat squealed, sniffing and clawing at the ball. Ronnie scowled at it. "I hate cats. Somebody oughta drowned that damn thing."

"Better not let Mrs. Mingle hear you talk like that," Seymour cautioned. "She'll put the evil eye on you."

"Bull!"

"Well, she grows them herbs and stuff and my old lady says—"

"Bull!"

"All right. But I wouldn't go monkeying around her or her old cat, either."

"I'll show you."

Before he knew it, Ronnie was opening the gate. He advanced towards the black tomcat as the boys gaped.

The cat crouched over the catnip, ears flattened against a velveteen skull. Ronnie hesitated a moment, gauging the glitter of claws, the glare of agate eyes. But the gang was watching—

"Scat!" he shouted. He advanced, waving his arms. The cat sidled backwards. Ronnie feinted with his hand and scooped up the catnip ball.

"See? I got it, you guys. I got—"

"Put that down!"

He didn't see the door open. He didn't see her walk down the steps. But suddenly she was there. Leaning on her cane, wearing a black dress that fitted tightly over her tiny frame, she seemed hardly any bigger than the cat which crouched at her side. Her hair was gray and wrinkled and dead, her face was grey and wrinkled and dead, but her eyes—

They were agate eyes, like the cat's. They glowed. And when she talked, she spit the way the cat did.

"Put that down, young man!"

Ronnie began to shake. It was only a chill, everybody gets chills now and then, and could he help it if he shook so hard the catnip just fell out of his hand?

He wasn't scared. He had to show the gang he wasn't scared of this skinny little dried-up old woman. It was hard to breathe, he was shaking so, but he managed. He filled his lungs and opened his mouth.

"You—you old witch!" he yelled.

The agate eyes widened. They were bigger than she was. All he could see were the eyes. Witch eyes. Now that he had said it, he knew it was true. Witch. She was a witch.

"You insolent puppy. I've a good mind to cut out your lying tongue!"

Geez, she wasn't kidding!

Now she was coming closer, and the cat was inching up on him, and then she raised the cane in the air, she was going to hit him, the witch was after him, oh Ma, no, don't oh—

Ronnie ran.

Could he help it? Geez, the guys ran too. They'd run before he did, even. He had to run, the old bat was crazy, anybody could see that. Besides, if he'd stayed she'd of tried to hit him and maybe he'd let her have it. He was only trying to keep out of trouble. That was all.

Ronnie told it to himself over and over at supper time. But that didn't do any good, telling it to himself. It was the guys he had to tell it to, and fast. He had to explain it before election tomorrow—

"Ronnie. What's the matter? You sick?"

"No, Ma."

"Then why don't you answer a person? I declare, you haven't said ten words since you came in the house. And you aren't eating your supper."

"Not hungry."

"Something bothering you, son?"

"No. Leave me alone."

"It's that election tomorrow, isn't it?"

"Leave me alone." Ronnie rose. "I'm goin' out."

"Ronnie!"

"I got to see Joe. Important."

"Back by nine, remember."

"Yeah. Sure."

He went outside. The night was cool. Windy for this time of year. Ronnie shivered a little as he turned the corner. Maybe a cigarette—

He lit a match and a shower of sparks spiraled to the sky. Ronnie began to walk, puffing nervously. He had to see Joe and the others and explain. Yeah, right now, too. If they told anybody else—

It was dark. The light on the corner was out, and the Ogdens weren't home. That made it darker, because Mrs. Mingle never showed a light in her cottage.

Mrs. Mingle. Her cottage was up ahead. He'd better cross the street.

What was the matter with him? Was he getting chicken-guts? Afraid of that damned old woman, that old witch! He puffed, gulped, expanded his chest. Just let her try anything. Just let her be hiding under the trees waiting to grab out at him with her big claws and hiss —what was he talking about, anyway? That was the cat. Nuts to her cat, and her too. He'd show them!

Ronnie walked past the dark shadow where Mrs. Mingle dwelt. He whistled defiance, and emphasized it by shooting his cigarette butt across the fence. Sparks flew and were swallowed by the mouth of the night.

Ronnie paused and peered over the fence. Everything was black and still. There was nothing to be afraid of. Everything was black—

Everything except that flicker. It came from up the path, under the porch. He could see the porch now because there was a light. Not a steady light; a wavering light. Like a fire. A fire—where his cigarette had landed! The cottage was beginning to burn!

Ronnie gulped and clung to the fence. Yes, it was on fire all right. Mrs. Mingle would come out and the firemen would come and they'd find the butt and see him and then—

He fled down the street. The wind cat howled behind him, the wind that fanned the flames that burned the cottage—

Ma was in bed. He managed to slow down and walk softly as he slipped into the house, up the stairs. He undressed in the dark and sought the white womb between the bed sheets. When he got the covers over his head he had another chill. Lying there, trembling, not daring to look out of the window and see the flare from the other side of the block, Ronnie's teeth chattered. He knew he was going to pass out in a minute.

Then he heard the screaming from far away. Fire engines. Some-body had called them. He needn't worry now. Why should the sound frighten him? It was only a siren, it wasn't Mrs. Mingle screaming, it couldn't be. She was all right. He was all right. Nobody knew . . .

Ronnie fell asleep with the wind and the siren wailing in his ears. His slumber was deep and only once was there an interruption. That was along towards morning, when he thought he heard a noise at the window. It was a scraping sound. The wind, of course. And it must have been the wind, too, that sobbed and whined and whimpered beneath the windowsill at dawn. It was only Ronnie's imagination, Ronnie's conscience, that transformed the sound into the wailing of a cat. . . .

"Ronnie!"

It wasn't the wind, it wasn't a cat. Ma was calling him.

"Ronnie! Oh, Ronnie!"

He opened his eyes, shielding them from the sun shafts.

"I declare, you might answer a person." He heard her grumbling to herself downstairs. Then she called again.

"Ronnie!"

"I'm coming, Ma."

He got out of bed, went to the bathroom, and dressed. She was waiting for him in the kitchen.

"Land sakes, you sure slept sound last night. Didn't you hear the fire engines?"

Ronnie dropped a slice of toast. "What engines?"

Ma's voice rose. "Don't you know? Why boy, it was just awful— Mrs. Mingle's cottage burned down."

"Yeah?" He had trouble picking up the toast again.

"The poor old lady—just think of it—trapped in there—"

He had to shut her up. He couldn't stand what was coming next. But what could he say, how could he stop her?

"Burned alive. The whole place was on fire when they got there. The Ogdens saw it when they came home and Mr. Ogden called the firemen, but it was too late. When I think of that old lady it just makes me—"

Without a word, Ronnie rose from the table and left the room. He didn't wait for his lunch. He didn't bother to examine himself in the mirror. He went outside, before he cried, or screamed, or hauled off and hit Ma in the puss.

The puss—

It was waiting for him on the front walk. The black bundle with the agate eyes. The cat.

Mrs. Mingle's cat, waiting for him to come out. Ronnie took a deep breath before he opened the gate. The cat didn't make a sound, didn't stir. It just hunched up on the sidewalk and stared at him.

He watched it for a moment, then cast about for a stick. There was a hunk of lath near the porch. He picked it up and swung it. Then he opened the gate.

"Scat!" he said.

The cat retreated. Ronnie walked away. The cat moved after him. Ronnie wheeled, brandishing the stick.

"Scram before I let you have it!"

The cat stood still.

Ronnie stared at it. Why hadn't the damn thing burned up in the fire? And what was it doing here?

He gripped the lath. It felt good between his fingers, splinters and all. Just let that mangy tom cat start anything—

He walked along, not looking back. What was the matter with him? Suppose the cat did follow him. It couldn't hurt him any. Neither could old Mingle. She was dead. The dirty witch. Talking about cutting his tongue out. Well, she got what was coming to her, all right. Too bad her scroungy cat was still around. If it didn't watch out, he'd fix it, too. He should worry now.

Nobody was going to find out about that cigarette. Mrs. Mingle was dead. He ought to be glad, everything was all right, sure, he felt great.

The shadow followed him down the street.

"Get out of here!"

Ronnie turned and heaved the lath at the cat. It hissed. Ronnie heard the wind hiss, heard his cigarette butt hiss, heard Mrs. Mingle hiss.

He began to run. The cat ran after him.

"Hey, Ronnie!"

Marvin Ogden was calling him. He couldn't stop now, not even to hit the punk. He ran on. The cat kept pace.

Then he was winded and he slowed down. It was just in time, too.

Up ahead was a crowd of kids, standing on the sidewalk in front of a heap of charred, smoking boards.

They were looking at Mingle's cottage—

Ronnie closed his eyes and darted back up the street. The cat followed.

He had to get rid of it before he went to school. What if people saw him with her cat? Maybe they'd start to talk. He had to get rid of it—

Ronnie ran clear down to Sinclair Street. The cat was right behind him. On the corner he picked up a stone and let it fly. The cat dodged. Then it sat down on the sidewalk and looked at him. Just looked.

Ronnie couldn't take his eyes off the cat. It stared so. Mrs. Mingle had stared too. But she was dead. And this was only a cat. A cat he had to get away from, fast.

The streetcar came down Sinclair Street. Ronnie found a dime in his pocket and boarded the car. The cat didn't move. He stood on the platform as the car pulled away and looked back at the cat. It just sat there.

Ronnie rode around the loop, then transferred to the Hollis Avenue bus. It brought him over to the school, ten minutes late. He got off and started to hurry across the street.

A shadow crossed the entrance to the building.

Ronnie saw the cat. It squatted there, waiting.

He ran.

That's all Ronnie remembered of the rest of the morning. He ran. He ran, and the cat followed. He couldn't go to school, he couldn't be there for the election, he couldn't get rid of the cat. He ran.

Up and down the streets, back and forth, all over the whole neighborhood; stopping and dodging and throwing stones and swearing and panting and sweating. But always the running, and always the cat right behind him. Once it started to chase him and before he knew it he was heading straight for the place where the burned smell filled the air, straight for the ruins of Mrs. Mingle's cottage. The cat wanted him to go there, wanted him to see—

Ronnie began to cry. He sobbed and panted all the way home. The cat didn't make a sound. It followed him. All right, let it. He'd fix it. He'd tell Ma. Ma would get rid of it for him. Ma.

"Ma!"

He yelled as he ran up the steps.

No answer. She was out. Marketing.

And the cat crept up the steps behind him.

Ronnie slammed the door, locked it. Ma had her key. He was safe now. Safe at home. Safe in bed—he wanted to go to bed and pull the covers over his head, wait for Ma to come and make everything all right.

There was a scratching at the door.

"Ma!" His scream echoed through the empty house.

He ran upstairs. The scratching died away.

And then he heard the footsteps on the porch, the slow footsteps; he heard the rattling and turning of the doorknob. It was old lady Mingle, coming from the grave. It was the witch, coming to get him. It was—

"Ma!"

"Ronnie, what's the matter? What you doing home from school?"

He heard her. It was all right. Just in time, Ronnie closed his mouth. He couldn't tell her about the cat. He mustn't ever tell her. Then everything would come out. He had to be careful what he said.

"I got sick to my stomach," he said. "Miss Sanders said I should come home and lay down."

Then Ma was up the stairs, helping him undress, asking should she get the doctor, fussing over him and putting him to bed. And he could cry and she didn't know it wasn't from a gut ache. What she didn't know wouldn't hurt her. It was all right.

Yes, it was all right now and he was in bed. Ma brought him some soup for lunch. He wanted to ask her about the cat, but he didn't dare. Besides, he couldn't hear it scratching. Must have run away when Ma came home.

Ronnie lay in bed and dozed as the afternoon shadows ran in long black ribbons across the bedroom floor. He smiled to himself. What a sucker he was! Afraid of a cat. Maybe there wasn't even a cat—all in his mind. Dope!

"Ronnie—you all right?" Ma called up from the foot of the stairs.

"Yes, Ma. I feel lots better."

Sure, he felt better. He could get up now and eat supper if he wanted. In just a minute he'd put his clothes on and go downstairs. He started to push the sheets off. It was dark in the room, now. Just about suppertime—

Then Ronnie heard it. A scratching. A scurrying. From the hall? No. It couldn't be the hall. Then where?

The window. It was open. And the scratching came from the ledge outside. He had to close it, fast. Ronnie jumped out of bed, barking his shin against a chair as he groped through the dusk. Then he was at the window, slamming it down, tight.

He heard the scratching.

And it came from *inside the room!*

Ronnie hurled himself upon the bed, clawing the covers up to his chin. His eyes bulged against the darkness.

Where was it?

He saw nothing but shadows. Which shadow moved?

Where was it?

Why didn't it yowl so he could locate it? Why didn't it make a noise? Yes, and why was it here? Why did it follow him? What was it trying to do to him?

Ronnie didn't know. All he knew was that he lay in bed, waiting, thinking of Mrs. Mingle and her cat and how she was a witch and died because he'd killed her. Or had he killed her? He was all mixed up, he couldn't remember, he didn't even know what was real and what wasn't real any more. He couldn't tell which shadow would move next.

And then he could.

The round shadow was moving. The round black ball was inching across the floor from beneath the window. It was the cat, all right, because shadows don't have claws that scrape. Shadows don't leap through the air and perch on the bedpost, grinning at you with yellow eyes and yellow teeth—grinning the way Mrs. Mingle grinned.

The cat was big. Its eyes were big. Its teeth were big, too.

Ronnie opened his mouth to scream.

Then the shadow was sailing through the air, springing at his face, at his open mouth. The claws fastened in his cheeks, forcing his jaws apart, and the head dipped down—

Far away, under the pain, someone was calling.

"Ronnie! Oh, Ronnie! What's the matter with you?"

Everything was fire and he lashed out and suddenly the shadow went away and he was sitting bolt upright in bed. His mouth worked but no sound came out. Nothing came out except that gushing red wetness.

"Ronnie! Why don't you answer me?"

A guttural sound came from deep within Ronnie's throat, but no words. There would never be any words.

"Ronnie—what's the matter? Has the cat got your tongue?"

Cat in Glass

(1989)

Nancy Etchemendy (born 1952)

Nancy Etchemendy is the author of four novels for young adults: *The Watchers of Space* (1980), *Stranger from the Stars* (1983), *The Crystal City* (1985), and *Figgy's Wings* (1992). She has published numerous science fiction, fantasy, and horror stories in a variety of magazines and anthologies. She currently lives in Menlo Park, California, with her husband and son. "Cat in Glass" was originally published in the July 1989 issue of *The Magazine of Fantasy and Science Fiction*. Its chilling tone and horrific vision will ensure its future as a classic of horror fiction.

I was once a respectable woman. Oh yes, I know that's what they all say when they've reached a pass like mine: I was well educated, well traveled, had lovely children and a nice husband with a good financial mind. How can anyone have fallen so far, except one who deserved to anyway? I've had time aplenty to consider the matter, lying here eyeless in this fine hospital bed while the stench of my wounds increases. The matrons who guard my room are tight-lipped. But I heard one of them whisper yesterday, when she thought I was asleep, "Jesus, how could anyone do such a thing?" The answer to all these questions is the same. I have fallen so far, and I have done what I have done, to save us each and every one from the *Cat in Glass*.

184

My entanglement with the cat began fifty-two years ago, when my sister, Delia, was attacked by an animal. It happened on an otherwise ordinary spring afternoon. There were no witnesses. My father was still in his office at the college, and I was dawdling along on my way home from first grade at Chesly Girls' Day School, counting cracks in the sidewalk. Delia, younger than I by three years, was alone with Fiona, the Irish woman who kept house for us. Fiona had just gone outside for a moment to hang laundry. She came in to check on Delia, and discovered a scene of almost unbelievable carnage. Oddly, she had heard no screams.

As I ran up the steps and opened our door, I heard screams indeed. Not Delia's—for Delia had nothing left to scream with—but Fiona's, as she stood in the front room with her hands over her eyes. She couldn't bear the sight. Unfortunately, six-year-olds have no such compunction. I stared long and hard, sick and trembling, yet entranced.

From the shoulders up, Delia was no longer recognizable as a human being. Her throat had been shredded and her jaw ripped away. Most of her hair and scalp were gone. There were long, bloody furrows in the creamy skin of her arms and legs. The organdy pinafore in which Fiona had dressed her that morning was clotted with blood, and the blood was still coming. Some of the walls were even spattered with it where the animal, whatever it was, had worried her in its frenzy. Her fists and heels banged jerkily against the floor. Our pet dog, Freddy, lay beside her, also bloody, but quite limp. Freddy's neck was broken.

I remember slowly raising my head—I must have been in shock by then—and meeting the bottomless gaze of the glass cat that sat on the hearth. Our father, a professor of art history, was very proud of this sculpture, for reasons I did not understand until many years later. I only knew that it was valuable and we were not allowed to touch it. A chaotic feline travesty, it was not the sort of thing you would want to touch anyway. Though basically catlike in shape, it bristled with transparent threads and shards. There was something at once wild and vaguely human about its face. I had never liked it much, and Delia had always been downright frightened of it. On this day, as I looked up from my little sister's ruins, the cat seemed to glare at me with bright, terrifying satisfaction.

I had experienced, a year before, the thing every child fears most:

the death of my mother. It had given me a kind of desperate strength, for I thought, at the tender age of six, that I had survived the worst life had to offer. Now, as I returned the mad stare of the glass cat, it came to me that I was wrong. The world was a much more evil place than I had ever imagined, and nothing would ever be the same again.

Delia died officially in the hospital a short time later. After a cursory investigation, the police laid the blame on Freddy. I still have the newspaper clipping, yellow now, and held together with even yellower cellophane tape. "The family dog lay dead near the victim, blood smearing its muzzle and forepaws. Sergeant Morton theorizes that the dog, a pit bull terrier and member of a breed specifically developed for vicious fighting, turned killer and attacked its tragic young owner. He also suggests that the child, during the death struggle, flung the murderous beast away with enough strength to break its neck."

Even I, a little girl, knew that this "theory" was lame; the neck of a pit bull is an almost impossible thing to break, even by a large, determined man. And Freddy, in spite of his breeding, had always been gentle, even protective, with us. Simply stated, the police were mystified, and this was the closest thing to a rational explanation they could produce. As far as they were concerned, that was the end of the matter. In fact, it had only just begun.

I was shipped off to my Aunt Josie's house for several months. What Father did during this time, I never knew, though I now suspect he spent those months in a sanitarium. In the course of a year, he had lost first his wife and then his daughter. Delia's death alone was the kind of outrage that might permanently have unhinged a lesser man. But a child has no way of knowing such things. I was bitterly angry at him for going away. Aunt Josie, though kind and good-hearted, was a virtual stranger to me, and I felt deserted. I had nightmares in which the glass cat slunk out of its place by the hearth and prowled across the countryside. I would hear its hard claws ticking along the floor outside the room where I slept. At those times, half-awake and screaming in the dark, no one could have comforted me except Father.

When he did return, the strain of his suffering showed. His face was thin and weary, and his hair dusted with new gray, as if he had stood outside too long on a frosty night. On the afternoon of his arrival, he sat with me on Aunt Josie's sofa, stroking my cheek while I cuddled gladly, my anger at least temporarily forgotten in the joy of having him back.

His voice, when he spoke, was as tired as his face. "Well, my darling Amy, what do you suppose we should do now?"

"I don't know," I said. I assumed that, as always in the past, he had something entertaining in mind—that he would suggest it, and then we would do it.

He sighed. "Shall we go home?"

I went practically rigid with fear. "Is the cat still there?"

Father looked at me, frowning slightly. "Do we have a cat?"

I nodded. "The big glass one."

He blinked, then made the connection. "Oh, the Chelichev, you mean? Well . . . I suppose it's still there. I hope so, in fact."

I clung to him, scrambling halfway up his shoulders in my panic. I could not manage to speak. All that came out of my mouth was an erratic series of whimpers.

"Shhhh, shhhh," said Father. I hid my face in the starched white cloth of his shirt, and heard him whisper, as if to himself, "How can a glass cat frighten a child who's seen the things you've seen?"

"I hate him! He's glad Delia died. And now he wants to get *me*."

Father hugged me fiercely. "You'll never see him again. I promise you," he said. And it was true, at least as long as he lived.

So the Chelichev *Cat in Glass* was packed away in a box and put into storage with the rest of our furnishings. Father sold the house, and we traveled for two years. When the horror had faded sufficiently, we returned home to begin a new life. Father went back to his professorship, and I to my studies at Chesly Girls' Day School. He bought a new house. The glass cat was not among the items he had sent up from storage. I did not ask him why. I was just as happy to forget about it, and forget it I did.

I neither saw the glass cat nor heard of it again until many years later. I was a grown woman by then, a schoolteacher in a town far from the one in which I'd spent my childhood. I was married to a banker, and had two lovely daughters and even a cat, which I finally permitted in spite of my abhorrence for them, because the girls begged so hard for one. I thought my life was settled, that it would progress smoothly toward a peaceful old age. But this was not to be. The glass cat had other plans.

The chain of events began with Father's death. It happened suddenly, on a snowy afternoon, as he graded papers in the tiny, snug office he had always had on campus. A heart attack, they said. He was found seated at his desk, Erik Satie's Dadaist composition "La Belle Excentrique" still spinning on the turntable of his record player.

I was not at all surprised to discover that he had left his affairs in some disarray It's not that he had debts or was a gambler. Nothing so serious. It's just that order was slightly contrary to his nature. I remember once, as a very young woman, chiding him for the modest level of chaos he preferred in his life. "Really, Father," I said. "Can't you admire Dadaism without living it?" He laughed and admitted that he didn't seem able to.

As Father's only living relative, I inherited his house and other property, including his personal possessions. There were deeds to be transferred, insurance reports to be filed, bills and loans to be paid. He did have an attorney, an old school friend of his who helped a great deal in organizing the storm of paperwork from a distance. The attorney also arranged for the sale of the house and hired someone to clean it out and ship the contents to us. In the course of the winter, a steady stream of cartons containing everything from scrapbooks to Chinese miniatures arrived at our doorstep. So I thought nothing of it when a large box labeled "fragile" was delivered one day by registered courier. There was a note from the attorney attached, explaining that he had just discovered it in a storage warehouse under Father's name, and had had them ship it to me unopened.

It was a dismal February afternoon, a Friday. I had just come home from teaching. My husband, Stephen, had taken the girls to the mountains for a weekend of skiing, a sport I disliked. I had stayed behind and was looking forward to a couple of days of quiet solitude. The wind drove spittles of rain at the windows as I knelt on the floor of the front room and opened the box. I can't explain to you quite what I felt when I pulled away the packing paper and found myself face-to-face with the glass cat. Something akin to uncovering a nest of cockroaches in a drawer of sachet, I suppose. And that was swiftly followed by a horrid and minutely detailed mental re-creation of Delia's death.

I swallowed my screams, struggling to replace them with something rational. "It's merely a glorified piece of glass." My voice bounced off the walls in the lonely house, hardly comforting.

I had an overpowering image of something inside me, something dark and featureless except for wide white eyes and scrabbling claws. Get us out of here! it cried, and I obliged, seizing my coat from the closet hook and stumbling out into the wind.

I ran in the direction of town, slowing only when one of my shoes fell off and I realized how I must look. Soon I found myself seated at a table in a diner warming my hands in the steam from a cup of coffee, trying to convince myself that I was just being silly. I nursed the coffee as long as I could. It was dusk by the time I felt able to return home. There I found the glass cat, still waiting for me.

I turned on the radio for company and made a fire in the fireplace. Then I sat down before the box and finished unpacking it. The sculpture was as horrible as I remembered, truly ugly and disquieting. I might never have understood why Father kept it if he had not enclosed this letter of explanation, neatly handwritten on his college stationery:

To whom it may concern:

This box contains a sculpture, *Cat in Glass*, designed and executed by the late Alexander Chelichev. Because of Chelichev's standing as a noted forerunner of Dadaism, a historical account of *Cat*'s genesis may be of interest to scholars.

I purchased *Cat* from the artist himself at his Zurich loft in December 1915, two months before the violent rampage that resulted in his confinement in a hospital for the criminally insane, and well before his artistic importance was widely recognized. (For the record, the asking price was forty-eight Swiss francs, plus a good meal with wine.) It is known that Chelichev had a wife and two children elsewhere in the city at that time, though he lived with them only sporadically. The following is the artist's statement about *Cat in Glass*, transcribed as accurately as possible from a conversation we held during dinner.

"I have struggled with the Devil all my life. He wants no rules. No order. His presence is everywhere in my work. I was beaten as a child, and when I became strong enough, I killed my father for it. I see you are skeptical, but it is true. Now I am a grown

Mysterious Cat Stories

man, and I find my father in myself. I have a wife and children, but I spend little time with them because I fear the father-devil in me. I do not beat my children. Instead, I make this cat. Into the glass I have poured this madness of mine. Better there than in the eyes of my daughters."

It is my belief that *Cat in Glass* was Chelichev's last finished creation.

Sincerely,
Lawrence Waters
Professor of Art History

I closed the box, sealed it with the note inside, and spent the next two nights in a hotel, pacing the floor, sleeping little. The following Monday, Stephen took the cat to an art dealer for appraisal. He came home late that afternoon excited and full of news about the great Alexander Chelichev.

He made himself a gin and tonic as he expounded. "That glass cat is priceless, Amy. Did you realize? If your father had sold it, he'd have been independently wealthy. He never let on."

I was putting dinner on the table. The weekend had been a terrible strain. This had been a difficult day on top of it—snowy, and the children in my school class were wild with pent-up energy. So were our daughters, Eleanor and Rose, aged seven and four, respectively. I could hear them quarreling in the playroom down the hall.

"Well, I'm glad to hear the horrid thing is worth something," I said. "Why don't we sell it and hire a maid?"

Stephen laughed as if I'd made an incredibly good joke. "A maid? You could hire a thousand maids for what that cat would bring at auction. It's a fascinating piece with an extraordinary history. You know, the value of something like this will increase with time. I think we'll do well to keep it awhile."

My fingers grew suddenly icy on the hot rim of the potato bowl. "I wasn't trying to be funny, Stephen. It's ugly and disgusting. If I could, I would make it disappear from the face of the earth."

He raised his eyebrows. "What's this? Rebellion? Look, if you really want a maid, I'll get you one."

"That's not the point. I won't have the damned thing in my house."

"I'd rather you didn't swear, Amelia. The children might hear."

"I don't care if they do."

The whole thing degenerated from there. I tried to explain the cat's connection with Delia's death. But Stephen had stopped listening by then. He sulked through dinner. Eleanor and Rose argued over who got which spoonful of peas. And I struggled with a steadily growing sense of dread that seemed much too large for the facts of the matter.

When dinner was over, Stephen announced with exaggerated brightness, "Girls. We'd like your help in deciding an important question."

"Oh goody," said Rose.

"What is it?" said Eleanor.

"Please don't," I said. It was all I could do to keep from shouting.

Stephen flashed me the boyish grin with which he had originally won my heart. "Oh, come on. Try to look at it objectively. You're just sensitive about this because of an irrational notion from your childhood. Let the girls be the judge. If they like it, why not keep it?"

I should have ended it there. I should have insisted. Hindsight is always perfect, as they say. But inside me a little seed of doubt had sprouted. Stephen was always so logical and so right, especially about financial matters. Maybe he was right about this, too.

He had brought the thing home from the appraiser without telling me. He was never above a little subterfuge if it got him his own way. Now he carried the carton in from the garage and unwrapped it in the middle of our warm hardwood floor with all the lights blazing. Nothing had changed. I found it as frightening as ever. I could feel cold sweat collecting on my forehead as I stared at it, all aglitter in a rainbow of refracted lamplight.

Eleanor was enthralled with it. She caught our real cat, a calico named Jelly, and held it up to the sculpture. "See, Jelly? You've got a handsome partner now." But Jelly twisted and hissed in Eleanor's arms until she let her go. Eleanor laughed and said Jelly was jealous.

Rose was almost as uncooperative as Jelly. She shrank away from the glass cat, peeking at it from between her father's knees. But Stephen would have none of that.

"Go on, Rose," he said. "It's just a kitty made of glass. Touch it and see." And he took her by the shoulders and pushed her gently toward it. She put out one hand, hesitantly, as she would have with a live cat who did not know her. I saw her finger touch a nodule of glass shards that might have been its nose. She drew back with a little yelp of pain. And that's how it began. So innocently.

"He bit me!" she cried.

"What happened?" said Stephen. "Did you break it?" He ran to the sculpture first, the brute, to make sure she hadn't damaged it.

She held her finger out to me. There was a tiny cut with a single drop of bright red blood oozing from it. "Mommy, it burns, it burns." She was no longer just crying. She was screaming.

We took her into the bathroom. Stephen held her while I washed the cut and pressed a cold cloth to it. The bleeding stopped in a moment, but still she screamed. Stephen grew angry. "What's this nonsense? It's a scratch. Just a scratch."

Rose jerked and kicked and bellowed. In Stephen's defense, I tell you now it was a terrifying sight, and he was never able to deal well with real fear, especially in himself. He always tried to mask it with anger. We had a neighbor who was a physician. "If you don't stop it, Rose, I'll call Dr. Pepperman. Is that what you want?" he said, as if Dr. Pepperman, a jolly septuagenarian, were anything but charming and gentle, as if threats were anything but asinine at such a time.

"For God's sake, get Pepperman! Can't you see something's terribly wrong?" I said.

And for once he listened to me. He grabbed Eleanor by the arm. "Come with me," he said, and stomped across the yard through the snow without so much as a coat. I believe he took Eleanor, also without a coat, only because he was so unnerved that he didn't want to face the darkness alone.

Rose was still screaming when Dr. Pepperman arrived fresh from his dinner, specks of gravy clinging to his mustache. He examined Rose's finger, and looked mildly puzzled when he had finished. "Can't see much wrong here. I'd say it's mostly a case of hysteria." He took a vial and a syringe from his small brown case and gave Rose an injection, ". . . to help settle her down," he said. It seemed to work. In a few minutes, Rose's screams had diminished to whimpers. Pepperman swabbed her finger with disinfectant and wrapped it loosely in gauze. "There, Rosie. Nothing like a bandage to make it feel better." He winked at us. "She should be fine in the morning. Take the gauze off as soon as she'll let you."

We put Rose to bed and sat with her till she fell asleep. Stephen unwrapped the gauze from her finger so the healing air could get to it. The cut was a bit red, but looked all right. Then we retired as well, reassured by the doctor, still mystified at Rose's reaction.

I awakened sometime after midnight. The house was muffled in the kind of silence brought by steady, soft snowfall. I thought I had heard a sound. Something odd. A scream? A groan? A snarl? Stephen still slept on the verge of a snore; whatever it was, it hadn't been loud enough to disturb him.

I crept out of bed and fumbled with my robe. There was a short flight of stairs between our room and the rooms where Rose and Eleanor slept. Eleanor, like her father, often snored at night, and I could hear her from the hallway now, probably deep in dreams. Rose's room was silent.

I went in and switched on the night-light. The bulb was very low wattage. I thought at first that the shadows were playing tricks on me. Rose's hand and arm looked black as a bruised banana. There was a peculiar odor in the air, like the smell of a butcher shop on a summer day. Heart galloping, I turned on the overhead light. Poor Rosie. She was so very still and clammy. And her arm was so very rotten.

They said Rose died from blood poisoning—a rare type most often associated with animal bites. I told them over and over again that it fit, that our child had indeed been bitten, by a cat, a most evil glass cat. Stephen was embarrassed. His own theory was that, far from blaming an apparently inanimate object, we ought to be suing Pepperman for malpractice. The doctors patted me sympathetically at first. Delusions brought on by grief, they said. It would pass. I would heal in time.

I made Stephen take the cat away. He said he would sell it, though in fact he lied to me. And we buried Rose. But I could not sleep. I paced the house each night, afraid to close my eyes because the cat was always there, glaring his satisfied glare, and waiting for new meat. And in the daytime, everything reminded me of Rosie. Fingerprints on the woodwork, the contents of the kitchen drawers, her favorite foods on the shelves of grocery stores. I could not teach. Every child had Rosie's face and Rosie's voice. Stephen and Eleanor were first kind, then gruff, then angry.

One morning I could find no reason to get dressed or to move from my place on the sofa. Stephen shouted at me, told me I was ridiculous, asked me if I had forgotten that I still had a daughter left who needed me. But, you see, I no longer believed that I or anyone else could make any difference in the world. Stephen and Eleanor would get along with or without me. I didn't matter. There was no God of order and cause. Only chaos, cruelty, and whim.

When it was clear to Stephen that his dear wife Amy had turned from an asset into a liability, he sent me to an institution, far away from everyone, where I could safely be forgotten. In time, I grew to like it there. I had no responsibilities at all. And if there was foulness and bedlam, it was no worse than the outside world.

There came a day, however, when they dressed me in a suit of new clothes and stood me outside the big glass and metal doors to wait; they didn't say for what. The air smelled good. It was springtime, and there were dandelions sprinkled like drops of fresh yellow paint across the lawn.

A car drove up, and a pretty young woman got out and took me by the arm.

"Hello, Mother," she said as we drove off down the road.

It was Eleanor, all grown up. For the first time since Rosie died, I wondered how long I had been away, and knew it must have been a very long while.

We drove a considerable distance, to a large suburban house, white, with a sprawling yard and a garage big enough for two cars. It was a mansion compared to the house in which Stephen and I had raised her. By way of making polite small talk, I asked if she were married, whether she had children. She climbed out of the car looking irritated. "Of course I'm married," she said. "You've met Jason. And you've seen pictures of Sarah and Elizabeth often enough." Of this I had no recollection.

She opened the gate in the picket fence, and we started up the neat stone walkway. The front door opened a few inches and small faces peered out. The door opened wider and two little girls ran onto the porch.

"Hello," I said. "And who are you?"

The older one, giggling behind her hand, said, "Don't you know, Grandma? I'm Sarah."

The younger girl stayed silent, staring at me with frank curiosity.

"That's Elizabeth. She's afraid of you," said Sarah.

I bent and looked into Elizabeth's eyes. They were brown and her hair was shining blonde, like Rosie's. "No need to be afraid of me, my dear. I'm just a harmless old woman."

Elizabeth frowned. "Are you crazy?" she asked.

Sarah giggled behind her hand again, and Eleanor breathed loudly through her nose as if this impertinence were simply overwhelming.

I smiled. I liked Elizabeth. Liked her very much. "They say I am," I said, "and it may very well be true."

A tiny smile crossed her face. She stretched on her tiptoes and kissed my cheek, hardly more than the touch of a warm breeze, then turned and ran away. Sarah followed her, and I watched them go, my heart dancing and shivering. I had loved no one in a very long time. I missed it, but dreaded it, too. For I had loved Delia and Rosie, and they were both dead.

The first thing I saw when I entered the house was Chelichev's *Cat in Glass*, glaring evilly from a place of obvious honor on a low pedestal near the sofa. My stomach felt suddenly shrunken.

"Where did you get that?" I said.

Eleanor looked irritated again. "From Daddy, of course."

"Stephen promised me he would sell it!"

"Well, I guess he didn't, did he?"

Anger heightened my pulse. "Where is he? I want to speak to him immediately."

"Mother, don't be absurd. He's been dead for ten years."

I lowered myself into a chair. I was shaking by then, and I fancied I saw a half-smile on the glass cat's cold jowls.

"Get me out of here," I said. A great weight crushed my lungs. I could barely breathe.

With a look, I must say, of genuine worry, Eleanor escorted me onto the porch and brought me a tumbler of ice water.

"Better?" she asked.

I breathed deeply. "A little. Eleanor, don't you realize that monstrosity killed your sister, and mine as well?"

"That simply isn't true."

"But it is, it is! I'm telling you now, get rid of it if you care for the lives of your children."

Eleanor went pale, whether from rage or fear I could not tell. "It isn't yours. You're legally incompetent, and I'll thank you to stay out of my affairs as much as possible till you have a place of your own. I'll move you to an apartment as soon as I can find one."

"An apartment? But I can't. . . ."

"Yes, you can. You're as well as you're ever going to be, Mother. You liked that hospital only because it was easy. Well, it costs a lot of money to keep you there, and we can't afford it anymore. You're just going to have to straighten up and start behaving like a human being again."

By then I was very close to tears, and very confused as well. Only one thing was clear to me, and that was the true nature of the glass cat. I said, in as steady a voice as I could muster, "Listen to me. That cat was made out of madness. It's evil. If you have a single ounce of brains, you'll put it up for auction this very afternoon."

"So I can get enough money to send you back to the hospital, I suppose? Well, I won't do it. That sculpture is priceless. The longer we keep it, the more it's worth."

She had Stephen's financial mind. I would never sway her, and I knew it. I wept in despair, hiding my face in my hands. I was thinking of Elizabeth. The sweet, soft skin of her little arms, the flame in her cheeks, the power of that small kiss. Human beings are such frail works of art, their lives so precarious, and here I was again, my wayward heart gone out to one of them. But the road back to the safety of isolation lay in ruins. The only way out was through.

Jason came home at dinnertime, and we ate a nice meal, seated around the sleek rosewood table in the dining room. He was kind, actually far kinder than Eleanor. He asked the children about their day and listened carefully while they replied. As did I, enraptured by their pink perfection, distraught at the memory of how imperfect a child's flesh can become. He did not interrupt. He did not demand. When Eleanor refused to give me coffee—she said she was afraid it would get me "hyped up"—he admonished her and poured me a cup himself. We talked about my father, whom he knew by reputation, and about art and the cities of Europe. All the while I felt in my bones the baleful gaze of the *Cat in Glass*, burning like the coldest ice through walls and furniture as if they did not exist.

Eleanor made up a cot for me in the guest room. She didn't want me to sleep in the bed, and she wouldn't tell me why. But I overheard

Jason arguing with her about it. "What's wrong with the bed?" he said.

"She's mentally ill," said Eleanor. She was whispering, but loudly. "Heaven only knows what filthy habits she's picked up. I won't risk her soiling a perfectly good mattress. If she does well on the cot for a few nights, then we can consider moving her to the bed."

They thought I was in the bathroom, performing whatever unspeakable acts it is that mentally ill people perform in places like that, I suppose. But they were wrong. I was sneaking past their door, on my way to the garage. Jason must have been quite a handyman in his spare time. I found a large selection of hammers on the wall, including an excellent short-handled sledge. I hid it under my bedding. They never even noticed.

The children came in and kissed me good night in a surreal reversal of roles. I lay in the dark on my cot for a long time, thinking of them, especially Elizabeth, the youngest and weakest, who would naturally be the most likely target of an animal's attack. I dozed, dreaming sometimes of a smiling Elizabeth-Rose-Delia, sifting snow, wading through drifts; sometimes of the glass cat, its fierce eyes smoldering, crystalline tongue brushing crystalline jaws. The night was well along when the dreams crashed down like broken mirrors into silence.

The house was quiet except for those ticks and thumps all houses make as they cool in the darkness. I got up and slid the hammer out from under the bedding, not even sure what I was going to do with it, knowing only that the time had come to act.

I crept out to the front room, where the cat sat waiting, as I knew it must. Moonlight gleamed in the chaos of its glass fur. I could feel its power, almost see it, a shimmering red aura the length of its malformed spine. The thing was moving, slowly, slowly, smiling now, oh yes, a real smile. I could smell its rotten breath.

For an instant I was frozen. Then I remembered the hammer, Jason's lovely short-handled sledge. And I raised it over my head, and brought it down in the first crashing blow.

The sound was wonderful. Better than cymbals, better even than holy trumpets. I was trembling all over, but I went on and on in an agony of satisfaction while glass fell like moonlit rain. There were screams. "Grandma, stop! Stop!" I swung the hammer back in the first part of another arc, heard something like the thunk of a fallen ripe melon, swung it down on the cat again. I couldn't see anymore. It came to me that there was glass in my eyes and blood in my mouth. But none of that mattered, a small price to pay for the long-overdue demise of Chelichev's *Cat in Glass.*

So you see how I have come to this, not without many sacrifices along the way. And now the last of all: the sockets where my eyes used to be are infected. They stink. Blood poisoning, I'm sure.

I wouldn't expect Eleanor to forgive me for ruining her prime investment. But I hoped Jason might bring the children a time or two anyway. No word except for the delivery of a single rose yesterday. The matron said it was white, and held it up for me to sniff, and she read me the card that came with it. "Elizabeth was a great one for forgiving. She would have wanted you to have this. Sleep well, Jason."

Which puzzled me.

"You don't even know what you've done, do you?" said the matron.

"I destroyed a valuable work of art," said I.

But she made no reply.

The Cat Mummy

(1924)

Arthur Weigall (1880–1934)

Weigall was an expert Egyptologist. He was the author of about 35 books, most of them historical and many on Egypt and its antiquities. For many years, he was the Inspector-General of Antiquities for the Egyptian Government and head of the Cairo Museum. He also worked closely with Lord Carnarvon and Howard Carter, who discovered the tomb of Pharaoh Tutankhamen in 1922. This account is from *Tutankhamen and Other Essays* (1924).

In the year 1909 Lord Carnarvon, who was then conducting excavations in the necropolis of the nobles of Thebes, discovered a hollow wooden figure of a large black cat, which we recognized, from other examples in the Cairo Museum, to be the shell in which a real embalmed cat was confined. The figure looked more like a small tiger as it sat in the sunlight at the edge of the pit in which it had been discovered, glaring at us with its yellow painted eyes and bristling its yellow whiskers. Its body was covered all over with a thick coating of smooth, shining pitch, and we could not at first detect the line along which the shell had been closed after it had received the mortal remains of the sacred animal within; but we knew from experience that the joint passed completely round the figure from the nose, over the top of the head, down the back, and along the breast—so that, when opened, the two sides would fall apart in equal halves.

The somber figure was carried down to the Nile and across the river to my house, where, by a mistake on the part of my Egyptian servant, it was deposited in my bedroom. Returning home at dead of night, I here found it seated in the middle of the floor directly in my path from the door to the matches; and for some moments I was constrained to sit beside it, rubbing my shins and my head.

I rang the bell, but receiving no answer, I walked to the kitchen, where I found the servants grouped distractedly around the butler, who had been stung by a scorpion and was in the throes of that short but intense agony. Soon he passed into a state of delirium, and believed himself to be pursued by a large gray cat, a fancy which did not surprise me since he had so lately assisted in carrying the figure to its ill-chosen resting-place in my bedroom.

At length I retired to bed, but the moonlight which now entered the room through the open French windows fell full upon the black figure of the cat; and for some time I lay awake watching the peculiarly weird creature as it stared past me at the wall. I estimated its age to be considerably more than three thousand years, and I tried to picture to myself the strange people who, in those distant times, had fashioned this curious coffin for a cat which had been to them half pet and half household god. A branch of a tree was swaying in the night breeze outside, and its shadows danced to and fro over the face of the cat, causing the yellow eyes to open and shut, as it were, and the mouth to grin. Once, as I was dropping off to sleep, I could have sworn that it had turned its head to look at me, and I could see the sullen expression of feline anger gathering upon its black visage as it did so. In the distance I could hear the melancholy wails of the unfortunate butler imploring those around him to keep the cat away from him, and it seemed to me that there came a glitter into the eyes of the figure as the low cries echoed down the passage.

At last I fell asleep, and for about an hour all was still. Then, suddenly, a report like that of a pistol rang through the room. I started up, and as I did so a large gray cat sprang either from or on to the bed, leapt across my knees, dug its claws into my hand, and dashed through the window into the garden. At the same moment I saw by the light of the moon that the two sides of the wooden figure had fallen apart and were rocking themselves to a standstill upon the floor, like two great empty shells. Between them sat the mummified figure of a cat, the bandages which swathed it round being ripped open at the neck, as though they had been burst outward.

I sprang out of bed and rapidly examined the divided shell; and it seemed to me that the humidity in the air here on the bank of the Nile had expanded the wood which had rested in the dry desert so long, and had caused the two halves to burst apart with the loud noise which I had heard. Then, going to the window, I scanned the moonlit garden; and there in the middle of the pathway I saw, not the gray cat which had scratched me, but my own pet tabby, standing with arched back and bristling fur, glaring into the bushes as though she saw ten feline devils therein.

I will leave the reader to decide whether the gray cat was the malevolent spirit which, after causing me to break my shins and my butler to be stung by a scorpion, had burst its way through the bandages and woodwork and had fled into the darkness; or whether the torn embalming cloths represented the natural destructive work of Time, and the gray cat was a night wanderer which had strayed into my room and had been frightened by the easily explained bursting apart of the two sides of the ancient Egyptian figure. Coincidence is a factor in life not always sufficiently considered; and the events I have related can be explained in a perfectly natural manner if one be inclined to do so.

The Jewel of Seven Stars

(1902)

Bram Stoker (1847–1912)

Originally from Dublin, Stoker in his own day was best known as the partner of Henry Irving in the running of the famous Lyceum Theatre in London, from 1878 to 1905. Today, his name is synonymous with the world's most famous vampire—Count Dracula. Stoker's creation of this cult hero has proven to be an endless cornucopia for movie makers, writers, and playwrights. It is now considered to be one of the all-time classics of horror literature. Unfortunately, *Dracula* (1897) has obscured his other works, some of which are equally deserving of attention. *The Jewel of Seven Stars* is an outstanding example of a work by Stoker that has fallen into unfortunate obscurity. Although we have abbreviated the novel in order to make it available to a wider audience, we guarantee that it still contains all the power and magic of the original.

"I knew you would come!"
The clasp of the hand can mean a great deal, even when it is not intended to mean anything especially. Following Miss Trelawny, I moved over to a dainty room which opened from the hall and looked out on the garden at the back of the house.
"I will thank you later for your goodness in coming to me in my trouble; but at present you can best help me when you know the facts."

"Go on," I said. "Tell me all you know." She went on at once:

"I was awakened by some sound; I do not know what. I only know that I found myself awake, with my heart beating wildly. My room is next to Father's, and I can often hear him moving about before I fall asleep. Last night I got up softly and stole to the door. There was not any noise of moving, and no kind of cry at all; but there was a queer kind of dragging sound, and a slow, heavy breathing. Oh! it was dreadful, waiting there in the dark and the silence, and fearing— fearing I did not know what!

"I pushed the door open all at once, switched on the electric light, and stepped into the room. I looked first at the bed. The sheets were all crumpled up, so that I knew Father had been in bed; but there was a great dark red patch in the center of the bed that made my heart stand still. As I was gazing at it the sound of the breathing came across the room, and my eyes followed to it. There was Father on his right side with the other arm under him. The track of blood went across the room up to the bed, and there was a pool all around him which looked terribly red and glittering as I bent over to examine him. The place where he lay was right in front of the big safe. He was in his pajamas. The left sleeve was torn, showing his bare arm, and stretched out toward the safe. It looked—oh! so terrible, patched all with blood, and with the flesh torn or cut all around a gold chain bangle on his wrist. I did not know he wore such a thing, and it seemed to give me a new shock of surprise."

She paused a moment; and as I wished to relieve her by a moment's divergence of thought, I said:

"Oh, that need not surprise you. You will see the most unlikely men wearing bangles. I have seen a judge condemn a man to death, and the wrist of the hand he held up had a gold bangle." She went on in a steadier voice:

"I did not lose a moment in summoning aid, for I feared he might bleed to death. We lifted father on a sofa; and the housekeeper, Mrs. Grant, tied a handkerchief round the cut. I sent off one man for the doctor and another for the police. When they had gone, I felt that, except for the servants, I was all alone in the house. Then I thought of you and, without waiting to think, I told the men to get a carriage ready at once, and I sent for you."

She paused. I did not like to say just then anything of how I felt. I looked at her; I think she understood, for her eyes were raised to mine for a moment and then fell, leaving her cheeks as red as peony roses. With a manifest effort she went on with her story:

"Doctor Winchester was with us in an incredibly short time; then a policeman, Sargeant Daw, arrived; and then you came."

There was a long pause, and I ventured to take her hand for an instant. We ascended to Mr. Trelawny's room, where we found everything exactly as she had described.

The Police Sergeant turned to Miss Trelawny and said:

"You say that you were outside the door when you heard the noise?"

"I was in my room when I heard the queer sound and I came out of my room at once. Father's door was shut, and I could see the whole landing and the upper slopes of the staircase. No one could have left by the door unknown to me, if that is what you mean!"

"That is just what I do mean, miss." He went to the windows.

"Were the shutters closed?" he asked Miss Trelawny in a casual way as though he expected the negative answer, which came.

"So far as I can see, the object was to bring that key to the lock of the safe. There seems to be some secret in the mechanism. It is a combination lock of seven letters; but there seems to be a way of locking even the combination." Then turning to the Doctor, he said:

"Have you anything you can tell me, Doctor?" Doctor Winchester answered at once:

"There is no wound on the head which could account for the state of stupor in which the patient continues. I must, therefore, take it that either he has been drugged or is under some hypnotic influence. So far as I can judge, he has not been drugged—at least by means of any drug of whose qualities I am aware."

The Detective began a systematic search of the writing-table in the room. In one of the drawers he found a letter sealed; this he brought at once across the room and handed to Miss Trelawny.

"A letter—directed to me—and in my Father's hand!" she said as she eagerly opened it. It said:

"MY DEAR DAUGHTER,—I want you to take this letter as an instruction—absolute and imperative, and admitting of no deviation whatever—in case anything untoward or unexpected should happen to me. If I should be suddenly and mysteriously stricken down—either by sickness, accident or attack—you must follow these directions implicitly. If I am not already in my bed-room when you are made cognizant of my state, I am to be brought there as quickly as possible. Thenceforth, until I am either conscious and able to give instructions on my own account I am never to be left alone—not for a single instant. From night-fall to sunrise at least two persons must remain in the room, awake and exercising themselves to my purpose. I should advise you, my dear Daughter, seeing that you have no relative to apply to, to get some friend whom you can trust to remain within the house. Once more, my dear Margaret, let me impress on you the need for observation. If I am taken ill or injured, this will be no ordinary occasion; and I wish to warn you, so that your guarding may be complete.

"Nothing in my room—I speak of the curios—must be re-moved or displaced in any way, or for any cause whatever. I have a special reason and a special purpose in the placing of each; so that any moving of them would thwart my plans.

"ABEL TRELAWNY."

That night we were not yet regularly organized for watching. Nurse Kennedy, who had been on duty all day, was lying down, as she had arranged to come on again by twelve o'clock. At nine o'clock Miss Trelawny and I went in to relieve the Doctor. He was bending over the bed as we came into the room.

"I am really and absolutely at my wits'-end to find any fit cause for this stupor. And as to these wounds"—he laid his finger gently on the bandaged wrist which lay outside the coverlet as he spoke, "Have you any strange pets here in the house; anything of an exceptional kind, such as a tiger-cat or anything out of the common?" Miss Trelawny smiled a sad smile, as she made answer:

"Oh no! Father does not like animals about the house, unless they are dead and mummied. Even my poor kitten was only allowed in the house on sufferance; and though he is the dearest and best-conducted cat in the world, he is now on a sort of parole, and is not allowed into this room."

As she was speaking a faint rattling of the door handle was heard. Instantly Miss Trelawny's face brightened. She sprang up and went over to the door, saying as she went:

"There he is! That is my Silvio. He stands on his hind legs and rattles the door handle when he wants to come into a room." She opened the door, lifted the cat, and came back with him in her arms. He was certainly a magnificent animal. A chinchilla gray Persian with long silky hair; a really lordly animal with a haughty bearing, despite his gentleness; and with great paws which spread out as he placed them on the ground. Whilst she was fondling him, he suddenly gave a wriggle like an eel and slipped out of her arms. He ran across the room and stood opposite a low table on which stood the mummy of an animal, and began to mew and snarl. Miss Trelawny was after him in an instant and lifted him in her arms, kicking and struggling and wriggling to get away; but not biting or scratching, for evidently he loved his beautiful mistress. He ceased to make a noise the moment he was in her arms; in a whisper she admonished him:

"O you naughty Silvio! You have broken your parole. Now, say goodnight to the gentlemen, and come away to mother's room!" As she was speaking she held out the cat's paw to me to shake. As I did so I could not but admire its size and beauty. "Why," said I, "his paw seems like a little boxing-glove full of claws." She smiled:

"So it ought to. Don't you notice that my Silvio has seven toes, see!" she opened the paw; and surely enough there were seven separate claws, each of them sheathed in a delicate, fine, shell-like case. As I gently stroked the foot the claws emerged and one of them accidentally—there was no anger now and the cat was purring—stuck into my hand. Instinctively I said as I drew back:

"Why, his claws are like razors!"

Doctor Winchester had come close to us and was bending over looking at the cat's claws. Whilst I was stroking the now quiescent cat, the Doctor went to the table and tore off a piece of blotting-paper from the writing-pad and came back. He laid the paper on his palm and, with a simple "pardon me!" to Miss Trelawny, placed the cat's paw on it and pressed it down with his other hand. The haughty cat seemed to resent somewhat the familiarity, and tried to draw its foot away. This was plainly what the Doctor wanted, for in the act the cat opened the sheaths of its claws and made several reefs in the soft paper. Then Miss Trelawny took her pet away. She returned in a couple of minutes; as she came in she said:

"It is most odd about that mummy! When Silvio came into the room first—indeed I took him in as a kitten to show to Father—he went on just the same way. He jumped up on the table, and tried to scratch and bite the mummy. That was what made Father so angry, and brought the decree of banishment on poor Silvio. Only his parole, given through me, kept him in the house."

Whilst she had been gone, Doctor Winchester had taken the bandage from her father's wrist. The wound was now quite clear, as the separate cuts showed out in fierce red lines. The Doctor held the blotting-paper down close to the wound. The cuts in the paper corresponded with the wounds in the wrist! No explanation was needed, as he said:

"It would have been better if master Silvio had not broken his parole!"

We were all silent for a little while. Suddenly Miss Trelawny said:

"But Silvio was not in here last night!"

"Are you sure? Could you prove that if necessary?" She hesitated before replying:

"I am certain of it; but I fear it would be difficult to prove. Silvio sleeps in a basket in my room. I certainly put him to bed last night; I remember distinctly laying his little blanket over him, and tucking him in. This morning I took him out of the basket myself. I certainly never noticed him in here; though, of course, that would not mean much, for I was too concerned about poor father, and too much occupied with him, to notice even Silvio."

The Doctor shook his head as he said with a certain sadness:

"Well, at any rate it is no use trying to prove anything now. Any cat in the world would have cleaned blood-marks—did any exist—from his paws in a hundredth part of the time that has elapsed."

Again we were all silent; and again the silence was broken by Miss Trelawny:

"But now that I think of it, it could not have been poor Silvio that injured Father. My door was shut when I first heard the sound; and Father's was shut when I listened at it. When I went in, the injury had been done; so that it must have been before Silvio could possibly have got in." This reasoning commended itself, especially to me as a barrister, for it was proof to satisfy a jury. It gave me a distinct pleasure to have Silvio acquitted of the crime—possibly because he was Miss Trelawny's cat and was loved by her. Silvio's mistress was manifestly pleased as I said:

"Verdict, 'not guilty!'" Doctor Winchester after a pause observed:

"My apologies to master Silvio on this occasion; but I am still puzzled to know why he is so keen against that mummy. Is he the same toward the other mummies in the house? There are, I suppose, a lot of them. I saw three in the hall as I came in."

"There are lots of them," she answered. "I sometimes don't know whether I am in a private house or the British Museum. But Silvio never concerns himself about any of them except that particular one. I suppose it must be because it is of an animal, not a man or a woman."

"Perhaps it is of a cat!" said the Doctor as he started up and went across the room to look at the mummy more closely. "Yes," he went on, "it is the mummy of a cat; and a very fine one, too. If it hadn't been a special favorite of some very special person it would never have received so much honor. See! A painted case and obsidian eyes—just like a human mummy. It is an extraordinary thing, that knowledge of kind to kind. Here is a dead cat—that is all; it is perhaps four or five thousand years old—and another cat of another breed, in what is practically another world, is ready to fly at it, just as it would if it were not dead. I should like to experiment a bit about that cat if you don't mind, Miss Trelawny." She hesitated before replying:

"Of course, do anything you may think necessary or wise; but I hope it will not be anything to hurt or worry my poor Silvio."

"Oh, Silvio will be all right. There are plenty of mummy cats to be had in Museum Street. I shall get one and place it here instead of that one. We shall then find out whether Silvio objects to all mummy cats, or only to this one in particular."

After a pause she went on: "But of course under the circumstances anything that is to be ultimately for his good must be done. I suppose there can't be anything very particular about the mummy of a cat."

Doctor Winchester said nothing. The room and all in it gave grounds for strange thoughts. There were so many mummies or mummy objects around which seem to for ever be releasing the penetrating odors of bitumen, and spices and gums. In far corners of the room were shadows of uncanny shape. More than once as I thought, the multitudinous presence of the dead and the past took such hold on me that I caught myself looking round fearfully as though some strange personality or influence was present. It was with a distinct sense of relief that I saw a new personality in the room in the shape of Nurse Kennedy, allowing the doctor and Miss Trelawny to get some rest. There was no doubt that that business-like, self-reliant, capable young woman added an element of security to such wild imaginings as my own. The only thing which it could not altogether abrogate was the strange Egyptian smell. You may put a mummy in a glass case and hermetically seal it so that no corroding air can get within; but all the same it will exhale its odor. One might think that four or five thousand years would exhaust the olfactory qualities of anything; but experience teaches us that these smells remain, and that their secrets are unknown to us. Today they are as much mysteries as they were when the embalmers put the body in the bath of natron. . . .

All at once I sat up. I had become lost in an absorbing reverie. The Egyptian smell had seemed to get on my nerves—on my memory—on my very will. Without stating my intention, I went downstairs and out of the house. I soon found a chemist's shop, and came away with a respirator.

Though I really cannot remember being asleep or waking from it, I saw a vision—I dreamed a dream. I scarcely know which.

I was still in the room, seated in the chair. I had on my respirator and knew that I breathed freely. The Nurse sat in her chair with her back toward me. She sat quite still. The sick man lay as still as the dead. The light was very, very low; the reflection of it under the green-shaded lamp was a dim relief to the darkness, rather than light. The green silk fringe of the lamp had merely the color of an emerald seen in the moonlight. The room, for all its darkness, was full of shadows. It seemed in my whirling thoughts as though all the real things had become shadows—shadows which moved, for they passed the dim outline of the high windows. I even thought there was sound, a faint sound as of the mew of a cat—the rustle of drapery and a metallic clink as of metal faintly touching metal. I sat as one entranced. At last I felt, as in nightmare, that this was sleep, and that in the passing of its portals all my will had gone.

All at once my senses were full awake. A shriek rang in my ears. The room was filled suddenly with a blaze of light. There was the sound of pistol shots—one, two; and a haze of white smoke in the room. When my waking eyes regained their power, I could have shrieked with horror myself at what I saw before me.

The sight which met my eyes had the horror of a dream within a dream, with the certainty of reality added. The room was as I had seen it last; except that the shadowy look had gone in the glare of the many lights, and every article in it stood stark and solidly real.

By the empty bed sat Nurse Kennedy, as my eyes had last seen her,

sitting bolt upright in the armchair beside the bed. She had placed a
pillow behind her, so that her back might be erect; but her neck was
fixed as that of one in a cataleptic trance. She was, to all intents and
purposes, turned into stone. The bedclothes were disarranged, as
though the patient had been drawn from under them without throwing them back. The corner of the upper sheet hung upon the floor;
close by it lay one of the bandages with which the Doctor had dressed
the wounded wrist. Another and another lay further along the floor,
as though forming a clue to where the sick man now lay. This was
almost exactly where he had been found on the previous night, under
the great safe. Again, the left arm lay toward the safe. But there had
been a new outrage, an attempt had been made to sever the arm close
to the bangle which held the tiny key. A heavy "kukri" knife—one of
the leaf-shaped knives which the Gurkhas and others of the hill tribes
of India use with such effect—had been taken from its place on the
wall, and with it the attempt had been made. It was manifest that just
at the moment of striking, the blow had been arrested, for only the
point of the knife and not the edge of the blade had struck the flesh.
As it was, the outer side of the arm had been cut to the bone and the
blood was pouring out. In addition, the former wound in front of the
arm had been cut or torn about terribly, one of the cuts seemed to jet
out blood as if with each pulsation of the heart. By the side of her
father knelt Miss Trelawny, her white nightdress stained with the
blood in which she knelt. In the middle of the room Sergeant Daw, in
his shirt and trousers and stocking feet, was putting fresh cartridges
into his revolver in a dazed mechanical kind of way. His eyes were red
and heavy, and he seemed only half awake, and less than half conscious of what was going on around him. Several servants, bearing
lights of various kinds, were clustered round the doorway.

As I rose from my chair and came forward, Miss Trelawny raised
her eyes toward me. When she saw me she shrieked and started to her
feet, pointing towards me. Never shall I forget the strange picture she
made, with her white drapery all smeared with blood which, as she
rose from the pool, ran in streaks toward her bare feet. I believe that I
had only been asleep; that whatever influence had worked on Mr.
Trelawny and Nurse Kennedy—and in less degree on Sergeant Daw
—had not touched me. The respirator had been of some service,
though it had not kept off the tragedy whose dire evidences were
before me. I can understand now the fright which my appearance

must have evoked. I had still on the respirator, which covered mouth and nose; my hair had been tossed in my sleep. Coming suddenly forward, thus enwrapped and disheveled, in that horrified crowd, I must have had, in the strange mixture of lights, an extraordinary and terrifying appearance. It was well that I recognized all this in time to avert another catastrophe; for the half-dazed, mechanically-acting Detective put in the cartridges and had raised his revolver to shoot at me when I succeeded in wrenching off the respirator and shouting to him to hold his hand.

Mrs. Grant took her mistress away and changed her clothes. She was back presently in a dressing-gown and slippers, and with the traces of blood removed from her hands. She was now much calmer, though she trembled sadly; and her face was ghastly white. It was so apparent to me that she did not know where to begin or whom to trust, so I said:

"Tell me what you remember!" The effort to recollect seemed to stimulate her; she became calmer as she spoke:

"I was asleep, and woke suddenly with the same horrible feeling on me that Father was in great and immediate danger. I jumped up and ran into his room. It was nearly pitch dark, but as I opened the door there was light enough to see Father's nightdress as he lay on the floor under the safe, just as on that first awful night. Then I think I must have gone mad for a moment." She stopped and shuddered. My eyes lit on Sergeant Daw, still fiddling in an aimless way with the revolver.

"Now tell us, Sergeant Daw, what did you fire at?" The policeman seemed to pull himself together with the habit of obedience.

"I went to sleep half-dressed—as I am now, with a revolver under my pillow. I thought I heard a scream; but I can't be sure, for I felt thick-headed as a man does when he is called too soon after an extra long stretch of work. Anyhow, my thoughts flew to the pistol. I took it out, and ran on to the landing. Then I heard a sort of scream, or rather a call for help, and ran into this room. The room was dark, for the lamp beside the Nurse was out, and the only light was that from the landing, coming through the open door. Miss Trelawny was kneeling on the floor beside her father, and was screaming. I thought I saw something move between me and the window; so, without thinking, and being half dazed and only half awake, I shot at it. It moved a little more to the right between the windows, and I shot again. Then you came up out of the big chair with all that muffling on your face. It seemed to me as if it had been you, being in the same direction as the thing I had fired at. And so I was about to fire again when you pulled off the wrap." Here I asked him—I was cross-examining now and felt at home:

"You say you thought I was the thing you fired at. What thing?" The man scratched his head, but made no reply.

"Come, sir," I said, "what thing; what was it like?" The answer came in a low voice:

"I don't know, sir. I thought there was something; but what it was I haven't the faintest notion."

When I went back to the sofa and took the tourniquet from Mrs. Grant, she went over and pulled up the blinds.

It would be hard to imagine anything more ghastly than the appearance of the room with the faint gray light of early morning coming in upon it. As the windows faced north, any light that came was a fixed gray light without any of the rosy possibility of dawn which comes in the eastern quarter of the heavens. The electric lights seemed dull and yet glaring; and every shadow was of a hard intensity. There was nothing of morning freshness; nothing of the softness of night. All was hard and cold, and inexpressibly dreary. The face of the senseless man on the sofa seemed of a ghastly yellow; and the Nurse's face had taken a suggestion of green from the shade of the lamp near her. Only Miss Trelawny's face looked white; and it was of a pallor which made my heart ache. It looked as if nothing on God's earth could ever again bring back to it the color of life and happiness.

Nurse Kennedy had slowly returned to her normal self late in the morning and Miss Trelawny slept into the afternoon. Before supper I was about to go out for a walk, when I noticed a man at the front door arguing with the butler. He claimed to be a colleague of Mr. Trelawny and insisted on seeing him. The butler refused to allow him in, saying Mr. Trelawny was too ill for visitors. I told the butler I would handle the matter. I took the man into the boudoir across the hall and sent for Margaret.

"I am a friend of Miss Trelawny's. My name is Ross."

"Thank you very much, Mr. Ross, for your kindness!" he said. "My name is Corbeck. I would give you my card, but they don't use cards where I've come from."

Miss Trelawny came very quickly and he began again:

"Good afternoon Miss Trelawny. My name is Eugene Corbeck. I am a Master of Arts and Doctor of Laws and Master of Surgery of Cambridge; Doctor of Letters of Oxford; Doctor of Science and Doctor of Languages of London University; Doctor of Philosophy of Berlin; Doctor of Oriental Languages of Paris. I have some other degrees, honorary and otherwise, but I need not trouble you with them. Those I have named will show you that I am sufficiently feathered with diplomas to fly into even a sickroom. Early in life I fell in with Egyptology. I must have been bitten by some powerful scarab, for I took it bad. I went out tomb-hunting; and managed to get a living of a sort, and to learn some things that you can't get out of books. I was in pretty low water when I met your Father, who was doing some explorations on his own account; and since then I haven't found that I have many unsatisfied wants. He is a real patron of the arts; no mad Egyptologist can ever hope for a better chief!

"I have been several times out on expeditions in Egypt for your Father. Many of his treasures—and he has some rare ones he has procured through me, either by my exploration or by purchase—or—or—otherwise. Your Father, Miss Trelawny, has a rare knowledge. He sometimes makes up his mind that he wants to find a particular thing, of whose existence—if it still exists—he has become aware; and he will follow it all over the world till he gets it. I've been on just such a chase now."

He paused, and an embarrassed look crept over his face. Suddenly he said:

"You are sure, Miss Trelawny, your Father is not well enough to see me today?"

She stood up, saying in a tone in which dignity and graciousness were blended:

"Come and see for yourself!" She moved toward her father's room; he followed, and I brought up the rear.

Mr. Corbeck entered the sick-room as though he knew it. I watched him narrowly, for somehow I felt that on this man depended much of our enlightenment regarding the strange matter in which we were involved.

"Tell me all about it. How it began and when!" Miss Trelawny looked at me appealingly; and forthwith I told him all that I knew. He seemed to make no motion during the whole time; but insensibly the bronze face became steel.

"Good! Now I know where my duty lies!"

"What do you mean?" I asked.

"Trelawny knows what he is doing. He had some definite purpose in all that he did; and we must not thwart him. He evidently expected something to happen, and guarded himself at all points."

"Not at all points!" I said impulsively. "There must have been a weak spot somewhere, or he wouldn't be lying here like that!" Somehow his impassiveness surprised me. Something like a smile flickered over his swarthy face as he answered me:

"This is not the end! Trelawny did not guard himself to no purpose. Doubtless, he expected this too; or at any rate the possibility of it."

Margaret and I spent the rest of the afternoon looking over the curio treasures of Mr. Trelawny. From what I had heard from Mr. Corbeck I began to have some idea of the vastness of his enterprise in the world of Egyptian research; and with this light everything around me began to have a new interest. The house seemed to be a veritable storehouse of marvels of antique art. In addition to the curios, big and little, in Mr. Trelawny's own room—from the great sarcophagi down to the scarabs of all kinds in the cabinets—the great hall, the staircase landings, the study, and even the boudoir were full of antique pieces which would have made a collector's mouth water.

The most interesting of the sarcophagi were undoubtedly the three in Mr. Trelawny's room. Of these, two were of dark stone. These were wrought with some hieroglyphs. But the third was strikingly different. It was of some yellow-brown substance. Here and there were patches almost transparent—certainly translucent. The whole chest was wrought with hundreds of minute hieroglyphics, the deep blue of their coloring showing up fresh and sharply edged in the yellow stone. It was very long, nearly nine feet; and perhaps a yard wide. The sides undulated, so that there was no hard line. Even the corners took such excellent curves that they pleased the eye. Inside was a raised space, outlined like a human figure. "Truly," I said, "this must have been made for a giant!"

"Or for a giantess!" said Margaret.

Close beside the sarcophagus was a low table of green stone with red veins in it, like bloodstone. On it rested a strange and very beautiful coffer or casket of stone of a peculiar shape. It was something like a small coffin, except that it was an irregular septahedron, there being two planes on each of the two sides, one end and a top and bottom. The stone was of a full green, the color of emerald without its gleam. The surface was almost that of a jewel. It was quite unlike anything I had ever seen, and did not resemble any stone or gem that I knew. In length it was about two feet and a half; in breadth about half this, and was nearly a foot high. I tried to lift up the lid but it was securely fixed. It fitted so exactly that the whole coffer seemed like a single piece of stone mysteriously hollowed from within. On the sides and edges of the table, on which the coffer rested, were some odd-looking protuberances.

On the other side of the great sarcophagus, on a small table, stood a case of about a foot square. Within, on a cushion of cloth of gold as fine as silk rested a mummy hand, so perfect that it startled one to see it. A woman's hand, fine and long, with slim tapering fingers and nearly as perfect as when it was given to the embalmer thousands of years before. In the embalming it had lost nothing of its beautiful shape; even the wrist seemed to maintain its pliability as the gentle curve lay on the cushion. The great peculiarity of it, as a hand, was that it had in all seven fingers, there being two middle and two index fingers. The upper end of the wrist was jagged, as though it had been broken off, and was stained with a red-brown stain.

"That is another of Father's mysteries. When I asked him about it he said that it was perhaps the most valuable thing he had, except one. When I asked him what that one was, he refused to tell me. 'I will tell you,' he said, 'all about it in good time.'"

Shortly after supper, Doctor Winchester arrived. He had a large parcel with him, which, when unwrapped, proved to be the mummy of a cat. With Miss Trelawny's permission he placed this in the boudoir; and Silvio was brought close to it. To the surprise of us all, however, except perhaps Doctor Winchester, he did not manifest the least annoyance; he took no notice of it whatever. He stood on the table close beside it, purring loudly. Then, following out his plan, the Doctor brought him into Mr. Trelawny's room, we all following. Doctor Winchester was excited; Miss Trelawny anxious. I was more than interested myself, for I began to have a glimmering of the Doctor's idea. The Detective was calmly and coldly superior: but Mr. Corbeck, who was an enthusiast, was full of eager curiosity.

The moment Doctor Winchester got into the room, Silvio began to mew and wriggle; and, jumping out of his arms, ran over to the cat mummy and began to scratch angrily at it. Miss Trelawny had some difficulty in taking him away; but so soon as he was out of the room he became quiet. When she came back there was a clamor of comments:

"I thought so!" from the Doctor.

"What can it mean?" from Miss Trelawny.

"That's a very strange thing!" from Mr. Corbeck.

"Odd! But it doesn't prove anything!" from the Detective.

Doctor Winchester turned to Mr. Corbeck:

"I want you, if you will, to translate some hieroglyphic for me."

"Certainly, with the greatest pleasure, so far as I can."

"There are two," he answered, handing him the first mummy cat. The scholar took it; and, after a short examination, said:

"There is nothing especial in this. It is an appeal to Bast, the Lady of Bubastis, to give her good bread and milk in the Elysian Fields. There may be more inside; and if you will care to unroll it, I will do my best. I do not think, however, that there is anything special. From the method of wrapping I should say it is from Delta; and of a late period, when such mummy work was common and cheap. What is the other inscription you wish me to see?"

"The inscription on Mr. Trelawny's mummy cat."

Mr. Corbeck's face fell. "No!" he said, "I cannot do that! I am, for the present, not prepared to discuss any of the things in Mr. Trelawny's room." Then turning to me, he said, "Mr. Ross, I understand that you are to have a spell of watching in the sick-room tonight. I shall get you a book which will help to pass the time for you. It will be necessary, or at least helpful, to understand other things which I shall tell you later."

The book was by one Nicholas van Huyn of Hoorn. In the preface he told how, attracted by the work of John Greaves of Merton College, *Pyramidographia*, he himself visited Egypt, exploring the ruins of many temples and tombs.

The narrative went on to tell how, after passing for several days through the mountains to the east of Aswan, the explorer came to a certain place. Here I give his own words, simply putting the translation into modern English:

"Toward evening we came to the entrance of a narrow, deep valley, running east and west. I wished to proceed through this; for the sun, now nearly down on the horizon, showed a wide opening beyond the narrowing of the cliffs. But the fellaheen absolutely refused to enter the valley at such a time, alleging that they might be caught by the night before they could emerge from the other end. At first they would give no reason for their fear. They had hitherto gone anywhere I wished, and at any time, without demur. On being pressed, however, they said that the place was the Valley of the Sorcerer, where none might come in the night. On being asked to tell of the Sorcerer, they refused. The next morning, however, when the sun was up and shining down the valley, their fears had somewhat passed away. Then they told me that a great Sorcerer in ancient days, a King or a Queen, they could not say which, was buried there. They could not give the name, persisting to the last that there was no name; and that anyone who should name it would waste away in life so that at death nothing of him would remain to be raised again in the Other World. In passing through the valley they kept together in a cluster, hurrying on in front of me. None dared to remain behind. They gave, as their reason for so proceeding, that the arms of the Sorcerer were long, and that it was dangerous to be the last. The which was of little comfort to me who of this necessity took that honorable post. In the narrowest part of the valley, on the south side, was a great cliff of rock, rising sheer, of smooth and even surface. Hereon were graven certain cabalistic signs, and many figures of men and animals, fishes, reptiles and birds; suns and stars; and many quaint symbols. The cliff faced exactly north. There was something about it so strange, and so different from the other carved rocks which I had visited, that I called a halt and spent the day in examining the rock front as well as I could with my telescope. The Egyptians of my company were terribly afraid, and used every kind of persuasion to induce me to pass on. I stayed till late in the afternoon, by which time I had failed to make out aright the entry of any tomb. By this time the men were rebellious; and I had to leave the valley if I did not wish my whole retinue to desert. But I secretly made up my mind to discover the tomb, and explore it. To this end I went further into the mountains, where I met with an Arab Sheik who was willing to take service with me. The Arabs were not bound by the same superstitious fears as the Egyptians; Sheik Abu Soma and his following were willing to take a part in the explorations.

"Being baffled of winning the tomb from below, and being unprovided with ladders to scale the face of the rock, I found a way by much circuitous journeying to the top of the cliff. Thence I caused myself to be lowered by ropes. I found that there was an entrance, closed however by a great stone slab. This was cut in the rock more than a hundred feet up, being two-thirds the height of the cliff. The hieroglyphic and cabalistic symbols cut in the rock were so managed as to disguise it. I used much force, and by many heavy strokes won a way into the tomb. The stone door having fallen into the entrance I passed over it into the tomb, noting as I went a long iron chain which hung coiled on a bracket close to the doorway.

"The tomb I found to be complete, after the manner of the finest Egyptian tombs, with chamber and shaft leading down to the corridor, ending in the Mummy Pit. All the walls of the chamber and the passage were carved with strange writings. We descended into the Mummy Pit. The huge sarcophagus in the deep pit was marvelously graven throughout with signs. The Arab chief and two others who ventured into the tomb with me, and who were evidently used to such grim explorations, managed to take the cover from the sarcophagus without breaking it.

"Within the sarcophagus was a body, manifestly of a woman, swathed with many wrappings of linen, as is usual with all mummies. Across the breast was one hand, unwrapped. Arm and hand were of dusky white, being of the hue of ivory that hath lain long in air. The skin and the nails were complete and whole, as though the body had been placed for burial overnight. I touched the hand and moved it, the arm being something flexible as a live arm; though stiff with long disuse. There was, too, an added wonder that on this ancient hand were no less than seven fingers. Sooth to say, it made me shudder and my flesh creep to touch that hand that had lain there undisturbed for so many thousands of years, and yet was like unto living flesh. Underneath the hand, as though guarded by it, lay a huge jewel of ruby; a great stone of wondrous bigness, for the ruby is in the main a small jewel. This one was of wondrous color, being as of fine blood whereon the light shineth. But its wonder lay not in its size or color, but in that the light of it shone from seven stars as clearly as though the stars were in reality there imprisoned. Taking this rare jewel, together with certain amulets of strangeness and richness being wrought of jewel-stones, I made haste to depart. I would have remained longer but that I feared so to do. For it came to me all at once that I was in a desert place, with strange men who were with me because they were not over-scrupulous. That we were in a lone cavern of the dead, a hundred feet above the ground, where none could find me were ill done to me, nor would any ever seek. But in secret I determined that I would come again, though with more secure following, as I saw many things of strange import in that wondrous tomb; including a casket of eccentric shape made of some strange stone, which was in the great sarcophagus itself. There was in the tomb also another coffer which, though of rare proportion and adornment, was more simply shaped. The cover was lightly cemented down with what seemed gum and Paris plaster, as though to insure that no air could penetrate. Within, closely packed, stood four jars finely wrought and carved with various adornments. I had before known that such burial urns as these were used to contain the entrails and other organs of the mummied dead; but on opening these we found that they held but oil. I was warned of my danger by seeing in the eyes of the Arabs certain covetous glances. Whereon, in order to hasten their departure, I wrought upon those fears of superstition which even in these callous men were apparent. The chief of the Bedouins ascended from the Mummy Pit to give the signal to those above to raise us; and I, not caring to remain with the men whom I mistrusted, followed him immediately. The others did not come at once; from which I feared that they were rifling the tomb afresh on their own account. At last they came. One of them, who ascended first, in landing at the top of the cliff lost his foothold and fell below. He was instantly killed. Before coming away I pulled into its place again, as well as I could, the slab of stone that covered the entrance to the tomb.

"When we all stood on the hill above the cliff, the burning sun that was bright and full of glory was good to see after the darkness and strange mystery of the tomb. Even was I glad that the poor Arab who fell down the cliff and lay dead below, lay in the sunlight and not in that gloomy cavern. I would fain have gone with my companions to seek him and give him sepulture of some kind; but the Sheik made light of it, and sent two of his men to see to it whilst we went on our way.

"That night as we camped, one of the men only returned, saying that a lion of the desert had killed his companion after they had buried the dead man in very deep sand without the valley, and had covered the spot where he lay with many great rocks, so that jackals or other preying beasts might not dig him up again as is their wont.

"Later, in the light of the fire round which the men sat or lay, I saw him exhibit to his fellows something white which they seemed to regard with special awe and reverence. So I drew near silently, and saw that it was none other than the white hand of the mummy which had lain protecting the Jewel in the great sarcophagus. I heard the Bedouin tell how he had found it on the body of him who had fallen from the cliff. There was no mistaking it, for there were the seven fingers which I had noted before. This man must have wrenched it off the dead body whilst his chief and I were otherwise engaged; and from the awe of the others I doubted not that he had hoped to use it as an Amulet, or charm. Whereas if powers it had, they were not for him who had taken it from the dead; since his death followed hard upon his theft. Already his Amulet had had an awesome baptism; for the wrist of the dead hand was stained with red as though it had been dipped in recent blood.

"That night I was in certain fear lest there should be some violence done to me; for if the poor dead hand was so valued as a charm, what must be the worth in such wise of the rare jewel which it had guarded.

"As I sank into the unconsciousness of sleep, I hid the graven Star Jewel in the hollow of my clenched hand.

"I waked out of sleep with the light of the morning sun on my face. I sat up and looked around me. The fire was out, and the camp was desolate; save for one figure which lay prone close to me. It was that of the Arab chief, who lay on his back, dead. His face was almost black; and his eyes were open, and staring horribly up at the sky, as though he saw there some dreadful vision. He had evidently been strangled; for on looking, I found on his throat the red marks where fingers had pressed. There seemed so many of these marks that I counted them. There were seven; and all parallel, except the thumb mark, as though made with one hand. This thrilled me as I thought of the mummy hand with the seven fingers.

"I paused not, but fled from the place. I journeyed on alone through the hot desert, till, by God's grace, I came upon an Arab tribe camping by a well, who gave me salt. With them I rested till they had set me on my way.

"I know not what became of the mummy hand. It doubtless is used as a charm of potence by some desert tribe."

Twice, whilst I had been reading this engrossing narrative, I had thought that I had seen across the page streaks of shade, which the weirdness of the subject had made to seem like the shadow of a hand. On the first of these occasions I found that the illusion came from the fringe of green silk around the lamp; but on the second I had looked up, and my eyes had lit on the mummy hand across the room on which the starlight was falling under the edge of the blind. I looked over at the bed; and it comforted me to think that the Nurse still sat there, calm and wakeful.

I sat looking at the book on the table before me; and so many strange thoughts crowded on me that my mind began to whirl. It was almost as if the light on the white fingers in front of me was beginning to have some hypnotic effect. All at once, all thoughts seemed to stop; and for an instant the world and time stood still.

There lay a real hand across the book! What was there to so overcome me, as was the case? I knew the hand that I saw on the book. Margaret Trelawny's hand was a joy to me to see; and yet at that moment, coming after other marvelous things, it had a strangely moving effect on me. It was but momentary, however, and had passed even before her voice had reached me.

"What disturbs you? What are you staring at the book for? I thought for an instant that you must have been overcome again!" I jumped up.

"I was reading," I said, "an old book from the library." As I spoke I closed it and put it under my arm. Nurse Kennedy was ready to go to bed; so Miss Trelawny watched with me in the room.

The next morning, Mr. Corbeck talked the whole matter over with me.

"I think you should know what followed Van Huyn's narrative. When Mr. Trelawny and I met, which we did through his seeking the assistance of other Egyptologists in his work, we talked over this as we did over many other things; and we determined to make search for the mysterious valley. Whilst we were waiting to start on the travel, for many things were required which Mr. Trelawny undertook to see to himself, I went to Holland to try if I could by any traces verify Van Huyn's narrative. I set me to work to find what had become of his treasures; for that such a traveler must have had great treasures was apparent. At last, in the shop of an old watchmaker and jeweler at Hoorn, I found what he considered his chiefest treasure: a great ruby, carven like a scarab, with seven stars in the shape of the constellation of the Plough,* and engraven with hieroglyphics. The jewel was put in security in Mr. Trelawny's great safe; and we started out on our journey of exploration in full hope.

"We got together a band of Arabs whom one or other of us had known in former trips to the desert, and whom we could trust; that is, we did not distrust them as much as others. We were numerous enough to protect ourselves from chance marauding bands.

"Well, after much wandering and trying every winding in the interminable jumble of hills, we came at last at nightfall on just such a valley as Van Huyn had described.

"The following morning Mr. Trelawny and I went alone into the tomb. Within, we found a great sarcophagus of yellow stone. But that I need not describe: you have seen it in Mr. Trelawny's chamber. There must, however, be one sense of disappointment. I could not help feeling how different must have been the sight which met the Dutch traveler's eyes when he looked within and found that white hand lying lifelike above the shrouding mummy cloths. It is true that a part of the arm was there, white and ivory like.

"I shall not trouble you with details of all we saw, or how we learned all we knew. Part of it was from knowledge common to scholars; part we read on the Stele in the tomb, and in the sculptures and hieroglyphic paintings on the walls.

"The tomb belonged to Queen Tera, who was of the Eleventh, or Theban, Dynasty of Egyptian Kings which held sway between twenty-ninth and twenty-fifth centuries before Christ. She succeeded as the only child of her father, Antef. She must have been a girl of extraordinary character as well as ability, for she was but a young girl when her father died. Her youth and sex encouraged the ambitious priesthood, which had then achieved immense power. They were then secretly ready to make an effort to transfer the governing power from a Kingship to a Hierarchy. But King Antef had suspected some such movement, and had taken the precaution of securing to his daughter the allegiance of the army. He had also had her taught

---

* The Big Dipper.

statecraft, and had even made her learned in the lore of the very priests themselves. He had used those of one cult against the other.

"But the King had gone to further lengths, and had had his daughter taught magic, by which she had power over Sleep and Will. This was real magic—'black' magic; not the magic of the temples, which, I may explain, was of the harmless or 'white' order, and was intended to impress rather than to effect. She had been an apt pupil; and had gone further than her teachers. She had won secrets from nature in strange ways; and had even gone to the lengths of going down into the tomb herself, having been swathed and coffined and left as dead for a whole month.

"Perhaps the most remarkable statement in the records, both on the Stele and in the mural writings, was that Queen Tera had power to compel the Gods. This, by the way, was not an isolated belief in Egyptian history; but was different in its cause. She had engraved on a ruby, carved like a scarab, and having seven stars of seven points, Master Words to compel all the Gods, both of the Upper and the Under Worlds.

"In the statement it was plainly set forth that the hatred of the priests was stored up for her, and that they would after her death try to suppress her name. This was a terrible revenge in Egyptian mythology; for without a name no one can after death be introduced to the Gods, or have prayers said for him. Therefore, she had intended her resurrection to be after a long time in a more northern land, under the constellation whose seven stars had ruled her birth. To this end, her hand was to be in the air—'unwrapped'—and in it the Jewel of Seven Stars, so that wherever was air she might move even as her Ka could move! This Mr. Trelawny and I agreed meant that her body could become astral at command, and so move, particle by particle, and become whole again when and where required.

"After extensive examinations of the tomb, we carefully removed all we could. With our heavy baggage, we set out on our laborious journey back to the Nile. The nights were an anxious time with us, for we feared attack from some marauding band. But more still we feared some of those with us. They were, after all, but predatory, unscrupulous men; and we had with us a considerable bulk of precious things. We had taken the mummy from the sarcophagus, and packed it for safety of travel in a separate case. During the first night two attempts were made to steal things from the cart; and two men were found dead in the morning.

"On the second night there came on a violent storm, one of those terrible simoons of the desert which makes one feel his helplessness. We were overwhelmed with the drifting sand. Some of our Bedouins had fled before the storm, hoping to find shelter; the rest of us endured with what patience we could. In the morning, when the storm had passed, we recovered from under the piles of sand what we could of our impedimenta. We found the case in which the mummy had been packed all broken, but the mummy itself could nowhere be found. We searched everywhere around, and dug up the sand which had piled around us; but in vain. Mr. Trelawny finally said to me:

" 'We must go back to the tomb in the Valley of the Sorcerer.'

" 'All right!' I answered. 'But why shall we go there?' His answer seemed to thrill through me as though it had struck some chord ready tuned within:

" 'We shall find the mummy there! I am sure of it!'

"The Arabs were surprised when we retraced our steps. There was a good deal of friction, and there were several desertions; so that it was with a diminished following that we took our way eastward again. Mr. Trelawny and I took ropes and torches, and again ascended to the tomb. It was evident that someone had been there in our absence, for the stone slab which protected the entrance to the tomb was lying flat inside, and a rope was dangling from the cliff summit. The first thing noticeable was the emptiness of the place.

"It was made more infinitely desolate still by the shrouded figure of the mummy of Queen Tera which lay on the floor where the great sarcophagus had stood! Beside it lay, in the strange contorted attitudes of violent death, three of the Arabs who had deserted from our party. Their faces were black, and their hands and necks were smeared with blood which had burst from mouth and nose and eyes.

"On the throat of each were the marks, now blackening, of a hand of seven fingers.

"Trelawny and I drew close, and clutched each other in awe and fear as we looked.

"For, most wonderful of all, across the breast of the mummied Queen lay a hand of seven fingers, ivory white, the wrist only showing a scar like a jagged red line, from which seemed to depend drops of blood.

"We got to Cairo all right, and from there to Alexandria. At Alexandria, Trelawny found waiting a cable stating that Mrs. Trelawny had died in giving birth to a daughter. Her stricken husband hurried off at once by the Orient Express; and I had to bring the treasures alone to the desolate house. Since he received that cable in the shipping office at Alexandria I have never seen a happy smile on his face.

"Work is the best thing in such a case; and to his work he devoted himself heart and soul. The strange tragedy of his loss and gain—for the child was born after the mother's death—took place during our second visit to the tomb of Queen Tera. He told me very little about his daughter; but I could see that he loved, almost idolized her. Yet he could never forget that her birth had cost her mother's life. She is unlike her mother; but in both feature and color she has a marvelous resemblance to the pictures of Queen Tera.

"Years later he sent for me early one morning. I was then studying in the British Museum, and had rooms in Hart Street. When I came, he was all on fire with excitement. The window blinds were down and the shutters closed. The ordinary lights in the room were not lit, but there were a lot of powerful electric lamps, fifty candle-power at least, arranged on one side of the room. The little bloodstone table on which the heptagonal coffer stands was drawn to the center of the room. The coffer looked exquisite in the glare of light which shone on it. It actually seemed to glow as if lit in some way from within.

" 'What do you think of it?' he asked.

" 'It is like a jewel,' I answered. 'You may well call it the "Sorcerer's Magic Coffer," if it often looks like that. It almost seems to be alive.'

"As I spoke he turned up the ordinary lights of the room and switched off the special ones. The effect on the stone box was surprising; in a second it lost all its glowing effect.

" 'Do you notice anything in the arrangement of the lamps?' he asked.

" 'No!'

" 'They were in the shape of the stars in the Plough, as the stars are in the ruby!' I listened as Trelawny went on to explain:

" 'For sixteen years I have never ceased to think of that adventure, or to try to find a clue to the mysteries which came before us; but never until last night did I seem to find a solution. It might be, I thought, that the light of the seven stars, shining in the right direction, might have some effect on the box, or something within it. I raised the blind and looked out. The Plough was high in the heavens, and both its stars and the Pole Star were straight opposite the window. I pulled the table with the coffer out into the light, and shifted it until the translucent patches were in the direction of the stars. Instantly the box began to glow, as you saw it under the lamps.

" 'All at once it came to me that if light could have some effect there should be in the tomb some means of producing light; for there could not be starlight in the Mummy Pit in the cavern. Then the whole thing seemed to become clear. On the bloodstone table, which has a hollow carved in its top, into which the bottom of the coffer fits, I laid the Magic Coffer; and I at once saw that the odd protuberances so carefully wrought in the substance of the stone corresponded in a way to the stars in the constellation. These, then, were to hold lights. So all we want are the lamps. Where are the lamps? I shall tell you: In the tomb! Do you remember wondering, when we examined the tomb, at the lack of one thing which is usually found in such a tomb?'

" 'Yes! There was no serdâb.'

"The Serdâb, I may perhaps explain," said Mr. Corbeck to me, "is a sort of niche built or hewn in the wall of a tomb. Those which have as yet been examined bear no inscriptions, and contain only effigies of the dead for whom the tomb was made." Then he went on with his narrative:

"Trelawny, when he saw that I had caught his meaning, went on speaking with something of his old enthusiasm:

" 'I have come to the conclusion that there must be a serdâb—a secret one. I am going to ask you to go out to Egypt again; to seek the tomb; to find the serdâb; and to bring back the lamps!'

"I started the next week for Egypt; and never rested till I stood again in the tomb. There, in the very spot where I had expected to find it, was the opening of the serdâb. And the serdâb was empty.

"But the Chapel was not empty; for the dried-up body of a man in Arab dress lay close under the opening, as though he had been stricken down. I examined all round the walls to see if Trelawny's surmise was correct; and I found that in all the positions of the stars as given, the Pointers of the Plough indicated a spot to the left hand, or south side, of the opening of the serdâb, where was a single star in gold.

"I pressed this, and it gave way. The stone which had marked the front of the serdâb, and which lay back against the wall within, moved slightly. On further examining the other side of the opening, I found a similar spot, indicated by other representations of the constellation; but this was itself a figure of the seven stars, and each was wrought in burnished gold. I pressed each star in turn; but without result. Then it struck me that if the opening spring was on the left, this on the right might have been intended for the simultaneous pressure of all the stars by one hand of seven fingers. By using both my hands, I managed to effect this.

"With a loud click, a metal figure seemed to dart from close to the opening of the serdâb; the stone slowly swung back to its place, and shut with a click. The glimpse which I had of the descending figure appalled me for the moment. It was like that grim guardian which, according to the Arabian historian Ibn Abd Alhokin, the builder of the Pyramids, King Saurid Ibn Salhouk placed in the Western Pyramid to defend its treasure: 'A marble figure, upright, with lance in hand; with on his head a serpent wreathed. When any approached, the serpent would bite him on one side, and twining about his throat and killing him, would return again to his place.'

"I knew well that such a figure was not wrought to pleasantry; and that to brave it was no child's play. The dead Arab at my feet was proof of what could be done! So I examined again along the wall; and found here and there chippings as if someone had been tapping with a heavy hammer. This then had been what happened: The grave-robber more expert at his work than we had been, and suspecting the presence of a hidden serdâb, had made essay to find it. He had struck the spring by chance; had released the avenging 'Treasurer,' as the Arabian writer designated him. The issue spoke for itself.

"Perhaps you do not know that the entrance to a serdâb is almost always very narrow; sometimes a hand can hardly be inserted. Two things I learned from this serdâb. The first was that the lamps, if lamps at all there had been, could not have been of large size; and secondly, that they would be in some way associated with Hathor, whose symbol, the hawk in a square with the right top corner forming a smaller square, was cut in relief on the wall within. Hathor is the goddess who in Egyptian mythology answers to Venus of the Greeks, in as far as she is the presiding deity of beauty and pleasure. In the Egyptian mythology, however, each God has many forms; and in some respects Hathor has to do with the idea of resurrection. There are seven forms or variants of the Goddess; why should not these correspond in some way to the seven lamps! That there had been such lamps, I was convinced. The first grave-robber had met his death; the second had found the contents of the serdâb.

"That was nearly three years ago; and for all that time I have been like the man in the Arabian Nights, seeking old lamps, not for new, but for cash. At last, not two months ago, I was shown by an old dealer in Mossul one lamp such as I had looked for. I wanted to see all his stock before buying; and one by one he produced, amongst masses of rubbish, seven different lamps. Each of them had a distinguishing mark; and each and all was some form of the symbol of Hathor. I got on as fast as it is possible to travel in such countries; and arrived in London with only the lamps and certain portable curios and papyri which I had picked up on my travels."

With all of this whirling through my mind, I resumed watch in Mr. Trelawny's room.

"Who are you? What are you doing here?"

Whatever ideas any of us had ever formed of his waking, I am quite sure that none of us expected to see him start up all awake and full master of himself. I was so surprised that I answered almost mechanically:

"Ross is my name. I have been watching by you! I am a Barrister. It is not, however, in that capacity I am here; but simply as a friend of your daughter. It was probably her knowledge of my being a lawyer which first determined her to ask me to come when she thought you had been murdered. Afterwards she was good enough to consider me to be a friend, and to allow me to remain in accordance with your expressed wish that someone should remain to watch."

"She thought I had been murdered! Was that last night?"

"No! three nights ago."

"Tell me all about it! All you know! Every detail! Omit nothing! But stay; first lock the door! I want to know, before I see anyone, exactly how things stand."

Accordingly, I told him every detail, even of the slightest which I could remember, of what had happened from the moment of my arrival at the house.

I met Margaret in the hall. The moment she saw me her eyes brightened, and she looked at me keenly.

"You have some good news for me?" she said. "Is Father better?"

"He is! Why did you think so?"

"I saw it in your face. I must go to him at once." She was hurrying away when I stopped her.

"He said he would send for you the moment he was dressed."

She sat down on the nearest chair and began to cry. I felt overcome myself. The sight of her joy and emotion quite unmanned me. She saw my emotion, and seemed to understand. She put out her hand. I held it hard, and kissed it. Such moments as these, the opportunities of lovers, are gifts of the gods! Up to this instant, though I knew I loved her, and though I believe she returned my affection, I had had only hope. Now, however, the self-surrender manifest in her willingness to let me squeeze her hand, the ardor of her pressure in return, and the glorious flush of love in her beautiful, deep, dark eyes as she lifted them to mine, were all the eloquences which the most impatient or exacting lover could expect or demand.

Presently a bell rang from the room. Margaret slipped from me, and looked back with warning finger on lip. She went over to her father's door and knocked softly.

"Come in!" said the strong voice.

"It is I, Father!" The voice was tremulous with love and hope.

There was a quick step inside the room; the door was hurriedly thrown open, and in an instant Margaret, who had sprung forward, was clasped in her father's arms.

Here the father and daughter went into the room together, and the door closed.

When I told Mr. Corbeck that Mr. Trelawny had quite recovered, he began to dance about like a wild man. I then found Sergeant Daw and took him into the study, so that we should be alone when I told him the news. It surprised even his iron self control when I told him the method of the waking. I was myself surprised in turn by his first words:

"And how did he explain the first attack? He was unconscious when the second was made."

Up to that moment the nature of the attack, which was the cause of my coming to the house, had never even crossed my mind, except when I had simply narrated the various occurrences in sequence to Mr. Trelawny.

"Do you know, it never occurred to me to ask him!" The Detective did not seem to think much of my answer:

"That is why so few cases are ever followed out," he said, "unless our people are in them. Your amateur detective never hunts down to the death. Well, Mr. Ross, I'm glad the case is over; for over it is, so far as I am concerned. I suppose that Mr. Trelawny knows his own business; and that now he is well again, he will take it up himself."

Soon after the Detective left, Mr. Trelawny called for me.

"Come in, Mr. Ross!" he said cordially, but with a certain formality which I dreaded.

"If things are as I fancy, we shall not have any secrets between us. Malcolm Ross knows so much of my affairs already, that I take it he must either let matters stop where they are and go away in silence, or else he must—know more. Margaret! are you willing to let Mr. Ross see your wrist?"

She threw one swift look of appeal in his eyes; but even as she did so she seemed to make up her mind. Without a word she raised her right hand, so that the bracelet of spreading wings which covered the wrist fell back, leaving the flesh bare. Then an icy chill shot through me.

On her wrist was a thin red jagged line, from which seemed to hang red stains like drops of blood!

She stood there, a veritable figure of patient pride. As we stood thus for some seconds, the deep, grave voice of her father seemed to sound a challenge in my ears:

"What do you say now?"

My answer was not in words. I caught Margaret's right hand in mine as it fell, and, holding it tight, whilst with the other I pushed back the golden cincture, stooped and kissed the wrist.

We were interrupted by a knock at the door. In answer to an impatient "Come in!" from Mr. Trelawny, Mr. Corbeck entered. All the enthusiasm of his youth, of which Mr. Corbeck had told us, seemed to have come back to him in an instant.

"So you have got the lamps!" he almost shouted. "Come to the library, where we will be alone, and tell me all about it!"

The next evening after supper Mr. Trelawny took us into the study where Mr. Corbeck and Doctor Winchester were waiting, saying as he passed in:

"The experiment which is before us is to try whether or no there is any force, any reality, in the old Magic. That there is some such existing power I firmly believe. It might not be possible to create, or arrange, or organize such power in our own time; but I take it that if in Old Time such a power existed, it may have some exceptional survival. After all, the Bible is not a myth; if the Witch at Endor could call up to Saul the spirit of Samuel, why may not there have been others with equal powers; and why may not one among them survive? Indeed, we are told in the Book of Samuel that the Witch of Endor was only one of many, and her being consulted by Saul was a matter of chance. He only sought one among the many whom he had driven out of Israel; 'all those that had Familiar Spirits, and the Wizards.' This Egyptian Queen, Tera, who reigned nearly two thousand years before Saul, had a Familiar, and was a Wizard too. See how the priests of her time, and those after it tried to wipe out her name from the face of the earth. Ay, and they succeeded so well that even Manetho, the historian of the Egyptian Kings, writing in the tenth century before Christ, with all the lore of the priesthood for forty centuries behind him, and with possibility of access to every existing record, could not even find her name. Did it strike any of you, in thinking of the late events, who or what her Familiar was?" There was an interruption, for Doctor Winchester struck one hand loudly on the other as he ejaculated:

"The cat! The mummy cat! I knew it!" Mr. Trelawny smiled over at him.

"You are right! There is every indication that the Familiar of the Wizard Queen was that cat which was mummied when she was, and was not only placed in her tomb, but was laid in the sarcophagus with her. That was what bit into my wrist, what cut me with sharp claws." He paused. Margaret's comment was a purely girlish one:

"Then my poor Silvio is acquitted. I am glad!" Her father stroked her hair and went on:

"This woman seems to have had an extraordinary foresight. Foresight far, far beyond her age and the philosophy of her time. She seems to have seen through the weakness of her own religion, and even prepared for emergence into a different world. From the first, her eyes seem to have been attracted to the seven stars of the Plough from the fact, as recorded in the hieroglyphics in her tomb, that at her birth a great aerolite fell, from whose heart was finally extracted that Jewel of Seven Stars which she regarded as the talisman of her life. The Magic Coffer, so wondrously wrought with seven sides also came from the aerolite. Seven was to her a magic number; and no wonder. With seven fingers on one hand, and seven toes on one foot. She was born, we learn in the Stele of her tomb, in the seventh month of the year—the month in which the presiding Goddess was Hathor, the Goddess of her own house, of the Antefs of the Theban line—the Goddess who in various forms symbolizes beauty, and pleasure, and resurrection. Again in this seventh month—which, by later Egyptian astronomy began on October 28th, and ran to the 27th of our November—on the seventh day the Pointer of the Plough just rises above the horizon of the sky at Thebes.

"In a marvelously strange way, therefore, are grouped into this woman's life these various things. The number seven; the Pole Star, with the constellation of seven stars; the God of the month, Hathor, who was her own particular God, the God of her family, the Antefs of the Theban Dynasty, whose Kings' symbol it was, and whose seven forms ruled love and the delights of life and resurrection. If ever there was ground for magic; for the power of symbolism carried into mystic use, it is here.

"Remember, too, that this woman was skilled in all the science of her time. Her wise and cautious father took care of that, knowing that by her own wisdom she must ultimately combat the intrigues of the Hierarchy. Bear in mind that in old Egypt the science of Astronomy began and was developed to an extraordinary height; and that Astrology followed Astronomy in its progress. And it is possible that in the later developments of science with regard to light rays, we may yet find that Astrology is on a scientific basis. Bear in mind also that the Egyptians knew sciences, of which today, despite all our advantages, we are profoundly ignorant. That Magic Coffer of Queen Tera is probably a magic box in more ways than one. It may—possibly it does —contain forces that we know not of. We cannot open it; it must be closed from within. How then was it closed? It is a coffer of solid stone, of amazing hardness, more like a jewel than an ordinary marble, with a lid equally solid; and yet all is so finely wrought that the finest tool made today cannot be inserted under the flange. How was it wrought to such perfection? How was the stone so chosen that those translucent patches match the relations of the seven stars of the constellation? How is it, or from what cause, that when the starlight shines on it, it glows from within—that when I fix the lamps in similar form the glow grows greater still; and yet the box is irresponsive to ordinary light however great? I tell you that that box hides some great mystery of science.

"In another way, too, there may be hidden in that box secrets which, for good or ill, may enlighten the world. We know from their records, and inferentially also, that the Egyptians studied the properties of herbs and minerals for magic purposes—white magic as well as black. We know that some of the wizards of old could induce from sleep dreams of any given kind. That this purpose was mainly effected by hypnotism, which was another art or science of Old Nile, I have little doubt. But still, they must have had a mastery of drugs that is far beyond anything we know. With our own pharmacopoeia we can, to a certain extent, induce dreams. But these old practitioners seemed to have been able to command at will any form or color of dreaming; could work round any given subject or thought in almost any way required. In that coffer, which you have seen, may rest a very armory of dreams. Indeed, some of the forces that lie within it may have been already used in my household.

"What I hold is, that the preparation of that box was made for a special occasion; as indeed were all the preparations of the tomb. Queen Tera did not trouble herself to guard against snakes and scorpions, in that rocky tomb cut in the sheer cliff face a hundred feet above the level of the valley, and fifty down from the summit. Her precautions were against the disturbances of human hands; against the jealousy and hatred of the priests, who, had they known of her real aims, would have tried to baffle them. I gather from the symbolic pictures in the tomb that she so far differed from the belief of her time that she looked for a resurrection in the flesh. It was doubtless this that intensified the hatred of the priesthood, and gave them an acceptable cause for obliterating the very existence, present and future, of one who had outraged their theories and blasphemed their gods. All that she might require in the accomplishment of the resurrection were contained in that almost hermetically sealed suite of chambers in the rock. In the great sarcophagus was the mummy of her Familiar, the cat, which from its great size I take to be a sort of tiger-cat. In the tomb, also in a strong receptacle, were the canopic jars usually containing those internal organs which are separately embalmed, but which in this case had no such contents. So that, I take it, there was in her case a departure in embalming; and that the organs were restored to the body, each in its proper place—if, indeed, they had ever been removed. If this surmise be true, we shall find that the brain of the Queen either was never extracted in the usual way, or, if so taken out, that it was duly replaced, instead of being enclosed within the mummy wrappings. The jars, instead of containing the organs, contained oil; probably for the lamps. Finally, in the sarcophagus there was the Magic Coffer on which her feet rested. Mark also, the care taken in the preservance of her power to control the elements. According to her belief, the open hand outside the wrappings controlled the Air, and the strange Jewel Stone with the shining stars controlled Fire. The symbolism inscribed on the soles of her feet gave sway over Land and Water. Mark how she guarded her secret in case of grave-wrecking or intrusion. None could open her Magic Coffer without the lamps, for we know now that ordinary light will not be effective. The great lid of the sarcophagus was not sealed down as usual, because she wished to control the air. But she hid the lamps, which in structure belong to the Magic Coffer, in a place where none could find them, except by following the secret guidance which she had prepared for only the eyes of wisdom. And even here she had guarded against chance discovery, by preparing a bolt of death for the unwary discoverer. To do this she had applied the lesson of the tradition of the avenging guard of the treasures of the pyramid built by her great predecessor of the Fourth Dynasty of the throne of Egypt.

"You have noted, I suppose, how there were, in the case of her tomb, certain deviations from the usual rules. For instance, the shaft of the Mummy Pit, which is usually filled up solid with stones and rubbish, was left open. Why was this? I take it that she had made arrangements for leaving the tomb when, after her resurrection, she should be a new woman, with a different personality, and less inured to the hardships that in her first existence she had suffered. So far as we can judge of her intent, all things needful for her exit into the world had been thought of, even to the iron chain, described by Van Huyn, close to the door in the rock, by which she might be able to lower herself to the ground. That she expected a long period to elapse was shown in the choice of material. An ordinary rope would be rendered weaker or unsafe in process of time, but she imagined, and rightly, that the iron would endure.

"What her intentions were when once she trod the open earth afresh we do not know, and we never shall, unless her own dead lips can soften and speak.

"Now, as to the Star Jewel! This she manifestly regarded as the greatest of her treasures. In the old Egyptian belief it was held that there were words, which, if used properly—for the method of speaking them was as important as the words themselves—could command the Lords of the Upper and the Lower Worlds. The 'hekau,' or word of power, was all-important in certain rituals. On the Jewel of Seven Stars, which, as you know, is carved into the image of a scarab, are graven in hieroglyphic two such hekau, one above, the other underneath. But you will understand better when you see it! Wait here! Do not stir!"

As he spoke, he rose and left the room. In two or three minutes he returned. He held in his hand a little golden box. This, as he resumed his seat, he placed before him on the table. We all leaned forward as he opened it.

On a lining of white satin lay a wondrous ruby of immense size, almost as big as the top of Margaret's little finger. Shining through its wondrous "pigeon's blood" color were seven different stars, each of seven points, in such position that they reproduced exactly the figure of the Plough. There could be no possible mistake as to this in the mind of anyone who had ever noted the constellation. On it were some hieroglyphic figures, cut with the most exquisite precision, as I could see when it came to my turn to use the magnifying glass, which Mr. Trelawny took from his pocket and handed to us.

When we all had seen it fully, Mr. Trelawny turned it over so that it rested on its back in a cavity made to hold it in the upper half of the box. The reverse was no less wonderful than the upper. It, too, had some hieroglyphic figures cut on it. Mr. Trelawny resumed his lecture:

"As you see, there are two words. The symbols on the top represent a single word, composed of one syllable prolonged with its determinatives. You know, all of you, I suppose, that the Egyptian language was phonetic, and that the hieroglyphic symbol represented the sound. The first symbol here, the hoe, means 'mer,' and the two pointed ellipses the prolongation of the final r: mer-r-r. The sitting figure with the hand to its face is what we call the 'determinative' of 'thought'; and the roll of papyrus that of 'abstraction.' Thus we get the word 'mer,' love, in its abstract, general, and fullest sense. This is the hekau which can command the Upper World.

"The symbolization of the word on the reverse is simpler, though the meaning is more abstruse. The first symbol means 'men,' 'abiding,' and the second, 'ab,' 'the heart.' So that we get 'abiding of heart,' or in our own language 'patience.' And this is the hekau to control the Lower World!"

He closed the box, and motioning us to remain as we were, he went back to his room to replace the Jewel in the safe. When he had returned and resumed his seat, he went on:

"That Jewel, with its mystic words, and which Queen Tera held under her hand in the sarcophagus, was to be an important factor—probably the most important—in the working out of the act of her resurrection. From the first I seemed by a sort of instinct to realize this. I kept the Jewel within my great safe, whence none could extract it; not even Queen Tera herself with her astral body."

"Her 'astral body'? What is that, Father?" There was keenness in Margaret's voice as she asked the question which surprised me a little; but Trelawny smiled as he spoke:

"The astral body, which is a part of Buddhist belief, long subsequent to the time I speak of, and which is an accepted fact of modern mysticism, had its rise in Ancient Egypt; at least, so far as we know. It is that the gifted individual can at will, quick as thought itself, transfer his body whithersoever he chooses, by the dissolution and reincarnation of particles. In the ancient belief there were several parts of a human being.

"First there is the 'Ka,' or 'Double,' which, as Doctor Budge explains, may be defined as 'an abstract individuality of personality' which was imbued with all the characteristic attributes of the individual it represented, and possessed an absolutely independent existence. It was free to move from place to place on earth at will; and it could enter into heaven and hold converse with the gods. Then there was the 'Ba,' or 'soul,' which dwelt in the 'Ka,' and had the power of becoming corporeal or incorporeal at will; 'it had both substance and form. . . . It had power to leave the tomb . . . It could revisit the body in the tomb . . . and could reincarnate it and hold converse with it.' Again there was the 'Khu,' the 'spiritual intelligence,' or spirit. It took the form of 'a shining, luminous, intangible shape of the body.' . . . Then, again, there was the 'Sekhem,' or 'power' of a man, his strength or vital force personified. These were the 'Khaibit,' or 'shadow,' the 'Ren,' or 'name,' the 'Khat,' or 'physical body,' and 'Ab,' the 'heart,' in which life was seated, went to the full making up of a man.

"Thus you will see, that if this division of functions, spiritual and bodily, ethereal and corporeal, ideal and actual, be accepted as exact, there are all the possibilities and capabilities of corporeal transference, guided always by an unimprisonable will or intelligence.

"Now comes the crown of my argument. The purpose of the attack on me was to get the safe open, so that the sacred Jewel of Seven Stars could be extracted. That immense door of the safe could not keep out her astral body, which could gather itself as well within as without the safe. And I doubt not that in the darkness of the night that mummied hand sought often the Talisman Jewel, and drew new inspiration from its touch. But despite all its power, the astral body could not remove the Jewel through the chinks of the safe. The Ruby is not astral; and it could only be moved in the ordinary way by the opening of the doors. To this end, the Queen used her astral body and the fierce force of her Familiar, to bring to the keyhole of the safe the master key which debarred her wish." He paused, and his daughter's voice came out sweet and clear, and full of intense feeling:

"Father, in the Egyptian belief, was the power of resurrection of a mummied body a general one, or was it limited? That is: could it achieve resurrection many times in the course of ages; or only once, and that one final?"

"There was but one resurrection," he answered. "In the common belief, the Spirit found joy in the Elysian Fields, where there was plenty of food and no fear of famine. Where there was moisture and deep-rooted reeds, and all the joys that are to be expected by the people of an arid land and burning clime."

Then Margaret spoke with an earnestness which showed the conviction of her inmost soul:

"To me, then, it is given to understand what was the dream of this great and far-thinking and high-souled lady of old; the dream that held her soul in patient waiting for its realization through the passing of all those tens of centuries. What were the lack of food or the plenitude of it; what were feast or famine to this woman, born in a palace, with the shadow of the Crown of the Two Egypts on her brows! What were reedy morasses or the tinkle of running water to her whose barges could sweep the great Nile from the mountains to the sea. What were petty joys and absence of petty fears to her, the raising of whose hand could hurl armies, or draw to the water-stairs of her palaces the commerce of the world! At whose word rose temples filled with all the artistic beauty of the Times of Old which it was her aim and pleasure to restore! Under whose guidance the solid rock yawned into the sepulcher that she designed!

"I can see her in her loneliness and in the silence of her mighty pride, dreaming her own dream of things far different from those around her. Of some other land, far, far away under the canopy of the silent night, lit by the cool, beautiful light of the stars. A land under that Northern star, whence blew the sweet winds that cooled the feverish desert air. A land of wholesome greenery, far, far away. Where were no scheming and malignant priesthood; whose ideas were to lead to power through gloomy temples and more gloomy caverns of the dead, through an endless ritual of death! A land where love was not base, but a divine possession of the soul! Where there might be some one kindred spirit which could speak to hers through mortal lips like her own; whose being could merge with hers in a sweet communion of soul to soul, even as their breaths could mingle in the ambient air! And in the realization of that dream she will surely be content to rest!"

Mr. Trelawny's face was full of delight. Holding his daughter's hand in his, he went on with his discourse:

"Now, as to the time at which Queen Tera intended her resurrection to take place! As you know, the stars shift their relative positions in the heavens. There can be no doubt whatever that astronomy was an exact science with the Egyptians at least a thousand years before the time of Queen Tera. Now, the stars that go to make up a constellation change in process of time their relative positions, and the Plough is a notable example. The changes in the position of stars in even forty centuries is so small as to be hardly noticeable by an eye not trained to minute observances, but they can by measured and verified. Did you, or any of you, notice how exactly the stars in the

Ruby correspond to the position of the stars in the Plough; or how the same holds with regard to the translucent places in the Magic Coffer? And yet when Queen Tera was laid in her tomb, neither the stars in the Jewel nor the translucent places in the Coffer corresponded to the position of the stars in the Constellation as they then were. Thus it is that to us and our time is given the opportunity of this wondrous peep into the old world, such as has been the privilege of none other of our time; which may never be again.

"Imagine what it will be for the world of thought if there can come back to us out of the unknown past one who can yield to us the lore stored in the great Library of Alexandria, and lost in its consuming flames. Not only history can be set right, and the teachings of science made veritable from their beginnings; but we can be placed on the road to the knowledge of lost arts, lost learning, lost sciences, so that our feet may tread on the indicated path to their ultimate and complete restoration. Oh, what possibilities are there in the coming of such a being into our midst!"

Mr. Trelawny took up another theme:

"We have now to settle definitely the exact hour at which the Great Experiment is to be made. The logical time is the seventh hour after sunset. On each of the occasions when action was taken in my house, this was the time chosen. As the sun sets tonight at eight, our hour is to be three in the morning!" He spoke in a matter-of-fact way, though with great gravity; but there was nothing of mystery in his words or manner.

In a lofty frame of mind, and with less anxiety than I had felt for days, I went to my room and lay down on the sofa.

I was awakened by Corbeck calling to me, hurriedly:

"Come as quickly as you can. Mr. Trelawny wants to see us at once. Hurry!"

I jumped up and ran down to the Mr. Trelawny's room. All were there except Margaret, who came immediately after me carrying Silvio in her arms. When the cat saw his old enemy he struggled to get down; but Margaret held him fast and soothed him. I looked at my watch. It was close to eight.

When Margaret was with us her father said directly, with a quiet insistence which was new to me:

"You believe, Margaret, that Queen Tera will not harm any of us in our attempt to assist in her resurrection?" After a pause Margaret answered in a low voice:

"Yes!"

In the pause her whole being, appearance, expression, voice, manner had changed. Even Silvio noticed it, and with a violent effort wriggled away from her arms; she did not seem to notice the act. I expected that the cat, when he had achieved his freedom, would have attacked the mummy; but on this occasion he did not. He seemed too cowed to approach it. He shrunk away, and with a piteous "miaou" came over and rubbed himself against my ankles. I took him up in my arms, and he nestled there content. Mr. Trelawny spoke again:

"You are sure of what you say! You believe it with all your soul?" Margaret's face had lost the abstracted look; it now seemed illuminated with the devotion of one to whom is given to speak of great things. She answered in a voice which, though quiet, vibrated with conviction:

"I know it! My knowledge is beyond belief!" Mr. Trelawny spoke again:

"Then you are so sure, that were you Queen Tera herself, you would be willing to prove it in any way that I might suggest?"

"Yes, any way!" the answer rang out fearlessly. He spoke again, in a voice in which was no note of doubt:

"Even in the abandonment of your Familiar to death—to annihilation?"

She paused, and I could see that she suffered—suffered horribly. There was in her eyes a hunted look, which no man can, unmoved, see in the eyes of his beloved. Finally she answered:

"Even that!"

Then stepping over to where the mummy cat stood on the little table, she placed her hand on it. She had now left the sunlight, and the shadows looked dark and deep over her. In a clear voice she said:

"Were I Tera, I would say 'Take all I have! This night is for the Gods alone!' "

As she spoke the sun dipped, and the cold shadow suddenly fell on us. We all stood still for a while. Silvio jumped from my arms and ran over to his mistress, rearing himself up against her dress as if asking to be lifted. He took no notice whatever of the mummy now.

Margaret was glorious with all her wonted sweetness as she said sadly:

"The sun is down, Father! Shall any of us see it again? The night of nights is come!"

Mr. Trelawny asked us men to come with him. We presently managed to move an oak table, which had stood against the wall in the hall, into his room. This we placed under the strong cluster of electric lights. Margaret looked on for a while; then all at once her face blanched, and in an agitated voice she said:

"What are you going to do, Father?"

"To unroll the mummy of the cat! Queen Tera will not need her Familiar tonight. If she should want him, it might be dangerous to us: so we shall make him safe. You are not alarmed, dear?"

"Oh no!" she answered quickly. "But I was thinking of my Silvio, and how I should feel if he had been the mummy that was to be unswathed!"

Mr. Trelawny got knives and scissors ready, and placed the cat on the table. It was a grim beginning to our work; and it made my heart sink when I thought of what might happen in that lonely house in the mid-gloom of the night. The sense of loneliness and isolation from the world was increased by the moaning of the wind which had now risen ominously.

There was an incredible number of bandages; and the tearing sound—they being stuck fast to each other by bitumen and gums and spices—and the little cloud of red pungent dust that arose, pressed on the senses of all of us. As the last wrappings came away, we saw the animal seated before us. He was all hunkered up; his hair and teeth and claws were complete. The eyes were closed, but the eyelids had not the fierce look which I expected. The whiskers had been pressed down on the side of the face by the bandaging; but when the pressure was taken away they stood out, just as they would have done in life. He was a magnificent creature, a tiger-cat of great size. But as we looked at him, our first glance of admiration changed to one of fear, and a shudder ran through each one of us; for here was a confirmation of the fears which we had endured.

His mouth and his claws were smeared with the dry, red stains of recent blood!

"It is as I expected," Mr. Trelawny said. "This promises well for what is to follow."

By this time Doctor Winchester was looking at the red stained paws. "As I expected!" he said. "He has seven claws, too!" Opening his pocket-book, he took out the piece of blotting-paper marked by Silvio's claws, on which was also marked in pencil a diagram of the cuts made on Mr. Trelawny's wrist. He placed the paper under the mummy cat's paw. The marks fitted exactly.

When we had carefully examined the cat, finding, however, nothing strange about it but its wonderful preservation, Mr. Trelawny lifted it from the table. Margaret started forward, crying out:

"Take care, Father! Take care! He may injure you!"

"Not now, my dear!" he answered as he moved towards the stairway. Her face fell. "Where are you going?" she asked in a faint voice.

"To the kitchen," he answered. "Fire will take away all danger for the future; even an astral body cannot materialize from ashes!" He signed to us to follow him. Margaret turned away with a sob. I went to her; but she motioned me back and whispered:

"No, no! Go with the others. Father may want you. Oh! it seems like murder! The poor Queen's pet. . . . !" The tears were dropping from under the fingers that covered her eyes.

In the kitchen was a fire of wood ready laid. To this Mr. Trelawny applied a match; in a few seconds the kindling had caught and the flames leaped. When the fire was solidly ablaze, he threw the body of the cat into it. For a few seconds it lay a dark mass amidst the flames, and the room was rank with the smell of burning hair. Then the dry body caught fire too. The inflammable substances used in embalming became new fuel, and the flames roared. A few minutes of fierce conflagration; and then we breathed freely. Queen Tera's Familiar was no more!

When we went back to the room we found Margaret sitting in the dark. Though she had been crying, her eyes were now dry. Her father said to us in a grave tone:

"Now we had better prepare for our great work. It will not do to leave anything to the last!" Margaret must have had a suspicion of what was coming, for it was with a sinking voice that she asked:

"What are you going to do now?" Mr. Trelawny too must have had a suspicion of her feelings, for he answered in a low tone:

"To unroll the mummy of Queen Tera!" She came close to him and said pleadingly in a whisper:

"Father, you are not going to unswathe her! All you men . . . ! And in the glare of light!"

"But why not, my dear?"

"Just think, Father, a woman! All alone! In such a way! In such a place! Oh! it's cruel, cruel!" She was manifestly much overcome. Her cheeks were flaming red, and her eyes were full of indignant tears. Her father saw her distress; and, sympathizing with it, began to comfort her.

"Not a woman, dear; a mummy! She has been dead nearly five thousand years!"

"What does that matter? Sex is not a matter of years! A woman is a woman, if she had been dead five thousand centuries! And you expect her to arise out of that long sleep! It could not be real death, if she is to rise out of it! You have led me to believe that she will come alive when the Coffer is opened!"

"I did, my dear; and I believe it! But if it isn't death that has been the matter with her all these years, it is something uncommonly like it. Then again, just think; it was men who embalmed her. They didn't have woman's rights or lady doctors in ancient Egypt, my dear!"

By this time Mr. Trelawny, assisted by Mr. Corbeck and Doctor Winchester, had raised the lid of the ironstone sarcophagus which contained the mummy of the Queen. It was a large one; but it was none too big. The mummy was both long and broad and high; and was of such weight that it was no easy task, even for the four of us, to lift it out. Under Mr. Trelawny's direction we laid it out on the table prepared for it.

Then, and then only, did the full horror of the whole thing burst upon me! There in the full glare of the light, the whole material and sordid side of death seemed staringly real. The outer wrappings, torn and loosened by rude touch, and with the color either darkened by dust or worn light by friction, seemed creased as by rough treatment; the jagged edges of the wrapping-cloths looked fringed; the painting was patchy, and the varnish chipped. The coverings were evidently many, for the bulk was great. But through all, showed that unhidable human figure, which seems to look more horrible when partially concealed than at any other time. What was before us was Death, and nothing else. All the romance and sentiment of fancy had disappeared. The two older men, enthusiasts who had often done such work, were not disconcerted; and Doctor Winchester seemed to hold himself in a business-like attitude, as if before the operating-table. But I felt low-spirited, and miserable, and ashamed; and besides I was pained and alarmed by Margaret's ghastly pallor.

Then the work began. The cat had been embalmed with coarser materials; here, all, when once the outer coverings were removed, was more delicately done. It seemed as if only the finest gums and spices had been used in this embalming. As the unrolling went on, the wrappings became finer, and the smell less laden with bitumen, but more pungent. Now and again Mr. Trelawny or Mr. Corbeck would point out some special drawing before laying the bandage on the pile behind them.

At last we knew that the wrappings were coming to an end. Already the proportions were reduced to those of a normal figure of the manifest height of the Queen. And as the end drew nearer, so Margaret's pallor grew; and her heart beat more and more wildly, till her breast heaved in a way that frightened me.

The final wrapping was a wide piece the whole length of the body. It being removed, a profusely full robe of white linen appeared, covering the body from the throat to the feet.

And such linen! We all bent over to look at it.

It was as fine as the finest silk. But never was spun or woven silk which lay in such gracious folds, constrict though they were by the close wrappings of the mummy cloth, and fixed into hardness by the passing of thousands of years.

Round the neck it was delicately embroidered in pure gold with tiny sprays of sycamore; and round the feet, similarly worked, was an endless line of lotus plants of unequal height, and with all the graceful abandon of natural growth.

Across the body, but manifestly not surrounding it, was a girdle of jewels. A wondrous girdle, which shone and glowed with all the forms and phases and colors of the sky!

Margaret raised her hands in ecstasy. She bent over to examine more closely; but suddenly drew back and stood fully erect at her grand height. She seemed to speak with the conviction of absolute knowledge as she said:

"That is no cerement! It was not meant for the clothing of death! It is a marriage robe!"

Mr. Trelawny leaned over and touched the linen robe. He lifted a fold at the neck, and I knew from the quick intake of his breath that something had surprised him. He lifted yet a little more; and then he, too, stood back and pointed, saying:

"Margaret is right! That dress is not intended to be worn by the dead! See! her figure is not robed in it. It is but laid upon her." He lifted the zone of jewels and handed it to Margaret. Then with both hands he raised the ample robe, and laid it across the arms which she extended in a natural impulse. Things of such beauty were too precious to be handled with any but the greatest care.

We all stood awed at the beauty of the figure which, save for the face cloth, now lay completely nude before us. Mr. Trelawny bent over, and with hands that trembled slightly, raised this linen cloth which was of the same fineness as the robe. As he stood back and the whole glorious beauty of the Queen was revealed, I felt a rush of shame sweep over me. It was not right that we should be there, gazing with irreverent eyes on such unclad beauty: It was indecent; it was almost sacrilegious! And yet the white wonder of that beautiful form was something to dream of. It was not like death at all; it was like a statue carven in ivory by the hand of a Praxteles. There was nothing of that horrible shrinkage which death seems to effect in a moment. There was none of the wrinkled toughness which seems to be a leading characteristic of most mummies. There was not the shrunken attenuation of a body dried in the sand, as I had seen before in museums. The flesh was full and round, as in a living person; and the skin was as smooth as satin. The color seemed extraordinary. It was like ivory, new ivory; except where the right arm, with shattered, bloodstained wrist and missing hand had lain bare to exposure in the sarcophagus for so many tens of centuries.

With a womanly impulse; with a mouth that drooped with pity, with eyes that flashed with anger, and cheeks that flamed, Margaret threw over the body the beautiful robe which lay across her arm. Only the face was then to be seen. This was more startling even than the body, for it seemed not dead, but alive. The eyelids were closed; but the long, black, curling lashes lay over on the cheeks. The full, red lips, though the mouth was not open, showed the tiniest white line of pearly teeth within. Her hair, glorious in quantity and glossy black as the raven's wing, was piled in great masses over the white forehead, on which a few curling tresses strayed like tendrils. This woman—I could not think of her as a mummy or a corpse—was the image of Margaret. She wore in her hair the "Disk and Plumes," which contained a glorious jewel; one noble pearl of moonlight luster, flanked by carven pieces of moonstone.

Mr. Trelawny was overcome as he looked. He quite broke down;

and when Margaret flew to him and held him close in her arms and comforted him, I heard him murmur brokenly:

"It looks as if you were dead, my child!"

There was a long silence. I could hear without the roar of the wind, which was now risen to a tempest. Mr. Trelawny's voice broke the spell:

"Later on we must try and find out the process of embalming. It is not like any that I know. There does not seem to have been any opening cut for the withdrawing of the viscera and organs, which apparently remain intact within the body. Then, again, there is no moisture in the flesh; but its place is supplied with something else, as though wax or stearine had been conveyed into the veins by some subtle process. I wonder could it be possible that at that time they could have used paraffin. It might have been, by some process that we know not, pumped into the veins, where it hardened!"

As the appointed hour drew near, we went about our separate duties. We looked first to the windows to see that they were closed, and we got ready our respirators to put them on when the time should be close at hand.

Then, under Margaret's guidance we carried the mummied body of Queen Tera and laid it on a couch. We put the sheet lightly over it, so that if she should wake she could at once slip from under it. The severed hand was placed in its true position on her breast, and under it the Jewel of Seven Stars which Mr. Trelawny had taken from the great safe. It seemed to flash and blaze as he put it in its place.

Margaret beckoned me, and I went out with her to bring in Silvio. He came to her purring. She took him up into her arms, and pressing him close to her bosom where he purred loudly, we went back to the room. I closed the door carefully behind me, feeling as I did so a strange thrill as of finality. There was to be no going back now. Then we put on our respirators, and took our places as had been arranged. I was to stand by the taps of the electric lights beside the door, ready to turn them off or on as Mr. Trelawny should direct. Doctor Winchester was to stand behind the couch so that he should not be between the mummy and the sarcophagus; he was to watch carefully what should take place with regard to the Queen. Margaret was to be beside him; she held Silvio ready to place him upon the couch or beside it when she might think right. Mr. Trelawny and Mr. Corbeck were to attend to the lighting of the lamps. When the hands of the clock were close to the hour, they stood ready with their linstocks.

The striking of the silver bell of the clock seemed to smite on our hearts like a knell of doom. One! Two! Three!

Before the third stroke the wicks of the lamps had caught, and I had turned out the electric light. In the dimness of the struggling lamps, and after the bright glow of the electric light, the room and all within it took weird shape, and all seemed in an instant to change. We waited with our hearts beating. I know mine did, and I fancied I could hear the pulsation of the others.

The seconds seemed to pass with leaden wings. It were as though all the world were standing still. The figures of the others stood out dimly, Margaret's white dress alone showing clearly in the gloom. The thick respirators which we all wore added to the strange appearance. The thin light of the lamps showed Mr. Trelawny's square jaw and strong mouth and the brown shaven face of Mr. Corbeck. Their eyes seemed to glare in the light. Across the room Doctor Winchester's eyes twinkled like stars, and Margaret's blazed like black suns. Silvio's eyes were like emeralds.

Would the lamps never burn up!

It was only a few seconds in all till they did blaze up. A slow, steady light, growing more and more bright, and changing in color from blue to crystal white. So they stayed for a couple of minutes without change in the coffer; till at last there began to appear all over it a delicate glow. This grew and grew, till it became like a blazing jewel, and then like a living thing whose essence of life was light. We waited and waited, our hearts seeming to stand still.

All at once there was a sound like a tiny muffled explosion and the cover lifted right up on a level plane a few inches; there was no mistaking anything now, for the whole room was full of a blaze of light. Then the cover, staying fast at one side rose slowly up on the other, as though yielding to some pressure of balance. The coffer still continued to glow; from it began to steal a faint greenish smoke. I could not smell it fully on account of the respirator; but, even through that, I was conscious of a strange pungent odor. Then this smoke began to grow thicker, and to roll out in volumes of ever increasing density till the whole room began to get obscure. The coffer still continued to glow; but the lamps began to grow dim. At first I thought that their light was being overpowered by the thick black smoke; but presently I saw that they were, one by one, burning out. They must have burned quickly to produce such fierce and vivid flames.

I waited and waited expecting every instant to hear the command to turn up the light; but none came. I waited still, and looked with harrowing intensity at the rolling billows of smoke still pouring out of the glowing casket, whilst the lamps sank down and went out one by one.

Finally there was but one lamp alight, and that was dimly blue and flickering. The only effective light in the room was from the glowing casket. I kept my eyes fixed toward Margaret; it was for her now that all my anxiety was claimed. I could just see her white frock beyond the still white shrouded figure on the couch. Silvio was troubled; his piteous mewing was the only sound in the room. Deeper and denser grew the black mist and its pungency began to assail my nostrils as well as my eyes. Now the volume of smoke coming from the coffer seemed to lessen, and the smoke itself to be less dense. Across the room I saw something white move where the couch was. There were several movements. I could just catch the quick glint of white through the dense smoke in the fading light; for now the glow of the coffer began quickly to subside. I could still hear Silvio, but his mewing came from close under; a moment later I could feel him piteously crouching on my foot.

Then the last spark of light disappeared, and through the Egyptian darkness I could see the faint line of white around the window blinds. I felt that the time had come to speak; so I pulled off my respirator and called out:

"Shall I turn up the light?" There was no answer; so before the thick smoke choked me, I called again but more loudly:

"Mr. Trelawny, shall I turn up the light?" He did not answer; but from across the room I heard Margaret's voice, sounding as sweet and clear as a bell:

"Yes, Malcolm!" I turned the tap and the lamps flashed out. But they were only dim points of light in the midst of that murky ball of smoke. In that thick atmosphere there was little possibility of illumination. I ran across to Margaret, guided by her white dress, and caught hold of her and held her hand. She recognized my anxiety and said at once:

"I am all right."

"Thank God!" I said. "How are the others? Quick, let us open all the windows and get rid of this smoke!" To my surprise, she answered in a sleepy way:

"They will be all right. They won't get any harm." I did not stop to inquire how or on what ground she formed such an opinion, but threw up the lower sashes of all the windows, and pulled down the upper. Then I threw open the door.

A few seconds made a perceptible change as the thick, black smoke began to roll out of the windows. Then the lights began to grow into strength and I could see the room. All the men were overcome. Beside the couch Doctor Winchester lay on his back as though he had sunk down and rolled over; and on the farther side of the sarcophagus, where they had stood, lay Mr. Trelawny and Mr. Corbeck. It was a relief to me to see that, though they were unconscious, all three were breathing heavily as though in a stupor. Margaret still stood behind the couch. She seemed at first to be in a partially dazed condition; but every instant appeared to get more command of herself. She stepped forward and helped me to raise her father and drag him close to a window. Together we placed the others similarly, and she flew down to the dining-room and returned with a decanter of brandy. It was not many minutes after we had opened the windows when all three were struggling back to consciousness. I looked round the room to see what had been the effect of the experiment.

The great sarcophagus was just as it had been. The coffer was open, and in it, scattered through certain divisions or partitions wrought in its own substance, was a scattering of black ashes. Over all, sarcophagus, coffer and, indeed, all in the room, was a sort of black film of greasy soot. I went over to the couch. The white sheet still lay over part of it; but it had been thrown back, as might be when one is stepping out of bed.

But there was no sign of Queen Tera! I took Margaret by the hand and led her over. She reluctantly left her father to whom she was administering, but she came docilely enough. I whispered to her as I held her hand:

"What has become of the Queen? Tell me! You were close at hand, and must have seen if anything happened!" She answered me very softly:

"There was nothing that I could see. Until the smoke grew too dense I kept my eyes on the couch, but there was no change. Then, when all grew so dark that I could not see, I thought I heard a move-ment close to me. It might have been Doctor Winchester who had sunk down overcome; but I could not be sure. I thought that it might be the Queen waking, so I put down poor Silvio. I did not see what became of him; but I felt as if he had deserted me when I heard him mewing over by the door. I hope he is not offended with me!" As if in answer, Silvio came running into the room and reared himself against her dress, pulling it as though clamoring to be taken up. She stooped down and took him up and began to pet and comfort him.

We examined the couch and all around it most carefully. But all we could find was a sort of ridge of impalpable dust, which gave out a strange dead odor. On the couch lay the jewel of the disk and plumes which the Queen had worn in her hair, and the Star Jewel which had words to command the Gods.

In the autumn Margaret and I were married. On the occasion she wore the jewel which Queen Tera had worn in her hair. On her breast, set in a ring of gold made like a twisted lotus stalk, she wore the strange Jewel of Seven Stars which held words to command the Gods of all the worlds. At the marriage the sunlight streaming through the chancel windows fell on it, and it seemed to glow like a living thing.

The graven words may have been of efficacy; for Margaret holds to them, and there is no other life in all the world so happy as my own.

We often think of the great Queen, and we talk of her freely. Once, when I said with a sigh that I was sorry she could not have waked into a new life in a new world, my wife, putting both her hands in mine and looking into my eyes with that faraway eloquent dreamy look which sometimes comes into her own, said lovingly:

"Do not grieve for her! Who knows, but she may have found the joy she sought? Love and patience are all that make for happiness in this world; or in the world of the past or of the future; of the living or the dead. She dreamed her dream; and that is all that any of us can ask!"

The Yellow Cat

(1915)

Wilbur Daniel Steele (1886–1970)

Steele was the author of about twenty books and plays, plus numerous short stories. As a young writer, his stories won the O. Henry Memorial Award so many times people began referring to it as the Wilbur Daniel Steele Memorial Award. Between 1919 and 1931, he won the award every year but two. He was born in North Carolina, but throughout his life he lived in many places all over the world. His last novel, *The Way to the Gold* (1955), was made into a movie. This tale originally appeared in the March 1915 issue of *Harper's Monthly Magazine* and was then included in his first collection of short stories, titled *Land's End and Other Stories* (1918).

At least once in my life I had had the good fortune to board a deserted vessel at sea. I say "good fortune" because it has left me the memory of a singular impression. I have felt a ghost of the same thing two or three times since then, when peeping through the doorway of an abandoned house.

Now that vessel was not dead. She was a good vessel a sound vessel, even a handsome vessel, in her blunt-bowed, coastwise way. She sailed under four lowers across as blue and glittering a sea as I have ever known, and there was not a point in her sailing that one could lay a finger upon as wrong. And yet, passing that schooner at two miles, one knew, somehow, that no hand was on her wheel. Sometimes I can imagine a vessel, stricken like that, moving over the empty spaces of the sea, carrying it off quite well were it not for that indefinable suggestion of a stagger; and I can think of all those ocean gods, in whom no landsman will ever believe, looking at one another and tapping their foreheads with just the shadow of a smile.

I wonder if they all scream—these ships that have lost their souls? Mine screamed. We heard her voice, like nothing I have ever heard before, when we rowed under her counter to read her name—the *Marionnette*, it was, of Halifax. I remember how it made me shiver, there in the full blaze of the sun, to hear her going on so, railing and screaming in that stark fashion. And I remember, too, how our footsteps, pattering through the vacant internals in search of that haggard utterance, made me think of the footsteps of hurrying warders roused in the night.

And we found a parrot in a cage; that was all. It wanted water. We gave it water and went away to look things over, keeping pretty close together, all of us. In the quarters the table was set for four. Two men had begun to eat, by the evidence of the plates. Nowhere in the vessel was there any sign of disorder, except one sea-chest broken out, evidently in haste. Her papers were gone and the stern davits were empty. That is how the case stood that day, and that is how it has stood to this. I saw this same *Marionnette* a week later, tied up to a Hoboken dock, where she awaited news from her owners, but even there, in the midst of all the waterfront bustle, I could not get rid of the feeling that she was still very far away—in a sort of shippish otherworld.

The thing happens now and then. Sometimes half a dozen years will go by without a solitary wanderer of this sort crossing the ocean paths, and then in a single season perhaps several of them will turn up: vacant waifs, impassive and mysterious—a quarter-column of tidings tucked away on the second page of the evening paper.

That is where I read the story about the *Abbie Rose*. I recollect how painfully awkward and out-of-place it looked there, cramped between ruled black edges and smelling of landsman's ink—this thing that had to do essentially with air and vast colored spaces. I forget the exact words of the heading—something like "Abandoned Craft Picked Up At Sea"—but I still have the clipping itself, couched in the formal patter of the marine-news writer:

"The first hint of another mystery of the sea came in today when the schooner *Abbie Rose* dropped anchor in the upper river, manned only by a crew of one. It appears that the outbound freighter *Mercury* sighted the *Abbie Rose* off Block Island on Thursday last, acting in a suspicious manner. A boat-party sent aboard found the schooner in perfect order and condition, sailing under four lower sails, the topsails being pursed up to the mastheads but not stowed. With the exception of a yellow cat, the vessel was found to be utterly deserted though her small boat still hung in the davits. No evidences of disorder were visible in any part of the craft. The dishes were washed up, the stove in the galley was still slightly warm to the touch, everything in its proper place with the exception of the vessel's papers, which were not to be found.

"All indications being for fair weather, Captain Rohmer of the *Mercury* detailed two of his company to bring the find back to this port, a distance of one hundred and fifteen miles. The only man available with a knowledge of the fore-and-aft rig was Stewart McCord, the second engineer. A seaman by the name of Björnsen was sent with him. McCord arrived this noon, after a very heavy voyage of five days, reporting that Björnsen had fallen overboard while shaking out the foretopsail. McCord himself showed evidences of the hardships he has passed through, being almost a nervous wreck."

Stewart McCord! Yes, Stewart McCord would have a knowledge of the fore-and-aft rig, or of almost anything else connected with the affairs of the sea. It happened that I used to know this fellow. I had even been quite chummy with him in the old days—that is, to the extent of drinking too many beers with him in certain hot-country ports. I remembered him as a stolid and deliberate sort of a person, with an amazing hodge-podge of learning, a stamp collection, and a theory about the effects of tropical sunshine on the Caucasian race, to which I have listened half of more than one night, stretched out naked on a freighter's deck. He has not impressed me as a fellow who would be bothered by his nerves.

And there was another thing about the story which struck me as rather queer. Perhaps it is a relic of my seafaring days, but I have always been a conscientious reader of the weather reports; and I could remember no weather in the past week sufficient to shake a man out of a top, especially a man by the name of Björnsen—a thoroughgoing seafaring name.

I was destined to hear more of this in the evening, from the ancient boatman who rowed me out on the upper river. He had been to sea in his day. He knew enough to wonder about this thing, even to indulge in a little superstitious awe about it.

"No sir-ee. Something *happened* to them four chaps. And another thing—"

I fancied I heard a sea-bird whining in the darkness overhead. A shape moved out of the gloom ahead, passed to the left, lofty and silent, and merged once more with the gloom behind—a barge at anchor, with the sea-grass clinging around her water-line.

"Funny about the other chap," the old fellow speculated. "Björn-sen—I b'lieve he called 'im. Now that story sounds to me kind of—" He feathered his oars with a suspicious jerk and peered at me. "This McCord a friend of yourn?" he inquired.

"In a way," I said.

"Hm-m—well—" He turned on his thwart to squint ahead. "There she is," he announced, with something of relief, I thought. It was hard at that time of night to make anything but a black blotch out of the *Abbie Rose*. Of course I could see that she was pot-bellied, like the rest of the coastwise sisterhood. And that McCord had not stowed his topsails. I could make them out, pursed at the mastheads and hanging down as far as the cross-trees, like huge, over-ripe pears. Then I recollected that he had found them so—probably had not touched them since; a queer way to leave tops, it seemed to me. I could see also the glowing tip of a cigar floating restlessly along the farther rail. I called: "McCord! Oh McCord!"

The spark came swimming across the deck. "Hello! Hello, there—ah—" There was a note of querulous uneasiness there that somehow jarred with my remembrance of this man.

"Ridgeway," I explained.

He echoed the name uncertainly, still with that suggestion of pee-vishness, hanging over the rail and peering down at us. "Oh! By gracious!" he exclaimed abruptly. "I'm glad to see you, Ridgeway. I had a boatman coming out before this, but I guess—well, I guess he'll be along. By gracious! I'm glad—"

"I'll not keep you," I told the gnome, putting the money in his palm and reaching for the rail. McCord lent me a hand on my wrist. Then when I stood squarely on the deck beside him he appeared to forget my presence, leaned forward heavily on the rail, and squinted after my waning boatman.

"Ahoy—boat!" he called out, sharply, shielding his lips with his hands. His violence seemed to bring him out of the blank, for he fell immediately to puffing strongly at his cigar and explaining in rather a shame-voiced way that he was beginning to think his own boatman had "passed him up."

"Come in and have a nip," he urged with an abrupt heartiness, clapping me on the shoulder.

"So you've—" I did not say what I had intended. I was thinking that in the old days McCord had made rather a fetish of touching nothing stronger than beer. Neither had he been of the shoulder-clapping sort. "So you've got something aboard?" I shifted.

"Dead men's liquor," he chuckled. It gave me a queer feeling in the pit of my stomach to hear him. I began to wish I had not come, but there was nothing for it now but to follow him into the afterhouse. The cabin itself might have been nine feet square, with three bunks occupying the port side. To the right opened the master's state-room, and a door in the forward bulkhead led to the galley.

I took in these features at a casual glance. Then, hardly knowing why I did it, I began to examine them with greater care.

"Have you a match?" I asked. My voice sounded very small, as though something unheard of had happened to all the air.

"Smoke?" he said. "I'll get you a cigar."

"No." I took the proffered match, scratched it on the side of the galley door, and passed out. There seemed to be a thousand pans there, throwing my match back at me from every wall of the boxlike compartment. Even McCord's eyes, in the doorway, were large and round and shining. He probably thought me crazy. Perhaps I was, a little. I ran the match along close to the ceiling and came upon a rusty hook a little aport of the center.

"There," I said. "Was there anything hanging from this—er—say a parrot—or something, McCord?" The match burned my fingers and went out.

"What do you mean?" McCord demanded from the doorway. I got myself back into the comfortable yellow glow of the cabin before I answered, and then it was a question.

"Do you happen to know anything about this craft's personal history?"

"No. What are you talking about! Why?"

"Well, I do," I offered. "For one thing, she's changed her name.

And it happens this isn't the first time she's—well, damn it all, four-teen years ago I helped pick up this whatever-she-is off the Virginia Capes—in the same sort of condition. There you are!" I was yapping like a nerve-strung puppy.

McCord leaned forward with his hands on the table, bringing his face beneath the fan of the hanging-lamp. For the first time I could mark how shockingly it had changed. It was almost colorless. The jaw had somehow lost its old-time security and the eyes seemed to be loose in their sockets. I had expected him to start at my announce-ment; he only blinked at the light.

"I am not surprised," he remarked at length. "After what I've seen and heard—" He lifted his fist and brought it down with a sudden crash on the table. "Man—let's have a nip!"

He was off before I could say a word, fumbling out of sight in the narrow state-room. Presently he reappeared, holding a glass in either hand and a dark bottle hugged between his elbows. Putting the glasses down, he held up the bottle between his eyes and the lamp, and its shadow, falling across his face, green and luminous at the core, gave him a ghastly look—like a mutilation or an unspeakable birth-mark. He shook the bottle gently and chuckled his "Dead men's liquor" again. Then he poured two half-glasses of the clear gin, swal-lowed his portion, and sat down.

"A parrot," he mused, a little of the liquor's color creeping into his cheeks. "No, this time it was a cat, Ridgeway. A yellow cat. She was—"

"*Was?*" I caught him up. "What's happened—what's become of her?"

"Vanished. Evaporated. I haven't seen her since night before last, when I caught her trying to lower the boat—"

"*Stop it!*" It was I who banged the table now, without any of the reserve of decency. "McCord, you're drunk—*drunk*, I tell you. A *cat!* Let a *cat* throw you off your head like this! She's probably hiding out below this minute, on affairs of her own."

"Hiding?" He regarded me for a moment with the queer superior-ity of the damned. "I guess you don't realize how many times I've been over this hulk, from decks to keelson, with a mallet and a foot-rule."

"Or fallen overboard," I shifted, with less assurance. "Like this fellow Björnsen. By the way, McCord—" I stopped there on account of the look in his eyes.

He reached out, poured himself a shot, swallowed it, and got up to shuffle about the confined quarters. I watched their restless circuit—my friend and his jumping shadow. He stopped and bent forward to examine a Sunday-supplement chromo tacked on the wall, and the two heads drew together, as though there was something to whisper. Of a sudden I seemed to hear the old gnome croaking. "Now that story sounds to me kind of—"

McCord straightened up and turned to face me.

"What do you know about Björnsen?" he demanded.

"Well—only what they had you saying in the papers," I told him.

"Pshaw!" He snapped his fingers, tossing the affair aside. "I found her log," he announced in quite another tone.

"You did, eh? I judged, from what I read in the paper, that there wasn't a sign."

"No, no; I happened on this the other night, under the mattress in there." He jerked his head toward the state-room. "Wait!" I heard him knocking things over in the dark and mumbling at them. After a moment he came out and threw on the table a long, cloth-covered ledger, of the common commercial sort. It lay open at about the middle, showing close script running indiscriminately across the column ruling.

"When I said 'log,' " he went on, "I guess I was going it a little strong. At least, I wouldn't want that sort of log found around my vessel. Let's call it a personal record. Here's his picture, somewhere—" He shook the book by its back and a common kodak blueprint fluttered to the table. It was the likeness of a solid man with a paunch, a huge square beard, small squinting eyes, and a bald head. "What do you make of him—a writing chap?"

"From the nose down, yes," I estimated. "From the nose up, he will 'tend to his own business if you will 'tend to yours, strictly."

McCord slapped his thigh. "By gracious! that's the fellow! He hates the Chinaman. He knows as well as anything he ought not to put down in black and white how intolerably he hates the Chinaman, and yet he must sneak off to his cubby-hole and suck his pencil, and—and how is it Stevenson has it?—the 'agony of composition,' you remember. Can you imagine the fellow, Ridgeway, bundling down here with the fever on him—"

"About the Chinaman," I broke in. "I think you said something about a Chinaman?"

"Yes. The cook, he must have been. I gather he wasn't the master's pick, by the reading-matter here. Probably clapped on to him by the owners—shifted from one of their others at the last moment; a queer trick.

"Listen." He picked up the book and, running over the pages with a selective thumb, read:

" '*August second.* First part, moderate southwesterly breeze—' and so forth—er—but here he comes to it:

" 'Anything can happen to a man at sea, even a funeral. In special to a Chinyman, who is of no account to social welfare, being a barbarian as I look at it.'

"Something of a philosopher, you see. And did you get the reserve in that 'even a funeral'? An artist, I tell you. But wait; let me catch him a bit wilder. Here:

" 'I'll get that mustard-colored—[This is back a couple of days.] Never can hear the bastard coming, in them carpet slippers. Turned round and found him standing right to my back this morning. Could have stuck a knife into me easy. "Look here!" says I, and fetched him a tap on the ear that will make him walk louder next time, I warrant. He could have stuck a knife into me easy.'

"A clear case of moral funk, I should say. Can you imagine the fellow, Ridgeway—"

"Yes, oh yes." I was ready with a phrase of my own. "A man handicapped with an imagination. You see he can't quite understand this 'barbarian,' who has him beaten by about thirty centuries of civilization—and his imagination has to have something to chew on, something to hit—a 'tap on the ear,' you know."

"By gracious! that's the ticket!" McCord pounded his knee. "And now we've got another chap going to pieces—Peters, he calls him. Refuses to eat dinner on August the third, claiming he caught the Chink making passes over the chowder-pot with his thumb. Can you believe it, Ridgeway—in this very cabin here?" Then he went on with a suggestion of haste, as though he had somehow made a slip. "Well, at any rate, the disease seems to be catching. Next day it's Bach, the second seaman, who begins to feel the gaff. Listen: " 'Back he comes to me tonight, complaining he's being watched. He claims the Chink has got the evil eye. Says he can see through a two-inch bulk-head, and the like. The Chink's laying in his bunk, turned the other way. "Why don't you go aboard of him?" says I. The Dutcher says nothing, but goes over to his own bunk and feels under the straw. When he comes back he's looking queer. "By God!" says he, "the devil has swiped my gun!" . . . Now if that's true there is going to be hell to pay in this vessel very quick. I figure I'm still master of this vessel.' "

"The evil eye," I grunted. "Consciences gone wrong there somewhere."

"Not altogether, Ridgeway. I can see that yellow man peeking. Now just figure yourself, say, eight thousand miles from home, out on the water alone with a crowd of heathen fanatics crazy from fright, looking around for guns and so on. Don't you believe you'd keep an eye around the corners, kind of—eh? I'll bet a hat he was taking it all in, lying there in his bunk, 'turned the other way.' Eh? I pity the poor cuss—Well, there's only one more entry after that. He's good and mad. Here:

" 'Now, by God! this is the end. My gun's gone too right out from under lock and key, by God! I been talking with Bach this morning. Not to let on, I had him in to clean my lamp. There's more ways than one, he says, and so do I.' "

McCord closed the book and dropped it on the table. "Finis," he said. "The rest is blank paper."

"Well!" I will confess I felt much better than I had for some time past. "There's *one* 'mystery of the sea' gone to pot, at any rate. And now, if you don't mind I think I'll have another of your nips, McCord."

He pushed my glass across the table and got up, and behind his back his shoulder rose to scour the corners of the room, like an incorruptible sentinel. I forgot to take up my gin, watching him. After an uneasy minute or so he came back to the table and pressed the tip of a forefinger on the book.

"Ridgeway," he said, "you don't seem to understand. This particular 'mystery of the sea' hasn't been scratched yet—not even *scratched*, Ridgeway." He sat down and leaned forward, fixing me with a didactic finger. "What happened?"

"Well, I have an idea the 'barbarian' got them, when it came to the pinch."

"And let the—remains over the side?"

"I should say."

"And then they came back and got the 'barbarian' and let *him* over the side, eh? There were none left, you remember."

"Oh, good Lord, I don't know!" I flared with a childish resentment at this catechising of his. But his finger remained there, challenging.

"I do," he announced. "The Chinaman put them over the side, as we have said. And then, after that, he died—of wounds about the head."

"So?" I still had sarcasm.

"You will remember," he went on, "that the skipper did not happen to mention a *yellow* cat in his confessions."

"McCord," I begged him, "please drop it. Why in thunder *should* he mention a cat?"

"True. Why *should* he mention a cat? I think one of the reasons why he should *not* mention a cat is because there did not happen to be a cat aboard at that time."

"Oh, all right!" I reached out and pulled the bottle to my side of the table. Then I took out my watch. "If you don't mind," I suggested, "I think we'd better be going ashore. I've got to get to my office rather early in the morning. What do you say?"

He said nothing for a moment, but his finger had dropped. He leaned back and stared straight into the core of the light above, his eyes squinting.

"He would have been from the south of China, probably." He seemed to be talking to himself. "There's a considerable sprinkling of the belief down there, I've heard. It's an uncanny business—this transmigration of souls—"

Personally, I had had enough of it. McCord's fingers came groping across the table for the bottle. I picked it up hastily and let it go through the open companionway where it died with a faint gurgle, out somewhere on the river.

"Now," I said to him, shaking the vagrant wrist, "either you come ashore with me or you go in there and get under the blankets. You're drunk, McCord—*drunk*. Do you hear me?"

"Ridgeway," he pronounced, bringing his eyes down to me and speaking very slowly. "You're a fool, if you can't see better than that. I'm not drunk. I'm sick. I haven't slept for three nights—and now I can't. And you say—you—" He went to pieces very suddenly, jumped up, pounded the leg of his chair on the decking, and shouted at me:

"And you say that, you—you landlubber, you office coddler! You're so comfortably sure that everything in the world is cut and dried. Come back to the water again and learn how to wonder—and stop talking like a damn fool. Do you know where—Is there anything in your municipal budget to tell me where Björnsen went? Listen!" He sat down, waving me to do the same, and went on with a sort of desperate repression.

"It happened on the first night after we took this hellion. I'd stood the wheel most of the afternoon—off and on, that is, because she sails herself uncommonly well. Just put her on reach, you know, and she carries it off pretty well—"

"I know," I nodded.

"Well, we mugged up about seven o'clock. There was a good deal of canned stuff in the galley, and Björnsen wasn't a bad hand with a kettle—a thoroughgoing Square-head he was—tall and lean and yellow-haired, with little fat, round cheeks and a white mustache. Not a bad chap at all. He took the wheel to stand till midnight, and I turned in, but I didn't drop off for quite a spell. I could hear his boots wandering around over my head, padding off forward, coming back again. I heard him whistling now and then—an outlandish air. Occasionally I could see the shadow of his head waving in a block of moonlight that lay on the decking right down there in front of the state-room door. It came from the companion; the cabin was dark because we were going easy on the oil. They hadn't left a great deal, for some reason or other."

McCord leaned back and described with his finger where the illumination had cut the decking.

"There! I could see it from my bunk, as I lay, you understand. I must have almost dropped off once when I heard him fiddling around out here in the cabin, and then he said something in a whisper, just to find out if I was still awake, I suppose. I asked him what the matter was. He came and poked his head in the door.

"'The breeze is going out,' says he. 'I was wondering if we couldn't get a little more sail on her.' Only I can't give you his fierce Square-head tang. 'How about the tops?' he suggested.

"I was so sleepy I didn't care, and I told him so. 'All right,' he says, 'but I thought I might shake out one of them tops.' Then I heard him blow at something outside. 'Scat, you—' Then: 'This cat's going to set me crazy, Mr. McCord,' he says, 'following me around everywhere.' He gave a kick, and I saw something yellow floating across the moonlight. It never made a sound—just floated. You wouldn't have known it ever lit anywhere, just like—"

McCord stopped and drummed a few beats on the table with his fist, as though to bring himself back to the straight narrative.

"I went to sleep," he began again. "I dreamed about a lot of things. I woke up sweating. You know how glad you are to wake up after a dream like that and find none of it is so? Well, I turned over and settled to go off again, and then I got a little more awake and thought to myself it must be pretty near time for me to go on deck. I scratched a match and looked at my watch 'That fellow must be either a good chap or asleep,' I said to myself. And I rolled out quick and went abovedecks. He wasn't at the wheel. I called him: 'Björnsen! Björnsen!' No answer."

McCord was really telling a story now. He paused for a long moment, one hand shielding an ear and his eyeballs turned far up.

"That was the first time I really went over the hulk," he ran on. "I got out a lantern and started at the forward end of the hold, and I worked aft, and there was nothing there. Not a sign, or a stain, or a scrap of clothing, or anything. You may believe that I began to feel funny inside. I went over the decks and the rails and the house itself—inch by inch. Not a trace. I went out aft again. The cat sat on the wheel-box, washing her face. I hadn't noticed the scar on her head before, running down between her ears—rather a new scar—three or four days old, I should say. It looked ghastly and blue-white in the flat moonlight. I ran over and grabbed her up to heave her over the side —you understand how upset I was. Now you know a cat will squirm around and grab something when you hold it like that, generally speaking. This one didn't. She just drooped and began to purr and looked up at me out of her moonlit eyes under that scar. I dropped her on the deck and backed off. You remember Björnsen had *kicked* her—and I didn't want anything like that happening to—"

The narrator turned upon me with a sudden heat, leaned over and shook his finger before my face.

"There you go!" he cried. "You, with your stout stone buildings and your policemen and your neighborhood church—you're so damn sure. But I'd just like to see you out there, alone, with the moon setting, and all the lights gone tall and queer, and a shipmate—" He lifted his hand overhead, the finger-tips pressed together and then suddenly separated as though he had released an impalpable something into the air.

"Go on," I told him.

"I felt more like you do, when it got light again, and warm and sunshiny. I said 'Bah!' to the whole business. I even fed the cat, and I slept awhile on the roof of the house—I was so sure. We lay dead most of the day, without a streak of air. But that night—! Well, that night I hadn't got over being sure yet. It takes quite a jolt, you know, to shake loose several dozen generations. A fair, steady breeze had come along, the glass was high, she was staying herself like a doll, and so I figured I could get a little rest lying below in the bunk, even if I didn't sleep.

"I tried not to sleep, in case something should come up—a squall or the like. But I think I must have dropped off once or twice. I remember I heard something fiddling around in the galley, and I hollered 'Scat!' and everything was quiet again. I rolled over and lay on my left side, staring at that square of moonlight outside my door for a long time. You'll think it was a dream—what I saw there."

"Go on," I said.

"Call this table-top the spot of light, roughly," he said. He placed a finger-tip at about the middle of the forward edge and drew it slowly toward the center. "Here, what would correspond with the upper side of the companion-way, there came down very gradually the shadow of a tail. I watched it streaking out there across the deck, wiggling the slightest bit now and then. When it had come down about halfway across the light, the solid part of the animal—its shadow, you understand—began to appear, quite big and round. But how could she hang there, done up in a ball, from the hatch?"

He shifted his finger back to the edge of the table and puddled it around to signify the shadowed body.

"I fished my gun out from behind my back. You see, I was feeling funny again. Then I started to slide one foot over the edge of the bunk, always with my eyes on that shadow. Now I swear I didn't make the sound of a pin dropping, but I had no more than moved a muscle when that shadowed thing twisted itself around in a flash—and there on the floor before me was the profile of a man's head, upside down, listening—a man's head with a tail of hair."

McCord got up hastily and stepped in front of the state-room door, where he bent down and scratched a match.

"See," he said, holding the tiny flame above a splintered scar on the boards. "You wouldn't think a man would be fool enough to shoot at a shadow?"

He came back and sat down.

"It seemed to me all hell had shaken loose. You've no idea, Ridgeway, the rumpus a gun raises in a box like this. I found out afterward the slug ricocheted into the galley, bringing down a couple of pans—and that helped. Oh yes, I got out of here quick enough. I stood there, half out of the companion, with my hands on the hatch and the gun between them, and my shadow running off across the top of the house shivering before my eyes like a dry leaf. There wasn't a whisper of sound in the world—just the pale water floating past and the sails towering up like a pair of twittering ghosts. And everything that crazy color—

"Well, in a minute I saw it, just abreast of the main-mast, crouched down in the shadow of the weather rail, sneaking off forward very slowly. This time I took a good long sight before I let go. Did you ever happen to see black-powder smoke in the moonlight? It puffed out perfectly round, like a big, pale balloon, this did, and for a second something was bounding through it—without a sound, you understand—something a shade solider than the smoke and big as a cow, it looked to me. It passed from the weather side to the lee and ducked behind the sweep of the mainsail like *that*—" McCord snapped his thumb and forefinger under the light.

"Go on," I said. "What did you do then?"

McCord regarded me for an instant from beneath his lids, uncertain. His fist hung above the table. "You're—" He hesitated, his lips working vacantly. A forefinger came out of the fist and gesticulated before my face. "If you're laughing, why, damn me, I'll—"

"Go on," I repeated. "What did you do then?"

"I followed the thing." He was still watching me sullenly. "I got up and went forward along the roof of the house, so as to have an eye on either rail. You understand, this business had to be done with. I kept straight along. Every shadow I wasn't absolutely sure of I *made* sure of—point-blank. And I rounded the thing up at the very stem—sitting on the butt of the bowsprit, Ridgeway, washing her yellow face under the moon. I didn't make any bones about it this time. I put the bad end of that gun against the scar on her head and squeezed the trigger.

It snicked on an empty shell. I tell you a fact; I was almost deafened by the report that didn't come.

"She followed me aft. I couldn't get away from her. I went and sat on the wheel-box and she came and sat on the edge of the house facing me. And there we stayed for upwards of an hour, without moving. Finally she went over and stuck her paw in the water-pan I'd set out for her; then she raised her head and looked at me and yawled. At sun-down there'd been two quarts of water in that pan. You wouldn't think a cat could get away with two quarts of water in—"

He broke off again and considered me with a sort of weary defiance.

"What's the use?" He spread out his hands in a gesture of hopelessness. "I knew you wouldn't believe it when I started. You *couldn't*. It would be a kind of blasphemy against the sacred institution of pavements. You're too damn smug, Ridgeway. I can't shake you. You haven't sat two days and two nights, keeping your eyes open by sheer teeth-gritting, until they got used to it and wouldn't shut any more. When I tell you I found that yellow thing snooping around the davits, and three bights of the boat-fall loosened out, plain on deck—you grin behind your collar. When I tell you she padded off forward and evaporated—flickered back to hell and hasn't been seen since, then— why, you explain to yourself that I'm drunk. I tell you—" He jerked his head back abruptly and turned to face the companionway, his lips still apart. He listened for a moment, then he shook himself out of it and went on:

"I tell you, Ridgeway, I've been over this hulk with a foot-rule. There's not a cubic inch I haven't accounted for, not a plank I—"

This time he got up and moved a step toward the companion, where he stood with his head bent forward and slightly to the side. After what might have been twenty seconds of this he whispered, "Do you hear?"

Far and far away down the reach a ferry-boat lifted its infinitesimal wail, and then the silence of the night river came down once more, profound and inscrutable. A corner of the wick above my head sputtered a little—that was all.

"Hear what?" I whispered back. He lifted a cautious finger toward the opening.

"Somebody. Listen."

The man's faculties must have been keyed up to the pitch of his nerves, for to me the night remained as voiceless as a subterranean cavern. I became intensely irritated with him, within my mind I cried out against this infatuated pantomime of his. And then, of a sudden, there *was* a sound—the dying rumor of a ripple, somewhere in the outside darkness, as though an object had been let into the water with extreme care.

"You heard?"

I nodded. The ticking of the watch in my vest pocket came to my ears, shucking off the leisurely seconds, while McCord's fingernails gnawed at the palms of his hands. The man was really sick. He wheeled on me and cried out, "My God! Ridgeway—why don't we go out?"

I, for one, refused to be a fool. I passed him and climbed out of the opening; he followed far enough to lean his elbows on the hatch, his feet and legs still within the secure glow of the cabin.

"You see, there's nothing." My wave of assurance was possibly a little over-done.

"Over there," he muttered, jerking his head toward the shore lights. "Something swimming."

I moved to the corner of the house and listened.

"River thieves," I argued. "The place is full of—"

"Ridgeway. Look behind you!"

Perhaps it *is* the pavements—but no matter; I am not ordinarily a jumping sort. And yet there was something in the quality of that voice beyond my shoulder that brought the sweat stinging through the pores of my scalp even while I was in the act of turning.

A cat sat there on the latch, expressionless and immobile in the gloom.

I did not say anything. I turned and went below. McCord was there already, standing on the farther side of the table. After a moment or so the cat followed and sat on her haunches at the foot of the ladder and stared at us without winking.

"I think she wants something to eat," I said to McCord.

He lit a lantern and went into the galley. Returning with a chunk of salt beef, he threw it into the farther corner. The cat went over and began to tear at it, her muscles playing with convulsive shadow-lines under the sagging yellow hide.

And now it was she who listened, to something beyond the reach of even McCord's faculties, her neck stiff and her ears flattened. I looked at McCord and found him brooding at the animal with a sort of listless malevolence. "*Quick!* She has kittens somewhere about." I shook his elbow sharply. "When she starts, now—"

"You don't seem to understand," he mumbled. "It wouldn't be any use."

She had turned now and was making for the ladder with the soundless agility of her race. I grasped McCord's wrist and dragged him after me, the lantern banging against his knees. When we came up the cat was already amidships, a scarcely discernible shadow at the margin of our lantern's ring. She stopped and looked back at us with her luminous eyes, appeared to hesitate, uneasy at our pursuit of her, shifted here and there with quick, soft bounds, and stopped to fawn with her back arched at the foot of the mast. Then she was off with an amazing suddenness into the shadows forward.

"Lively now!" I yelled at McCord. He came pounding along behind me, still protesting that it was of no use. Abreast of the foremast I took the lantern from him to hold above my head.

"You see," he complained, peering here and there over the illuminated deck. "I tell you, Ridgeway, this thing—" But my eyes were in another quarter, and I slapped him on the shoulder.

"An engineer—an engineer to the core," I cried at him. "Look aloft, man."

Our quarry was almost to the cross-trees, clambering up the shrouds with a smartness no sailor has ever come to, her yellow body, cut by the moving shadows of the ratlines, a queer sight against the mat of the night. McCord closed his mouth and opened it again for two words: "By gracious!" The following instant he had the lantern and was after her. I watched him go up above my head—a ponderous, swaying climber into the sky—come to the cross-trees, and squat there with his knees clamped around the mast. The clear star of the lantern shot this way and that for a moment, then it disappeared, and in its place there sprang out a bag of yellow light, like a fire-balloon at anchor in the heavens. I could see the shadows of his head and hand moving monstrously over the inner surface of the sail, and muffled exclamations without meaning came down to me. After a moment he drew out his head and called: "All right—they're here. Heads! there below!"

I ducked at his warning, and something spanked on the planking a yard from my feet. I stepped over to the vague blur on the deck and picked up a slipper—a slipper covered with some woven straw stuff and soled with a matted felt, perhaps a half-inch thick. Another struck somewhere abaft the mast, and then McCord reappeared above and began to stagger down the shrouds. Under his left arm he hugged a curious assortment of litter, a sheaf of papers, a brace of revolvers, a gray kimono, and a soiled apron.

"Well," he said when he had come to deck, "I feel like a man who has gone to hell and come back again. You know I'd come to the place where I really believed that about the cat. When you think of it—By gracious! we haven't come so far from the jungle, after all."

We went aft and below and sat down at the table as we had been. McCord broke a prolonged silence.

"I'm sort of glad he got away—poor cuss! He's probably climbing up a wharf this minute, shivering and scared to death. Over toward the gas-tanks, by the way he was swimming. By gracious! now that the world's turned over straight again, I feel I could sleep a solid week. Poor cuss! can you imagine him, Ridgeway—"

"Yes," I broke in. "I think I can. He must have lost his nerve when he made out your smoke and shinnied up there to stow away, taking the ship's papers with him. He would have attached some profound importance to them—remember, the 'barbarian,' eight thousand miles from home. Probably couldn't read a word. I suppose the cat followed him—the traditional source of food. He must have wanted water badly."

"I should say! He wouldn't have taken the chances he did."

"Well," I announced, "at any rate, I can say it now—there's another 'mystery of the sea' gone to pot."

McCord lifted his heavy lids.

"No," he mumbled. "The mystery is that a man who has been to sea all his life could sail around for three days with a man bundled up in his top and not know it. When I think of him peeking down at me —and playing off that damn cat—probably without realizing it— scared to death—by gracious! Ridgeway, there was a pair of funks aboard this craft, eh? Now—now—I could sleep—"

"I should think you could." McCord did not answer.

"By the way," I speculated. "I guess you were right about Björnsen,

McCord—that is, his fooling with the foretop. He must have been caught all of a bunch, eh?" Again McCord failed to answer. I looked up, mildly surprised, and found his head hanging back over his chair and his mouth opened wide. He was asleep.

Ancient Gods

(1992)

Kim Smith (born 1955)

Kim Smith is an up-and-coming author—primarily of erotic fiction —who has only recently entered the world of publishing. In addition to being a writer and editor, she is a book dealer who specializes in horror, fantasy, and science fiction. Smith is also a practicing Wiccan and resides in Spring Valley, California, with five cats and a pig.

 WARNING: This story may upset the more sensitive cat lover. Such persons should bypass this tale.

My hair has gone gray, and no doubt from the vantage point of your youth I seem a harmless and foolish enough old woman. Yet in my younger days I thought I knew all there was in the world to know, and I did a great deal of harm through my ignorance.

As a young woman of twenty I took service with a respectably well-off family from London, who had just acquired a rambling old house in an area of the South Downs. The house sat in a grouping of four others in a little hollow and the township proper was a longish walk out of a little valley. Brackley House it was called in the village, so named for an ancient family that once resided there.

The family I went to work for was as ordinary and unremarkable a grouping as could be imagined. Mr. Rothery's parents had died the year before, leaving him enough money to resign his banking job and retire to the countryside to try his hand at writing articles for botanical journals. From my lofty intellectual height I thought him the most boring man I had ever met. Mrs. Rothery was considerably younger than her husband. A most unimaginative woman, her greatest ambition at the time was to restore the old still room. Their children were likewise ordinary—bordering on dull. The boy, Charles Jr., was a sturdy child without any wildness in his nature, for which circumstance I was grateful. Jane, the little girl, was four, and gave some promise for turning out to be more intelligent than her sibling. My task was easy enough—to look after the children and give them lessons. Yet I could not refrain from feeling that my hard-won education gave me superiority over these gentry, who—like the parents who endowed them with an easy lifestyle—were essentially soft and unworldly. The wages were excellent, my room was in a quiet part of the house, and I had plenty of time to pursue my one great passion— reading. Really, I had more than most girls of my age and station can hope for, but I was still not content. As you shall see, this unfortunate attitude resulted in tragedy for all connected with me.

The South Downs have a dreamy quality to them, with their ancient, rounded slopes and quaint valleys. I often spent my days off reading by a small pond I found not far from the house—Moore's Deep, it was called. The village was also named for it. As time passed I adopted the placid and slow moving rhythm of the locals. I envisioned a stately procession of such days: unremarkable, indulgent, never-ending.

The start of the trouble was nothing notable in and of itself. One wash day I was lending the scullery maid a hand hanging up the linen to dry when I noticed a mangy looking cat skulk out from the hedge. It was dirty white, with no markings. Its body was covered in scabs and scars. The creature's entire visage repelled me, even though I am normally fond of cats. The maid gave a sharp squeak of fear when she caught sight of it coming closer and, clutching the wet laundry to her chest, began backing toward the house. Thinking the thing was probably rabid, I began waving a damp tea towel and snapping it in the cat's direction. It merely turned bored eyes in my direction and took another step forward. I stamped and called out "Shoo! Scat!", while moving toward it. I must have presented a ridiculous figure, there on the lawn, flapping the towel and shouting and stamping, while the cat simply stopped and yawned at me. When I was within a few paces of it, the cat lost its bored expression and a mad light grew in its eyes. It crouched down low, growling deep in its throat. Before I could react, it sprang forward and slashed out at me, catching the back of my hand with its claws. The pain was agonizing. I screamed and dropped the towel. The cat slowly backed away, still crouching, until it gained the hedge, where it disappeared.

The wounds were painful but not serious and I cleaned them thoroughly, knowing that a cat scratch can turn rotten and gangrenous faster than any other sort of wound. The maid was completely undone by the events of the afternoon. It took all my skill to convince her that we must finish setting out the wash. The cat did not reappear that day.

When Mr. Rothery returned from his botanical society meeting in London, I made a point of telling him about the cat. I was concerned for the children's safety, as well as my own. A cat mad enough to attack a human was nothing to fool with. He assured me that if the creature returned while he was about, he would be happy to shoot it and thus end the problem. With this I had to be satisfied, though in my heart I felt an unease all out of proportion to the events.

The next day I did errands in the village and had the ill fortune to encounter our neighbor, Mrs. Munro, on the street. Mrs. Munro is one of those annoying people whose own lives are so dull that they must make a point of prying at and into everyone else's. In this capacity, she apparently had witnessed my mauling from her window and now saw fit to comment on it.

"Good Afternoon, Miss Fowles," she chirped.

"How do you do, Mrs. Munro," says I, to be polite.

"And how is your injury, Miss Fowles?"

"I do not expect to die from it, thank you." She leaned toward me with a conspiratorial gleam in her tiny black eyes.

"That cat is not a normal beast, you know." "Clearly not," I said, "Clearly it is mad."

"Well, mad or not, that beast has been a plague hereabouts for as many years as I can recall. More than one has tried to track it down and kill it, but as you can see, no one has succeeded."

Attempting to disengage from the conversation I moved away, saying, "Perhaps Mr. Rothery will succeed where others have failed, Mrs. Munro. Good day."

Some few days later I was reading under a tree while the children played quietly, when out of the corner of my eye I caught sight of Mrs. Munro advancing on me. She plumped her over-stuffed figure onto the seat next to me and after bowing to the barest amenities, went to the heart of her visit.

"Tell me, Miss Fowles, has anyone from the house been feeding that cat?"

"No indeed. Why do you ask?"

"It has been coming around the back steps the last three nights, or did you not know?"

A sense of alarm swept through me at this news. "No, I did not know. If anyone here has been feeding it, I'll put a stop to it immediately."

Mrs. Munro arched her eyebrows significantly at me. "That would be ill-advised, I think. The cook that worked for the family who owned Brackley House before the Rothery's used to feed the cat every night when the rest of the house was asleep. Indeed, she was able to pet and play with it where no else could. With her it seemed tame, but with anyone else it acted in its usual mad manner. Eventually the mistress of the house discovered what was afoot and the master put a stop to it because the mistress had a horror of cats ever since she was a little girl. Well," Mrs. Munro went on to relate in hushed tones, "not even a week later, the trap door to the cellar fell shut on Mr. Colchester's arm. Gangrene set in and it had to be amputated at the shoulder. That's why they sold the house and moved to Scotland to live with Mrs. Colchester's sister. He always swore that he saw the cat looking down on him, just before the door fell shut."

"Surely you do not mean to suggest that the cat engineered that accident, Mrs. Munro," said I, unable to conceal my contempt. I need not have concerned myself, she was oblivious to all such attacks.

She fixed me with an arch look and said "Mark my words. There is more to all this than you know. Someday you'll know what I mean. And if I were you, I'd see to it that whoever is feeding the cat continues to do so."

In spite of what I considered my firm grip on reality, I confess I did spend the next few nights keeping watch at the back steps at various times. The cat did not appear and I began to assume that it had left the area. Then one morning I happened to rise much earlier than usual, after a night of tossing and turning, and I caught the parlor maid bringing in a dish from the back steps that bore traces of greasy scraps. I pounced on her, much like a cat myself. "Just what do you think you're about here, Morgan, to be feeding that vicious thing?" She started and dropped the bowl, which split apart with a crack.

Blushing furiously, she stood her ground, "It isn't a bad cat, Miss Fowles, only starved and suffering from neglect. Since I started feeding it, it's gotten quite tame." She looked at me defiantly. "I only feed it what would otherwise be thrown out."

"Don't you know how it scratched me?" I asked. "Don't you think it has proved its evil temper sufficiently?"

"You'll excuse me, Miss, but I imagine that you frightened it out of its wits with all that shouting. It probably thought you were intent on hurting it."

I fixed her with my best "I come from the upstairs and therefore rule you" sort of look and said, "This must end. There will be no more nonsense about encouraging such a dangerous animal to remain near the house. What if it scratched one of the children?" I exacted a grudging promise from Morgan and went back upstairs feeling very self-satisfied.

Thereafter, I noticed that the cat was again lurking about the hedges. At first I accused Morgan of violating her promise, but she protested so vehemently that I relented, knowing that she was not one to lie about anything. What I did finally was to formulate my own plan, which I thought was a good solution and showed my wit and intelligence. I resolved to feed the cat myself—oh yes, *feed* it indeed.

On my next trip into town I made a stop at the chemist's. In spite of my resolve, my nerves were in a terrible state and I was sure that Mr. Smithers, the chemist, would notice. I felt guilty enough about my plan and I did not want it generally known that the Rothery's governess was either prey to folly or intending to do away with a local legend. I need not have concerned myself. My request for rat poison was taken in stride and I was out of the shop before I had a chance to fully realize that I had beneath my arm the means to be rid of the pestilent animal once and for all. I carefully hid the packet in my room and began a campaign of luring the cat back to the house with table scraps.

Over a period of days, though I never saw the cat myself, he must have come anyway, for the bowl was always licked clean in the morning. When several days had passed thus, I then proceeded to lace some very good bits of beef with the rat poison, until I felt I had a sufficient quantity to do the creature to death. I set out the bowl and stationed myself where I had a good view of the back steps.

There was an unearthly quiet about the house during my vigil. The sounds of coals falling through the oven grate seemed loud as cannon shots to my stretched nerves. I shivered and wished I could sit nearer the banked coals. Strong moonlight shone into the room and on the yard, illuminating everything with an arcane white glow. I had just begun to nod, when a motion in the yard caught my eye. It was the cat, come to feed. He stalked across the grass with the arrogance of a god. His tail lashed the moonlight and his eyes showed green in the cold, white light. He went to the bowl as though he were taking a sacrifice, eating greedily, disdainfully. He ate every bite.

Once he had finished with his poisoned meal, he stalked leisurely out into the moonlight again and then commenced to roll about like a kitten, playing with moonbeams, jumping up to slap at shadows. I clenched my hands into fists of impatience and waited for the first spasms to take him. They began suddenly, halting his playful leaps in mid-air. He rolled around madly, his body arching convulsively. I rose to better see the end, despising myself for it, but utterly unable to help myself. To my surprise, even though he weakened rapidly, he did not expire immediately. He managed to begin dragging himself into the hedge and though my mind screamed at me to go out and finish him, my heart quailed at the vicious thing I had done and I was rooted to the spot. The cat disappeared into the hedge, and I made my way upstairs with leaden feet, trying to convince myself that the poison had done its job.

The weather turned fine a week or so later and I took the children with me out to Moore's Deep for the afternoon to play in the grassy meadows surrounding the pond. After exacting from them a promise not to roam out of ear shot, I took a seat under a shade tree and began to read my latest volume of verse.

It might have been ten minutes, it certainly was not more than twenty, when Jane's shrill screaming cut shockingly through the placid afternoon air. I ran as quickly as my clumsy skirts would allow me, and reached her only moments later. She stood in the grass, a hand clapped over one eye, still screaming. Charles stood nearby, a stunned expression on his face. And crouching in the grass before them both was the cat! Healthy and mad as ever. How had the cat escaped injury from the poison? I saw it eat the poisoned meat with my own eyes. I saw it begin its convulsions. By all natural laws, it should have been dead, yet here it had come again, healthy and mean tempered as ever.

Prying Jane's hand away from her face, I feared the worst. What was revealed, though, was a long, deep scratch that ran from just under the eyelid across her cheek. Bright blood welled from the wound and ran down her face, but I could see that it was not as serious as it might have been had the eye itself been involved. I turned to Charles, "What happened?" His voice shaking with shock, he told me about the cat they had found laying in the grass. Jane—the trusting soul—rushed forward to pet it. According to Charles, the cat seemed friendly enough until Jane had bent quite close to it, and then it lashed out with a lightening quick slash at the little girl's face. Holding Jane's hand tightly in mine and bidding her to cease her crying, I took Charles' hand in my other and began to back slowly away from the cat. It made no move to follow. When we were out of sight, I carried the still hysterical Jane back to the house in my arms. As we walked, the sun was dimmed behind gathering clouds and I could see that we were in for an early summer storm. I realized then that I had left the book by the tree. I cleaned Jane up, put her in a fresh gown, and left the children in the cook's charge while I hurried back to retrieve the book before the coming rain could spoil it.

The book lay where I had abandoned it, and I slipped it into my pocket and turned to go back to the house. There on the path, between me and the house, stood the cat. In the gathering gloom the creature seemed to swell and grow larger than was natural. I stepped to the side, trying to go around it. It arched its back, hissed and sidled into my path with a horrid twisting kind of motion. I moved in the opposite direction, and again, the beast blocked my progress. From its throat issued a ghastly mewling cry. With its dirty white fur all on end, it seemed the size of a dog. I advanced slowly and this time it allowed me to move forward, though it stayed in my path for several yards, capering and twisting and mewling. A bolt of lightening rent the air close by, the flash momentarily blinding me. When I could see again, the cat was gone. Lashing rain began to fall. Though I ran for all my worth, I was soaked through by the time I gained the house. Unfortunately the book was ruined despite my efforts.

Mr. Rothery's anger was immense on learning of the attack on his daughter. He declared that he would henceforth dedicate himself to the eradication of "that menace." Although I applauded his decision, yet I felt a cold dread. I continually saw in my mind's eye the way the cat looked at me as it blocked my path. Impossible though it was, I could have sworn that there was intelligence burning in its eyes and that intelligent gaze imparted to me an implacable thirst for revenge on I who had tried to kill it, and all those around me.

The next day Mr. Rothery began his campaign, arming himself with an old rifle and stomping around the surrounding area like a vengeful spirit. It would have been amusing if I had been able to shake free of the unease that now haunted me. While I was not about to arm myself and join in the hunt with Mr. Rothery, I decided that I could do a bit of sleuthing and at least arm myself by learning more about this local, legendary menace. I discarded the idea of going to Mrs. Munro for more information, since I could not bear the thought of subjecting myself to her irritating presence. So, I took myself to that time honored repository of local lore, the town vicar, in this case a charming man named Mr. Warfield.

Mr. Warfield was that classic treasure of British country life: a widower of advanced middle-age, with a gruff but kind housekeeper done up in gray braids, and an addiction to endless pots of tea (laced in the evening with brandy), and an enormous appetite for local gossip and color.

The vicarage was quiet as I approached, knocking at the servant's door rather than the formal front door. Mrs. Maddigan, the housekeeper let me in and invited me to tea and scones until the vicar returned from his constitutional.

Mr. Warfield greeted me warmly, and when he heard my business, showed keen interest. We sat in the cozy parlor and he began to relate the following tale:

"As you probably know, this good land of ours was not always ruled by Christian creeds. Indeed, Christianity has never really put down very deep roots here, though I suppose it borders on heresy for someone of my line of work to say so. The fact is that here, as no where else, the pagan cults found their expression. We live with the emblems of these pagan ways even now. When the Romans arrived, they found stone monuments that defied explanation; for how could the primitive, wild men and women they encountered have engineered the feat of moving and placing such huge stones?

"If further evidence of the unusual nature of pagan England is needed, then just go look at the church before you leave today. Look up high at the pillars and cornices and you'll see grinning down at you the face of the Green Man, the same fertility god that was worshipped here thousands of years since. And how did he get into a good Christian church? Because the builders know that, in spite of all we say to the contrary, the ancient gods are best kept at bay by giving them their due. I don't believe Christ would have minded, had he known.

"Now, up until the time of the Reformation, there was a ring of stones here in Moore's Deep. In point of fact, this stone circle stood on the very spot that Brackley House now occupies. Legend has it that when the Roundheads pulled down and hauled away the stones, they released a powerful spell that had been cast on the stones. They say that the old gods took vengeance on the criminals in the form of a giant cat that crept into their houses night after night, until each of the men was found dead in his bed, his face torn mostly off.

"A gruesome tale, to be sure. Yet if you go anyplace where there are still stones standing, you'd find tremendous resistance to their removal, and behind that reluctance you would most likely find a dread of the consequences. Yes, indeed, the ancient gods have not lost their power over our minds.

"As to the cat, it disappeared until the manor house was built some fifty years later. At that time, stories started that a giant white cat was seen around the premises. Local lore has it that so long as the house's inhabitants feed the cat, it is content to allow them to stay. But if they fail in their offerings, then the cat sees to it that they quickly change. And if they go so far as to attempt to rid themselves of it—well, it is said that the same hideous fate as the desecraters of the stone circle will be visited on all who dwell in the house."

He leaned toward me, a look of kind concern on his face. "My dear, though I know that the cat you have been having difficulty with cannot be the same cat the legends speak of, I want you to know that I will help you in anyway I can. Do not hesitate to call on me should the need arise."

I thanked him and made my way home. When I returned to the

house I found it in chaos. Mr. Rothery had found his quarry, out near the pond where it had attacked Jane. When he raised the rifle to fire, the mechanism malfunctioned and the rifle exploded. The local doctor had been called and remained at the house for several hours, doing his best to repair the damage wrought by the jagged shrapnel. At last he came downstairs, his face saddened. "I could not save the eye, I am sorry to say. He will live, provided the wounds do not become morbid. There will be a lot of scarring." He looked at Mrs. Rothery with great pity. "He will need a great deal of compassion when the bandages are removed, Madame. Above all, you should try not to show shock or repulsion at any time. Each of you will need to learn to clean the wounds and change the bandages." He demonstrated what we must do and then departed. I busied myself calming the children, who were naturally hysterical over their father's accident. It was well past 2 A.M. when I was finally able to fall into an exhausted sleep for a few hours.

While I slept, a dream came to me of the sort that is so clear that it seems it cannot be a dream at all. I dreamed that I woke to see the cat leap to the foot of my bed, its eyes catching the light from the grate in baleful glimmers. I understood that I was to rise and follow it. Like the subject of a hypnotic trance, I rose and paced after it down the hall. Occasionally it looked back at me with a smirking glance that was frightening for the humanness it lent the feline features. It led me through the kitchen and into the ancient cellar, which in the dream glowed with a dull, pale green light. Before my gaze, the scene changed and the walls of the house melted away until I was standing alone, naked, on a small rise, surrounded by tall stones that stood up like jagged teeth in the moonlight. I was myself, Mary Fowles, and at the same time I was another woman of an older age, intent on a dreadful magic. As this other woman, I understood that I was a priestess. The Romans had conquered my land, bringing with them the deadening creeds of Christianity. Where once my land had spoken with a green, vital voice, it now cried out in death agonies. The people abandoned their ties to the land, and their desertion served to begin to kill the land's spirit. Even I who had been trained to hear and heed the voices of trees, rivers, rocks and clouds, could scarcely make them out. The land begged for vengeance as it died and, therefore, I was embarked on a perilous path—to set wards and watches on the land within my reach, to try to build a refuge for some small part of the land's spirit, and to set a guardian over it for all time.

The stone altar before me held a cat, a huge white cat, drugged into stillness with herbs. In my hands I gripped a cold stone knife, wrought with my own hands, bound with spells that gave it razor sharpness and true aim. With my feet apart and planted firmly on the breast of my mother, the soil, I raised supplicating hands to the moon and began the long invocations. I called the mother to me by her strongest name, I invoked the consort god by his most ancient appellations. Incense I cast into the flames that danced on the altar, breathing in the intoxicating smoke until I lost touch with my body and seemed to walk the starry paths as a goddess myself. I danced then, using sounds and words that the goddess gave to me, my feet moving in patterns as old as time. I danced until my feet were raw and still I danced, immune to pain and lost in ecstatic union.

Just before dawn . . . just before the day came with its dominating male influence to dispel the power I had grown in the mother's dark womb, the power in me reached its peak, and I carried out the final act of this great making. Standing before the altar, I gave a last salute to my mother goddess and plunged the stone knife into my heart. Blood warm as sunlight poured over my naked belly, pooling on the body of the cat. As I sank to my knees in shock and mortal pain, I rejoiced, for the making was strong and good and would remain here, sleeping, until it was needed.

The dream ended. I came to myself in total darkness, my fingers caked with dirt. In the darkness I could hear someone whimpering, and at last I realized that it was me.

Slowly, hesitantly, I groped my way to a wall and from there to the cellar door. As I crawled into the kitchen, I realized to my horror that I was naked. I gained my room without being discovered and in the dawning light I inspected myself in the mirror. Dirt was smeared over me in patterns that looked disturbingly like blood. I filled a basin with chilly water and washed again and again to rid myself of the dirt and the smell of mold.

In spite of my exhaustion, I had no sleep before I had to tend to Mr. Rothery, who tossed in a delirium of pain in spite of the soothing elixirs we administered him. The doctor was right, it was not easy to control my reaction on first seeing the wounds. Jagged metal had made a hash out of the right side of his face. The remains of the eye had been removed and the flaccid lid was terrible to see. During the process of cleaning the wounds Mr. Rothery mercifully lost consciousness. I wished often that I could do the same, yet I was condemned by a strong constitution to witness every ghastly, painful moment of it.

The moon rose full and cold three nights later. I went to bed feeling stifled by the smells of the sickroom, and left my window raised and the curtains open, falling asleep in a broad shaft of clean moonlight. Sometime in the dregs of the night, I dreamed of the cat again. As before, I followed the cat through the house to the cellar where, once again, the ancient altar rose before me. This time, though, I seemed to see a happier time, before the land began to die. As the priestess, I went at the rising of the moon to the stone circle baring my body proudly, shamelessly to the moonlight, speaking the words of praise and power, and gave greeting to the ancient gods. Power surged in me as I gave the ritual greetings and received in return solutions to troubles among my people, and visions to give them hope and keep their feet on the path. Under the moon I danced, sometimes alone, sometimes in the company of four or five others. Sometimes a male was present and I lay with him in ecstatic union, offering my pleasure to the god and goddess. As suddenly as a falling curtain, the visions that had gripped me abruptly vanished. Light shone around me, the light of a lantern. I looked down at my hands to realize that, while my mind had been absent my body had been occupied with digging into the black loam. My nails were half torn away and my fingers oozed blood. Beneath my feet, a smooth stone slab lay revealed.

The next morning I begged leave of Mrs. Rothery and fled to the vicar's house as soon as I could. Fortunately, he was in. I must have looked as dreadful as I felt, for his face was filled with alarm at the sight of me. When he and Mrs. Maddigan had pressed tea laced with brandy on me, the vicar persuaded me to tell him of my difficulties. I related all—left nothing out. Truthfully, I expected to be admonished for giving way to superstitious dread. However, Mr. Warfield's look of concern deepened as I told my tale and when I reached the end, he clasped my hand and said, "Show me what you found in the cellar."

When we reached the house, he told Mrs. Rothery that he thought I discovered an item of archaeological interest in the cellar and that he had come to verify this. We took lanterns and descended. Mr.

Warfield knelt and broke away some soil with a small trowel he had brought along. The slab revealed by his efforts was some four feet in length and two feet in width. Other than some stains, which my imagination believed must be ancient blood, the object was unremarkable. Yet the sight of it filled me with terror and I could not bring myself to come further into the cellar than the foot of the stairs.

When the three of us returned to the kitchen, he related to my employer his thoughts on the matter in a voice that was calm and rational, in spite of the irrational subject matter. There was, he believed, some ancient, infernal force at work in the house and village. The cat played a major role, he was certain of that, though not of its particular place in the puzzle. The evident danger to the house's inhabitants forced him to conclude that strong measures were called for and though the Church of England did not officially recognize exorcism, he intended to perform such a rite, with Mrs. Rothery's permission.

On hearing that he planned an exorcism, I felt a fearful cold sweep through me. I begged him not to proceed, but he gently refused to yield and set off for the vicarage to fetch the necessary implements. I sat at the kitchen table in misery, waiting for his return, my sense of danger overwhelmingly sharp.

He returned in a few hours, his face positively lit from within with anticipation. I could tell that this was something he had secretly hoped to do for a long time. He strode cheerfully down the stairs and knelt by the altar stone, laying out his tools. I watched from the head of the stairs, there being no power on earth that could persuade me to enter the cellar.

From the darkest corner of the cellar, a slight movement caught my eye and my blood turned to ice. Here was the cat, stalking into the ring of lantern light. I tried to call out, but my voice froze in my throat. Something must have alerted Mr. Warfield, though, for at the last moment he looked up—just in time to see the cat launch itself at his face. His screams were dreadful as he writhed on the dirt floor, desperately trying to pry the fiend's claws loose. Holy water spilled in a silver stream over the ancient altar as its crystal container was sent flying. The lantern was knocked over and the light went out. I heard Mrs. Rothery behind me gasp and begin running for another lantern. And I? It was as though I were rooted to the kitchen floor, staring into the darkness. The sounds of struggle continued below, until I heard a rending sound, as of wood fracturing, and the thud of something heavy falling. Mrs. Rothery ran up behind me with a lit lantern at that moment and by its light we could see the vicar laying across the stone altar, a heavy wooden beam knocked loose in the struggle laying squarely across his back. His head twisted to look at us, it seemed, but the ravaged sockets would see no more. The vicar was dead.

The cat rushed by me and leaped through an open window in the kitchen. Its passage seemed to release me from my paralysis. Together we flew down the steps. I kneeled by the vicar, probing for signs of life. There were none. Like the bursting of a dam, my horrible guilt spilled over and a fit of weeping took me. In a voice that seemed to belong to another I heard myself confess to the poisoning of the cat, to the warnings given by Mrs. Munro, to every horrid, guilty thought and feeling in me, as though the vicar's spirit might somehow absolve me of the responsibility. When the storm of words abated, the eerie quiet of the cellar reasserted itself. I raised my face, covered in blood and dirt, and saw Mrs. Rothery standing over me, her face set in lines of strength that had never been there before she left her comfortable London life and came to live in Moore's Deep. I looked at her, pleading silently for forgiveness. She pulled her gaze from me, as though I were too loathsome to bear looking at, and turned to go. As she slowly climbed the stairs, she looked back to say one thing only— "Feed the cat, Mary."

In time the ghastly wounds Mr. Rothery received healed over. The right side of his face remained a nightmare, but with his wife's tender care he eventually came out of suicidal despair. His children grew accustomed to his appearance and stopped having nightmares over the dreadful events of that summer.

Jane married a banker last year. Charles achieved more success than I had originally imagined him capable of and is studying at Cambridge. The Rotherys died together in a flu epidemic several years ago and by the terms of their will I received the house in trust for the children until my death, at which time it has been ordered to be torn down and a public arboretum built on the site. The events of that horrible summer seem impossibly distant now, yet still sometimes on a night when the moon is full and comes winding into my room, I see the ravaged face of Mr. Rothery and the broken body of the vicar rising to remind me of my guilt, lest I forget. I will never leave this house. By my guilt I have been woven into the town's tapestry as intimately as those whose ancestral roots reside here.

As I said in the beginning, I seem harmless enough. Yet looks can be deceiving, eh? And now, please excuse me. I must go to feed the cat.

The Haunted Manor House

(1913)

Ms. Hartnoll

As told to

Elliott O'Donnell (1872–1965)

O'Donnell was a well-known writer and British ghost hunter. The following account is from his book, *Animal Ghosts: or Animal Hauntings and the Hereafter* (1913).

 WARNING: This story may upset the more sensitive cat lover. Such persons should bypass this tale.

Up to the age of nineteen, I resided with my parents in the Manor House, Oxenby. It was an old building, dating back, I believe, to the reign of Edward VI [1547–1553], and had originally served as the residence of noble families. Built, or, rather, faced with split flints, and edged and buttressed with cut grey stone, it had a majestic though very gloomy appearance, and seen from afar resembled nothing so much as a huge and grotesquely decorated sarcophagus. In the centre of its frowning and menacing front was the device of a cat,

constructed out of black shingles, and having white shingles for the
eyes; the effect being curiously realistic, especially on moonlight
nights, when anything more lifelike and sinister could scarcely have
been conceived. The artist, whoever he was, had a more than human
knowledge of cats—he portrayed not merely their bodies but their
souls.

In style the front of the house was somewhat castellated. Two semi-
circular bows, or half towers, placed at a suitable distance from each
other, rose from the base to the summit of the edifice, to the height of
four or five stairs; and were pierced, at every floor, with rows of
stone-mullioned windows. The flat wall between had larger windows,
lighting the great hall, gallery, and upper apartments. These windows
were wholly composed of stained glass, engraved with every imagin-
able fantastic design—imps, satyrs, dragons, witches, queer-shaped
trees, hands, eyes, circles, triangles and cats.

The towers, half included in the building, were completely circular
within, and contained the winding stairs of the mansion; and whoever
ascended them when a storm was raging seemed rising by a whirlwind
to the clouds.

In the upper rooms even the wildest screams of the hurricane were
drowned in the rattling clamour of the assaulted casements. When a
gale of wind took the building in front, it rocked it to the foundations,
and, at such times, threatened its instant demolition.

Midway between the towers there stood forth a heavy stone porch
with a Gothic gateway, surmounted by a battlemented parapet, made
gable fashion, the apex of which was garnished by a pair of dolphins,
rampant and antagonistic, whose corkscrew tails seemed contorted—
especially at night—by the last agonies of rage convulsed. The porch
doors stood open, except in tremendous weather; the inner ones were
regularly shut and barred after all who entered. They led into a wide
vaulted and lofty hall, the walls of which were decorated with faded
tapestry, that rose, and fell, and rustled in the most mysterious fashion every time there was the suspicion—and often barely the suspicion—of a breeze.

Interspersed with the tapestry—and in great contrast to its antiq-
uity—were quite modern and very ordinary portraits of my family.
The general fittings and furniture, both of the hall and house, were
sombre and handsome—truss-beams, corbels, girders and panels were
of the blackest oak; and the general effect of all this, augmented, if

anything, by the windows, which were too high and narrow to admit of much light, was much the same as that produced by the interior of a subterranean chapel or charnel house.

From the hall proceeded doorways and passages, more than my memory can now particularize. Of these portals, one at each end conducted to the tower stairs, others to reception rooms and domestic offices.

The whole of the house being too large for us, only one wing—the right and newer of the two—was occupied, the other was unfurnished, and generally shut up. I say generally because there were times when either my mother or father—the servants never ventured there—forgot to lock the doors, and the handles yielding to my daring fingers, I surreptitiously crept in.

Everywhere—even in daylight, even on the sunniest of mornings— were dark shadows that hung around the angles and recesses of the rooms, the deep cupboards, the passages, and silent, winding staircases.

There was one corridor—long, low, vaulted—where these shadows assembled in particular. I can see them now, as I saw them then, as they have come to me many times in my dreams, grouped about the doorways, flitting to and fro on the bare, dismal boards, and congregated in menacing clusters at the head of the sepulchral staircase leading to the cellars. Generally, and excepting at times when the weather was particularly violent, the silence here was so emphatic that I could never feel it was altogether natural, but rather that it was assumed especially for my benefit—to intimidate me. If I moved, if I coughed, almost if I breathed, the whole passage was filled with hoarse reverberating echoes, that, in my affrighted ears, appeared to terminate in a series of mirthless, malevolent chuckles. Once, when fascinated beyond control, I stole on tiptoe along the passage, momentarily expecting a door to fly open and something grim and horrible to pounce out on me, I was brought to a standstill by a loud, clanging noise, as if a pail or some such utensil were set down very roughly on a stone floor. Then there was the sound of rushing footsteps and of someone hastily ascending the cellar staircase. In fearful anticipation as to what I should see—for there was something in the sounds that told me they were not made by anything human—I stood in the middle of the passage and stared. Up, up, up they came, until I saw the dark, indefinite shape of something very horrid, but which I could not—I dare not—define. It was accompanied by the clanging of a pail. I tried to scream, but my tongue cleaving to the roof of my mouth prevented my uttering a syllable, and when I essayed to move, I found I was temporarily paralysed. The thing came rushing down on me. I grew icy cold all over, and when it was within a few feet of me, my horror was so great, I fainted.

On recovering consciousness, it was some minutes before I summoned up courage to open my eyes, but when I did so, they alighted on nothing but the empty passage—the thing had disappeared.

On another occasion, when I was clandestinely paying a visit to the unused wing, and was in the act of mounting one of the staircases leading from the corridor I have just described, to the first floor, there was the sound of a furious scuffle overhead, and something dashed down the stairs past me. I instinctively looked up, and there, glaring down at me from over the balustrade, was a very white face. It was that of a man, but very badly proportioned—the forehead being low and receding, and the rest of the face too long and narrow. The crown rose to a kind of peak the ears were pointed and set very low down and far back. The mouth was very cruel and thin-lipped; the teeth were yellow and uneven. There was no hair on the face, but that on the head was red and matted. The eyes were obliquely set, pale blue, and full of an expression so absolutely malignant that every atom of blood in my veins seemed to congeal as I met their gaze. I could not clearly see the body of the thing, as it was hazy and indistinct, but the impression I got of it was that it was clad in some sort of tight-fitting, fantastic garment. As the landing was in semi-darkness, and the face at all events was most startlingly visible, I concluded it brought with it a light of its own, though there was none of that lurid glow attached to it, which I subsequently learned is almost inseparable from spirit phenomena seen under similar conditions.

For some seconds, I was too overcome with terror to move, but my faculties at length reasserting themselves, I turned round and flew to the other wing of the house with the utmost precipitation.

One would have thought that after these experiences nothing would have induced me to have run the risk of another such encounter, yet only a few days after the incident of the head, I was again impelled by a fascination I could not withstand to visit the same quarters. In sickly anticipation of what my eyes would alight on, I stole to the foot of the staircase and peeped cautiously up. To my infinite joy there was nothing there but a bright patch of sunshine, that, in the most unusual fashion, had forced its way through from one of the slits of windows near at hand.

After gazing at it long enough to assure myself it was only sunshine, I quitted the spot, and proceeded on my way down the vaulted corridor. Just as I was passing one of the doors, it opened. I stopped—terrified. What could it be? Bit by bit, inch by inch, I watched the gap slowly widen. At last, just as I felt I must either go mad or die, something appeared—and, to my utter astonishment, it was a big, black cat! Limping painfully, it came towards me with a curious, gliding motion, and I perceived with a thrill of horror that it had been very cruelly maltreated. One of its eyes looked as if it had been gouged out—its ears were lacerated, whilst the paw of one of its hindlegs had either been torn or hacked off. As I drew back from it, it made a feeble and pathetic effort to reach me and rub itself against my legs, as is the way with cats, but in so doing it fell down, and uttering a half purr, half gurgle, vanished—seeming to sink through the hard oak boards.

That evening my youngest brother met with an accident in the barn at the back of the house, and died. Though I did not then associate his death with the apparition of the cat, the latter shocked me much, for I was extremely fond of animals. I did not dare venture in the wing again for nearly two years.

When next I did so, it was early one June morning—between five and six, and none of the family, saving my father, who was out in the fields looking after his men, were as yet up. I explored the dreaded corridor and staircase, and was crossing the floor of one of the rooms I had hitherto regarded as immune from ghostly influences, when there was an icy rush of wind, the door behind me slammed to violently, and a heavy object struck me with great force in the hollow of my back. With a cry of surprise and agony I turned sharply round, and there, lying on the floor, stretched out in the last convulsions of death, was the big black cat, maimed and bleeding as it had been on the previous occasion. How I got out of the room I don't recollect. I was too horror-stricken to know exactly what I was doing, but I distinctly remember that, as I tugged the door open, there was a low, gleeful chuckle, and something slipped by me and disappeared in the direction of the corridor. At noon that day my mother had a seizure of apoplexy, and died at midnight.

Again there was a lapse of years—this time nearly four—when, sent on an errand for my father, I turned the key of one of the doors leading into the empty wing, and once again found myself within the haunted precincts. All was just as it had been on the occasion of my last visit—gloom, stillness and cobwebs reigned everywhere, whilst permeating the atmosphere was a feeling of intense sadness and depression.

I did what was required of me as quickly as possible, and was crossing one of the rooms to make my exit, when a dark shadow fell athwart the threshold of the door, and I saw the cat.

That evening my father dropped dead as he was hastening home through the fields. He had long suffered from heart disease.

After his death we—that is to say, my brother, sisters and self—were obliged to leave the house and go out into the world to earn our living. We never went there again, and never heard if any of the subsequent tenants experienced similar manifestations.

Elliott O'Donnell's conclusion

This is as nearly as I can recollect Mrs. Hartnoll's story. But as it is a good many years since I heard it, there is just a possibility of some of the details—the smaller ones at all events—having escaped my memory.

When I was grown up, I stayed for a few weeks near Oxenby, and met, at a garden party, a Mr. and Mrs. Wheeler, the then occupants of the Manor House.

I asked if they believed in ghosts, and told them I had always heard their house was haunted.

"Well," they said, "we never believed in ghosts till we came to Oxenby, but we have seen and heard such strange things since we have been in the Manor House that we are now prepared to believe anything."

They then went on to tell me that they—and many of their visitors and servants—had seen the phantasms of a very hideous and malignant old man, clad in tight-fitting hosiery of medieval days, and a maimed and bleeding big, black cat, that seemed sometimes to drop from the ceiling and sometimes to be thrown at them. In one of the passages all sorts of queer sounds, such as whinings, moanings, screeches, clangings of pails and rattlings of chains, were heard, whilst something, no one could ever see distinctly, but which they all felt to be indescribably nasty, rushed up the cellar steps and flew past, as if engaged in a desperate chase. Indeed, the disturbances were of so constant and harrowing a nature, that the wing had to be vacated and was eventually locked up.

The Wheelers excavated in different parts of the haunted wing and found, in the cellar, at a depth of some eight or nine feet, the skeletons of three men and two women; whilst in the wainscoting of the passage they discovered the bones of a boy, all of which remains they had properly interred in the churchyard. According to local tradition, handed down through many centuries by word of mouth, the house originally belonged to a knight, who, with his wife, was killed out hunting. He had only one child, a boy of about ten, who became a ward in chancery. The man appointed by the Crown as guardian to this child proved an inhuman monster, and after ill-treating the lad in every conceivable manner, eventually murdered him and tried to substitute a bastard boy of his own in his place. For a time the fraud succeeded, but on its being eventually found out, the murderer and his offspring were both brought to trial and hanged.

During his occupation of the house, many people were seen to enter the premises, but never leave them, and the place got the most sinister reputation. Among other deeds credited to the murderer and his offspring was the mutilation and boiling of a cat—the particular pet of the young heir, who was compelled to witness the whole revolting process. Years later, a subsequent owner of the property had a monument erected in the churchyard to the memory of this poor, abused child, and on the front of the house constructed the device of the cat.

Though it is impossible to determine what amount of truth there may be in this tradition, it certainly seems to accord with the hauntings, and to supply some sort of explanation to them. The ghostly head on the banisters might well be that of the low and brutal guardian, whose spirit would be the exact counterpart of his mind. The figure seen, and noises heard in the passage, point to the re-enaction of some tragedy, possibly the murder of the heir, or the slaughter of his cat, in either of which a bucket might easily have played a grimly significant part. And if human murderers and their victims have phantasms, why should not animals have phantasms too? Why should not the phenomenon of the cat seen by Mrs. Hartnoll and the Wheelers have been the actual phantasm of an earthbound cat?

No amount of reasoning—religious or otherwise—has as yet annihilated the possibility of all forms of earthly life possessing spirits.

Sir Walter Scott's Cat

(1817)

Washington Irving (1783-1859)

Irving is best known for his famous stories "Rip Van Winkle" and "The Legend of Sleepy Hollow," which appeared in a collection of miscellany titled *Sketchbooks*. This book played a major role in the development of the American short story. He was the first American writer to achieve fame both at home and abroad. During his lengthy travels, he had occasion to strike up a close friendship with Sir Walter Scott, which resulted in the piece included here. This excerpt is from his essay "Abbotsford," which was written during his visit to Sir Walter Scott's mansion of the same name in Scotland. Although the essay was written in 1817, it was not published until 1935.

Writing about

Sir Walter Scott (1771-1832)

Sir Walter Scott was the inventor of the historical novel and was the first to portray peasant characters sympathetically and realistically. He was the author of *Ivanhoe* and the story-poem *The Lady of the Lake*. Scott's intimate knowledge of Scottish folklore is reflected throughout his writings.

Among the other important and privileged members of the household who figured in attendance at the dinner, was a large gray cat, who, I observed, was regaled from time to time with titbits from the table. This sage grimalkin was a favorite of both master and mistress, and slept at night in their room; and Scott laughingly observed that one of the least wise parts of their establishment was that the window was left open at night for puss to go in and out. The cat assumed a kind of ascendancy among the quadrupeds—sitting in state in Scott's arm-chair, and occasionally stationing himself on a chair beside the door, as if to review his subjects as they passed, giving each dog a cuff beside the ears as he went by. This clapper-clawing was always taken in good part; it appeared to be, in fact, a mere act of sovereignty on the part of grimalkin, to remind the others of their vassalage; which they acknowledged by the most perfect acquiescence. A general harmony prevailed between sovereign and subjects, and they would all sleep together in the sunshine.

The evening passed away delightfully in this quaint-looking apartment, half study, half drawing-room. Scott read several passages from the old romance of Arthur, with a fine deep sonorous voice, and a gravity of tone that seemed to suit the antiquated, black-letter volume. It was a rich treat to hear such a work, read by such a person, and in such place; and his appearance as he sat reading, in a large armed chair, with his favorite hound Maida at his feet, and surrounded by books and relics, and border trophies, would have formed an admirable and most characteristic picture.

While Scott was reading, the sage grimalkin already mentioned had taken his seat in a chair beside the fire, and remained with fixed eye and grave demeanor, as if listening to the reader. I observed to Scott that his cat seemed to have a black-letter taste in literature.

"Ah," said he, "these cats are a very mysterious kind of folk. There is always more passing in their minds than we are aware of. It comes no doubt from their being so familiar with witches and warlocks." He went on to tell a little story about a gude [sic] man who was returning to his cottage one night, when, in a lonely out-of-the-way place, he met with a funeral procession of cats all in mourning, bearing one of their race to the grave in a coffin covered with a black velvet pall. The worthy man, astonished and half frightened at so strange a pageant, hastened home and told what he had seen to his wife and children. Scarce had he finished, when a great black cat that sat beside the fire raised himself up, exclaimed "Then I am king of the cats!" and vanished up the chimney. The funeral seen by the gude man was one of the cat dynasty.

"Our grimalkin here," added Scott, "sometimes reminds me of the story, by the airs of sovereignty which he assumes; and I am apt to treat him with respect from the idea that he may be a great prince incog., and may some time or other come to the throne."

Tobermory

(1911)

Saki (Hector Hugh Munro; 1870–1916)

Under the pen name "Saki," H. H. Munro produced a body of fantastic literature that stands out as some of the finest of the genre. This Scottish author was actually born in Burma, though his family brought him to Britain when he was two years old. He was a well-known author and journalist by the time he went off to fight in World War I. His career was cut unfortunately short when he was struck down by a German sniper in France. True to his famous cynical, darkly humorous style, his last recorded words were "Put that bloody cigarette out!" This story, which is typical of his satires on British society, is from his book *The Chronicles of Clovis* (1911).

It was a chill, rain-washed afternoon of a late August day, that indefinite season when partridges are still in security or cold storage, and there is nothing to hunt—unless one is bounded on the north by the Bristol Channel, in which case one may lawfully gallop after fat red stags. Lady Blemley's house party was not bounded on the north by the Bristol Channel, hence there was a full gathering of her guests round the tea table on this particular afternoon. And, in spite of the blankness of the season and the triteness of the occasion, there was no trace in the company of that fatigued restlessness which means a dread of the pianola and a subdued hankering for auction bridge. The undisguised openmouthed attention of the entire party was fixed on the homely negative personality of Mr. Cornelius Appin. Of all her guests, he was the one who had come to Lady Blemley with the vaguest reputation. Someone had said he was "clever," and he had gotten his invitation in the moderate expectation, on the part of his hostess, that some portion at least of his cleverness would be contributed to the general entertainment. Until teatime that day she had been unable to discover in what direction, if any, his cleverness lay. He was neither a wit nor a croquet champion, a hypnotic force nor a begetter of amateur theatricals. Neither did his exterior suggest the sort of man in whom women are willing to pardon a generous measure of mental deficiency. He had subsided into mere Mr. Appin, and the Cornelius seemed a piece of transparent baptismal bluff. And now he was claiming to have launched on the world a discovery beside which the invention of gunpowder, of the printing press, and of steam locomotion were inconsiderable trifles. Science had made bewildering strides in many directions during recent decades, but this thing seemed to belong to the domain of miracle rather than to scientific achievement.

"And do you really ask us to believe," Sir Wilfrid was saying, "that you have discovered a means for instructing animals in the art of human speech, and that dear old Tobermory has proved your first successful pupil?"

"It is a problem at which I have worked for the last seventeen years," said Mr. Appin, "but only during the last eight or nine months have I been rewarded with glimmerings of success. Of course I have experimented with thousands of animals, but latterly only with cats, those wonderful creatures which have assimilated themselves so marvelously with our civilization while retaining all their highly developed feral instincts. Here and there among cats one comes across an outstanding superior intellect, just as one does among the ruck of human beings, and when I made the acquaintance of Tobermory a week ago I saw at once that I was in contact with a 'Beyond-cat' of extraordinary intelligence. I had gone far along the road to success in recent experiments; with Tobermory, as you call him, I have reached the goal."

Mr. Appin concluded his remarkable statement in a voice which he strove to divest of a triumphant inflection. No one said "Rats," though Clovis's lips moved in a monosyllabic contortion which probably invoked those rodents of disbelief.

"And do you mean to say," asked Miss Resker, after a slight pause, "that you have taught Tobermory to say and understand easy sentences of one syllable?"

"My dear Miss Resker," said the wonder-worker patiently, "one teaches little children and savages and backward adults in that piecemeal fashion; when one has once solved the problem of making a beginning with an animal of highly developed intelligence one has no need for those halting methods. Tobermory can speak our language with perfect correctness."

This time Clovis very distinctly said, "Beyond-rats!" Sir Wilfrid was more polite, but equally skeptical.

"Hadn't we better have the cat in and judge for ourselves?" suggested Lady Blemley.

Sir Wilfrid went in search of the animal, and the company settled themselves down to the languid expectation of witnessing some more or less adroit drawing-room ventriloquism.

In a minute Sir Wilfrid was back in the room, his face white beneath its tan and his eyes dilated with excitement.

"By Gad, it's true!"

His agitation was unmistakably genuine, and his hearers started forward in a thrill of awakened interest.

Collapsing into an armchair he continued breathlessly: "I found him dozing in the smoking room, and called out to him to come for his tea. He blinked at me in his usual way, and I said, 'Come on, Toby; don't keep us waiting'; and, by Gad! he drawled out in a most horribly natural voice that he'd come when he dashed well pleased! I nearly jumped out of my skin!"

Appin had preached to absolutely incredulous hearers; Sir Wilfrid's statement carried instant conviction. A Babel-like chorus of startled exclamation arose, amid which the scientist sat mutely enjoying the first fruit of his stupendous discovery.

In the midst of the clamor Tobermory entered the room and made his way with velvet tread and studied unconcern across to the group seated round the tea table.

A sudden hush of awkwardness and constraint fell on the company. Somehow there seemed an element of embarrassment in addressing on equal terms a domestic cat of acknowledged dental ability.

"Will you have some milk, Tobermory?" asked Lady Blemley in a rather strained voice.

"I don't mind if I do," was the response, couched in a tone of even indifference. A shiver of suppressed excitement went through the listeners, and Lady Blemley might be excused for pouring out the saucerful of milk rather unsteadily.

"I'm afraid I've spilled a good deal of it," she said apologetically.

"After all, it's not my Axminster," was Tobermory's rejoinder.

Another silence fell on the group, and then Miss Resker, in her best district-visitor manner, asked if the human language had been difficult to learn. Tobermory looked squarely at her for a moment and then fixed his gaze serenely on the middle distance. It was obvious that boring questions lay outside his scheme of life.

"What do you think of human intelligence?" asked Mavis Pellington lamely.

"Of whose intelligence in particular?" asked Tobermory coldly.

"Oh, well, mine for instance," said Mavis, with a feeble laugh.

"You put me in an embarrassing position," said Tobermory, whose tone and attitude certainly did not suggest a shred of embarrassment. "When your inclusion in this house party was suggested Sir Wilfrid protested that you were the most brainless woman of his acquaintance, and that there was a wide distinction between hospitality and the care of the feebleminded. Lady Blemley replied that your lack of brain power was the precise quality which had earned you your invitation, as you were the only person she could think of who might be idiotic enough to buy their old car. You know, the one they call 'The Envy of Sisyphus,' because it goes quite nicely uphill if you push it."

Lady Blemley's protestations would have had greater effect if she had not casually suggested to Mavis only that morning that the car in question would be just the thing for her down at her Devonshire home.

Major Barfield plunged in heavily to effect a diversion.

"How about your carryings-on with the tortoiseshell puss up at the stables, eh?"

The moment he had said it everyone realized the blunder.

"One does not usually discuss these matters in public," said Tobermory frigidly. "From a slight observation of your ways since you've been in this house I should imagine you'd find it inconvenient if I were to shift the conversation on to your own little affairs."

The panic which ensued was not confined to the major.

"Would you like to go and see if cook has got your dinner ready?"

suggested Lady Blemley hurriedly, affecting to ignore the fact that it wanted at least two hours to Tobermory's dinnertime.

"Thanks," said Tobermory, "not quite so soon after my tea. I don't want to die of indigestion."

"Cats have nine lives, you know," said Sir Wilfrid heartily.

"Possibly," answered Tobermory; "but only one liver."

"Adelaide!" said Mrs. Cornett, "do you mean to encourage that cat to go out and gossip about us in the servants' hall?"

The panic had indeed become general. A narrow ornamental balustrade ran in front of most of the bedroom windows at the Towers, and it was recalled with dismay that this had formed a favorite promenade for Tobermory at all hours, whence he could watch the pigeons—and heaven knew what else besides. If he intended to become reminiscent in his present outspoken strain, the effect would be something more than disconcerting. Mrs. Cornett, who spent much time at her toilet table, and whose complexion was reputed to be of a nomadic though punctual disposition, looked as ill at ease as the major. Miss Scrawen, who wrote fiercely sensuous poetry and led a blameless life, merely displayed irritation; if you are methodical and virtuous in private you don't necessarily want everyone to know it. Bertie van Tahn, who was so depraved at seventeen that he had long ago given up trying to be any worse, turned a dull shade of gardenia white, but he did not commit the error of dashing out of the room like Odo Finsberry, a young gentleman who was understood to be reading for the Church and who was possibly disturbed at the thought of scandals he might hear concerning other people. Clovis had the presence of mind to maintain a composed exterior; privately he was calculating how long it would take to procure a box of fancy mice through the agency of the Exchange and Mart as a species of hush money.

Even in a delicate situation like the present, Agnes Resker could not endure to remain too long in the background.

"Why did I ever come down here?" she asked dramatically. Tobermory immediately accepted the opening.

"Judging by what you said to Mrs. Cornett on the croquet lawn yesterday, you were out for food. You described the Blemleys as the dullest people to stay with that you knew, but said they were clever enough to employ a first-rate cook; otherwise they'd find it difficult to get anyone to come down a second time."

"There's not a word of truth in it! I appeal to Mrs. Cornett—" exclaimed the discomfited Agnes.

"Mrs. Cornett repeated your remark afterwards to Bertie van Tahn," continued Tobermory, "and said, 'That woman is a regular Hunger Marcher; she'd go anywhere for four square meals a day,' and Bertie van Tahn said—"

At this point the chronicle mercifully ceased. Tobermory had caught a glimpse of the big yellow tom from the rectory working his way through the shrubbery toward the stable wing. In a flash he had vanished through the open French window.

With the disappearance of his too brilliant pupil Cornelius Appin found himself beset by a hurricane of bitter upbraiding, anxious inquiry, and frightened entreaty. The responsibility for the situation lay with him, and he must prevent matters from becoming worse. Could Tobermory impart his dangerous gift to other cats? was the first question he had to answer. It was possible, he replied, that he might have initiated his intimate friend the stable puss into his new accomplishment, but it was unlikely that his teaching could have taken a wider range as yet.

"Then," said Mrs. Cornett, "Tobermory may be a valuable cat and a great pet; but I'm sure you'll agree, Adelaide, that both he and the stable cat must be done away with without delay."

"You don't suppose I've enjoyed the last quarter of an hour, do you?" said Lady Blemley bitterly. "My husband and I are very fond of Tobermory—at least, we were before this horrible accomplishment was infused into him; but now, of course, the only thing is to have him destroyed as soon as possible."

"We can put some strychnine in the scraps he always gets at dinnertime," said Sir Wilfrid, "and I will go and drown the stable cat myself. The coachman will be very sore at losing his pet, but I'll say a very catching form of mange has broken out in both cats and we're afraid of it spreading to the kennels."

"But my great discovery!" expostulated Mr. Appin. "After all my years of research and experiment—"

"You can go and experiment on the shorthorns at the farm, who are under proper control," said Mrs. Cornett, "or the elephants at the Zoological Gardens. They're said to be highly intelligent, and they have this recommendation, that they don't come creeping about our bedrooms and under chairs, and so forth."

An archangel ecstatically proclaiming the millennium, and then finding that it clashed unpardonably with Henley and would have to be indefinitely postponed, could hardly have felt more crestfallen than Cornelius Appin at the reception of his wonderful achievement. Public opinion, however, was against him; in fact, had the general voice been consulted on the subject it is probable that a strong minority vote would have been in favor of including him in the strychnine diet.

Defective train arrangements and a nervous desire to see matters brought to a finish prevented an immediate dispersal of the party, but dinner that evening was not a social success. Sir Wilfrid had had rather a trying time with the stable cat and subsequently with the coachman. Agnes Resker ostentatiously limited her repast to a morsel of dry toast, which she bit as though it were a personal enemy; while Mavis Pellington maintained a vindictive silence throughout the meal. Lady Blemley kept up a flow of what she hoped was conversation, but her attention was fixed on the doorway. A plateful of carefully dosed fish scraps was in readiness on the sideboard, but sweets and savory and dessert went their way, and no Tobermory appeared either in the dining room or kitchen.

The sepulchral dinner was cheerful compared with the subsequent vigil in the smoking room. Eating and drinking had at least supplied a distraction and cloak to the prevailing embarrassment. Bridge was out of the question in the general tension of nerves and tempers, and after Odo Finsberry had given a lugubrious rendering of "Mélisande in the Wood" to a frigid audience, music was tacitly avoided. At eleven the servants went to bed, announcing that the small window in the pantry had been left open as usual for Tobermory's private use. The guests read steadily through the current batch of magazines, and fell back gradually on the Badminton Library and bound volumes of *Punch*. Lady Blemley made periodic visits to the pantry, returning each time with an expression of listless depression which forestalled questioning.

At two o'clock Clovis broke the dominating silence.

"He won't turn up tonight. He's probably in the local newspaper office at the present moment, dictating the first installment of his reminiscences. Lady What's-her-name's book won't be in it. It will be the event of the day."

Having made this contribution to the general cheerfulness, Clovis went to bed. At long intervals the various members of the house party followed his example.

The servants taking round the early tea made a uniform announcement in reply to a uniform question. Tobermory had not returned.

Breakfast was, if anything, a more unpleasant function than dinner had been, but before its conclusion the situation was relieved. Tobermory's corpse was brought in from the shrubbery, where a gardener had just discovered it. From the bites on his throat and the yellow fur which coated his claws it was evident that he had fallen in unequal combat with the big tom from the rectory.

By midday most of the guests had quitted the Towers, and after lunch Lady Blemley had sufficiently recovered her spirits to write an extremely nasty letter to the rectory about the loss of her valuable pet.

Tobermory had been Appin's one successful pupil, and he was destined to have no successor. A few weeks later an elephant in the Dresden Zoological Garden, which had shown no previous signs of irritability, broke loose and killed an Englishman who had apparently been teasing it. The victim's name was variously reported in the papers as Oppin and Eppelin, but his front name was faithfully rendered Cornelius.

"If he was trying German irregular verbs on the poor beast," said Clovis, "he deserved all he got."